UNEXPECTED GUESTS

"Keep going!" Simon screamed, "Don't stop!" They continued right into the middle of the nearly four thousand as yet unidentified party crashers. Surprised by the move, the new arrivals gave little resistance to the maneuver. Simon led the charge through the center of the horde himself, pushing men away on either side of the column, the aggressors hitting their shields with an assortment of metal rods, two-by-fours, baseball bats, and other blunt instruments while screaming at them in what was clearly a foreign tongue. When they had broken through, again Simon found no signs of the police. Robert looked at Simon, not knowing what to do next.

"Brent, turn us around!" Simon cried out, "We're the northern line now!"

MELCHIZEDEK

BOOK ONE: KINGS AND PRIESTS

A Christian Novel by Michael S. Cordima

Original cover and illustration designs by Michael S. Cordima
Cover painting by G.A.C.
Cover formatting and final design by MelHak (Fiverr.com)
Alternate cover by Jesh_art_studio (Fiverr.com)
Back cover illustration by dawaeboo (Fiverr.com)
Act illustrations by Brandonsmait (Fiverr.com)
Maps by creativesyntax (Fiverr.com)
Proof Reader/Editing by Michael S. Cordima

Scripture verses taken from the World English Bible (American Standard, 1901) Public domain, non-apocryphal version: https://ebible.org/pdf/engwebp/

First Printing, 2020

ISBN-13: 978-0-578-70750-1

Distribution: www.MelchizedekNovel.com

Acknowledgements:

To all who encouraged and helped me stay on task during this long journey. To Ben and Pheobe whose friendship is worth more to me than gold. To my uncle Thomas, for pushing me forward when I needed it most. To the rest of my family and friends for supporting me and giving me time and space to complete this work, and of course, to my Holy Father. You have changed me forever, and I am eternally grateful for your loving kindness in my life. You are the author and perfecter of my faith and much of this book, and it is my hope that your Son Jesus would be glorified by the words within and not myself.

Thank you.

For Brad

A good friend and a kind soul that always had a new song to sing for his Lord and Savior.

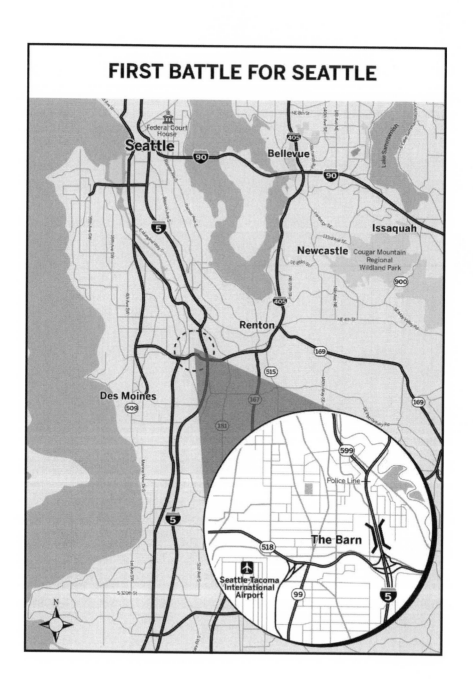

FIRST BATTLE FOR SEATTLE

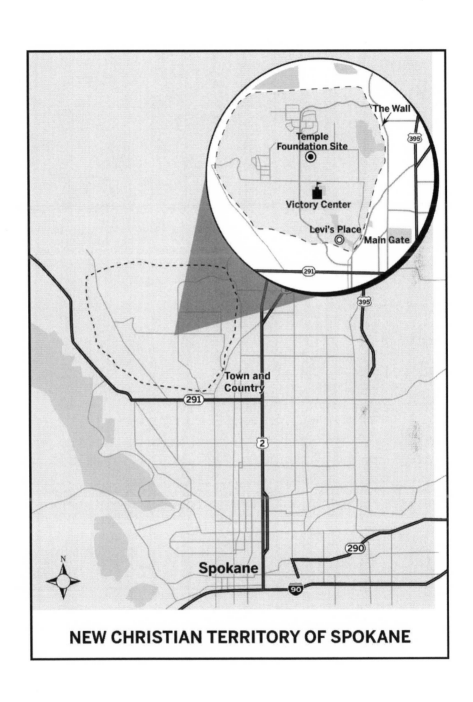

NEW CHRISTIAN TERRITORY OF SPOKANE

The Twelfth Amendment of the Constitution of the United States in regard to the Electoral College:

...The person having the greatest Number of votes for President, shall be the President, if such number be a majority of the whole number of Electors appointed; and if no person have such majority, then from the persons having the highest numbers not exceeding three on the list of those voted for as President, the House of Representatives shall choose immediately, by ballot, the President. But in choosing the President, the votes shall be taken by states, the representation from each state having one vote; a quorum for this purpose shall consist of a member or members from two-thirds of the states, and a majority of all the states shall be necessary to a choice. And if the House of Representatives shall not choose a President whenever the right of choice shall devolve upon them, before the fourth day of March next following, then the Vice-President shall act as President, as in the case of the death or other constitutional disability of the President-The person having the greatest number of votes as Vice-President, shall be the Vice-President, if such number be a majority of the whole number of Electors appointed, and if no person have a majority, then from the two highest numbers on the list, the Senate shall choose the Vice-President; a quorum for the purpose shall consist of two-thirds of the whole number of Senators, and a majority of the whole number shall be necessary to a choice. But no person constitutionally ineligible to the office of President shall be eligible to that of Vice-President of the United States.

Knowing their thoughts, Jesus said to them, "Every kingdom divided against itself is brought to desolation, and every city or house divided against itself will not stand."-**Matthew, 12:25**

Prologue

Supreme Court Building
Washington D.C.
Tuesday, March22nd, 10AM EST

A sober-looking man briskly made his way up the wide concrete slabs that lay beside First Street, his fine, dirty blonde hair swaying side to side with each intentional step. He wore black slacks and boots, and a red wool shirt. Eight large black buttons were stitched into the shirt's heavy fabric, four on either side of his chest. Together, they held in place a trapezoid-shaped bib that covered most of the area from his waist up to the shirt's collar. He was clean-shaven and had pale blue eyes, eyes that he used as he moved through the hustle and bustle that existed on the sidewalk on that bright morning, to monitor each soul that he passed by.

Watching every face and action as he scanned the other visitors, he carefully cataloged any sound or gesture that seemed out of place, just as he had been trained to do. Concealing his surveillance by feigning disinterest, he took into account the tones in their voices and the mannerisms of their movements, making a mental note of each one. Tall and thin, normally he would have easilystood out from those around him in such an environment,but neither his conspicuous stature, nor his confidentdemeanor had drawn attention up to that point, as theincreasingly unruly element he was walking into had bigger fish to fry than he.

Drawing nearer to his goal, he found himself maneuvering through a slew of screaming dissidents, every one of them carrying signs strewn with all manner of slogans and insults across their placards. Meant asmessages to those in power, the words wereultimately useless, having lost their meaning over a decade henceduring the propaganda battlefield that inevitably arose at the inception of the digital age known as the Hypnotic War. They were not alone of course, having been surrounded by a group of would-be independent internet reporters that were nearly as numerous. The opportunistic information peddlers, as always, were using their First Amendment rights to flaunt the latest in Snap Camera technology that was strapped to the ends of their fingertips. They were recording the entire fiasco from behind the safety of their wide contagion stopping masks and slap-goggles that conveniently concealed their identities, while also protecting them from communicable disease. *What a mess.* The man thought, realizing with some trepidation that it was one in which he was about to willingly become a part of, as he stepped up to the first of two military checkpoints.

Two small foldable tables were there, set up on either side of a short set of wide marble steps that stood between the sidewalk and a large plaza area, but only one of them was occupied. Behind it sat a female soldier. Not far behind her to one side were five more, two male, two female, and another that looked as if they were either in the process of changing their gender or did not claim one at all. Each of them stood completely still, staring straight ahead and through him as he approached, every one holding an automatic rifle in their white knuckled hands.

"Your credentials, please," The soldier behind the table said flatly. Without hesitating, the tall visitor reached out his right hand. The female soldier then picked up a small scanning device from a cradle that had been holding it upright on the table top, and waved it over his right arm while carefully watching a small screen that was protruding from its handle.

She put the device back in its cradle, and reached into a small box that was next to her right foot. From it, she took out a plastic badge with an alligator clip on one end. "Mr. Robert Valley," she said. She looked down at a list that appeared on a tablet which was sitting on the table next to the cradle. When she found his name on the list, she gave him the badge and smiled back. "They are expecting you inside in the north conference room. Could you lean down, please? I have to check your eyes." Robert obliged and leaned toward her. She stood up and looked closely at his irises. "Look up please, now look down. Thank you." She sat back down. "I am required to let you know that there are no recording devices allowed on the premises at this time beyond the second checkpoint. Do you have any electronic devices of any kind on your person?" Robert shook his head. "Good. Private Arnold will now pat you down, and use a metal detector. Then he will lead you to your destination, and stand by the door until you are finished. He will then escort you back here, to return your badge before you leave."

One of the soldiers standing behind her, a pale and tepid looking young man, stepped forward around the table and walked up to him as if he were executing some kind of silent military drill. Robert turned to face the boy, and looked down at him. Standing six-foot-four on a good day, he was easily head and shoulders over his escort. Through a series of well-practiced motions the boy placed his rifle on the table, and began to pat Robert down. Robert extended his arms, and waited as the soldier waved a small device around his torso and appendages before retrieving his weapon.

Robert clipped the badge to his shirt, "Uh, thank you." he said to the woman. He walked up the short set of steps that led to the plaza, an area they would need to cross in order to get to the portico on the other side and the main entrance. Private Arnold marched dutifully to his right as they went, his footfalls sounding off loudly. Robert looked at the young man. "So, you're my private Arnold huh?" The soldier did not respond. "If something happens, are you supposed to make sure ah get to da' choppa?" He spoke with a slight accent. The soldier continued marching, careful to keep his eyes facing forward, and gave no reaction to the levity Robert was trying to bring to the situation. "Yeah, that's what I thought. You've probably never seen that one anyway." He looked around at the soldiers stationed on either side of the plaza, and at the second checkpoint at the top of another, much larger stairway, careful not to turn his head as he did so. "Yup, real professionals around here," he said. He looked down toward his escort again, mentally noting different aspects of the boy's uniform and equipment. "Cream of the crop, I'm tellin' ya."

At least forty representatives of major corporately owned media outlets had camped out around and between two turquoise blue fountains that adorned the southern side of the plaza. As he and the boy walked by, several of them took notice of his shirt, and started taking pictures. As some of the reporters attempted to approach him, their Snap Cameras pointing in his direction ahead of them, several more soldiers standing guard around the areas where they were allowed to congregate quickly sprung into action, preventing any of them from getting closer than a few meters from his position. They stopped and yelled at the troops, their fingers pointing around at everything and everyone but themselves, an irony that did not escape Robert's notice. He smirked at them and leaned in close to his mute escort again, "You know a few years ago when I came here to testify, they laughed and made jokes about these uniforms." He pointed to his shirt. "Now look at 'em.

They can't even get inside the building." He smiled and waved at the onlookers.

Two imposingly hooded monolithic statues stood on either side of the bottom of the second stairway. Looking up as he walked, Robert took a moment to admire the grand columns and neoclassical artwork that sat above the portico. Several philosophers were depicted there in a large Parthenon-like motif, eternally frozen in endless debate. Beneath them, just above the entablature and engraved in large letters, were the words: EQUAL JUSTICE UNDER LAW. *Rest easy boys,* Robert thought to himself. *We'll take it from here.*

They walked up the hard and unyielding steps, and past the incredibly tall columns of the portico. Robert showed his badge to another soldier, who was sitting at another small table just outside of the opened seventeen foot bronze doors that made the building's main entrance. The soldier waved him by, and he nodded at two more men who were standing on either side of the large entryway as he walked in. Arnold picked up his pace and walked ahead of him. "This way, mister Valley," he said.

The hallway was long, with a marble floor and a ceiling that looked as if it could have been thirty feet high. Several well-dressed lawyers and other political operatives stopped what they were doing and stood, watching him in silence. They stared at him as he walked past, putting an end to the sounds of echoing conversations that had filled the immense space when they'd first entered. Unphased by the sudden change in mood upon his approach, he continued to look up as he walked, as if preferring the echo of his own footsteps to the ramblings of others, who in his mind were no longer relevant. He took in the grand sight, appreciating the different, but equally impressive columns that lined the inside of the great hall of justice, noting the high level of detail that had been put into its intricately decorated coffered ceiling, and did not even acknowledge those they passed by, not even giving them the satisfaction of looking in their general direction.

At the far end of the hall, Robert could see into the main judicial chamber where decisions had been made that had affected the lives of so many. At that moment it was empty, but still impressive. Beyond the audience seats, a small lectern and a wide wooden bench,one that was large enough to accommodate them all, nine tall black chairs stood out from a backdrop of giant red velvet curtains that hung behind them. But long before they could reach the Eastern side of the building where the room was located, Arnold stopped and turned to face a different door on the north side of the hall. He marched to the door, and stood beside it without saying a word.

Robert followed him and gave him an unsure glance before reaching out and opening the door himself. Inside, the curtains of a few windows had been pulled to their sides, allowing for some sunlight to come in from a courtyard outside, which partially illuminated the room. No artificial lights were turned on, forcing his eyes to adjust to the dim environment. When they did, he was able to see a long dark conference room with a large oak table in its center, surrounded by twenty heavy looking chairs. All of them were made of the same dark, grainy wood. Upon entering, a strange musty odor hit his nostrils, the kind one might encounter while riding in an old car that had been well cared for, but rarely left the place where it was kept. Beyond the table on the far side of the room, he could make out three men who were standing and facing in the opposite direction. One of them wore a suit and the other two were in flat green military style outfits, the type used by officers. They were looking at a large portrait that hung on the far wall of the conference room, the man in the suit pointing out something to the others with his left index finger, while saying something that Robert couldn't quite make out. After hearing the heavy door close behind him, they turned around.

"Ah, perfect timing." the man in the suit said, clasping and rubbing his hands together as he looked Robert over. "Robert Valley, I presume?"

"That would be me." Robert said. He walked across the room to meet them. He couldn't help but notice that they were not sitting down as he approached, nor did they invite him to. He shook hands with the man in the suit and the man closest to him, who was in uniform. Three stars were attached to the collars of the second man's shirt, and a manila folder was tucked under his left arm. The third man didn't move or say a word. Robert could see that he was clearly a subordinate or assistant to the general.

The man in the suit introduced himself. "I am Justice Jerald Marrow, and this is General Kent. I take it Simon wasn't able to join us today?"

"Simon is still in Detroit overseeing the final touches of our latest project there. He likes to handle things personally until he is sure everything is running smoothly."

"Of course, we've been told there is no direct way to reach him, and that he prefers it that way. Just to be clear, you are his second in command, correct? I don't want to assume too much from what I hear in the news."

"I am." Robert said.

"Well, please ask mister Raimes to consider having an ID chip installed. He is a national treasure after all. We would hate to lose him. I'm sure he has many enemies in his chosen line of work." the Justice said.

"I'll let him know of your concerns."

"The General told me you've visited the Supreme Court before."

"Yes, a case went through the ninth circuit a few years ago. Some folks down south didn't think we should have been able to search or detain civilians, as we were a private organization. Even when the neighborhoods we were helping were burning to the ground and our people were randomly being attacked. They said it was a breach of fourth amendment rights."

"I do remember that one! That was a big win for you. If I remember, after that your little project really started to take off."

"That's right. We already had a long track record with local authorities on a case by case basis with such incidents in other cities, and made sure that everything was recorded through a drone grid in case anyone was mistreated in any way. After reviewing the videos we took of the incidents, the court sided with us, because we'd only gone in after our assistance had already been accepted by the mayor and because we were there to protect and dispense aid only. It was determined that our people were merely protecting themselves as volunteers in a hostile situation, and as such had a right in the face of senseless, unorganized and unsanctioned violence, to perform individual searches and detainments of violent members of the populace on the spot as responsible, independent members of the citizenry."

Justice Marrow nodded. "I take it mister Raimes has given you full authority here?"

"Simon has given me authority over all affairs pertaining to the Shotgun Relief Army, and has instructed me to provide any requested assistance we can to the government without terms."

The Judge looked at General Kent, who gave him a slight nod. "Very well," Marrow said, "Tell me Robert, how much do you know about what's been going on here in D.C. since last November?" he asked.

"I know that there was a tie in the Electoral College, and that when the House went to vote for a new president, some kind of digital paper trail was leaked to the press. It revealed that foreign billionaires, and at least one country that we don't get along with, bribed some House members, including the Speaker, so they would select a particular candidate. If I remember right, the guy they wanted in was someone very influential in the Senate. All I saw in the news after that was something about how the Senate had become unable as a body to investigate what had happened in the House, and then everything just went to hell."

"Not bad, but that's not all of it." Justice Marrow said, "In the event that the House is unable to select a replacement, the Constitution states that the Vice President is to become an interim president after the twentieth of January.Because the apparent corruption in both the House and the Senate appears to be widespread, and since the Vice President has suddenly become ill, too ill to serve, we now find ourselves past the March fourth deadline specified in the Twelfth Amendment, by which Congress was to select a new POTUS, without even a temporary one to take the reins."

Marrow walked around the long oak table, opposite to where Robert was standing. He placed his hands on it and leaned forward, "In response to this direst of circumstances, the majority party in Congress have passed emergency legislation and offered this equal branch of the government a unique honor, the responsibility of overseeing the day to day federal operations of the nation through our judicial system until an impartial investigation can be completed and another election date set." It wasn't difficult for Robert to discern by the Justice's tone that he was being a bit sarcastic with the last part of his statement. After a short pause, Justice Marrow's voice returned to normal. "In the meantime, to avoid a complete breakdown of government at the federal level, and to make sure that peace is enforced for the foreseeable future, all federal affairs will be handled by federal judges in each state. They will have full authority over local governorships and mayors under threat of immediate military action."

"Martial law?" Robert asked.

"We're trying to avoid using that term," General Kent broke his silence, his voice was flat and grating, like someone who had spent the entirety of their youth smoking menthols. It wasn't until his Adam's apple started moving up and down, that Robert saw the large scar that ran down the right side of the man's neck. "As far as the public and media are concerned, no such thing is occurring. For now, we're keeping the military out of it. We don't want panic or an uprising to come from this, so we're keeping the Armed Forces on alert, but for now, they are only being used to secure our borders and for continued protection from our foreign enemies."

The Justice waited for the General to finish and continued. "As the most recently appointed member of this court, it is tradition that I take on a number of responsibilities that the other, more senior members would like to avoid. Therefore the other Justices, in their divine wisdom have given to me the responsibility of being a liaison to your organization, which brings us to why we asked for you to come here. I'm sure you know what happens next."

"Some will suspect that you've grabbed power for yourselves, and have no intention of giving it back." Robert said.

"Precisely," Marrow stood upright again, and moved to a small cabinet that was set against the wall beyond his side of the table. He opened it, and took out a small glass and a bottle of what appeared to be Scotch. He motioned to Robert, "Would you like some?" Tempted by the offer, Robert felt his right hand move slightly forward, but he caught himself, remembering his past failings, and realized that the gesture may have been a test. He waved his hand as he pulled it back, and shook his head instead, as if to signal that he wasn't interested. Marrow looked at the others, who also declined in a similar manner. Marrow, looking a little disappointed, poured some for himself. He lifted the half empty glass of hard liquor to his lips, and drank most of it in one gulp before continuing. "Despite the fact that the Hypnotic War has been over for several years now, and accountability measures put in place for members of the press and other free media who omit, slander, or attempt to manipulate the population, a large portion of Americans still receive their information from extremely biased sources on all sides of the political landscape."

He lifted his glass and motioned toward the doorway, "The National Guard troops you saw posted outside are not precaution, they are an unfortunate necessity. Similar arrangements have been made at state capitols and Federal Court buildings across the country until we can sort out this mess. We have temporarily left the Constitution behind in this, and need to make sure that order is maintained. We are on thin ice here." He drank again and swallowed the remaining Scotch in his glass, then proceeded to pour himself another.

"So you want us to represent you, to be an arm of the Court?" Robert asked.

"No!" Marrow began to cough and then started to laugh. He waved a dismissive hand into the air, which traveled through a ray of light coming in through one of the windows behind him, briefly casting a shadow on Robert's face. "Not at all, we asked you here because the people trust Simon. Well, most of them do anyway. They believe he is impartial and not connected to the politics of this town. Without any help, he has become a household name, inspiring stability even among those who despise him, because of what *all* of you have accomplished over the last several years under his leadership. Transforming some of the worst of our inner cities into safe zones, while working with authorities to remove undesirable elements and providing aid and work programs to help those who live within. Achieving such a thing using only a modicum of violence is no small feat."

"It's almost as if we're doing the government's work for them already, I know." Robert said.

General Kent cleared his throat, "We are offering your organization limited support," he said. "Assistance with finding and recruiting more volunteers, a large budget with little to no oversight, and few strings attached. In exchange, you would be required to make yourselves and your people available to assist the National Guard and Armed Services as needed. With our help your outfit could finally come into the twenty-first century. Unfortunately, this help won't come quickly, it will take a few months to get it approved, but I think we'll be able to get around Congress and go straight to the Pentagon for a modest hand out. In the meantime, we will need assistance with a particular problem."

"You mean Seattle." Robert said.

General Kent passed the manila folder to Robert, "These last few years, the A.I. riots have been going like clockwork." he said. "They are, as you know the worst in the country, and the most covered by every type of news media. Local authorities tell us they are predictable though. When they aren't trying to stop or divert traffic downtown, they typically try to take the highway near SeaTac airport to disrupt transportation and commerce throughout the Tri-City area, and when they fail there, they usually move to other areas of the city, where they loot until they are dispersed, or their ring leaders are arrested."

"I thought the leaders were arrested last fall when they protested the election results." Robert opened the folder and started flipping through its contents.

"The last ones were, yes. But we have intelligence that shows at least one, a Tammy Shelton and two others who are as of yet still unidentified, are planning on taking charge of the riots in the Pacific Northwest this year. Any information you can get on the other two while you're there would be useful. If you manage to find and detain them, you can hand them over to the Guard after things settle down. We have already instructed Leavenworth Prison to provide transportation vehicles. They will meet you in Kansas City at your headquarters before you leave. You can use them for anyone you take into custody while you're there."

"Custody?" Robert asked, looking up from the folder.

"Well, you were an FBI agent for over ten years, weren't you?" Marrow asked. "Consider yourself and any others you see fit who are partaking in this police action, deputized. As of today, the Shotgun Army will be considered a voluntary civilian police force, operating under government supervision. You now have the authority to arrest and detain anyone you see fit who is in the area we have directed you to from the moment you arrive, whether they are attacking your people or not, under the humanitarian rules set forth by the Geneva Convention, of course. This way, we won't have to worry about any more of those pesky court cases. Just try not to kill anyone after you've arrested them."

"We're familiar with Tammy and the True Bolsheviks. She shouldn't be a problem." Robert said. He closed the folder.

"Good!" Marrow said. "I would say that you have no idea what good this will do for the country, but I know that you do. Having civilian volunteers using nonlethal force to put down the largest of the riots, well, it's what the people out there need to see. They need to know that they are the ones in control, not us, and not the anarchists. Simon has done a great job making his army a very diverse and positive force, not to mention everything he's done to make our young men feel useful again. We just want to help him to do what he does best. Help those in need, and protect the innocent."

General Kent chimed in again, "Most of the National Guard in the area will be moved to the Capitol in Olympia to protect it from anyone who might be coming in from the south. We can give you some support to make sure anything that happens on the highway doesn't spread into the city. The local police will have a small force north of the airport to stop anyone from advancing toward Bellevue or North Seattle."

"Bellevue. Of course, have to protect those who have the most to lose." Robert said. The general gave the judge an uneasy glance. "Sorry. Please continue, General."

"If looting or violence spreads to any other parts of the area, they too may be called away. When you arrive, you will meet with a small Guard group which you will relieve. They will be heading to the federal courthouse north of the city. Putting down the riot will be *your* job. The Guard won't have the time or manpower to deal with anything else. We will be depending on you. All of you."

Robert nodded and squared his shoulders. "You won't be disappointed. The New Hope for All organization and the Shotgun Relief Army thank you for this opportunity, and will do our best to make sure that the greater Seattle area is safe. I'm sure Simon will want to get out there as soon as I notify him."

"Then you'd better get going. It's supposed to warm up in a few days. As soon as the latest storm front ends, we expect they will be coming out in force. Here is the information package on our operations in the area and how to reach our officers there." The assistant reached around the general and passed Robert a small envelope. "As you already have a high level clearance due to your background, I trust that you will be able to keep it safe and understand the consequences of not doing so."

"I do." Robert said.

"Excellent!" Marrow said. "Thank you for your time, and God speed."

Robert placed the envelope in the folder and shook their hands again. He left the room and walked out of the building. Private Arnold sprang into action as Robert briskly walked by and followed him back to the bottom of the wide marble steps that stood in front of the western entrance, and across the plaza. When they reached the sidewalk, Robert returned his visitor's badge to the woman at the first checkpoint. He gave Arnold a small nod as the young man got back in line with his fellow soldiers, and went back through the crowd to the exact location on the side of the street where he'd first arrived.

When he was in clear view at the edge of the curb, a black low profile Connected Autonomous Vehicle, which had been waiting for him two blocks to the south, pulled up to the curb. The door on its side silently slid forward, and he got in. He sat down on a plush leather seat, and looked to his left. Already seated next to him, another man was looking out of the opposing window. He was wearing a red bib shirt of his own, his eyes covered with a pair of round rimmed sunglasses with gold tinted reflecting lenses. A few of the buttons on his shirt were not fastened, so that the top left side of his bib fell over his upper chest in the shape of a triangle. Without a sound, the door closed by itself, and the CAV began to move again.

Robert passed the folder to the man, tapping it against his right arm. The man looked away from the heavily tinted window, and down at the folder. He took it and opened it up on his lap.

"So?" he said. He stopped reading for a moment and looked at Robert.

Robert looked back at the first checkpoint for a moment. "So, they have their security badges sitting in a box on the curb. That, and if I wanted to, I could have transferred a virus or poison to a Supreme Court Justice *and* a three star general with a hand shake and no one would have known until it was too late." he said.

The man tilted his head and looked at Robert over the rims of his glasses. "We're not trying to break into the Supreme Court Robert, at least not yet anyway." he said.

"I know. It just bothers me." Robert said. He looked at his right arm. "When are you going to let me remove the stupid ID chip in my arm? I don't belong to the government anymore."

"Soon, for now it's better if they think they can track you. I want them to feel comfortable. They know that I don't have one. If neither of us did, this meeting might not have even happened. So?" he asked again.

"So, they bought it when I said you were still in Detroit."

"That means their surveillance algorithm still isn't sure about what I look like from the ground or in the air. That's good news, at least. Those look-alikes you found were a good idea."

"They aren't just for your safety, they'll also keep you from getting nailed with a 'face crime' infraction and will hold off the scammers for a while, not to mention the fakers who just want to belittle you."

"I thought face crime was just a rumor?"

"Trust me, it's not. We used to pick people up off the street around sensitive areas using random drone footage all the time. The A.I. could even tell what they were thinking by their temperature, facial expressions, and how they walked. We used a lot of stuff like that to catch people when I was in the bureau."

"And I thought they just did that in China." the man said. "What else?"

"You called it boss. They're giving you almost full autonomy in Seattle. We can even arrest and detain without immediately handing people over to the local authorities." He hit the other man on the shoulder. "How did you know all this would happen, Simon?"

"I didn't know that the Supreme Court would be the ones to take control." Simon said. "Once they did, it was only a matter of time before they reached out to us though. We positioned ourselves well, but time is exactly what we won't have much of after Seattle has been dealt with. We'll need to capitalize on this opportunity as much as we can. This is the end game, Robert. We need to be sure that when everything falls apart, everyone will be begging for us to lead. That means reminding them that we are out there and capable of taking control. It's time for the world to see what we can do."

"And if they don't?"

"Don't what?"

"Come begging."

"Then plan 'B' goes into effect."

"Ooooh, plan 'B'." Robert rubbed his hands together impersonating Marrow. "Um, what's plan 'B' again?" He raised an eyebrow at Simon.

Simon took off his sunglasses and gave him an intensely dissatisfied look, "We've discussed this before, you'll know when I tell you, but it shouldn't come to that. You know Robert, sometimes I wonder if you still work for the Bureau."

Robert rose up his hands as if to show that he had given up, and shrugged. "Just wondering if I need to cancel Christmas!" he said. "Do you think the Justices are behind the Vice President's sudden leave of absence?"

"There's no way to know right now. My sources tell me no one can get near the man, save for his personal physician. If he dies, we might learn more about what happened. Until then, we must assume it could have been any one of a number of factions that had something to gain from the chaos that's transpired in government circles since he stepped down. He could also be faking it, trying to find a way out of a bad situation, or worse, someone powerful could be blackmailing him or threatening his family, perhaps the same people who were caught influencing Congress, not that any of it matters now anyway. There will be plenty of time to look into it after the smoke clears. In the meantime, we need to look at this for the opportunity that it is, and not allow ourselves to get distracted in the minutia of the situation."

"His honor said that it would take some time to get us any requests for new tech, possibly several months. He plans to go straight to the Pentagon."

"He's going to use it as a carrot. We'll just move forward with our original plan then. We don't need any more hardware to accomplish our goals. By this time next year, everything will be different...everything." Simon put his glasses back on and looked out the window again.

"Whatever you say boss, whatever you say." Robert stretched out his legs and lay back in his seat. You got the plane tickets?" he asked.

"They're waiting for us at the airport. I want you to get out of the CAV before I do. I'll wait until the CAV returns to the rental lot and change, then board the plane separately. Buy yourself a seat front and center in coach. I'll find a spot near the back as usual." Simon said.

"You just want to be closer to the bathrooms in case you get airsick again, or maybe the stewardesses?" Robert raised his eyebrows and nudged Simon with his left elbow.

"Ha-ha. Let's just keep our minds on task, shall we?"

"One day, Simon, one day I'm going to rub off on you, and I *will* be there to see it, oh yes I will." He stretched out his arms and yawned. "I already feel jetlagged. I'm going to take a nap. Wake me up when we get there." Robert closed his eyes and started to doze off.

Simon looked out of his window again. Since they'd arrived, he'd taken the time to admire the monuments and memorials that dotted the capitol. He enjoyed also observing those who went about their business in and around them, most largely ignorant of the sacrifices of the past that had been made so they could live as they did. It entered his mind that they were equally oblivious to the more modern pains that people like him endured every day to keep the world from imploding in on them. Mindlessly, they pursued their dreams without a care for the larger world around them. There were exceptions to the rule of course, but most were easily manipulated, their thoughts force fed to them on a daily basis by those in power to keep them under control. Free to live but not to think. *That will change.* He thought. *I'll be the one to change it, and when I do, people in the future will look up at my monument and remember me, every last one of them.*

Then he saw something through his window that startled him, something that shouldn't have been there. A slightly overweight man in a worn black suit, his hair combed over in a vain attempt to cover the top of his partially bald head, was standing on the sidewalk on the other side of the street. He was talking to someone who did not seem particularly interested in what he was saying, another man wearing a white collared shirt, who was facing in the other direction. As he watched, the man in the white shirt looked down at his watch several times, and shifted his footing as if agitated, the man in the old suit purposefully blocking his path while trying to speak to him. The man in the white shirt stopped shifting his stance, and began waving his hands around, no doubt yelling for the other man to get out of his way. After having his say, the man in the suit relented and allowed him to pass by, and he continued on his way into a nearby building.

That's when the CAV they were in passed by the scene. As it did, the overweight man turned and stared in Simon's general direction with a slightly confused look upon his face. This lasted only for a moment though, before he turned around and followed after the person he'd bothered. Simon leaned away from the window, knowing no one should have been able to see through the heavy, one way tint that was infused into the glass, not without using some kind of advanced tech which this man did not appear to possess, at least from what he could tell by looking at him. *It couldn't be him, no, it couldn't be. Simon thought.*

Robert began to snore, making Simon jump in his seat. After giving his subordinate a disagreeable look, he turned his attention back to the scenery outside. The man had vanished into the same building. He took a deep breath, lay back in his own seat and closed his eyes. *No, of course it's not. I just need some rest.*

****

Fourteen hours later and more than twenty-three hundred miles to the west, a tense looking young man in a black wool winter jacket paced back and forth on a sidewalk of his own. He had smooth features and thick black hair, his hands and feet fidgeting as he anxiously waited on the edge of the busy Seattle street corner. He too watched as an expensive car with rounded, sleek lines drove up to the curb in front of him. The car that approached him was not automated though. In fact, he didn't know exactly what kind of vehicle it was, nor did he care. It came to a stop, and the passenger door slid open. Inside, he saw an attractive woman lean over toward the driver giving him a peck on the cheek. As she did this, she placed her left hand over the man's right thigh. Then she grabbed her purse and started to turn when the man behind the wheel cracked a smile and made an awkward attempt to wink at her.

Having already turned to see if someone were waiting for her on the sidewalk, she missed the not so subtle sign of affection, and didn't look at the man behind the wheel again until she had gotten out, turning only briefly to give the driver a polite smile and a small wave goodbye as the door closed, and the car began to move back into traffic.*Another satisfied deviant, no doubt.*The young man thought to himself, now frozen in place. His fingers curled into fists inside the coat's oversized pockets. She walked up to him, looked directly into his eyes, grabbed onto the lapels of his jacket and smiled, half drunk on herself. She was wearing her special contacts again. She had set them so that they slowly morphed randomly from one bright pastel color to the next. On a face as beautiful as hers, the effect was mesmerizing. He hated her contacts. On at least one occasion, he could have sworn that she'd changed the true color of her eyes beneath them, and used the fact that he'd remembered her real eye color wrong against him. He pulled away from her.

"I can't do this anymore." he said.

"You can't do what?" She looked back in the direction the car was driving, "Him? He's just a friend, Jerry. He gave me a ride here to see you!"

Jerry gave her a knowing look. "You couldn't have ordered a CAV? I'm not stupid, Noel, he winked at you for crying out loud!"

"Did he?" She looked back again, the hint of a smile appearing at the corners of her lips. Then she looked at Jerry, realizing her mistake. Her mouth dropped open but nothing came out.

Jerry pointed at her. "I'm not into this crap. Other guys might be willing to risk getting an incurable disease, but I'm not. Antibiotics don't work anymore, Noel, and there's no telling what people might have-"

"Oh for-" She threw her hands up and reached into her purse, "We've all been vaccinated Jerry!" Seeing through the faux display of frustration, Jerry recognized it for what it really was, yet another in a long line of sad attempts to avoid the issue. Jerry looked on as she rummaged around for something, anything that could be turned into a reason to change the subject. Then, finding herself out of excuses, she dropped her arms to her sides and looked at Jerry again. "You know who I am, Jerry."

"Oh yeah, I know!" he said.

"Not this again!" she yelled at him. "Don't be so salty Jerry. Most of the guys I know go around doing whoever they want. Well it's my turn now, our turn." She pointed at herself as she spoke.

"You know I'm not like those guys." Jerry said.

"Yeah, and you're like, the only one who isn't. That's why I like you Jerry, but I need *my time*. Do you understand?"

"I understand." Jerry said. "You think you know how things should be, but you don't. You really do-"

"We are who we are Jerry." she said. "Our experiences define us, and we can't change who we are. Our experiences are all we have in this life, and I still want to have more experiences with you, but if you don't want them with me, then...do you." She waved an arm in the air.

"You know I don't go in for that existential B.S. Noel. Saying you believe that nothing has meaning and the truth of reality cannot be known from one side of your mouth, while making up your own meaning from the other side, preaching it to others so that you won't feel bad about all of the different ways you take advantage of people. I can't stand it. Stop pretending that you can reason your way out of your guilt. I can't stand watching you do it to yourself, living a lie like that. It's too much for me to bear."

"You're the one living the lie Jerry! You're the one who won't admit what you are. I know you, I've been with you-"

"Just because I act a certain way while having sex with someone doesn't mean that's who I want to be all of the time!" he yelled back at her. "It certainly doesn't mean that getting into bed with people is the only thing I aspire to do with my life! Seriously, who do you think I am?"

She rolled her eyes and put her hands up in a defensive manner, "Obviously not who I thought." She turned around and started walking away from him. She raised an arm in the air and waved. "Call me when you come to your senses and get over yourself. Until then, you can have fun playing at home with your rent-a-dolls!"

She left Jerry standing on the sidewalk to contemplate his mistake, shifting her weight from side to side a little more than usual as she headed off, in a clear attempt to show Jerry what he was missing. When she had finished crossing the street from which she'd arrived, she let down her long dark hair and let it flow in the breezy cool night air, and though he waited to see if she would, she didn't look back.

Jerry felt a fit of anger surge up from inside his chest. *Why? Why does she have to be this way?* He thought. *Why am I not good enough for her?* He turned toward the bar where they were supposed to have their date. Through a large window, he could see their mutual friends sitting on bar stools, enjoying their drinks and laughing. He and Noel were supposed to join them that night for the first time as a real couple. Obviously, without Jerry on her arm, Noel already had a backup plan with someone else.

"Maybe she just wants sex." A voice said from somewhere nearby. Jerry turned around. Sitting next to a street lamp and a few trash bags, just a few yards away from where he had waited for the last hour, was an old homeless man he hadn't noticed the entire time. He was looking in the direction that Noel had stormed off in, his eyes were opened wide, and he was swaying slowly from side to side. He had a large scruffy beard, and was wearing dark and dirty looking clothes that were full of holes. Jerry guessed it wouldn't be long before he started losing them one article at a time. He thought about helping the guy out, but decided it was best not to get involved. Instead, he looked up across the street at the thousands of lights that illuminated the buildings of the Seattle skyline, giving his mind time to wonder, as it often did, about the stories of those who were behind every window, or responsible for any one of the hundreds of drones that were flying purposefully through the night air to and fro between them, allowing himself a momentary distraction from his own problems. After a few seconds of indecision about what he should do with what was left of his evening, he made up his mind, and started the long walk back to his apartment building.

When he started walking, he heard the man on the sidewalk mumble something. "...you know."

Jerry turned, curious as to what the man had just said. "What was that?" he asked.

The hobo's wide eyes turned slowly in Jerry's direction. He gulped and blinked once before speaking again. Then, with a small sluggish slur, he said, "There's a reason...she left you." He looked down at the sidewalk as he said the last few words. Then he looked up at Jerry again and continued with a high pitched voice, now clearly speaking in the universal language of drunk, "Don't worry, man. Everything will be alright. He's got you man, God's got you." The man nodded a few times and then looked down at the pavement again. What Jerry could only see as a sad shell of a human being, then started pulling at one of the holes in his own worn out jacket. The insulation was coming out of it, and he was trying to keep the hole closed, attempting to hold the fabric together with his fingers.

Jerry looked down at his own wool coat. It was hardly new, and he had three others just like it in storage at his apartment. As it wasn't necessarily freezing, and since his own health was not something that he cared about in that moment, he checked the pockets to make sure he hadn't forgotten anything in them, and took it off. He then knelt down next to the man and handed the heavy coat to him. The man's eyes grew wide as he took it from Jerry's hands. A large smile crossed the homeless man's face. "He does have you. I know you know, I can tell. God bless you man, bless you."

Jerry nodded, and had started walking again when he heard his Omni-Glass beeping in his right pants pocket. "What the, who's-?"

he said to himself. Frustrated, he took a small white carrying case out of his pocket and opened it. Then he took a single contact-like lens out of it, and placed it into his right eye. As it came alive, he saw a small message at the bottom right of his vision, indicating that a call was coming through from a scrambled private line. He cleared his mind of distractions. *Omni, answer call, audio only.* He thought. He started to walk away from the bar's entrance. The call picked up and he heard a man's voice.

"Jerry!" it said. "I have a job for you. Big bonus, some risk might be involved though."

Jerry turned around and looked down the street one last time. Noel was still nowhere to be seen. The drunk on the sidewalk had covered himself in Jerry's old coat and had passed out. He looked into the bar one more time at the people inside. *They're really more Noel's friends than mine anyway.*

"I'm not busy," he said. "What do you have for me?"

SARINA

MISIKASHI-1750

Then Moses set apart three cities beyond the Jordan toward the sunrise, that the man slayer might flee there, who kills his neighbor unintentionally and didn't hate him in time past, and that fleeing to one of these cities he might live.
-Deuteronomy, 4:41-42

Chapter One

I-5 Corridor north of SEATAC International Airport
Seattle, Washington State
Friday, March 25[th,] 8:19AM PST

A strong gust of cool wind that originated from Puget Sound blew eastward through the city and over the highway, dissipating the latest round of teargas. As the smoke cleared, the chaos and confusion that was prevailing just north of the Seattle-Tacoma airport came into focus for a third party who was watching astutely from the sidelines. Feeling like he was late for a party he wasn't invited to, Jerry Farron stood atop a rusted out abandoned van that was parked on the side of a road that ran parallel to the Interstate in the south end of Seattle's industrial district. He was shivering slightly, wearing only a pair of jeans and a tee shirt despite the cold morning air, but was too distracted by his quarry to notice.

With some assistance from an augmented reality lens in his right eye, he could see virtually everything that was happening on the highway. The lens was synced to a drone that was hovering some sixty feet above the burgeoning confrontation. With a critical expression on his face, he looked over the progress that the various groups involved had made since his arrival. The purpose of the protest was nothing new. Every year, the unions organized and came out in an attempt to attract media attention to the most recent round of layoffs caused by advancements in Artificial Intelligence and robotic automation. In their latest effort, they had joined up with the most recent iterations of a variety of social rights and other advocacy groups. Each had their own reasons for being there, and together made a formidable force, which was good news for him, as it meant the authorities would be too busy to notice his presence.

Omni, Focus zoom, twenty percent. He thought to himself. A new window appeared in the display that was projected onto the lens. Included within was an even closer look at the action. Able to see the players in more detail, Jerry made out the easily identifiable red and pink arm bands of the True Bolsheviks, who appeared to be taking the lead. They were marching north ahead of the others toward a series of wooden and plastic barricades that had been set up by the local police. The officers stood dutifully behind them in riot gear, their unyielding forms standing ready to stop any advance on their position.

Not far behind the True Bolshevik's main force, four or five union groups that had scattered when the last volley of gas canisters was fired in their direction, started to regroup. Their numbers were smaller than those of their successors when counted all together, but they were better armed, most having come to the occasion wielding chains, wooden planks, and other varied blunt instruments in their hands. They shared their positions with the local chapter of the Democratic Socialist Republican party, otherwise known as the DSR, their members wearing bright blue sashes or bandanas somewhere on their person in a vain effort to separate themselves from the others. Keeping up the façade of being the only group in the conflict that 'cared about the people', the DSR was currently in the process of removing any who had been affected by the teargas while the True Bolsheviks provided medical attention for any that had been injured or burned in the most recent face-off using converted medical vans to the south.

In general, the rioters appeared to be more organized than previous times Jerry had been sent out to report on their activities and were no longer the unruly, chaotic mob he had become accustomed to seeing when they started their yearly round of protests each spring. They were still a ramshackle group to be sure, but also appeared to be much more coordinated than they had been in previous years, and the day was still young. Noticing how aggressive they were as well, Jerry supposed that the protesters who did not appreciate violence had been sent into the city center for the time being, where the majority of activist groups usually congregated with their picket signs and amplifiers so those who lived and worked downtown could see their quippy catchphrases and hear their endless speeches. *This riot has been going on since rush hour last night, which means some of the protesters haven't gotten any sleep yet.* Jerry thought to himself. *Maybe it will burn out by evening like the one that happened last fall.* But these thoughts did not comfort him. It was still only 7AM, and things were different. America was under new management, one that the people had not elected.

He let out a sigh, and looked on in disbelief as his breath hung in the air for a moment in the morning cold. "Well, at least it's not raining." he said to himself out loud. He'd been watching the situation unfold since daybreak, not only using the Omni-Glass lens to scout out the event and record it's progress, but to tap into some of the hundreds of publicly streamed real time news reports available to him as well which allowed him to see every part of the engagement as it was happening from multiple points of view. He wasn't there to gawk at it like some spectator though, or to report on the riot even if that was his usual role. When the teargas had blown away completely, he saw his opening. It was time to head for the highway. There was money to be made.

"Do you see that?" A small female voice reverberated through his cranium.

"Yeah, yeah I see it." he responded. "I'm heading in. Have you spotted me yet?"

"Wait a sec, yeah, I see you. Blue jeans and...are you wearing a white shirt? Are you trying to draw attention to yourself?" The voice sounded irritated.

Jerry looked down at himself. She was right. "Hold on." He reached down to the bottom right side of his un-tucked tee shirt and felt along its bottom edge until his fingers found a concealed button that was sewn into the seam. He pressed it three times changing his shirt from white to blue, then red and finally black.

"Flat black?" she said, "You can't do better than flat black?"

Not knowing which of the multitude of drones that were flying around the area she was watching him from, he simply looked up in the general direction of the highway and raised an eyebrow. "Ok, fashion Gestapo, fine." he said and pushed a second button that was next to the first, each press causing an image or slogan of some kind to appear on the front of or around his torso. He cycled through several of the available options which ranged from reasonably playful to outright insulting before finally stopping on one that resonated with him. It appeared in large red block letters over the dark fabric spelling the words, 'DO YOU!'

"Better?" he said, lifting up his arms.

"Much. You'll fit right in."

Jerry took off a lightweight backpack he'd brought with him and set it down next to his right foot. Out from it, he took a dark blue towel and a water bottle. He poured some water onto the towel and wrapped it around his head, covering his mouth and nose and tied it tightly behind his neck. *Hope this holds.* He thought. *Didn't have time to get a cheap mask and can't blend in with my expensive one, so this will have to do.* He reached into the backpack again, took out an expensive looking pair of sunglasses, and put them on. He focused his thoughts into another command. *Omni, sync to ProtoMark Glasses, and bring up structural outlines.* The interface in his lens vanished and reappeared in both lenses of the glasses giving the interface a deeper and larger space to work with.

Through the glasses, he could see the orange outlines of several burning vehicles that had been moved onto the highway by the protesters earlier that morning and people marching toward them through the smoke. Behind the burning cars more outlines revealed information about the surrounding buildings along with their entrances and exits, handy information to have should he need to make a quick getaway or find somewhere to hide or lay low for a few minutes. The augmented data being fed through his lens and into the glasses also revealed the structure of the highway itself. At the moment, it looked as if the union members were finished regrouping and were about to make another charge. Jerry planned to be with them when they did.

"Are you sure you can't get IDs from the drone feed?" he asked. Several seconds passed before he received a response.

"No, the smoke from the cars they set on fire in the northbound lanes is blocking my view. We knew this would happen, the same thing happened last year and we missed our opportunity, that's why Tom asked you to go out there. We need to know who the leaders are this time around before they get arrested. They can't be the same organizers of the last riot because all of them are either in jail or out of the country. They have to be on the highway because no leaders have shown up to speak downtown. They aren't gathering peacefully this time either. Some of the protesters have started looting and setting fires to street level businesses there. No one knows who put this together yet, and we could really make out well by selling anything you can record that has their faces in it, but we need it now."

"And how am I supposed to know who they are?"

"You know the answer to that Jerry, don't joke around. Just take the time to look at anyone barking orders, organizing anything or taking shelter behind the others while still trying to look important."

Jerry looked northeast, no longer using the feed from the drone. He focused his thoughts again. *Omni, outline people who are wearing helmets with visors in blue.* Multiple figures that were standing on the northbound side of the highway changed from orange to blue. Their outlines indicated that most of them were carrying riot shields, obviously the local police force. There must have been two or three hundred of them. The protesters, estimated to have been about the same in number earlier that morning, were growing in their ranks. They could just turn south and head toward the ramps that led to the airport terminals, essentially stopping all transportation in and out of SeaTac, but they seemed content for the time being drumming up attention in the news by lighting the Interstate on fire, perhaps with the hope that by doing so more people might show up and join their cause.

The cold wind began to pick up again, pushing its way through the nearby buildings. He raised an arm up to block the harsh breeze, turning his face away from it just long enough to notice how the rays of the sun seemed to sparkle off of the tall skyscrapers to the north. It was still rising, and for a few seconds, the reflection the eastern skyline made against their nearly flawless surfaces made it appear as if there were two great balls of flame in opposition to one another, destined to eventually meet somewhere far above the rest of the world. But of course, one of them was an illusion and would soon vanish long before the real McCoy would reach its zenith.

He was glad he'd put on the glasses as he might have been blinded by the bright visage, but also noticed that in the light of day the newer structures that were erected after the calamity looked nothing like they did at night. Seeing the Cascade Mountains in the reflection of the giant mirror that was downtown Seattle he also realized that he hadn't been this far out from the city center for a while. He found himself staring at the sheer beauty of the sight, the stark contrast of the tall pristine pillars standing behind the rundown section of the city where he stood as if Seattle were some mystical place full of justice and beauty. But of course, he knew the truth.

"What are you doing? Go now!" the voice yelled at him.

"Sorry, on my way." he said.

He climbed down from the van and crossed the street to the parking lot where he'd had a CAV taxi drop him off. It had taken some work to find the right wording so that the Connected Automated Vehicle would leave him where there was no formal address, but he'd managed. Apparently saying "Let me out now or I'll sue." a few times in a row was a back door to getting a CAV to let someone out anywhere. He was not unfamiliar with the place he'd made the CAV stop, having trespassed through that particular parking lot before. He'd used the same route several times to reach the highway whenever he needed to report on a situation developing near SeaTac be it hostage or terrorist related or one of the many protests like the one he was about to go into, usually designed to get attention for one cause or another or to force a local politician's hand on some issue in exchange for getting traffic to the airport going again.

The van he was standing on was located across the street from a fenced in storage lot on Airport Way that was owned by a small shipping company called Aloha Freight Services LLC. The lot was full of shipping containers, old machinery and any number of types of transportable materials typically used for a wide variety of construction projects, many of which had been there for years waiting for an industrious buyer to come along and utilize them for some grand project but no one had come. A few years earlier, he'd found a route behind and through the long rows of forklifts and piles of scrap metal that allowed him to avoid the one, solitary security camera which overlooked the entire lot while doing a report on thefts in the area.

During an interview, he was allowed to see videos recorded by the security cameras that monitored the property. Remembering at the time that he wasn't far from the place where the Interstate protests most frequently occurred, he'd noticed that the top corner of a large steel cargo container, which was well worn by the elements and surrounded by high grass, had been placed close to the highway and concealed a portion of the fence which he could climb over without being seen. After navigating his way through the lot, he climbed the fence and began to make his way up the grassy shoulder of the highway to the southbound CAV dedicated lane that ran along the outside of the others, which were still reserved for gas powered vehicles.

When he reached the top of the shoulder, Jerry could see that the CAV lane was still operating. A short line of CAVs, possibly a dozen in number, were heading toward him from the north, likely on their way to the airport. Jerry didn't understand why the lane was still open as he doubted that heading to the airport in a private CAV while a riot was in progress nearby would have been a smart move for anyone especially since only the wealthiest of the wealthy had their own automated vehicles, the rest being owned by taxi services that protected their investments by programming them to avoid operating in any conditions that might cause them damage. He watched as several of the private CAVs drove past as he moved to the guardrail next to the emergency lane. A few of them slowed down, giving their passengers more time to gawk at what was happening in the other lanes. *Yeah Timmy,* Jerry thought to himself. *On the way to the Bahamas we saw all these poor people fighting on the highway for some strange reason. It turned out to be the most exciting part of the trip!*

Without his Omni-Glass, he wouldn't have been able to make out the majority of the protesters. With it, he was able to see multiple layers of them, it's weak Artificial Intelligence instantly connecting to the Omni web database where it was capable of comparing and identifying each and every object that was in his field of view, right down to every bolt in a car or each visible stone on the side of the road depending on the amount of detail he wanted it to see. For the time being, he'd changed the settings to identify only those objects he needed to be aware of in a riot. As such, the Omni-Glass was able to identify a variety of weapons and other things commonly used in violent situations, as well as a few more common objects like beer bottles and large rocks. These were outlined in yellow when they were identified as being in a person's hands or flying through the air. The aspect of the A.I. that he would need most on that day though, was the custom made search engine that quickly allowed him to identify and catalog human faces without governmental interference or permission.

He climbed over the guardrail. As another CAV traveled within a few feet from his position down the highway at full speed, his Omni-Glass attempted to make out the shapes of the people within through its tinted windows. Just as he thought, most people in the CAVs were looking at the fires while others simply appeared to be doing mundane activities like reviewing documents, talking to others, or sleeping.

He waited for the next small break in traffic, enough for him to step out into the lane. As soon as he did, the very next vehicle quickly and smoothly slowed to a complete stop finishing the maneuver within inches of him. The darkened windows concealed the people inside, but his glasses showed the outline of at least two surprised passengers who moved suddenly, reacting to the CAVs sudden decrease in speed. The CAV he'd stopped was definitely owned by a private party. It was black and sleek and had an elaborate silver grill on the front, reminding him of old Cadillac SUVs. Other CAVs immediately began to slow down and stop behind it, fast creating a line of twenty or so vehicles before he could reach the other side. He raised his hand to block his face so that it would not be seen or recorded by any onboard cameras. A calm, robotic male voice originating from the vehicle began to speak. "Jay walking in a CAV lane can result in a five hundred dollar fine and even jail time. Please remove yourself from the roadway." He changed his flat hand into another well known shape as he passed, without looking at the CAV as he did so. As soon as he was out of the way, the autonomous cars quietly started moving again, continuing along their predetermined route.

Without looking back, he crossed the grassy median and vaulted over a low line of concrete barriers that ran along the side of the regular southbound lanes of the highway. Picking up his pace, he kept his eyes on the northbound lanes, occasionally looking south to see if the protesters he was planning to conceal himself within, had started to advance. It appeared as if some of them had already begun to press through the smoke that was still

billowing out of several of the burning vehicles they themselves
had set fire to before sunrise. Most of these were old steel or
fiberglass jalopies that still used fossil fuels to run before new
government regulations essentially made them useless.

He crossed the smaller median between the south and
northbound lanes and saw an opportunity to enter the fray at a spot
where there was a lot of smoke that could shield him from
detection. Deciding to take it, he took a deep breath and ran
headlong into the smoldering fumes, quickly blending into the
crowd of protesters. Once among their ranks, he took off his
backpack again and from it took out a folded tire iron. He pressed a
button on its side, unfolding it and locked it into its extended
position. That's when he caught the attention of two DSR members
standing nearby. They, after looking down at the two words bluntly
displayed on his shirt, lifted their thumbs, and nodded in approval.
They were wearing plain, white surgical masks and what looked
like old hockey pads on their knees and elbows over their clothes,
sections of much larger pieces of defensive gear that had been torn
off and reassembled into something more practical. He walked
through the smoke toward them.

As he approached, Jerry noticed that one of them had a
feminine shape and that they were holding hands with one another.
When he was within five feet of their position, the A.I. in his
Omni-Glass began comparing what it could see of their facial
oddities and nonsymmetrical attributes with known identities that
were listed on a variety of social networking sites and several
lesser known government databases even though they were
partially covered by handkerchiefs. Doing this wasn't legal of
course, in fact, it was quite dangerous, requiring a series of illegal
hacks he'd collected or bought over the last two years specifically
designed to locate and mess with highly protected servers in such a
way that they were tricked into operating as if the hack infiltrating
their systems was either just another update or a check disk
routine. If he were arrested while using the software in a public
area, it could land him in jail for several years, but since the hacks
were made only to collect photographs and videos, he figured it
was unlikely that anything too bad would happen to him even if he
were caught. At least he hoped that was the case.

"Where do you want me?" He walked over to the couple,
acting as if he had met them before.

"Looks like you could break some shields with that thing!" the
woman said. By her voice, Jerry could tell that she was both young
and nervous. Almost as soon as she spoke the A.I. in his Omni-
Glass lens found a match from a list it had already compiled by her
body type, estimated size and shape of her upper facial features,
their general location just south of Seattle and an estimation of

how far someone with her appearance and behavior would be willing travel to go to a riot. Another small pop-up window appeared in his vision, this one showing him what she looked like when she wasn't hiding behind a mask. It notified him that her name was Ellen Margaret Stapleton, a twenty two year old university student from the Seattle area. The guy was probably her boyfriend, and they were both most likely there to prove to themselves that they cared for the little people or so that they could brag to their friends about how they had "participated".

"Is the big guy up there in the front or organizing everything from the back?" he asked them. He'd been down this road before. These kids weren't experienced but as they were clearly associated with an influential group being college students, there was a good chance that they had been close to one of the ring leaders earlier that day and might know where he or she was.

"Tammy is in the back with the support group." the boy said. "I think Aaron and Chavez are somewhere near the front of the crowd throwing Molotov's." The A.I. gave Jerry two possible identities for the young man in its final analysis of his voice just as he'd suspected. Both were university students, only one of which was listed as being single. But Jerry's mind wasn't on the information being presented to him about these two. It had already moved onto bigger and more important things.

"Tammy Shelton?" he said. He had heard of her before. She ran for Mayor of Seattle in the last election for the Communist Party.

"Yeah. Wait, who are you?"

"James Ardent," Jerry said without missing a beat. "I'm with the anarchists. I worked with Tammy a couple of months ago."

"Oh." the boy said, sounding unsure of himself. Even through the handkerchief on the kid's face, Jerry could tell he wasn't buying it.

"Time to break some shields!" Jerry said and ran north in the direction of the amassing crowd.

"Did you get that?" he said.

"I got it." the voice in his head responded. "It would be better to have actual live video confirmation that Tammy Shelton is there herself, but I'm not sure you'll have the time. We need to get you out of there before you get arrested for threatening police with a weapon. Seriously, why did you bring that?"

"It's served its purpose." He folded the tire iron and threw it under one of the burning cars.

"Now I just have to find Aaron and this guy Chavez. Any idea who they might be?"

"Aaron may be Aaron Fornier, the homeless advocate from LA. You know, that guy who started the riots there after the quake, the one that forced the state to provide shelter and food for the homeless survivors, long term."

"I know him." he said.

"Nothing for any Chavez, it could be an alias. Wait, don't turn around. Someone is talking to that couple. They might have seen you get rid of your tire iron."

"Damn, thought the smoke was too thick."

"Sending you a visual, you see him?" Yet another window appeared in his glasses. It showed a bird's eye view of the area. He saw himself from above, through a break in the smoke in front of the others. Not far behind him, someone was running in his direction, waving what looked like a heavy chain above their head.

"Oh, you guys are paying me extra for this!" Jerry said. He waited until the aggressor was close enough to hit, ducked as the assailant swung the heavy chain over his head, turned around, and kicked the man in his left knee, making him fall to the ground in agony. He then clenched his fists as tightly as he could and punched the aggressor with a hard left hook. The sad excuse for an insurgent's head hit the pavement, and he was down for the count.

"Gee, that was easier than I thought it would be, must have been another overzealous teenager." Jerry kicked the body of his attacker over and took a red surgical mask off of his face so that he could take a better look at him. Beneath the bandana was the soft face of a kid who couldn't have been more than sixteen or seventeen years old. He had long dark hair and smooth features and was wearing a black tee shirt that briefly caught Jerry's attention. Printed on the front in white was the artistically interpreted outline and features of some mid-twentieth century celebrity that Jerry couldn't quite pin down in his memory. The man in the picture had a troubled look with squinting eyes and was wearing a leather jacket. He held a cigarette between two of his fingers in the closed fist of one hand and a bright blue pixilated sword in the other. Underneath the odd portrait, and over a splash of red, large white letters were printed in a strange font that read 'Griefer'. *Great, a minor.* Jerry thought. *I'd better get out of here ASAP.*

"You're a badass, Jerry!" The woman's voice returned. "You ever do anything like that before?"

"Uh, nope!" Jerry said. He kicked the chain under another burning vehicle and noticed that the unfortunate anarchist that had tried to take him down had a trash can lid strapped to his back that was rigged with two leather straps for handles. Jerry took the makeshift shield and ran through the heat and smoke toward the mounting sounds of chaos that lay ahead.

A moment later, and he was close enough to the tumult of the colliding forces to see that it mainly consisted of a decent sized contingent of the True Bolsheviks and an unyielding line of police officers, most of them holding riot shields. A few dozen police on horseback moved through the line and started pushing south, a strategy they reserved for intimidating the opposition, but it only emboldened them. Before the riders, over a thousand protesters that were scattered about the entire width of the interstate reciprocated by attacking like the tide, pushing back at their "oppressors" in small alternating groups of five to ten at an almost rhythmic pace, each small wave retreating like clock-work in order to allow for the next attack. They would then double back to get more Molotov cocktails or to bandage their wounds before heading into danger again.

Meanwhile, through small breaks in the smoke above the commotion, Jerry witnessed a large cloud of drones of all shapes and sizes, was gathering. There were more there than he had ever seen at a riot or at any event in recent memory. The robotic cloud moved into the air space above their heads, each one carrying a camera, streaming all they could capture on video to the leaders of both sides, and to the rest of the world. *Great, it'll be a miracle if I get out of here unseen now.* He thought.

Normally the local protesters he had come to know, would have been more cautious in a conflict of that kind, throwing the flaming cocktails and whatever else they could get their hands on, from a safe distance. On that day however, they seemed to be more desperate than usual. As he'd suspected before he arrived on the highway, the gravity of the situation was escalating. Then, over the shouts and reverberating sounds of clashing metal and shattering glass Jerry heard someone ahead close to the police line yelling something though a megaphone. He couldn't make out what was being said, but whatever it was it had an immediate effect on the protesters ahead of him. Quickly changing their tactics, all of the protesters rushed the police line at the same time in an attempted blitz. They tried to force their way through the riot troops, successfully pushing the line back a few yards. They also began throwing their cocktails and other objects over the heads of the police, setting small fires behind their position and causing some of them standing at the rear of their formation to catch fire as they gave ground.

Knowing that the cops could see outlines through the smoke just as he could using their visors and that their A.I. was doing its own series of investigations so that they could pick up the worst offenders at a later time, Jerry stopped observing the spectacle and started looking at every face he could. He was short on time. The protest turned riot was turning into a war, something that he hadn't anticipated, and he didn't want to get caught on the wrong side of things when the big guns were brought in.

He was also protecting an investment. An entire year's bonus had gone into getting the lens and glasses. Not only that, but both would have been useless if he hadn't also sought out and bought hacks for them and had them installed and tested by someone who knew how to do both without getting caught. This meant that the hacks weren't cheap either, but without them, the Omni-Glass A.I. wouldn't be able to do more than search through public records and easily accessible accounts on a few popular community sites. Without the hacks, his Omni-Glass and ProtoMark glasses were just expensive toys, but the software he had added to them made them priceless. It would be hard for him to recover from losing them should they happen to break or be lost as he had become dependent on the edge they gave him in the field.

Jerry used the shield to cover his face as much as he could while pressing through the thick waves of smoke that swirled around him, detected a hint of teargas in the air, and began to cough. The coughing fit that ensued, forced him to turn his eyes so that he noticed a small group of men throwing Molotov Cocktails from behind a burned out vehicle not far from the police line to his right. As he got closer, he could see that there four men were in the group. Three of them were throwing lit bottles over the car as the fourth, which was kneeling next to a large duffle bag filled with bottles, used a cheap lighter to set more of them aflame, passing them forward in quick succession. Then, while steadying himself so that the A.I. could focus, he saw it, an unclaimed bullhorn was there lying on the ground between them. Two of the men had lost any face coverings they may have brought with them when they'd arrived, and like Jerry, the thick smoke and lingering vapors from the last round of teargas were causing all of them to cough violently and often.

He began moving closer to the car that the men were behind and saw a middle aged woman who was kneeling not far from his position. She was alone in the center of one of the lanes with her face down and was in the middle of having her own coughing fit except that hers wasn't stopping. Seeing an opportunity to get closer without revealing himself, Jerry ran to her side and put his arm around her while still covering most of his face with the shield. He was much closer after doing this, within ten yards of the group when what sounded like gun fire broke out, and a volley of rubber bullets rained down on all of them. Some ricocheted off of the car the four men were behind, while a few of them hit the trash can lid. One bounced off of the pavement and hit Jerry squarely in the right thigh, causing him to cry out in pain. Fighting through it, he looked under the shield long enough for the A.I. to confirm that the man lighting the cocktails was in fact, one Aaron Fornier. There were still three others left to identify though, one of which the A.I. couldn't make heads or tails of despite having nothing on his face that could have complicated the search.

"I got nothing on these guys, and the cops are getting closer." Jerry said. In response to the police firing baton rounds into the crowds, the protesters that hadn't yet run for cover or off of the highway completely began to rush the shield line again, this time every one of them screaming a slogan over and over that sounded something like "You can't stop us copper top!" in muddled unison. That's when the already nearly unbearable sound of the confrontation became deafening. At one point, Jerry felt like he was in the middle of the grand finale of a firework display.

"Nothing here either. Can you get closer?" the voice responded.

"No, too risky. Damn, no time. Wait, can you see us here on the ground from the drone?" Jerry hunched down even more than he already had been, moved the shield up to his face, and pretended to adjust his bandana so that no one could see that he was speaking to someone who wasn't present.

"Uh, barely. What did you have in mind?" the voice asked.

"Try to get a fix on the protesters. Go infrared if you need to."

"Ok, got heat signatures, good thing that car is nearly burned out already."

"Alright," Jerry continued, "Now, watch their heads."

"What?"

His face still covered, Jerry turned away from the blaring noise ahead of his position and screamed, "CHAVEZ!" at the top of his lungs. Unable to see for himself what effect his trick had on the group of men, he asked the voice, "Well?"

"The third man from you, he's the one. He was the only one that looked in your direction. He still is. You need to get closer if we're going to get a good rendering of his face though. All I can see from here is a blur."

Jerry peeked under the shield again when a group of reinforcements from the south ran past him on both sides. Two young women that were among them sporting blue bandanas on their arms grabbed the middle aged woman he had been kneeling next to and took her away on a stretcher. One of them gave Jerry a congratulatory thumb up. Jerry gave her one in return. His excuse for hiding from his target no longer present, he took a moment to gather his courage and stood up again, looking in the direction of the men as he rose to his feet, the right corner of his mouth curling upward, his goal now within reach. In that instant, a great booming sound came from the center of the police line, and without thinking, he turned to face it.

He saw something that looked like a small blurry object coming at him out of the smoke faster than the A.I. could identify, and suddenly the world around him became hazy. He thought for a second that his glasses had malfunctioned, leaving him blind, and he reached for them, but they were no longer on his face for his hand to grasp. His vision began to narrow and fade, and for a fleeting moment, he could hear something that overtook the unruly shouts and chanting of the protesters that surrounded him on the interstate that day, full of angst, anger, and the occasional lewd insult. No, the noise that filled his mind was far more intense. It was the shrill and piercing cries of thousands of people in utter despair. The kind of hopeless and fearful wailing that only comes when death is near and all is lost, and as the darkness from which they poured came to claim him, so was he.

If you see the oppression of the poor, and the violent taking away of justice and righteousness in a district, don't marvel at the matter, for one official is eyed by a higher one, and there are officials over them. Moreover the profit of the earth is for all. The king profits from the field. He who loves silver shall not be satisfied with silver; nor he who loves abundance, with increase: this also is vanity.
-Ecclesiastes, 5:8-10

Chapter Two

I-5 Corridor north of SEATAC International Airport
Seattle, Washington State
Friday, March 25[th,] 9:02AM PST

Jerry was about to wake up, he just didn't know it yet. The flat, persistent thumping of hundreds of footfalls began to echo through his ears, followed by an annoyingly loud and consistent beeping sound that came and went in beat with an incessant throbbing. The pulsating sensation originated from somewhere deep within his skull, drowning his thoughts in recurring bouts of pain. "OH, MAN!" He began to sit up. The worst hangover he'd ever had didn't even come close to this. To him, it felt like someone had hit him in the side of his head with a hammer.

He opened his eyes and allowed them a moment to focus. He was in what looked like a makeshift hospital in the back of an elongated van. *I must have been moved to the support area for the protesters.* He thought. They had hooked him up to a heart monitor that was bolted into the side of the vehicle. The monitor was only a few inches away from his right ear, and as things came into focus, he felt the oxygen mask that had been placed over his mouth and nose. He took off the mask and looked around. Three other people were there with him, each of them lying on stretchers that were rigged to fold out from the sides of the van.

There were eight stretchers all together, four of them still folded above where he sat, making the most of the small space. The others were out cold as he had been, and as his senses began to come back to him, he noticed that one of them was wearing a very familiar looking tee shirt. The young man he'd knocked out on the highway was lying down just two spaces away from him still out cold. "Time to go," Jerry said to himself.

He disconnected the heart monitor from his chest and got up. As he climbed out of the back of the van, the still rising sun shone through breaks in the smoke and hit his eyes, momentarily blinding him. For a second, his head felt like it would explode from the inside out, and he staggered and almost fell. He grabbed one of the open doors on the back of the van to catch himself when one hand accidentally touched something that was attached to his forehead. Standing straight again, he reached up and felt his head a second time, feeling with his fingers a bandage which someone had wrapped around it. It was then that he realized both his glasses and backpack were missing.

He turned around and looked into the van for his possessions. They were gone. Suddenly the pounding fire in his head no longer mattered. He thought about going back into the riot area to look for his things and started walking in that direction before he was stopped by what looked like a nurse in a pink overcoat.

"Hold on, you took quite a hit to the head. You shouldn't be out here hero." the woman said. She had shoulder length dark brown hair, was slightly overweight and wasn't very tall. Jerry had trouble making her out, but the A.I. in his Omni-Glass lens was on the job. It listed her as Tammy Shelton.

"Tammy." Jerry said.

"That's right, hon," she spoke with a slight southern drawl, "Don't worry we'll take good care of you." She took a cold pack out of one of several large pockets that were on the front of her coat and started shaking it.

"It's ok," Jerry said. "I'm ok. What do you mean 'hero'?"

"Why, you protected that poor woman while she was waiting for help. From the rubber bullets, I mean. We all saw it through one of our drones. That shield you were carrying was like a beacon. She was asphyxiating on the smoke from the cars, she could have died. You gave her cover until one of the DSR teams could get to her. You saved her hon!" The smile she gave him next was big and friendly. "And everyone's going to remember what you did for a long, long time." She lifted up the bandage on his head and put the cold pack under it. "Oh, that's some bump you got there!"

Jerry winced, feeling a spike of pain wash over his skull, but he fought through it. "What do you mean?" he asked.

"Oh, they *said* you were one of the ones who just jumped in locally. You watch the news?"

"Uh, no, not really," Jerry said, he did his best to smile back.

"That's alright hon," she said, "Ooh, this is loose." She looked at his bandage and started redressing it. "You see, the Supreme Court took over the government last week because of the electoral mess and some junk going on in the congress that happened while they were voting for a new president. I know it's confusing, but that's what they're supposed to do when there's a tie. But the court taking over part isn't in the Constitution. They may think they have the power to do it temporarily because they're one third of the government, but they're not legitimate." she said, "I'm sorry hon, is this over your head? I tend to go on and on, sometimes it's too much for people. Hope I didn't lose you."

"No, not at all, so you're saying this is more than just a protest?"

"Of course!" she said, "We've got groups all over the country today protesting, but the largest groups are here. Thousands more are on their way!" Somehow her big smile became even bigger as she spoke. "When we take Seattle and then Olympia, everyone sitting on the sidelines will hopefully join in. We're finally gonna bury this dinosaur of a government and really make one by and for the people!" She finished redressing his bandage. "I'm sayin' all this because you're gonna be a big part of it. Everyone is sharing the video of you helping that woman. It's really helped to boost our numbers here this mornin'. We might need you to represent us in a video or go on the news later. Is that alright with you hon?" She gave him a concerned look.

"Uh, yeah! Sure!" Jerry did his best to look excited, but by then, he wasn't really paying attention to Tammy's words. Through the fog of pain that his mind was enduring, his brain could only focus on how much time he had before the protester he'd beaten down woke up. Jerry pointed at the cold pack Tammy had put under his bandage and said, "Thanks. Uh, no problem, I'm just gonna sit down for a sec next to the van if that's alright, better air out here."

"Ok." she said. "Just take it easy."

"Sure thing," He moved to the side of the van, it was completely pink on the outside from top to bottom. "Can you hear me, Brenda? Are you there? Did you get that?"

The voice in his head began to speak again. "I got it. I kept recording on my end in case you woke up so we could find you. I think your Omni-Glass shut down for a moment while you were out cold."

"I set it so that it camouflages itself when I black out so no one who checks my eyes can see it. But without a direct command, it still transmits. It's a kidnapping feature." Jerry said. Another surge of pain went from one side of his head to the other.

"Are you ok? I saw what happened. Looks like your vitals are alright now, though."

"I'm good. Got a splitting headache and lost my glasses, though. What *did* happen?" he asked.

"Oh, you didn't see it?" Brenda responded, "You took a teargas can to the head." She opened a video in his Omni-Glass lens, showing him from above again. In the playback, he was standing up next to a woman in the middle of the highway as some DSR members were taking her away.

A moment later, the police fired a volley of tear gas canisters into the advancing crowd. One of them made it over their heads and could be seen shooting off in his direction before hitting him squarely in the forehead and down he went. In the instant that the canister made contact, he could see his glasses as they flew off of his face and out of frame, lost somewhere in the billowing smoke. Soon after, hundreds of protesters and police covered the entire picture, their feet likely stomping over the three thousand dollar pair of glasses in the ensuing clash. Soon the protesters began to retreat, and he saw two New Bolshevik protesters, their pink bandanas proudly displayed on their upper arms, bravely risk the tear gas to take him out of harm's way.

"It's gone viral." she said. "She was right, you're a hero." Brenda let out a small laugh that seemed to bounce around the inside of his skull.

"Ha, ha, ha." Jerry started to laugh back sarcastically, but his attempt at mocking the voice in his head quickly turned into a cough. He cleared his throat. "Not for long. Think Tom will reimburse me for them?"

"Maybe, you should come in and talk to him about it yourself, though. Looks like you've accomplished your mission out there. He wants to talk to you in person."

"He wants me at the office?" Jerry was surprised. These days he did most of his work from home like the majority of the website's employees.

"He has another job for you." she said, "But we can't talk about it right now, he's still gathering intel."

Jerry took a deep breath. "Alright, tell him I'm on my way. Can you send a personalized CAV to the closest address point from where I got on the highway?"

"That's almost half a mile away from where you were!"

"I'll just have to run it."

Jerry waited until no one nearby was looking in his direction and started jogging northward again, forcing himself to put weight on the leg that had been hit by one of the baton rounds. Pushing through the shooting pains that had begun to feel like they were coursing through his entire body, he retraced his steps and climbed back over the same concrete barriers he'd crossed earlier that morning, crossing the southbound lane toward CAV lane. While crossing, he noticed that the CAV lane was empty, meaning that the CAVs had been stopped somewhere to the north, cutting off the greater Seattle area from the airport completely. He looked northward but couldn't see anything other than smoke and the odd rag-tag protester milling around the edges of the conflict area. That's when Brenda began to speak again. "Oooh, I didn't know you were an Aquarius Jerry!" she said.

"What? What are you looking at over there, Brenda?"

"Oh, just your company profile. So what happened, child trauma? Usually, driven Aquarians have started a business by the time they're your age."

"I don't believe in any of that crap." Jerry said. "ANY of it, everyone is different and spiritual stuff is nonsensical. It's like trying to predict when and where a snowflake will fall. You're almost never right, but if you wait long enough, a snowflake will fall right where you said it would and that somehow makes it ok to believe you had it right from the beginning. It's all just a bunch of childish nonsense."

"Well, they are saying that scientists think that where you are born and when might have something to do with your brain's development while in the womb." Brenda's tone indicated that she hadn't listened to anything that Jerry had just said. "'The gravitational pull of the planets in different configurations during pregnancy may actually influence the long term thought processes of a developing fetal brain, resulting in minor differences in behavior and personality traits which have been found to be surprisingly consistent across a large percentage of the population when taking into account when and where they were originally conceived.' I am reading directly from the article."

"If scientists were correct all the time, Seattle would still be under water." Jerry retorted. He arrived at the location where he'd first gotten onto the highway. He turned around and looked south once more before heading down to the parking lot to make sure he wasn't being followed and climbed over the fence. "And Fife and Puyallup would have gotten more of a warning. Scientists aren't gods, Brenda. They're just regular people who hope they'll be remembered as gods just like the rest of us. Personally, I don't think any single person alive today will be remembered at all. The future will remember us as a bunch of confused animals that couldn't stop themselves from fighting over resources." He felt the throbbing return to his head again, and moved a hand up to the bandage. "You're giving me a headache."

"Well, either way, it will be good to see you in person."

"Same here, Brenda. Tell Tom to have the on call doctor meet us there. Hey, what are you wearing today?"

"Oh, you!" She snapped. "The CAV is on its way, see you soon."

"I don't know Brenda, I got hit pretty hard, might even have a concussion. Who knows what could happen?" A grin coming over his face, Jerry climbed down the knoll that met with the highway and began to climb the fence surrounding the storage lot.

"Very funny, Jerry, just make sure you don't say anything like that to anyone at the office today, you could get us all fired." she said.

"Don't worry darlin', your hero's on his way. I'll save you from your boring office life."

"Oh, Jerry. If only," she said with a sigh.

Once again, Jerry stealthily slid around and between the storage containers and piles of retired steel and crouched under a part of the fence on the other side that he had already broken through months earlier. He passed the spot where the derelict van he'd stood on earlier that morning had sat, the rims of its long since deteriorated tires buried six or more inches in the earth, but no longer. The van was missing. All that remained of it were two long black streaks that crossed the street. Confused, he looked around for the van in a bit of a daze, before continuing down the street toward where the CAV was supposed to arrive.

The noise from the highway became louder behind him as he went, smoke and teargas drifting even farther away from the highway than it had before, reaching him even up to a hundred yards away from the hellish scene as he made his escape. He turned back for a moment and saw the bright orange glow of several recently lit flames amidst the haze. *They must be bringing in more cars to burn from the surrounding area.* He thought. *Anything they can get their hands on by the look of it.*

He held his breath as best he could and, with a slight limp, began to pick up his pace again. Every other step sent a wave of pain up his leg to his spine. The waves hit the base of his skull and cascaded around the sides of his head, meeting together again at the point of the original impact. He wondered now if there were stitches under the bandage. He raised his hand to his head once more. *Well, I'll find out when I get to the office, I guess.*

On the surface, he may have given Brenda the impression that he was happy to meet up in his old stomping ground, but in actuality, Jerry hated the office. To him the whole idea of having a place to physically meet to do their kind of work was borderline obscene. He knew it was all for show, but as far as he was concerned it was an antiquated concept that had outlived its welcome when antibiotics stopped being effective and multi gigabyte download speeds became the norm.

When he'd first started working at the Internet news site two years earlier, that is before he made the decision to go independent and pursue a career as a freelance investigative reporter. It was different then, or at least it seemed different at the time. Perhaps he was just too naive to notice. Perhaps he was just excited to be working in a busy news hub in downtown Seattle. It didn't matter, no matter how he perceived working there in the past, Brenda was right, if even the smallest flirtation were witnessed by the wrong offended party, all hell could break loose, but that wasn't even the worst of it. The truth was that almost everyone there was doing much more than simply flirting with one another, sometimes even in the same building during work hours. Jerry was no saint, but the extreme hypocrisy of the environment had slowly gotten to him. Of course he never would have admitted as much to anyone there at the time as doing so could have easily left him without a job.

Every other story the Introspector published during the time he worked for them made the average working Joe, and anyone else for that matter that wasn't part of the journalistic elite, look like the sexually depraved ones. In fact he noticed that most news outlets he'd interacted with followed a similar pattern, often accusing less fortunate blue collar working people of the same or worse behavior that they themselves participated in every day when in truth it just didn't happen as often in the places that they were reporting on as it did in their own high rises. In reality it was people like those who worked at the Introspector and a lot of other news outlets in and around the city who were living it up behind the scenes while they profited by making it harder for the average laborer to get along with their coworkers.

As much as he loved what he did, he often wondered if he was participating, if not helping to create the same wrongs he had gotten into the industry to right in the first place. After all, the editors, web specialists, and pundits that sat comfortably passing judgment in their ivory towers didn't have to see the heart broken faces of those who were losing their jobs after decades of promises to the contrary or deal with the painful reality of government support that never really came, at least not in the way the average person was told it would. Having started as a grunt doing the stories no one else wanted, he did.

From their high positions, many of those he was forced to work with while earning his chops didn't care that the people they made a living off of mocking and ridiculing were slowly transforming into passionless slaves. This wasn't only because of the increase in automation that made the average worker more desperate with each passing day, but also because of the one sided perspectives that flooded the culture through an opportunistic media that could influence a work environment at the speed of a visually appealing viral opinion piece that was half written by an A.I. on some lazy editor's commute to work. In the end, Jerry could only conclude that such efforts were just another way that the new aristocracy kept the little people in line.

He had come to terms with the fact that he sympathized a little with the protesters, at least those who weren't trying to use the rest for their own ends. Sympathy was where it ended for him, though. He'd been through enough to know that life was about looking out for himself, something he did and did well.

Down the street, he saw the CAV drive into view. To him, CAVs had always looked strange, almost alien, too round and smooth to be a car. Starting to become faint as the sun's sparkling reflections began to bounce off of nearby surfaces disorienting him even more, the automated car took on the appearance of a giant red gel pill, the kind one might take to stave off a bad cold before going to bed. Like a big shiny capsule, it glistened as it moved down the street, reflecting the clouds above on its flawlessly polished shell with no clear beginning or end to its design. It slowed down for a second, scanning the immediate area for its fare. Too far for a facial scan, Jerry frantically waved his hands in the air and called out, "Hey! Hey, over here!" The CAV reacted and drove itself over to his position. Jerry saw it turn and head in his direction. He stopped running and took a moment to catch his breath, placing his hands on his knees.

When the CAV reached him, he walked up to the side door and waited. "Facial imprint identified." The CAV spoke in a very soft, almost relaxing male voice. The door slid open. "Welcome to Lofti's latest in automated vehicle entertainment." It continued. "Would you like to see a movie or play an augmented video game? Our new system can sync with any Omni or Omni compatible peripheral device to provide..."

"SHUT-UP," Jerry said loudly as he entered the vehicle causing another spike of pain to course through his head, centered in his right temple. The car stopped speaking. Inside were two long leather seats that faced one another. In the center between them was a console with four small screens, each one aimed at one of the seats at forty-five-degree angles. A wide variety of ports for charging just about any kind of device were available to use below each screen. The center of the console was a flat transparent table top in which a small touch screen map of the area was positioned so that it could be used to select a destination. Jerry lay down on one of the seats. The door slid closed behind him, and the voice stated, "Ten minutes to the preprogrammed destination. Please be aware that it may take thirty minutes due to unusual traffic activity in the immediate vicinity that is currently preventing this and other CAVs from using the highway at the closest intersecting points to our current location. Thank you, and enjoy your ride."

The car began to move and pick up speed. Jerry looked up and stared blankly at the silent animated advertisements that were slowly moving along the interior sides of the CAV's darkened windows. One ad was for tickets to a holographic concert. It showed two handsome young men in black and white suits singing in unison. Below them, in large moving letters, it said, 'See the Valiant Brothers live and in concert as they have never been seen before! Get your tickets now!' Another showed a group of people in white shirts giving food and toiletries to thankful looking families in a generic American city. More words appeared. They said, 'Help American cities by giving to your fellow man! Call the number below and be a part of the New Hope For All movement and remember, everyone deserves a helping hand.' Normally Jerry would ask the CAV to turn the ads off, but with his head still pulsating and the feeling of dizziness overwhelming his senses, he was too impaired to care. Feeling the inside of the vehicle beginning to spin around him, he closed his eyes and tried to focus on something that would take his mind off of the pain.

In his mind's eye a vision of Noel materialized, her bright smile and flowing hair glowing in the natural light of the sun, the entire city behind her. They were on the roof of his office building when he'd first started working there back when she was a receptionist for an import business that was renting out space in the same building. It was where they'd first met. During lunch one day in the cafeteria, she said she'd wondered what the view must have been like from the top floor. He dared her to race him up the stairwell.*She looked so beautiful on that day,* he thought, *So...perfect.*

But I tell you, love your enemies, bless those who curse you, do good to those who hate you, and pray for those who mistreat you and persecute you, that you may be children of your Father who is in heaven. For he makes his sun to rise on the evil and the good, and sends rain on the just and the unjust. For if you love those who love you, what reward do you have? **-Matthew, 5:44-46**

Chapter Three

Denny Triangle, downtown area
Seattle, Washington State
Friday, March 25[th,] 9:43AM PST

"You have arrived at your destination. Please depart from the vehicle. Please do not forget to remove any belongings you may have brought with you." Jerry could hear the CAV speaking to him again. The message must have repeated two or three times before it was joined by Brenda's footsteps as the sound of her heels came to his ears through the CAV's open door. He'd been staring at the ceiling of the transport unable to rest. As the CAV slowed to a stop, he noticed that the throbbing pain in his head had finally ended its attempt to match the size of the entire expanding universe, at least for the time being. In the bottom right of his Omni-Glass display, he saw the time. It was nine forty-five.

Brenda was an attractive forty-two year old divorcee and mother of two. Jerry knew this information because when he first started working at the Introspector, he'd hacked his way into the profiles of all of the women who were working there that were better than average in appearance based on his own highly subjective set of standards, in the off chance that he might one day want to go out with them. Before he met Noel, Brenda had made it onto his short list. She could easily have passed for someone in their mid-thirties. Her hair was thick and blonde, rolling down her shoulders in large wavy locks. When she came to get him in the

CAV, she was wearing a lavender colored jacket with a black button-up blouse underneath and dark suit pants. She was still wearing her headset, and was busy speaking to someone through it as she came out of the parking garage elevator. With a poised urgency Jerry himself had witnessed firsthand a thousand times before, she looked side to side as she approached, making sure no one was present to catch her in the act of bringing a wounded and possibly wanted journalist into the building. She leaned into the CAV and helped Jerry sit upright.

"I convinced the security guards to turn the cameras off down here and on the express elevator as a favor. Come on, we only have a few minutes." She pulled him out of the car. As he stood, he began to feel a little dizzy but was otherwise alright and able to keep his balance.

"It's ok." he said. "I'm alright, I'm feeling better."

"You look terrible, kiddo." she said, stopping for a moment to inspect the bandage on his head.

"Come on," he said to her, "Let's go. The doc can look at that."

"He got here five minutes ago." she said, "He's waiting for you in Tom's office. Oh, it's freezing out here! Seriously Jerry, if I didn't know you better, I'd think you were trying to catch a superbug or something."

They reached the express elevator and went up to the fifty-sixth floor. Still holding Jerry up with her right arm, Brenda hit the elevator button with her left hand before moving it to her headset, which partially covered her left ear, holding it in place. "Change the setting on your shirt. You can't look anything like you do in the video when you go in there. Tom just told me he has a fresh shirt for you. Weren't you cold out there?"

Jerry reached down and changed the pattern on the tee shirt to a bright yellow Hawaiian flower pattern. "The flames kept me warm." he said and gave her a lopsided grin. Brenda began to sniff the air in the elevator then Jerry's shirt. "Wooo! You smell like tear gas. Do us a favor, and don't get too close to anyone you don't know while you're here. At least not until we get you something else to wear."

The elevator stopped on the eighth floor. A janitor entered, pushing his equipment into the tight space with them. Brenda looked at Jerry's bandage again. She lifted it up. "Good, no stitches. It might not be that bad, after all." She turned her attention to the janitor, reached in her left pants pocket, and took out a wad of bills. She gave some of them to the day laborer and took a Seahawks baseball cap off of his head. She removed Jerry's bandage and put the cap on his head, covering up the large bruised bulge in the process. Then she looked back at the janitor and said, "No ves nada. Comprende?"

"Si senorita, gracias," All Jerry could tell about the man in his current state was that he looked to be old as dirt. His sleeves were rolled up, revealing volume upon volume of Catholic imagery tattooed on his forearms. He noticed that the man was also wearing a large silver cross on a snake chain necklace and appeared to be very satisfied with the exchange.

The janitor got off at the twelfth floor, where the building's main lounge and food court were located. It was also where most of the Introspector's employees used to go to eat during work hours when he worked out of the office. When they got off the elevator on the twenty-fourth, Brenda hurriedly pushed Jerry down the hallway, attempting to avoid any prying eyes that might have been nearby. "Keep your head down." she said. A facial scanner reacted as they approached the automatic doors that led to the main offices of the Seattle Introspector.The doors then opened, allowing them to proceed to the front desk. There, Brenda told a young and less than experienced receptionist that Jerry did not need to be logged in as he would only be there for a few minutes and that she would be his chaperone during the short visit, a common practice at the office whenanonymous witnesses or whistleblowers were brought in. The receptionist hit a button under her desk, opening a second set of doors that lead to the main production floor.

Jerry hadn't been to the office for nearly a year. This put him in the perfect position to judge any changes that had been done to the space in his absence. He noticed several major improvements had been made since his last visit. Together, the offices of the Seattle Introspector consumed most of the floor of the Darryle Heart building on Fourth Avenue. It was very bright inside, the main work area flooded with natural light that came in through large transparent aluminum windows which lined the southern and western sides of the building. To Jerry, it appeared as if nearly all of the surfaces in the shared workspace had recently been repainted from their original mundane gray to tones of white, including the cubicles and desks whose plain flat surfaces people could more easily use augmented tech with without having to waste precious time making environmental adjustments to their devices.

The place had higher ceilings than he remembered, with soft LED lamps hanging down to provide better, softer lighting in the evening hours. On the northern side, several meeting areas had been installed separated by a series of tall partitions, each containing long white tables. As always, lines of open cubicles took up most of the office, filling its center. The biggest difference was a large elevated informal area that had been placed close to the windows facing west. It was three feet higher than the rest of the production floor and was furnished with several plush leather couches and rounded artistic style coffee tables.

Having been away for so long, it was strange for Jerry to see the high energy of the place. It was full of people speed walking to and fro, an amazing sight for a location that was meant to impress potential investors more than anything else. They walked around and past him and Brenda as if they weren't even there. People high on caffeine, cog pills, and god knew what else, rushing to meet deadlines or attend meetings. They were well dressed too, some wearing bug resistant gloves, designer masks, and slap-goggles to lessen their chances of catching a dangerous cold or flu while away from their usual working spaces at home.

The excitement of the room was almost palpable to the senses, and seeing what he'd been missing caused a wave of nostalgia to hit Jerry unexpectedly as if he'd found an old keepsake that he didn't know was lost. Several small meetings were happening simultaneously on the northern end of the room while individual reporters and editors went about their work in the cubicles using Omni-Glass tech, writing on virtual keyboards, or by Mind-Print automated dictation. One thing the Introspector was known for was their diligence in making sure that their journalists didn't cheat by using A.I. to write their stories for them.

"Go over there to the window. Here, this is for your hands." Brenda gave him a disinfectant wipe. Where she got it from, Jerry had no idea. "Remember, don't talk to anyone you don't know. We've got a lot of...overly ambitious interns these days. I'm going to make sure Tom isn't in a meeting." She wiped a tear from the side of her face and looked at her hand. "Wow, we really need to get you a new shirt. The fumes are starting to irritate my eyes!"

Jerry nodded. He used the wipe and threw it in a trash bin under a nearby desk. Then he took another look around and realized he hardly recognized anyone. The place was full of new faces, people who acted and dressed much more professionally than what he was used to. He obediently moved to one of the large windows on the southwestern side of the building and looked out. Looking straight ahead, he could see most of the city south of the Space Needle, Puget Sound to the west, and the smoke still rising to the south near the airport.

He lifted up the cap on his head and checked his wound using a reflection in one of the enormous glass panes to make sure there were no stitches or worse an open wound. An untreatable staph infection was the last thing he needed. When he had confirmed there weren't any, he relaxed and allowed his eyes to focus outward again, this time looking farther, past the clouds of smoke and into the distance, all the way to what used to be the Port of Tacoma, once a busy port, now only a few small lights blinking at the end of a long dark line.

His eyes followed what was left of the hardened lava flow and rocky debris trail all the way to the horizon where the Rainier spire stood defiantly like a strange piece of abstract art that came from someplace other than Earth. He could remember when Mt. Rainier used to dwarf the rest of the skyline, strong and unmovable like a second moon. But it was gone now. Replaced by something new, something different, something less than the magnificent mountain it had once been. He would often look at the spire from his own apartment window as a reminder that even the biggest and most steady parts of people's lives can not only leave them in an instant, but can also leave a long path of destruction when they go.

A small delivery drone caught his attention as it approached the building and flew passed the window. It slowed down for a moment and turned so that its' guidance camera faced him. Not knowing if a computer program or a person was in control of the machine that was looking at him, Jerry lifted up his hand and waved. The drone turned back to its original course and continued on its way, indifferent to Jerry's friendly gesture.

"Jerry, is that you?" Jerry turned around. It was Percival Lars Orinson or Perry as everyone in the office knew him. He was young and thin, in his mid-twenties and moderately tall with straight dark hair with a natural sheen that Jerry had always been a little jealous of. He couldn't conceal his odd awkwardness, though. Perry bounced side to side as he walked and had a strange intensity in his eyes that was hard to ignore. He was in his usual attire, a short sleeved dress shirt, and Khakis and was wearing a pair of augmented reading glasses that he used exclusively for keeping up on current events throughout the work day, making him a go-to source of information for anyone that didn't have their own syncable tech handy. As he came closer, Jerry could see that he was currently keeping track of the latest performance of a particular set of stock options.

One thing Jerry always admired about Perry was his taste in expensive shoes. On that day, his feet were covered by a pair of very comfortable looking Italian loafers that must have cost a small fortune. Perry came from a wealthy family that lived on the other side of the country in upstate New York. Years earlier, when Jerry still worked in the office, Perry told him that he'd moved to the west coast to get away from the stagnated journalistic culture there and because he had a taste for Asian Fusion and Mongolian grill. Jerry suspected it was more than that but never pressed him on the subject.

"Hey Perry," Jerry said. "Good to see you man. You still seeing that girl from, umm..." Jerry thought hard for a second. "Indonesia, wasn't it?"

"Yeah, we're getting hitched next spring." Perry's face lit up. He gave Jerry a very wide but awkward looking grin and raised his eyebrows twice in a slightly suggestive manner. "Glad to hear it."

"You're invited to the wedding if you'd like to come."

"I'd love to, send me an invite. I see you haven't traded up for an Omni-Glass yet."

Perry tapped the side of his glasses. "Nope. I can see just fine with these, don't have to take some irritating thing out of my eye if I just want to curl up with a good book either." He shrugged. "I don't know, maybe I'm old fashioned, but putting tech in my body that could be hacked just feels wrong, you know? No offense, Tom told me you got an upgrade. What is it? An audio chip?"

"The works. Hey, what's with all of the good looking stiffs? Looks like some changes have happened since I was last here."

"Well, it *has* been over a year since you last dropped by, you know." Perry said. "An up and coming web development group bought us out a few months back and expanded the scope of our reporting. Now we focus mostly on economic stuff. You should have gotten an email about it. Anyway, they came in and upgraded the place because they want to use the Introspector as their main location for linking day to day stories from their platforms. They have tons of customers whose sites will be connecting to our stories and economic data." Perry extended his arms wide as he spoke. Somehow he was able to convey all of the information while maintaining a smile. "They said it was because we do the best job updating our site with info throughout the day or something like that. So, what brings you in? I'm getting bored around here. You always got the good stories, lots of travel and excitement!" He hit Jerry's left shoulder. "Would love to get in on any action you might be working on man, the new people they've been bringing in have no imagination at all, I swear most of them are using an A.I. to write their stuff. I'm just waiting to catch some of them red handed." Perry started rubbing his hands together, then his brow moved downward, and his nose crinkled up. He looked at Jerry's shirt and took a whiff. "Oh, man! It burns!" he said loudly. "What's on your shirt?"

Jerry smiled and lifted up his hat revealing the large reddish bump that was poking out from beneath it. He leaned closer to Perry. "It's classified." he said in a hushed, low tone. Perry's eyes widened.

Brenda walked up to both of them with a cup of coffee in her hand. Jerry hit Perry in the shoulder and pointed at her. They both watched her as she walked toward them, perfect posture, chin up, and confident. She began to blush a little and started to smile when she noticed both of them studying her appearance.

"Hi Perry," she said. "Here, Jerry, you look like you could use some." Jerry took the cup.

"Thanks." he said.

Brenda looked out the window. There was a blue sky outside which was rare in Seattle, especially in early spring. "Except for the riots and the cold, today certainly is a beautiful one."

"Riots, plural?" Jerry said, "They don't usually move on from the highway until after the first day."

"You haven't heard?" Perry said. He pointed toward the Sound. There's already another protest going on downtown blocking Alaskan Way, one at the city center that some think is really just a gathering point for a march on the courthouse and another at the statehouse in Olympia. It's not about jobs or raising the Uni-income for the average Joe anymore, they're protesting last week's Supreme Court takeover."

"I knew about the Court," Jerry said. "From what I saw on the highway I suspect things are going to get worse there before they get any better. It was the worst I've seen it in years. The most organized too. I figured the takeover had something to do with it."

"Too bad those congressmen got caught taking bribes." Brenda said. "You'd think they would have fixed the Electoral College by now. Good for business, though."

Jerry sipped his coffee and was amazed at how good it tasted. The décor wasn't the only thing that had improved. "I don't think that anyone ever expected there would be a tie after all the votes were recounted." Jerry said. "Now we might end up getting someone nobody even voted for. It's a crazy system."

Perry chimed in, "It's too bad the Vice President or acting President...whatever, took ill before they could make him POTUS. I don't know, I think it's good that Congress asked the courts to step in. Someone had to."

All three of them looked out of the window. Jerry looked to the southwest. *Omni, focused zoom times three.* He thought. The square-shaped window appeared again. Using directional thought commands, he aimed it downtown and saw that smoke was indeed rising from Alaskan Way near the Sound and in other nearby areas. He then turned around and faced the office, looking away from the windows and just next to where Brenda was standing. *Omni, give me a visual of the city and what is happening outside in real time.* He waited as the lens loaded orange outlines of the many tightly configured buildings beyond the northern walls, overlapping his view of the office area he'd just walked through. Anticipating what he was looking for it pinpointed and labeled a heat bloom just south of The Rock and Roll Hall of Fame before his thought command was finished.

"Today is going to be some news day." Jerry said.

"You don't know the half of it." Brenda said, a corner of her mouth curling upward. "Come on," She tilted her head in the direction of the big man's office. "Tom is ready for you, you too, Perry." Perry's eyes got wide again. He followed them to Tom's office in a state of bouncing excitement, his entire body bobbing up and down as he followed them.

Brenda walked ahead and opened the wide opaque sliding door to Tom's office. She waved Jerry and Perry in and closed the door behind them. Walking into the office was like walking into another world. Everything on the inside was wood grain and steel. A large digitally interactive touch board that Jerry almost took for a high end billiard table with several elevated chairs around it stood only about two yards from the entrance. Beyond the table was another twenty feet of empty space that ended at Tom's desk. In between, various ornaments from Tom's travels were displayed on an arranged group of small pedestals to one side. Along the opposite wall was a small library of books on literary history, editorial analysis, and team building. Among them, the occasional family vacation photo had been placed. Each picture neatly separated the different subjects on the book shelves, but they were a bit on the small side, so that the people depicted in them were hard to make out from the middle of the room.

A wide ornamental rug from Turkey that Jerry had once seen at Tom's Gig Harbor home during a holiday party he'd hosted a few years earlier covered what appeared to be genuine hardwood flooring in the space between. His desk stood in front of two corner windows that faced south and east. It was the same solid oak desk he had always used, and on it, the same old placard showing his name and position in the company sat front and center, 'Tom Merrick – Head Editor'. Tom was standing up behind it, reviewing some papers in a manila folder when he looked up past the desk and the four plush leather chairs that were between it and his guests and saw the trio.

"Moving up in the world," Jerry said.

"Jerry!" Tom dropped the folder on his desk and opened his arms wide. He was wearing a robin's egg blue dress shirt with an elaborate silver and black striped tie. His equally silver hair was well styled and combed back. Not the same man Jerry had remembered when he began working for him three years earlier. Tom reached his hand out over his desk, and Jerry shook it. Immediately after, Tom took a small tube of hand sanitizer out of one of his desk drawers and used it. *Always safe to shake hands with Tom.* Jerry thought.

"Good to see you, Tom." he said. "I see you've finally gotten the office you've always wanted." Brenda walked around him and left the room through a thin side door just off of its north side. If she hadn't opened it, he never would have noticed that it was there.

"Sit down, please! You too, Perry, it's good to see you as well." Tom said. Jerry and Perry sat in the two center most leather chairs. Jerry finished off his coffee quickly and put the empty paper cup on Tom's desk next to the nameplate. Perry was looking around at the office and grew wide eyed again as if he had never been in the boss' office before, but Jerry was feeling a little uneasy. When he'd worked at the Introspector, Tom used to come in every morning with a hangover, his hair a complete mess, and his shirt un-tucked. Brenda would get there early every morning to "clean him up." Jerry never quite knew what many of those clean up sessions entailed, but everyone in the office had their own similar theories. The man before him was a new Tom, one that had finally made it in his life and knew it. Thinking more clearly as the throbbing in his head faded, he was able to piece together that the whole new ownership with perks thing at the office also explained why Brenda appeared to be somewhat more confident and less anxiety ridden than he remembered as well.

Outside, a cloud moved, revealing the still rising sun to the east. Jerry lifted up his hand to block the incoming light. "Oh," Tom turned around and looked out of the window behind him. "Sorry about that. I'm still getting used to the new configuration of my office. Watch this!" He raised his pointer finger as if to emphasize what he was about to do. He looked back at the window. "Window, tint, eighty percent." Jerry watched as both windows grew darker until the sunlight was no longer an issue. Several soft lights embedded in the ceiling turned on to compensate.

"Wow." Perry said flatly, not particularly impressed.

"It's great, Tom. Thanks." Jerry said. "So, what's going on, to be honest, I was hoping on taking the rest of the day off. I took quite a hit this morning." He pointed at his forehead.

"Well, that's just it." Tom said.

Brenda came back out of the side room with a wet comb in one hand and a white, long sleeve dress shirt in the other. She was followed by a man in a white lab coat who was carrying what looked like something between a small briefcase and a first aid kit. She motioned to Jerry to stand up, and walked around him so she could pull his seat back. Jerry obliged and stood up.

Brenda took off the hat and his tee shirt, revealing his pale skin and two dark tattoos, one being a tribal style scorpion that was located on the left pectoral muscle of his chest. The other an image of a serpent-like dragon that spiraled down and around his right arm ending just before the wrist, the lower end of it depicting the face and claws of the beast in great detail. Both images appeared to move across his skin, adjusting slightly in different directions before returning back into their original positions, changing just enough to give the illusion that they were living things.

The doctor began to look at the bump on his head while she helped him put on the plain dress shirt. "You see," Tom said while turning the monitor on his desk in Jerry's direction. "The drone video of what you did out there this morning is getting a lot of traction on the net and with the major news conglomerates. They've been trying to find you over the last hour to thank you, but it looks like the guy you took that shield from just woke up and is telling a different story. We have to get you out of here now so that we can say we sent you out of town before the riots even started. The last thing we need right now is for the Feds to find out we've been sending free agents into dangerous situations to spy on people using illegal apps that hack into government and corporate databases."

"That's funny, and here I thought they were the same thing." Jerry said.

Tom motioned to Perry. "Perry will write the article about the three new leaders quoting an anonymous source." He looked at Perry sternly. "By noon, Perry. Brenda will fill you in with the details." Perry nodded, and Tom continued, "You will be elsewhere with a solid alibi just in case they manage to get a facial ID. You may not have noticed but you lost your towel when they loaded you up on the stretcher. Thankfully there's way too much smoke in the video to make out your face, but other videos are surfacing. They estimate at least four thousand drones are out there today between the local authorities, the National Guard, and private news outlets, not to mention all of the independent reporters, lookie-loos, and the protesters themselves. And yes, I noticed the glasses, and yes, I will replace them myself *if* you pull off this next assignment for me."

Brenda finished buttoning up Jerry's new shirt and started tucking it into his pants when Jerry placed his hands on hers and looked down at her as if to say that it was OK to leave it un-tucked. She gave him a slightly disappointed look, used the comb to cover the bump on his head by moving some of his straight black hair forward and to one side and waved off the doctor.

The doctor frowned at Brenda and looked at Tom. "He's got a mild concussion, but he'll be alright." he said. He looked at Jerry. "Just make sure you get some rest tonight. Don't do anything exciting. If your sight begins to blur, lie down." He reached into one of his lab coat's large pockets and pulled out a small plastic bottle. He opened it, took out a small yellow pill, and gave it to Jerry. "Take this, it will stop the pain."

"Thanks." Jerry said. Brenda led the doctor out the same way he'd come in. Jerry looked quizzically at the nearly invisible door. Then he noticed that Perry was staring up at him in stunned admiration after having realized that Jerry was the man in the video. He patted Perry on the shoulder and sat down again.

Tom continued. "The great news is that we're gonna get a lot of money from the video evidence you got us this morning. Multiple news agencies are willing to pay a pretty penny for what you got today, and even though you didn't quite get this 'Chavez' character's face, the boys down the hall are working on clearing up the few blurry images you did get of him so we can try to make an educated guess down the road as to who he really is. I'm gonna add seven large to your next bonus for this one kiddo, two more than usual, because you won't get the credit when the article comes out. But seriously Jerry, thanks for going out there today. You really helped us out on this one."

"Just doing my job Tom," Jerry said. "So where is it you want me to go now?"

"Come, take a look." They could hear the excitement rising in Tom's voice again. He stood up and walked over to the interactive data display table near the entrance of the room. Jerry and Perry followed. "Table, bring up Spokane." The flat black surface of the table turned white, showing an obscure logo that consisted of two bright blue Japanese Hiragana characters that vanished nearly as quickly as they had appeared. They were replaced almost immediately by a map of the city of Spokane.

"Spokane?" Jerry's tone became irate. "Nothing ever goes on there! Are you just hiding me, or is there a story that's actually worth something that I can write about? For crying out loud, you just gave my best story to Perry! No offence, Perry."

"None taken," Perry said. He was looking curiously at a virtual control panel that had appeared on the table.

"Just watch this!" Tom said, even more excited. He pointed a finger upward. "Table, create a three dimensional holographic display of the area." From the ceiling above them, a small panel slid open, revealing a holographic projector. It moved into place aiming downward at the table's surface and sprung to life, working in concert with several other pinhole projectors that surrounded the edge of the table top to levitate millions of microscopic plasma discharges, resulting in a high resolution three dimensional representation of the city. Instinctively Jerry reached out toward the image with his right hand. "Don't touch it!" Tom said. "You might get burned. The lasers cross in mid-air and generate a lot of heat with each micropixel they create. It's like plasma. That's what the team that installed it told me anyway. This thing takes a lot of juice to work." Then he continued, "Table, zoom in on the northern half of the map and highlight any new structural features added in the last year according to satellite imagery."

They watched as the map zoomed in, giving Jerry a brief sense of vertigo as his mind was tricked into feeling like it was falling from the sky down and through the clouds that were represented in the holographic image. When it was done zooming, a few dozen green outlines appeared highlighting what looked like several new office and residential buildings and a few larger unidentifiable structures while another thicker green line stretched around an entire section of northwestern Spokane on the outskirts of town. Tom gave another command, "Table, create time-lapsed holographic display. Parameters: Recent structural developments. The last five months in a single five second interval."

A few seconds later, the time-lapse Tom requested began, clearly showing structures being erected, including homes and some sort of large concrete foundation in the middle of the area. What stood out however, were the hundreds of short, thin, green lines that slowly began to surround them all. At first the lines were unconnected, then, suddenly they joined together, making a perimeter around a large area some three or four miles across at its widest point.

"What the hell is that?" Perry asked.

"A wall," Tom said. "Over the last several years, something like ten or twenty thousand members of otherwise unaffiliated prosperity based Christian churches from across the country, have been busy, slowly buying up property in north Spokane and some of its outlying areas. They've voted in their own local leadership, changed zoning laws, and started building their own little walls on their properties. Turns out, these were just foundations for what was coming later. Last month, the Spokane City Council unanimously voted to allow them to connect the walls while no one was paying attention. They also removed height restrictions. The last parts went up last week. They brought in two automated brick layers to do it and to increase the height of the walls that were already made. Now, almost a fifth of the largest city in eastern Washington State is behind a twenty-foot wall, and today with riots happening around the country because of the political mess in D.C., they hope to finish the entrance and put in a ten ton steel gate at the only entrance." He used his finger to point out where the entryway stood. "Yesterday it was just another suburb of Spokane, later today when the gate is installed it will become the second largest gated community in the world. Needless to say, the locals are a little miffed that no one told them about it."

"Holy crap," Jerry said.

"Daaaamn," said Perry.

"That's not all, over the last few weeks no one in the area has been able to send out any video from the area or even call people who live there unless they have an old landline phone. There seems to be a hidden signal jammer somewhere in the middle that scrambles any radio based wireless communication systems inside the wall. Even Lifi systems don't work there. My sources say that drones are falling flat just before they reach it on every side."

"How high does the jamming signal go?" Perry asked.

"No one knows yet. High enough to make any remote commercial or private drones fall to the ground. We don't know if higher flying military and police drones have encountered any issues yet. No higher flying commercial or private planes have reported anything, though." Tom said.

"How did you get the info on this?" Jerry asked Tom, his eyes glued to the image.

"Some local conspiracy nuts have been watching the situation for some time. When the automated brick layer was brought in, one of them sounded the alarm and called us. They didn't trust the national media outlets and didn't think they'd report it anyway even if they did. The official story from the mayor is that it's an experimental self-sustaining gated community." The expression on Tom's face changed to one of disgust, "Normally I wouldn't give any credence to reports like these but it is happening, and from what they've told us there are a lot of people still living in the area that had no say in the project, and are now walled in against their will. I think that whoever is really behind this might be jumping the gun. They probably thought now was a good time to finish the project because so much is going on everywhere else. I want you to get in there somehow before they set up that gate this afternoon and find out what is really going on. You'll have to leave your Omni-Glass with us. If the authorities here find anything that makes them think you're the one in the video, they'll be able to track your movements through its signal, and we don't want them to see that you're on the move after we said you were. It will be better off here, shut off and in my safe. If they try to say you were on the highway this morning, we'll tell them that you were already in Spokane and lost your Omni-Glass weeks ago."

"That means no Brenda." Jerry said.

Brenda reappeared behind them from the magic door. "That's right, sorry. I know how much you depend on me." Jerry noticed that she was fastening a button on her shirt, and her hair didn't quite look as perfect as it had when she'd left the room. "No support, no exit strategy. You're going solo on this one."

"You should consider using cash and leave your wallet with me too." Tom continued. He reached in his pocket and gave Jerry a few two hundred dollar bills. Jerry gave him his wallet. "That should last you a few days, we wouldn't want anyone to find out who you are before you get there. We also don't know what kinds of people are calling the shots in there. They may be harmless, but they also might be looking to pull another Utah, and with the judicial system calling the shots there is no telling how unpredictable the situation might get. You'll need anonymity."

Omni-off. Jerry thought to himself. The lines and shapes that made the customized interface he worked with every day disappeared from his vision. He took the lens out of his right eye, put it in the small white case he kept in his pants pocket and gave it to Tom. "I'm not worried about finding a way back, what I need to know is how am I supposed to get there with the riots going on and how I'm supposed to ID the ringleaders of the place without my lens?"

"Well, the second part is easy," Tom said. He walked back to his desk, opened a drawer and took out a small ring-bound pad of paper and a pencil. "Old style detective work." He put the pencil through the ringed binding and threw the pad at Jerry, who caught it with his left hand. Tom reached back into the drawer and took out a white pill bottle. "You need some Cog Pills? My latest prescription came in from Switzerland yesterday."

Jerry started to reach out with his other hand then pulled back. "Umm...thanks but I think I'll wait until I get back. I appreciate it but if I accidentally end up in the wrong place at the wrong time, I'd hate to be charged with transportation of illegal drugs. I only really need them for when I'm writing my articles anyway, not when I'm in the field.

"You never *get* caught, Jerry, that's why I'm sending you in the first place. You can get in and out of anywhere, and you're a good writer to boot. Still, you're probably right. Me, I can't even make it into work without them these days. Keeps me alert, you know? Hell, half of this new crew is on 'em." Tom loosely waved a hand toward his office door.

Jerry looked down at the small pad of paper in his hand. "What is this, a hundred years old?"

"We don't need video for this one, just names and the location of that jammer. If you can disable it, we can be the first ones to send a drone in there to see what they're really up to."

"You still haven't answered my first question."

"The answer to that one is the reason I didn't throw Perry out of my office a few minutes ago."

"What?" Perry asked. "Oooh, right, you want to borrow Sarina."

"We'd like to borrow Sarina." Tom said.

"Uh, who is Sarina?" Jerry asked, perplexed.

"Beware! Keep yourselves from covetousness, for a man's life doesn't consist of the abundance of the things which he possesses." **-Luke, 12:15**

Chapter Four

Denny Triangle, Downtown Area
Seattle, Washington State
Friday, March 25[th,] 10:55AM PST

Jerry left Tom's office with Brenda in tow carrying one of Tom's dark blue sport jackets. When they reached the receptionist area, she put it on him and fixed his collar. She then used her hands to smooth out the wrinkles, moving her fingers across his chest. Jerry looked at her, a somber expression on his face. "Thank you, Brenda." he said.

Brenda took a deep breath. "You might be fifteen years younger than me, but I still consider you an equal and competent colleague." she said. She hadn't moved her gaze from his collar. Her right hand moved over his heart, and she looked him in the eyes. "You look better like this you know. I still want to tuck your shirt in, though. She reached down to his waist. Once again, Jerry stopped her hands with his. "Well, at least you won't look like a strobe light out there shining through the smoke with this jacket on." she said. "And it will keep you warm."

"I have a favor to ask Brenda," Jerry said.

"What is it?"

"I need you to call Noel for me. We fought again, and I haven't had a chance to..."

Brenda smiled softly and tilted her head. "You and that girl, I'll never understand it. She doesn't deserve you Jerry." She looked down at his neck and gently touched his collar again. "Don't worry

I'll let her know we're sending you on an assignment and that you'll call her when you get back. Hopefully she won't be around when you do, though. Oh, and you have about ten minutes to get out of here. After that, the cameras on the basement level will start recording again."

"Thanks, Brenda, I owe you one."

The express elevator opened, and a member of the cleaning staff came out. Jerry went down the hall and walked in. He turned around to look at Brenda one more time and hit the button to the basement level of the building, where Sarina would hopefully be waiting for him in the parking garage. As the doors began to close, he looked directly into Brenda's eyes and started to tuck in his shirt. Brenda blushed again, covered a bright and widening smile with her right hand, and before the doors finished closing, looked as if she were going to cry. Jerry smiled back. A few moments later, when the doors opened again, he walked out of the parking garage and into the bright sunlight to meet his new ride.

****

Standing there on the curb waiting for a very different kind of woman than he had earlier that week, the gears in Jerry's mind began to turn. Spokane only had two small news organizations, both of which had a limited number of Internet subscribers and both of which were almost sure to downplay the events transpiring there as they were known to be very loyal to their community and usually tried to avoid reporting scandal and corruption in their picturesque city as much as possible. If he got there quickly enough, the story could be his and his alone.

'East German Commie Christians come to Washington?', 'Separation of Church in our State?', 'Christian fanatics claim Spokane: Local politicians bought, Intolerant or Racist?', 'Religious hypocrites keep out the riff-raff'. Jerry began to imagine the amount of spin that would be applied to the story once it broke. The headlines alone were worth millions. For Jerry, it could mean Pulitzer, national syndication in an even bigger net news distributor than the Introspector. To others, it might have been small news, but to Jerry, it was a unique opportunity that could lead to TV interviews, even a book deal.

The possibilities crowded his mind, each one vying for attention over the others. Distracted, Jerry fumbled and dropped the keys Perry had given him while taking them out from his right pants pocket. As he leaned over to pick them up, he heard the loud revving of Perry's next generation Misikashi, self-balancing motorcycle. Sleek wasn't an adequate enough word to describe what it looked like. Unlike the big round pill that was the average

CAV, Misikashi semi-automated motorcycles were known for their multitude of self-adjusting smooth surfaces that jutted out of their symmetrical aerodynamic forms. Each section of their flawless outer covering was independently programmed to move slightly in response to the speed the bike was travelling for optimum energy conservation.As he approached it, he noticed it had no plates, meaning it wasn't registered.

Perry had summoned it from his own apartment's parking garage, which wasn't much further away from the office than Jerry's place less than a mile away. Still holding the notepad and pencil Tom had given him in one hand, Jerry hesitated for a moment before putting them in his back pocket as he climbed onto the smooth, shape fitting seat on the technological marvel. He looked at the key Perry had given him. It was thick with three buttons on the back end. One said 'Alarm', the next 'Helmet' and the last 'Find me'. Jerry put the key in a keyhole next to the digital odometer like Perry had instructed him to in the office. When he did, on a center display that was located just above the gas tank, Perry's smiling face appeared. By what he saw of the view behind him, Jerry could tell that Perry was sitting in front of the computer terminal on Tom's desk.

"There you are. Beauty ain't she?" Perry said. "It's one of the best on the market. It can do zero to sixty in one point nine seconds!"

Jerry began to shake. He had never driven a car on his own let alone a motorcycle. "So, this is what you've been putting all of your money into." he replied.

"No mine. Last year after you started working from home, Tom gave me a tough assignment. He told me if I couldn't get the story everyone in Seattle was trying to get about the illegal A.I. races that had been going on late at night around the city he'd put me back on the court beat and make me report on local civic events. So, I went to my dad and asked him to buy me the bike. He's full of cash, and I'd never asked him for anything before, so he was more than happy to help me out with my career path in a way that didn't involve bribing someone for a change. So yeah, you remember that article that came out last fall?"

"Didn't some guys from a motorcycle gang who killed a cop get pinched because of that article? You got an award for it, didn't you?"

"Yeah, but no one published my picture. Guess I'm not that photogenic. Anyway, my cover was still intact so I just kept going out. Eventually I wrote my own hack for the bike for navigating through traffic. That algorithm is what Sarina really is. She learns each time she goes out and runs her own simulations. In a tight situation she can do some crazy stuff so be careful."

"Perry, I didn't know you had it in you." Jerry said, smiling back at the screen.

"Well, I may not be a ladies' man like you, but I do have a life you know. A little more practice, and with Sarina's help, I could be racing professionally one day. Who knows?" Seeing that Jerry's posture become more rigid as he spoke, Perry continued with a softer tone. "Don't worry, man, the bike you're on is completely self-driving. I'll just put in the location you need to get to from here, along with the desired time frame you want to get there in. If anything gets in your way that Sarina has trouble getting around, she'll give you an option to go into full A.I. mode, ignoring the regular driving restrictions put on most bikes. That's why you can't get caught. I don't want the cops to know I've got an illegal A.I. onboard. Stupid bureaucrats think some deep learning navigation software on one motorcycle is going to take over the world." Perry waved his hands around, his face still stuck in its perpetual grin. He genuinely looked like a mad scientist for a moment. "Only say yes to the option Sarina gives you if you can tell there is no other way to get where you want to go. Sarina is usually able to figure her way through stuff pretty well on her own in semi-autonomous mode most of the time though, she was designed to race against other A.I. bikes to see which could find the fastest routes through the city, so she knows it like the back of her, well uh, hand I guess you could say. If you need to stop, just let go of the handle bars, both of them. The bike will slow itself down and stop on the side of the road. You don't need to do a thing. Afterward, just hit the green 'GO' on the screen, and she will start up again."

Jerry heard a clacking sound from the right side of the bike. Perry's voice came over the motorcycle's main speaker again. "That's the helmet. I've unlocked its hanger. Unhook it and put it on, it looks like you're going to need it."

"What do you mean?" Jerry asked.

"Well, I've decided to take a look at the latest developments. The police have closed off the I-90 tunnel heading to the Lacy Murrow Bridge, West of Mercer Island. Either the folks in Bellevue got nervous, or they're trying to stop the rioters from using that route to get into the city from the East. Either way, you're going to have to go south to Route 405 through Renton to get to I-90 East now. Should be a clear shot though, I mean, after you pass the riot area that is. The National Guard troops that are usually dispatched to protect the airport haven't made it up from Olympia yet. They shouldn't be long, so you'd better get going. They're probably going to block off the 405 when they get to it."

"Great. Will this thing drive down a CAV lane?"

"Oh yeah, if you want to do that, just say her name and tell her which lane to move into. I've used those lanes to get away from the fuzz on more than one occasion. Good luck Jerry, I have to cut the transmission now to make sure you aren't tracked through a com signal."

"Take it easy, Perry, and...thanks." Jerry said.

He watched as Perry gave him a quick two fingered salute, and the connection ended. The screen changed from Perry's smiling face to a map of the area. Jerry put the helmet on. When he locked the chin strap into place, a head's up display appeared on the inside of the visor. The operating system got to work identifying and outlining his surroundings in green lines, much like his Omni-Glass did each time it booted up. The helmet was different though, as the only computer it was synced to was housed somewhere in the motorcycle's innards. Everything Jerry could see, the A.I. would figure out on its own without assistance, and it would still be figuring things out on its own while Jerry rode. A shiver went down his spine thinking about it. He looked in the rear view mirrors to adjust them before taking off and for a moment was put at ease when his mind shifted gears by thinking instead about how the helmet was going to ruin his hair and make him look like a bum.

He grabbed onto the handlebars, and the motorcycle moved forward, slowly gaining speed as it moved onto the road. Soon Sarina was weaving in and out of lanes, moving precariously between the other vehicles that it shared them with. The A.I. performed just as Perry said it would, effortlessly gliding around several sharp turns on its way to the only accessible interstate ramp in town and toward the mayhem that he'd left just over an hour earlier. Soon he would be headed back in the opposite direction, right into the thick of it. *Hopefully the protesters haven't moved to the southbound side of the highway yet.* He thought.

Sarina started to maneuver more swiftly, occasionally avoiding other vehicles and pot holes without warning, catching Jerry off guard. "Ok, ok, ok...." Jerry kept saying to himself. Only then did he realize that for the second time that day, he was voluntarily putting himself at risk for a story. Something he had promised Noel he would never do again only a few weeks before. Seeing a tight turn ahead, Jerry pushed his thoughts aside and focused his eyes on the road.

Don't weary yourself to be rich. In your wisdom, show restraint. Why do you set your eyes on that which is not? For it certainly sprouts wings like an eagle and flies in the sky. **-Proverbs 23:4-5**

Chapter Five

Denny Triangle, Downtown Area
Seattle, Washington State
Friday, March 25[th,] 11AM PST

The streets were filled with people both trying to get to work and trying to get out of town. Jerry thought he saw a group of looters breaking into a pawn shop in broad daylight, a sign that law and order in the area was evaporating. Over the last few years, the anti A.I. protests had been steadily growing. The slow but sure replacing of all forms of work by mechanical and software automation was creating a permanent underclass in the western part of Washington State which could not be remedied by attempts to provide a universal income for its inhabitants. Food and rent combined with the added cost of clothing and education were just too expensive for most of the residents in the Tri-City area to keep up with, even with financial assistance. Raising a family on a twenty-five grand a year stipend was just not possible anymore, especially for those who chose to gamble away their limited funds or spend it on addictive substances, not to mention all of the charlatans in the area that were always preying off of the poorest of the poor.

Along with the almost unlimited supply of drug dealers, gangs, and conmen that were responsible for the majority of these problems were the prosperity churches, most of which had collapsed during the heavily publicized Henry Alstead scandal. There were still plenty of small time false prophets in the greater

Seattle area to make up for them however, and when the Alstead empire fell along with the network of other local pastors he was associated with, they were more than willing to fill the vacuum. After the story broke about Alstead's great network of embezzlement and abuse, crimes that extended far beyond the borders of Washington state and even those of the United States, even more, lower income residents than what had been projected began to pour out onto the streets demanding more money and job opportunities. It got so bad at one point that whenever higher-ups with the federal government came to town, everyone who did have a job and wasn't protesting usually decided to stay home rather than risk being harmed while going to work. The political mayhem that was going on in D.C. was only making an already bad situation even worse. As he approached the highway, Jerry saw even more looters breaking windows and setting fires as they carried away their stolen goods, the kind of scene he hadn't witnessed since the days that followed the Mt. Rainier calamity.

When he hit the highway, the motorcycle came to a complete standstill. Just like Perry said, it looked as if the tunnel had been closed to I-90 east, but Sarina had a plan. He looked at a map that was displayed on the bike's main screen located just above the emergency gas tank. Perry's algorithm wanted to take him along a few side roads and alleyways to bypass thirty minutes of traffic. Sarina would first have to find a way to navigate through the rioters. From there, it would be a three and a half hour drive to his destination if the solar powered batteries in the bike's outer shell held out. Jerry looked up for a few seconds. *If the clear skies hold up, there shouldn't be any problems. The bike should have enough time to recharge in transit, until we reach the mountains anyway.*

He looked down again. A second, much longer route had appeared on the screen while he was looking away, and a few seconds later, the message Perry had mentioned to him earlier appeared on the interface. It said, 'Disregard regular driving parameters to make time?' Two buttons appeared below the message labeled 'YES' and 'NO'. Feeling more comfortable and confident with his ride and noting that the second route could potentially add another hour to his time, Jerry smiled and tapped the 'Yes' option.

The motorcycle lurched forward again. Sarina's engine was powerful and tuned perfectly. Jerry gripped the handlebars as hard as he could and noticed that he no longer had any control over the direction of the front wheel. Whatever force was controlling it was far stronger than he was. After swerving around a group of CAVs and a few older analog vehicles that were heading up the ramp with him, the bike found its way to the emergency lane and took off. In a matter of seconds, Jerry was traveling at 140 kilometers an hour and holding on for dear life. On the screen, he could see the onboard A.I. making calculations far faster than any man could ever think. The speed at which it began to calculate its position and course of action was a far cry from what he had seen the onboard computer do only a few minutes earlier.

According to the activity read out on the bottom right of the screen the motorcycle was sensing objects using proximity lasers, sound waves and infrared sensors to locate objects up to one hundred meters away but it only appeared to show objects ahead in his visor when they were in direct line of sight. When he looked back up at the road, he noticed that the map had been added to his visor. Even with everything else that was going on, Sarina was accommodating him, adjusting to the behavior of its new rider. The map appeared in the form of a yellow square above and to the right of the rest of the spastic green lines that consumed the center of his vision as Sarina frantically attempted to identify everything that passed by. Using the map, he was able to get a better idea of what was coming next and to him what he saw looked like hell itself.

****

Of all the things Jerry had planned to do that day, driving through a riot on a motorcycle he couldn't control wasn't one of them. In his visor, emergency vehicles and police appeared as red outlines, which was helpful to him since there was so much smoke and fire ahead on both sides of the highway, that Jerry couldn't possibly have seen them on his own. The only good thing about the situation he'd found himself in was that thesmoke was *so* thick, it was unlikely that anyone would be able to catch him on camera going through it. Meanwhile, beyond the police line, the rioters began to multiply in his visor until they appeared as one large green mass, an obstacle that the A.I. seemed confident it could break through, if the trajectory it appeared to be pursuing on the map was any indication.

As Jerry approached the police cruisers from behind while heading south, Sarina began to increase in speed. The motorcycle shot between two of the gas powered police cars that were parked perpendicular to the lanes, which were meant to block traffic and went straight into the smoke. He saw the outlines of a few police move as they either frantically jumped out of his way or turned their heads in his direction, but by the time any noticed him apart from the onslaught of raining fire that was coming at them from the protesters in the opposite direction, it was too late as Sarina was far too fast for them to get a lock on. Then unexpectedly, an excessively sensual female voice came through the helmet's speakers. "Please hold on tightly." it said, followed by a short playful giggle. *Of course Perry would choose that*. Jerry thought and tightened his grip on the handle bars. Immediately after he did this, the motorcycle slowed down so quickly that its rear tire lifted straight up into the air. Before Jerry had time to react, he noticed that the bike was continuing to drive on its front wheel. As blood rushed to his head, he could feel the bike gaining speed again. His legs began to flail, forcing him to focus his strength into them in order to regain his balance so he wouldn't fall off. This was not what he thought the A.I. had been talking about when it had told him to 'hold on'.

Soon the bike was traveling less than twenty miles an hour, swerving through the crowd while balancing on its front wheel. Though he couldn't help but look downward, the helmet's visor still showed him what was up ahead as if he were still sitting upright. Jerry could see the wire frames of each person that they passed but couldn't lift his head high enough to see more than their legs with his own eyes. Some of the people in the crowd were throwing a variety of objects in his general direction. A few of them who were on the ground hurt and waiting for assistance, likely due to having been hit with sonic emitters or rubber bullets stared at the motorcycle in amazement as it passed by. But it wasn't over yet. Ahead were even more people and dozens of vehicles, most of which were on fire spanning the entire highway, including the CAV lanes.

As he approached the seemingly insurmountable barrier, he managed to look up long enough to see that the rioters had lined them up side by side and at least ten deep so that there was little if any chance of anything getting through save for those who could squeeze the wounded through on foot. Confused by this, he looked at the map in his visor again to see if the trajectory Sarina had planned to take had changed. To his horror, the line Sarina was following had changed so that it was constantly fluctuating, changing with every new scenario that Sarina could come up with. One of these included going right through the vehicles themselves.

The voice returned. "Unlocking rear wheel axel," it said, another small giggling sound followed, one that would resonate in Jerry's mind for years afterward whenever he realized that he'd done something especially stupid, like trusting an illegal A.I. with his life. "Wait, wha-" Jerry said. Before he could finish, the rear end of the bike crashed back to the ground and immediately began to peel out.

Jerry began to panic. He remembered the almost cartoonish movements of an A.I. motorcycle he had seen in a video on some online forum some months previous. In it, an A.I. like Sarina inadvertently killed its driver while attempting to illegally navigate its way through a busy intersection in LA. The video was never verified as real as far as he knew, but that didn't make it any less shocking to watch. He was deciding whether or not he should ditch the motorcycle altogether and find another way through the lines of burning vehicles ahead when the front tire began to rise. It stopped forty-five degrees above the ground, and the bike began to lean to the right, heading toward an old premillennial car, the front end of which was particularly low because its tires had been slashed by the protesters to prevent it from being moved. Then Jerry felt something inside the bike shift, and the motorcycle began to bounce on its rear wheel. The front tire rose again until it was pointing almost straight up toward the sky, and all Jerry could see through the digital readout in his visor was smoke. Each bounce was higher than the last, and on the third, feeling the heat from the flames, Jerry put his head down, pressed his chin firmly against his chest, and screamed, "HOLY SHIT!"

The third bounce had lifted the motorcycle nearly four feet from the ground. When it finally returned to earth, the rear tire of the motorcycle landed on the front end of the disabled vehicle with a hard crash. The front tire lowered onto the roof but only made contact long enough to crack the windshield as the rear tire began to peel out again, this time across the hood and up the windshield, partially breaking through so that small shards of glass were sprayed in every direction as Sarina accelerated. Then the motorcycle shot off like a rocket, both tires peeling out as they gained traction for the launch. Flying through the air, Jerry could feel the weight of the back tire moving again. Unlocked from its original position but still controlled by Sarina, the rear wheel moved below him side to side like a pendulum allowing the bike to bounce off the sides of other vehicles that had been placed behind the first. Sarina bounded forward relentlessly, leaving a trail of broken glass, twisted metal, and screaming protesters in its wake. The next impact Jerry felt was on his left side, then the right, then the left again.

Finally, with the front tire still in the air, Sarina somehow managed to leap onto the top of a support van in one of the southbound lanes, and with one last deftly executed aerial feat landed, both tires touching down on the grassy median. The front tire touched down with a screeching sound, and Sarina took off like a bullet toward the I-405 North interchange. All of this happened in only a handful of seconds, too fast for Jerry's mind to process. In shock and not believing or fully understanding what had just happened, Jerry opened his eyes, remembering that he had shut them when the cycle first launched itself into the air. His heart was beating faster than it ever had in years, and his arms and legs were sore from hanging on to the motorcycle while he was upside down. He couldn't think straight or relax the grip his hands and legs had on Sarina's frame for several minutes. Later, he would compare the experience to Perry as being comparable to riding a mechanical bull off a cliff.

Listen, my beloved brothers. Didn't God choose those who are poor in this world to be rich in faith, and heirs of the Kingdom which he promised to those who love him? But you have dishonored the poor man.
-James, 2:5-6

Chapter Six

Temple Foundation Temporary Meeting House
Christian Territory of Spokane
Friday, March 25[th,] 11AM PST

Not far from a newly laid foundation that was almost as large as a football field, a temporary, single-story community meeting house stood. It was made with a pine frame and plywood sheets, all of which were painted gray. Much of the insulation and sheetrock had not yet been installed, causing the temperature inside to remain colder than out for most of the day. Several small sections of the tile floor were also unfinished, forcing those who had prepared the room that morning to cover those areas with several small rugs.

A few dozen concerned church leaders slowly filed in through the small building's propped open double doors two or three at a time, many of them still wearing their winter jackets. A few stopped to assist the older attendees up the small set of steps that led to the entrance. Inside, twelve long plastic tables had been arranged together in the shape of a large open rectangle. Pinned to the sheetrock and wooden studs that surrounded the unfinished room were a wide variety of notices and photos of local and foreign missionaries along with more recent pictures taken at a recent ground breaking ceremony. A small bathroom and office were at the south end of the building, used almost exclusively by contractors and coordinators during the construction of the Temple Foundation building, the true and soon to be realized community center and veritable future hub of the Christian Territory of Spokane.

The impromptu gathering was full of mumbling and friendly small talk as its members lined up to get their coffee. More than forty men and women were gathered around the twenty-three pastors who, after shaking hands and saying polite hellos to the rest of those present, eventually sat at the haphazardly assembled tables. The rest continued milling around and speaking to one another in small cliques as the meeting began, some brought in extra chairs for those who couldn't stand for long periods from a storage area that was located somewhere not far from the construction site. As the meeting started, their voices lowered and then fell completely silent. For a moment, a tense undercurrent could be felt, a hint of insecurity that floated just beneath the surface of the otherwise calm and collected veneer manifesting only in fleeting glances and knowing stares while they waited for the meeting to begin.

"Good morning, everyone, and thank you for coming," A tall, handsome man in an expensive pinstriped suit moved to the head of the table and sat down. He moved his chair closer to the table and straightened his jacket, like a man attending a business conference he had an aura of supreme confidence that brought smiles to the faces of everyone in the room, causing the tension to dissipate. He had a noticeable tan and extremely bright teeth. In front of him, a plastic plaque had been placed that said, 'Pastor Edwin Alstead'. He bowed his head, and everyone in the room followed suit. "Lord, thank you for your provision and your guidance." he said. "Thank you for bringing everyone here safely, we know your plans for our lives have been revealed and justified by recent events, and we pray that you will continue to give us wisdom as we pursue your love and your blessings."

He lifted his head and looked around the room. When he was sure that the eyes of everyone there were on him, he formally started the meeting by taking a small gavel from a briefcase he had brought with him and hitting it on the table. "This Temple Foundation meeting is now in session." He carefully placed the gavel back into his briefcase before continuing. "I called this meeting because many of you contacted me and expressed regret regarding our last minute decision to connect the walls." he said. "I would just like to say that all of the issues we are experiencing right now were not unexpected. We knew there would be no way to do this final step without upsetting certain elements in the community, no matter when we would eventually decide to complete its construction. Just know that the police are outside of the main entrance right now and have told me that they will increase their presence throughout the day as we get ready to install the gate when it arrives this afternoon. They have assured me that peace will be maintained, and everything should go smoothly as planned. There is no reason to be concerned."

"And what if it doesn't?" A woman sitting at the far end of the table spoke up. Her plaque indicated that she was Pastor Susan Favorton. She was wearing a purple dress and enough jewelry to make a bank robber think twice about where to get their next score. "The reports coming in from Seattle say there are now three riots going on in that city alone. Even more riots have started in Olympia and Tacoma, and in other major cities around the country. Judges are fighting amongst themselves since they were given direct authority to guide local municipalities. According to an email I received this morning from the mayor of Spokane, one of them may even arrive at our gate with a small army as soon as tomorrow! Not to mention the crazy mob that at this very moment is forming outside of this community and openly threatening to burn down our homes should they manage to get in! It's not about demands anymore for these people. They want to destroy our way of life!"

"Look, we don't need to worry, everything is in hand." An older man spoke up. He sat near the center of the table, his back to the front entrance. Several onlookers stood directly behind him. The place was so packed full of people, it forced one of them to press uncomfortably up against the back of his chair. He wore several large gold and silver rings and was dressed in a light brown suit. A large polished tie clip that was shaped like a cross shone in the dimly lit room, its golden sheen reflecting the long florescent lights that hung from the low ceiling. According to his nameplate, he was known as Pastor Mitch Branson. "Once the gate is set, everyone will forget about the protesters. They will return to their homes when the riots have settled down again on the other side of the state." His hands shook as he spoke. "God brought us here one by one so that we might share in His bounty and His protection, we all know that. Whatever we do will work out, we are in His will I am sure of it."

A younger, slim African American pastor in a large dark trench coat, chimed in. Pastor Obobwey was the name that sat on the table before him, "That's easy for you to say, you have a helicopter sitting in your backyard and a clear shot to Canada! I have a flock of real Christian men women and children to look out for!"

"Are you saying that I don't?" Branson shot back.

"Please calm down! Please!" another man spoke up from the far end of the table. In front of him was a folded piece of paper that said, 'Pastor G. Greeley, Miraculous Dawn Community Church of Cleveland', written in red marker by his own hand. He was the most sensibly dressed, wearing a plaid shirt, a simple, inexpensive wrist watch, and an old pair of reading spectacles. "I think what my colleague means is that we took the opportunity to connect the walls now because we thought that the change in government coinciding with the usual spring rioting in Seattle would distract the authorities from what we were doing. This was *our* agreed calculation. It was all decided right here in this room, and all of us are culpable. I really hope that you are not implying that it was all God's doing when it was clearly our own."

"But what do we do?" The woman piped up again. "The cat's out of the bag. This judge is on her way! There are barbarians standing at the gate, and it isn't even installed yet. What do we do?"

Then from the small office, an attendee who until that time had gone unnoticed limped into the meeting room. Even though his posture was slightly bent to one side, he was still taller than everyone else currently standing. His white hair, and well groomed and equally white beard somehow shone as he stood in the rays of natural light that came through the still open double doors so that a glow appeared to come off of his wrinkled and worn looking face. He was wearing a large brown sweater with a snowflake pattern that was woven into it and blue jeans and was leaning heavily on a cane that he gripped with his right hand. The cane was thick and long, made of a single piece of dark wood that was straight and smooth. The handle was the color of gold formed in the shape of a Lion's head with a long mane with two red ruby-like stones set into the eye sockets. Others had noted that from a certain angle, it looked less like a lion and more like a cobra, much like a certain staff that was once raised up in a desert long ago. "Do not be anxious brothers and sisters." he said, "I just checked the weather. At this very moment, a storm is heading this way. I'm sure God will protect us. We shouldn't encounter any more troubles. Even secular law and the mayor himself are on our side now. There is no reason to be nervous. We came here on faith and we must continue in it. There is no turning back now."

"George is right," Alstead said, hitting his fist on the plastic table top. "We only need to wait this out a little longer and it will all settle down. In the meantime, keep everyone on alert in case more men are needed when the work on the gate is finished. We will meet back here after our services on Sunday evening to discuss our other...differences now that we will have to work closer together as a single community. Mr. Harmin, if you would please pray us out."

Everyone bowed their heads as the man with the cane spoke in a loud voice. "Mighty and gracious Lord, the Lord who gave the promise to Abraham to give him a land of his own that he could pass down to his descendants, the Lord who called Nehemiah to restore the nation that was lost, we call on you to protect and guide us. Please forgive us for our lack of faith and remove all anxiety from our hearts. Help us to not miss the mark. Correct us and reveal what needs to be revealed in us so that we will not miss in the future or be led astray from your divine purpose for us in this world. In the name of Jesus, we pray, Amen."

"Amen." they all said in unison, and each left to their work.

The centurion answered, "Lord, I'm not worthy for you to come under my roof. Just say the word, and my servant will be healed. For I am also a man under authority, having under myself soldiers. I tell this one, 'Go,' and he goes; and tell another, 'Come,' and he comes; and tell my servant, 'Do this,' and he does it." **-Matthew, 8:8-9**

Chapter Seven

I-5 Corridor north of SEATAC International Airport
Seattle, Washington State
Friday, March 25[th,] 11:22AM PST

The National Guard arrived on the highway sooner than expected, forcing Sarina to take an unanticipated detour down Interurban Avenue through Tukwila, causing the bike to slow as it engaged regular traffic again, giving Jerry a moment to breathe. They were still traveling much faster than the posted speed limit, and within a few minutes the mechanized monstrosity, as Jerry began to see it in his mind, brought him back onto the highway heading east on Interstate 405. Somewhere during the short detour, the option to return to regular parameters had appeared on the main screen, but Jerry was too petrified and distracted by his own thoughts to notice, taking the opportunity instead to ensure that his clothes weren't on fire.

It wasn't much longer before he was cruising eastward onto I-90 and heading toward the deep green of the Cascade mountain range. They drove through Issaquah and were halfway to Preston that he noticed his eyes were stinging, and he was feeling ill. Then he remembered that though he had done so quickly, he had still driven through a cloud of tear gas, and even though the helmet he wore was snug and likely came with some type of filter installed in its air vents, it was hardly air tight.

He slowly built up the courage to let go of the handlebars. When he did, the motorcycle behaved just as Perry said it would,

quickly slowing down before it pulled over to the side of the road
and stopped. Allowing his heart a few seconds to return to its usual
rhythm, he began to wonder if the illegal A.I. would have stopped
its acrobatic feats had he decided to let go while driving through
the rioters. The possibilities of what it was capable of frightened
him. *Would it have stopped at all if I fell off?* He asked himself.
The only answer he could come up with was that he didn't know
for sure. Combined with the irritating gas that had started to feel
like it had entered his nostrils and was creeping down his throat,
the question scared him enough to make him take off the helmet
and puke on the side of the road. He got off the motorcycle and sat
down behind Sarina in the grass on the side of the highway.

He noticed that his heart was still racing and clutched the grass
with his hands while taking deep breaths in an attempt to calm
down. When he had gathered himself a little, he spoke to the bike.
"Sarina," he said gruffly, his voice still hoarse from the remains of
teargas and vomit that still coated his throat. He coughed several
times and spit on the ground before trying again. "Sarina, if I had
let go while the regular parameters were off, would you have
turned around and picked me up?" Sarina's voice returned, coming
from the speakers in the helmet that lay beside him. As Jerry heard
it, he raised the inside of the helmet to his right ear. "This A.I. does
not include rescue and retrieval procedures. Had you fallen and
called out, however, I would have instructed the vehicle to return
to your location. That is, assuming you had not been separated
from the helmet during the fall."

Jerry asked it another question, "And if you'd lost me, then
what would you have done?"

Sarina's response was fast and sure, "Having lost my rider, I
would have returned to my point of origin. That is what I am
programmed to do in semi-autonomous mode." The voice giggled
at him again.

Jerry smiled at himself and shook his head. "Of course," he
said and began to stand back up. He noticed something felt wrong.
He felt lighter somehow. He looked down at himself for a moment
and then began to empty out his pockets, but there was nothing in
them. Then he remembered the money Tom had given him. He
looked back in the direction he'd just come from.

"AAAAAAAAGGGGHHHHH!" he screamed, and kicked
Perry's motorcycle hard. It moved slightly and righted itself. Jerry
scowled and stared at it angrily. It looked as if nothing had even
touched it.

Jerry took a deep breath and leaned forward, putting his hands
on his knees. He shook his head for a moment and caught himself
in one of the side mirrors of the motorcycle, able to see his own
reflection in his bent over position. He attempted to improve his

appearance by moving his fingers through his hair, while taking a moment to inspect the receding lump on his forehead. He then moved his hand to the place on his leg where the batton round had hit him, amazed at how well the pain pills the doctor had given him in Tom's office were working.

Having completed the cursory self-examination, he turned and looked down the highway in the direction of his destination to the east. From where he stood, I-90 looked like a never ending path that stretched through a sea of wilderness into the distance and then upward toward the sky before reaching the horizon. He had only been over the Cascades once before by road. He was with Noel at the time, heading to Glacier Park, but his focus then had been on her natural beauty, not on that of their surroundings. Alone and in silence, he took another moment to look around. *I've really been inside too long, ever since I did that cartel story over the border. Maybe I've lost my nerve.* He recalled that there was supposed to be a desert covered in several feet of ash, a veritable wasteland leftover from the calamity on the other side of all the green hills and seemingly never ending fir trees that surrounded him. *Time to see it for myself.* He thought. He put the helmet back on and grabbed one of the handle bars. A green 'Go' button appeared on the center screen on the bike.

"Semi-autonomous mode again," he said, taking a deep breath before following it up with "Yeah, let's do that." He tapped the button and held on tightly again as Sarina drove them both back onto the road.

****

As Jerry wound his way up interstate 90 through the wilderness of western Washington, the twists and turns of the highway began to remind him of Noel, the curves of her body and her dark flowing hair. *I'll go back to her*. He thought. *I'll act all submissive and do whatever she wants, but eventually, my testosterone and lack of patience with her lies and her late nights out will get the better of me. I'll end up yelling at her again, but this time she'll call the cops on me or get a restraining order or something or worse.* Jerry did not intend to be ensnared in a one way relationship trap for a third time, but part of him desperately wanted to, a part he was becoming more aware of with each passing day. He recalled feeling the irrational need to be with Noel a few weeks after their first break up, the same feeling that had started to rear its ugly head as he rode, making his heart feel weak. *I've given in before and look where that got me, heart sick and doing stupid things.*

Was it loneliness? Lust? He didn't know and didn't want to. Then something clicked in his mind, a sharp revelation that broke its way through his mental defenses. He wasn't going to deal with the problem at all. Whatever it was that kept driving him back to her, he knew that he *would* go back again, and again, and again until something horrible happened to him unless he got some help. Cringing at the thought, Jerry didn't notice that he'd closed his eyes.

"Warning!Multiple irregular moving objects ahead!" Sarina's voice had returned, but she sounded different. Something about her tone seemed wrong. Gone was the calm, relaxing demeanor Jerry had gotten used to. The new voice in his helmet was a little too loud and a bit too rushed in the way that it spoke to be from the same program.

When he opened his eyes again, he saw a small doe standing in the road, not two car lengths ahead of him. It was staring directly at him, almost paralyzed as the bike approached at high speed around a sharp corner and was moving side to side as if not sure which direction it should go next. Figuring that the motorcycle was manually built at least something like a regular bicycle, Jerry grabbed what he was pretty sure were the brakes on the handlebars and squeezed them as tight as he could so that the cycle slid at a slight angle. His body lurched forward as the front tire wound down, bringing the motorcycle to a stop almost on top of the spot where the animal was standing. His heart began to beat violently again as he saw just how close he had come to colliding with the two large eyes that were staring at him innocently just a few inches from his left forearm.

No longer teetering with indecision, the young deer lifted its head, arching its neck in his direction. It breathed in deeply through its large nostrils and continued to gaze up at him through the visor. Staring back into the fawn's wide eyes, Jerry felt his body instinctively begin to breathe in and out in time with the animal causing his perception of time to slow and forcing him to relax. Meanwhile, the green wire frames in his visor scrambled, unable to make sense of what was standing in the road. Green lines shot off in every direction, bouncing off of the edges of his new friend until it had created a three dimensional outline around it. Their task completed, the lines were followed by a series of photographs that appeared in the top left corner of the visor's interface, most consisting of different species of four legged fauna, the onboard computer cycling through them faster than a magician could flip through a deck of cards while shuffling. They finally stopped on a picture of a reindeer with several white spots on its body and a big round red nose that looked like it was air brushed on the side of a vehicle. Sarina then matched the wording beneath it to the animal, labeling the deer as a "Rudolph".

Jerry was confused at the strange result until he remembered that Sarina wasn't connected to outside sources of information like his Omni-Glass was. It was probably the first time the onboard A.I. had even seen a deer, and it was most likely doing the best it could, given the limited amount of information it had access to. Then as suddenly as the bike had jerked to a stop, the doe turned its head and darted off to the shoulder on the southern side of the road.

He could do nothing but look on as it leaped up an embankment and into the dense forest. Watching as it swiftly made its way under the low lying branches and around tree trunks, his gaze followed the deer as it met up with several others of its kind which had been observing the entire event from a short distance behind the tree line. He couldn't tell exactly how many there were, only that there were some smaller ones among them and at least one large buck. He saw the deer he'd almost hit take one final brief look at him and the motorcycle before disappearing into the thick shadows that lay beneath the trees. For a third time in as many hours, he had narrowly escaped serious harm. Paralyzed in the middle of the road sitting on what had turned out to be something more akin to a not-so-smart missile than the intelligent self-actualized mode of transportation he had been sold on, Jerry found himself reanalyzing his recent life decisions while wondering if there would be a fourth.

Clack!

Jerry was still frozen, his hands firmly glued to the handlebars, his fingers still pressing down hard on what he thought were the brakes. His mind continued to consider the fact that earlier that morning, he could have been hurt, should have been even...badly. He wasn't an action hero for crying out loud, and people all around him were getting hurt. What made him so special? Noel was right. She'd told him many times in the past that he shouldn't take so many chances with his life. His number had to be up sometime, and between that day and all of the other times he'd taken risks to get a bonus or a good story and got out without a scratch, it was quite possible that whatever that number was, it would be coming up sooner rather than later.

Clack!

Startled, Jerry jumped in his seat, his mind catching up with the fact that something was hitting the side of his helmet. He turned to his left and saw the butt end of a flashlight and immediately knew what was standing next to him before the bright golden badge and dark blue uniform even came into focus. He let go of the brakes and lifted his visor with his left hand, careful not to release his grip on the right handlebar completely.

"You ok?" The officer was middle-aged and shaped like a pear. He had a kind smile and warm eyes. Jerry was relieved to see someone, anyone in that moment. He let down his shoulders and breathed deeply, nodding his head in response. "Saw that caravan you almost hit before *you* did, looks like." The cop continued. He was now looking at the side of the motorcycle, his eyes getting wider the longer he took it in. The officer looked at Jerry again, quizzically. "Some ride you got there, you drunk or something? You should have seen that group of deer from a mile away, plenty of time to slow down."

Jerry opened his visor. "Sorry, officer." he said, "Just lost in my thoughts, don't get out of the city that much, I think I started to doze off a little."

"Where ya' headed?" the cop asked.

"Spokane. I have uh, family there." He felt blood flowing into his face and realized that he must have looked pale.

The cop gave Jerry a confused look. "Ok." he said, "Just be careful, there's a service area coming up in a few miles. It has a recharging station if you need it." He touched Jerry's jacket with the butt of his flashlight. "I think you might want to buy a heavier jacket there too if you plan on going over the mountains. It isn't summer yet. Make sure you at least stop to get a cup of coffee anyways". The officer turned around and looked behind them. "Oh, and uh, if you don't mind, I need you to get off the road for a sec." Jerry obliged, letting go of the hand grips. He was careful to rest his forearms on the handlebars, so that the officer wouldn't see that he'd given up control of the motorbike. Sarina moved to the side of the highway. Once he was out of the way, the officer used his flashlight to wave by several vehicles that had come up behind him after he'd stopped. The officer had driven his cruiser around them in the breakdown lane, before getting out of it to talk to him. While he waited for the others to pass, Jerry wondered how long he had been there, paralyzed before the cop showed up.

He was getting ready to get back on the road when he saw several police cruisers, an empty prison bus and three personnel carriers passing by in the other direction on their way to the Tri-City area. Things back home must have been getting serious. Fortunately, the National Guard had gone into the cities of Seattle, Tacoma, and Olympia on more than one occasion over the last several years to quell the riots. Though alarming, they weren't an all-together unfamiliar sight. Once they went by, some twenty or so vehicles in all, the officer put his flashlight away and began to turn back to his cruiser not far from where Jerry was gawking at the passing traffic.

"What's going on, officer?" Jerry asked, feigning ignorance. *Maybe I can get some inside info off this guy about the government's response to the riots that Tom might be willing to pay for.*

"Just get that cup of coffee, son." the cop said and got back into his cruiser.

Jerry lowered his visor. "Sarina," he said, "Why didn't the officer notice that you don't have license plates?"

Sarina answered, "Perry added photorealistic screens at both plate locations along with instructions for use in my programming whenever figures of authority are identified nearby. I simply displayed previously recorded plates onto them. The police officer didn't notice because he did not look at them more closely."

"Perry, you da' man." Jerry said to himself out loud. Since the cop looked to be headed in the same direction he was going, Jerry decided to follow him.

****

The service area turned out to be another fifteen miles up the highway. Jerry was obviously not planning to stop for coffee as the Police officer had instructed, but his interest in the activities of the authorities peaked when he saw even more military, and police vehicles were recharging or filling up on gas there. Curious as to why, Jerry decided to stop, stretch his legs for a minute, and do a little investigating.

"How's your battery, Sarina?" he asked.

"The battery is at eighty percent. If the current amount of cloud cover holds for the next two hours, I should have no issues with reaching the requested destination within the desired time frame."

The service center was a decent sized place with a large parking lot that desperately needed to be repaved and a very tall 'Charlie's' sign that he had seen above the tree line from two miles out. Of course, it helped that he had just crossed over a high ridge and was on his way back down the other side of the first true rise of the mountain range when he'd first spotted it. The sign was actually a refreshing sight after seeing nothing but trees. Living so long in the city with its miles and miles of urban sprawl and smog that steadily extended year by year into the outlying areas around it could make one forget that quaint, isolated locations like it even existed.

The place was busy. Along with the other vehicles, five or six large CAV haulers were in the process of being recharged with a few more sitting in line behind them. A young man in ripped jeans, a black tee shirt, and a beard that hadn't really filled in yet walked around each of the charging stations connecting and disconnecting the cables. Nearby, two gas powered diesel tractor trailers were filling their tanks, their respective drivers standing between the motorized behemoths bragging about the differences in their rigs. Two police cruisers were parked on the opposite side of the pumps, the officers responsible for them also filling up while two more personnel carriers waited for their turns. On the other side of the building, a civilian electric car idled quietly while three children inside fought over what looked like a stuffed animal as their mother reprimanded them through an opened rear window. Five or six more police cars were parked in the spaces near the front door of a small restaurant that was attached to the convenience store behind the charging hubs, but Jerry couldn't see their drivers which meant they were likely all inside, drinking coffee and eating doughnuts.

Jerry headed into the parking lot from the off ramp and steered clear of the main building as he approached, parking the motorcycle behind a large propane tank on the edge of the property near the tree line so the police wouldn't see it. Breathing in deeply as he took off the helmet, he was surprised by how clean the forest air felt to his lungs. How long had it been since he and Noel had taken that trip to Glacier Park? Two years? Three? He wasn't sure. *I'll have to ask her when I get back to-* The thought made him cringe again, bringing some of the dull throbbing back along with it. He waited for the pain to pass and secured the helmet on its lockable hook on the side of the bike. His composure regained, he marched into the building with no small amount of determination brimming up inside him.

After walking through a pair of glass double doors that he was amazed to find he had to push to go through, his suspicions were verified. Inside and to the right, there was a small gift shop and the convenience store. The restaurant was to his left. It had several small tables and a short counter. Eight bar stools were firmly attached to the floor in front of it, seven of them were occupied. The place was full of police, twenty-five or thirty of them by the look of it. Jerry's interest began to grow. He was seeing another side of the riots, one that started far outside of the city in the middle of nowhere. Thinking that the perspectives of the locals and the police might make a good story in its own right, he went to the counter where a manager and one waitress were frantically filling coffee mugs.

All of the booths and tables were filled as well, forcing three of the officers to engage one another in conversation near the entrance, standing with coffee in hand while even more went in and out of the men's bathroom. Jerry noticed that some of them had stripes along their dark slacks and hats, meaning they were with the state police. Thinking back to his near miss on the highway, he remembered that the one who had invited him there didn't have stripes, which meant that he must have been from a nearby town.

The camaraderie was amazing to watch. Jerry's impression of the police up to that point had always been that state troopers traditionally did not mingle with local officers. In fact, he'd always thought that they were more competitors than friends, neither side particularly liking the other very much, but from where he stood in that crowded restaurant, it seemed like they were old drinking buddies, or coffee buddies at least. *I guess viral transmission regs for small spaces don't apply to the police in rural areas.* He thought to himself. The noise of their chatter filled the room, carrying the sounds of stories about family events and mishaps on the job to wreck loose sons and daughters to the current costs for tuition for their kids, car repairs, taxes, and home improvement projects.

Seeing so many people in one place share their stories with one another so effortlessly was a rare thing for Jerry since most of the people he knew only communicated through online interactions using small personal devices one-on-one or in small groups. The closest he'd witnessed anything even close was when he and Noel went out drinking with their friends except when they talked, they usually didn't open up to one another in a genuine way, at least not until they'd had plenty to drink that is. He certainly never expected to see a bunch of police talking so openly about their private lives in a public space as conspicuous as a restaurant at a highway recharging station.

"I see you took my advice." Sitting at the counter not far from the register next to the only open stool left was the officer that he had spoken to after his near animal maiming experience. Several of the other officers began to look in his direction, and the entire place dropped two decibels.

"That the guy?" one officer across the room asked.

"That's him, alright." another officer two tables down stated, without taking his eyes off of Jerry, "The guy that almost killed Bambi *and* his mother!"

Some of the older officers began to laugh, and Jerry watched as some of the local cops that must have passed him on the road began describing to the others what had happened, resulting in some giggles and more staring. Jerry had no idea what a 'Bambi' was, save that by the way it was being used it must have been an old reference to something associated with deer. He shook off the obvious joke as he'd had to for so many others while in similar situations and approached the cop with which he was already acquainted.

"Name's Sam," the officer said, "Sam Reaton." He raised his coffee mug in Jerry's direction.

"Mine's Aaron, Aaron Williams. What's going on here, Sam?" Jerry asked.

"Tell you what," Sam said, motioning to the manager behind the counter with his hand and then pointing to Jerry. "Why don't you let me buy you that coffee, Aaron," Jerry noticed that Sam was not as young as he had first appeared. Upon closer inspection his hair was filled with more gray than Jerry had originally noticed, and there were some very distinctive lines around his eyes that when they'd been on the road had been covered up by a pair of large reflective sunglasses. The skin under his chin was drooping as well. It only took a moment of observing him close up for Jerry to figure out that it was Sam's relaxed and friendly nature that made him seem younger than he actually was.

Jerry sat down on the empty stool next to Sam. The stool was free because it stood almost directly across from the register, and there was barely any counter space in front of it. A young man, probably in his late twenties, neatly dressed in a white work shirt and slacks moved back and forth behind the counter around a waitress in a kind of dance that they both seemed to be used to performing in the small space. Reacting to Sam's words, he filled a cup of coffee and placed it down in front of Jerry without needing to be asked directly. "Thanks." Sam said to the waiter plainly. The waiter smiled and nodded. Jerry put his hands on the mug, only then noticing how incredibly cold they were. A shiver abruptly ran through his system, adjusting to the new information. He took a sip and looked at Sam with a friendly smile.

"Why are all of you here?" Jerry asked.

"Here? Well, uh..." Sam looked around at his fellow officers to see if anyone was within earshot then repositioned himself so that he could speak to Jerry more directly. "We're the backup. All us old fogies here, we usually come whenever there's a commotion around the Sound. The National Guard calls us up in case anyone needs to be removed for 'disturbing the peace'. Been meeting on and off with the Staties here for at least four or five months now in preparation for days like this."

"That explains the bus." Jerry said. "So why aren't you there now?"

"Well, no one's been arrested yet." Sam said. "We're just waiting for the call. But from what I've heard, the National Guard should be calling us in anytime now."

Jerry nodded, "Have you heard about the wall being built in the northern part of Spokane? That's where I'm headed. Uh, where my family is, I mean."

"That mess?" Sam didn't sound at all concerned. "Nothing that needs any doing by us, the locals there can fix their own problems. It'll all work out."

He could tell that Sam was holding something back, but unfortunately, there wasn't time for any more questions. A loud scratching sound began squawking through the speakers of every one of the hand held radios that rested in the belts of the officers, "Ten thirty-four, ten thirty-four, all available officers on deck, over!"

A state trooper wearing a long brimmed hat walked in through the front door and yelled to everyone inside, "Looks like its Olympia. Everyone finish up your coffee, it's time to head out!"

"Well, that's our call." Sam said. He stood up. "If you're headed to Spokane today, try to understand that community is a fragile thing and...keep your head down if you're heading through the north end of town." With that, Sam paid the bill for the coffee. As he did, Jerry noticed a cross that was pinned to the officer's left collar. While he was looking at it, Sam said, "You noticed my pin. It was blessed, you know. My wife got it for me years ago. I wear it to work every day."

Jerry looked up toward Sam's smiling face. It was beaming with pride. Confused and a little saddened, Jerry nodded toward the pin and said back, "You'd think there would be a conflict of interest, you being a representative of the law and all."

Sam's smile suddenly turned into a hardened frown. "The law exists for and because of what it represents my friend. And faith has gotten me through more than a few bad days on the job. You should know what I mean by that, you had a guardian angel watching over you this morning." He pointed at Jerry's chest with his index finger and looked him square in the eye, "And you know it." And with that, he patted Jerry on the shoulder and filed out of the restaurant with the rest of the officers. Jerry sat in silence watching as each of them put on their hats and walked out of the building toward the danger that was awaiting them. A few continued to talk as they went, but most fell silent and checked their gear to make sure they weren't leaving anything behind.

After all of them had left, Jerry finished his coffee and gave a quick nod to the manager before heading back outside. Stepping out the door, he felt the warmth of the sun hit his skin. He watched as all but one of the police cars crossed the highway and got back on heading west. He turned and looked eastward again. Not much farther and he would arrive in plain country, and then the desert. He looked up at the sky. There were some dark clouds to the northeast that were travelling inland at a pretty good clip. Then he heard a voice coming out of a radio in the only cruiser that hadn't left yet, "That's right it was black, looked expensive. If you think you've got it, call in the VIN number and the license plate if you can find one. Did you see anyone with it?"

Jerry looked in the direction of Perry's motorcycle. Three State policemen were standing next to the propane tank. One of them, the one with his thumb on his radio, swiveled his head around and looked Jerry up and down for a moment. Jerry smiled and gave another nod and a short two fingered salute and turned in the opposite direction. He took off his sport jacket, slinging it over his left arm, which he moved near to his stomach, concealing it while he walked. He headed toward the electric power stations where four or five cars now waited in line to be powered up. Behind him, he heard the officer speaking into his radio. "Nope, no one suspicious looking. That and the keys were left in it. Someone probably stole it so they could go for a joy ride or get on the news. I'll stick around for a few minutes, and if nobody shows up, I'll call a truck. Once we return it to the owner they probably won't want to press charges unless they know who it was that did it. The thing still looks pristine. Do you really think this is the one you guys are looking for?"

The voice on the radio started speaking again, "Fits the description. No one saw what model it was, but they were pretty sure it was a Misikashi 1750." The voice faded as Jerry walked around the charging stations, smiling and nodding at the people filling up on electric current as he went. He picked up his pace a little, turned around the corner of the building, and walked toward the regular gas pumps. A tractor-trailer that was hauling a huge milk container with a strange picture of a smiling farmer next to a cow painted on the side of it was there. The driver of the hauler was at that moment sitting on the edge of the step-up on the passenger side of the cab biting his fingernails and spitting them out onto the ground one by one. He was balding and rough looking, wearing a pair of genuinely faded jeans that were strewn with black oil smears and an oversized red tee shirt with several small holes developing along its edges. Jerry noticed that the truck had Idaho plates.

"Hey!" Jerry put on a friendly face and walked up to him. "I was wondering if you could help me, my CAV broke down on the way up here. It had to be towed back to Seattle, but I have to get to my sister in Spokane. She's in the hospital with cancer there and might not have long to live." The expression on the man's face didn't change at all, but he did stop chewing on himself, the fingers on his left hand remaining frozen in his mouth. Jerry continued, "I figured if I stuck around here long enough, I might be able to get a ride from someone passing through." Finally, the man's expression softened a bit. He lowered his hand from his face and looked Jerry up and down in a similar manner as the police officer had, no doubt noticing the formalness of his outerwear.

The man began to nod and spit out another fingernail. "Yeah, I can help you out. It's only a few hours." He paused for a moment and looked down again, then, he kicked the ground where the fingernails had fallen. His gaze returned to Jerry. "You can sit in the passenger seat, just give me a minute so's I can move some stuff out of the way." He reached out his left hand to Jerry and put his right hand in his pants pocket. Jerry forced himself to put on a wide grin and took it.

"Name's Marty." the man said. "What's yours?"

"Johnny," Jerry said, still smiling. "Johnny Barren. Nice to meet you, Marty."

For when Gentiles who don't have the law do by nature the things of the law, these, not having the law, are a law to themselves, in that they show the work of the law written in their hearts, their conscience testifying with them, and their thoughts among themselves accusing or else excusing them. **-Romans, 2:14-15**

Chapter Eight

Interstate 90, Eastbound Lane
Twenty minutes west of Ellensburg, WA
Friday, March 25[th,] 12:40PM PST

The cab of Marty's tractor-trailer smelled like a combination of alcohol, bubble gum, and air freshener. The alcohol, no doubt from the wide variety of empty whiskey bottles Marty had lined up neatly just behind the driver's seat and the pine scent from the air freshener hanging from an oversized rear view mirror. For the first hour, while Marty talked, Jerry looked around the cab for what was causing the bubblegum odor. Then he saw Marty take a pack of chewing gum out of the breast pocket of Marty's shirt. Seeing that Jerry was eying it, Marty offered him a piece, which he politely declined.

Around the windshield, pictures of Marty's adventures as a truck driver were tucked into every available crack and lining. Fishing trips and vacations that he had gone on over the years with family and friends were given equal space around the window. On the dashboard, bills and work related papers were strewn about. Some of them slid to and fro, at times piling up close to the windshield when they went around tighter turns before moving apart again to the edge of the dash. Each time they moved toward his side of the cab, Jerry's natural reflexes were tempted to reach out and catch them before they fell in his lap, but they never did. *I probably shouldn't touch anything in here,* He thought. *He's probably been all over. No telling what germs are in this cab.* In the center of the dashboard on top of the CB radio, a small plastic statue of Saint Mary had been placed, held there by some type of glue. Something that Jerry hadn't seen since he was a small child.

A little way into the trip, Jerry noticed that his seat was sticky on one side. Marty had taken a moment to remove a mountain of trash from where he was now sitting, mostly consisting of fast food bags and wrappers from snacks likely bought from highway service centers like the one they had just left. There was no telling how long the trash had been sitting there before he'd climbed in. Because of this, Jerry tried not to touch anything that was in the cab of the truck more than he needed to.

Despite those minor inconveniences, the ride was quite comfortable. Marty turned out to be a pretty solid guy and amusing to boot. He regaled Jerry with stories about the crazy things he had seen while hauling different loads around the country, from bad car crashes to UFOs. Wide awake from the second cup of coffee he'd had that morning, Jerry was more than willing to listen. He liked meeting new people, especially those that were interesting and unusual. So many people he came across in the city were bland, blindly materialistic, or insufferably predictable. Of course, he would never tell anyone there that he thought this, at least not while he was sober anyway. Besides, he'd often considered himself just as bland and materialistic as the next city fellow, it was just part of what came with growing up in one.

Sitting there, listening to Marty's stories, it struck him that he had almost forgotten what it was like to talk to someone whose opinions and perspectives were not tied exclusively to an urban background. Meanwhile, he kept his own answers to Marty's inquiries short, sweet, and close to the vest. Not that it was difficult to conceal the true nature and purpose of his trip to Spokane or the ordeal he'd just been through from the guy. Once Marty felt comfortable with him, he was quite the chatterbox, taking most of the air out of the cab for himself anyway.

There was plenty of scenery to pass the time watching as well. When they entered a region some sixty miles into the desert where the latest turbine windmills were installed, he asked Marty if he was worried about losing his job to the newer automated haulers. "Sure I am," he said, "But I think there are still some companies like the one that ships the milk I just finished hauling that prefer an experienced driver who can get their goods where they need to be safely you know? Better than dealin' with insurance later if there's an accident with a CAV and losin' good customers, you know? I mean, my track record speaks for itself. I haven't been late on a haul for over twenty years. Until these CAVs grow enough brains to notice when someone else is driving funny 'cause they're having a coronary or something from over a mile away and knows how to get around *that* type of situation while also callin' 911 for help, I'm pretty sure my job is safe. Well, for now anyways."

They moved past the hundreds of elevated wind absorbing machines that were scattered on either side of the road, each of them slowly turning when even the slightest breeze touched their twisted abstract shapes. It was while he was admiring the sheer number of them that had been installed across the landscape that Jerry noticed something on the horizon, a long line of buses that was heading toward them in the opposite direction. When they passed a few minutes later, he saw that some were bare bone prison transports like those he had seen before reaching the service station. The others looked to be charter buses. These were painted black with wide red stripes that went down either side.

Two of the transports that were near the front of the long parade were equipped with giant plows. They were suspended several feet from their grills and held in place by steel bars that were welded to the vehicle's frames. Bolted just below the windows of the rest of the buses were several layers of metal sheeting. They were at least five feet wide and painted to match the uniform color scheme, at least the outside layer anyway. *Why beneath the windows?* Jerry asked himself. *Why not over them? Some kind of shielding, maybe? If so, then why make it so they can be taken off so easily?* Jerry was unable to see the advantage of adding so much weight to gas powered vehicles whose purpose already was to carry large amounts of people over long distances, especially when they might attract criticism from the general public for their lack of efficiency. Looking into the windows as they flew by, he could tell that the charter buses passing them were not filled with police but with volunteers. The men and women that he could see sitting idly inside were wearing different colored western style bib shirts, the kind of all-purpose outerwear that cowboys donned in the days before things like cars became fashionable.

"Shotguns," Jerry said under his breath, his eyes locked on the procession. Marty who was in the middle of telling Jerry a story about a gray orb that he'd once seen over a military base near Maine, stopped talking and joined him in glaring at the long stream of traveling peacekeepers. Jerry counted forty-two buses in all.

"Yup, Shotguns alright," Marty said. "I heard that they were coming this way. Other truckers 'been talking about it all morning on the CB."

"I've never seen so many in one place." Jerry said.

"Well, from what I saw when I pulled out of Seattle early this morning, they're probably gonna need 'em. The police had to give some of us drivers an escort out of the city you know. I've seen firsthand what these guys have been able to do to clean up some nasty places. They're all volunteers, you know. Some are former military and police force folks. They don't just look out for the elderly and infirm either. They work with young people, give 'em a purpose, you know what I mean?"

Jerry looked at Marty. "What do you think of their leader, the guy who started the nonprofit thing, and the Shotgun Relief Army?"

Marty looked at the buses again. "Well, there's no denyin' he's done a lot of good for the country, getting aid to all those people in dangerous places over the years ain't an easy thing to do, I know, I've been to some of 'dem places. Now that the government's changed, the Supreme Court's probably gonna be relying on him to keep the peace in certain areas, is my guess. They probably don't want people to think they're takin' over or nothin' while they sort out those scandals so's they can finally decide who the next president is gonna be. That's what the news on the radio's been saying all week anyways." He looked at his left index finger and stopped talking for a moment to bite another fingernail. Then he opened his window and spit it out. "What's his name? Maims?"

"Raimes, Simon M. Raimes." Jerry said.

"Yeah, that's him. There is one thing about him that bothers me though."

"What's that?"

"Well, from what I heard over the CB just before I picked you up, he's got his work cut out for him in Seattle. I only saw what it was like in the north part of the city. From what I've heard, things were much worse down near the airport, walking right into a hornet's nest he is. And I watched them close that tunnel on I-90 on my way out." He turned and looked Jerry in the eyes to accentuate his next point. "But take it from an old truck driver who's seen just about everything, he may advertise himself as some great do-gooder, but I ain't never met a real man o' peace who thought that driving half way across the country looking for a fight was a good idea."

Jerry couldn't help but wonder if Marty was on to something. Simon Raimes was notorious for having never done a press conference or an interview. He had only given a few small speeches to his close supporters far away from any cameras and the occasional unpublicized private visit to the corporations that had given large donations to his nonprofit the New Hope for All Foundation, its original charter being to work with police to take back drug and gang infested neighborhoods in large urban areas. Combined with the fact that he never seemed to leave his humanitarian work, one could understand why an air of humility had formed around him, one that the press was unable or unwilling to penetrate. Unfortunately, despite the great impact he was having on society, the man remained something of a mystery. He didn't seem to have any kind of social media footprint or even a credit history before starting his organization, which made it difficult for journalists to get anything on him that might have made an interesting story.

It was also nearly impossible to get an honest comment from those who were closest to him, as they were all extremely loyal to the man. Not that any reputable news outlets were likely to print anything negative about him anyway, since public approval was definitely on Raime's side. Add in the recent court rulings that essentially ended the Hypnotic War, which made it easy for individuals to sue into oblivion any news publication that accused them of wrong doing without at least some kind of verifiable evidence, and Simon Raimes could have been considered untouchable in a way that few others were.

Of course, those obstacles weren't enough to deter armchair warriors and conspiracy nuts around the world from trying to take the man down a peg or two, and over the last year several stories about supposed sexual indiscretions and other accusations appeared randomly on the internet. Most were either immediately debunked or ignored by the general public, never taking traction, however. Soon after, the trolls and the press alike just began to see him as a somewhat unwanted but necessary neutral fixture of the new American landscape. He was even given the title 'Man of the year' in a widely publicized net magazine but didn't show up to accept the award, nor did he comment on it. The picture of him on the website that gave the award was obscured as no one was even sure what he looked like, having been surrounded by doubles at that point for years and with no photos available of him online that could be found, something almost unheard of in the digital age. Despite his clandestine nature, he did seem to be as advertised though, an impartial force for stability in uncertain times, a fact that made even his most dedicated enemies a little more comfortable at night in their beds.

Jerry had a different opinion about the altruistic figure, a hunch that he couldn't quite put his finger on. To him, something was off about the whole thing, like Raimes was someone who was simply too perfect to be real, someone who came across as being a little too involved in his work to be trustworthy. Jerry could understand why in a time of constant conflict, one in which he was a fairly controversial figure, Raimes would want to avoid attention, but he also couldn't help but think that something else was going on.

In some places, Raimes had started to become something of a folk hero, more known and liked than politicians or celebrities. Independent artists across the country had even taken to painting vague images of him in public areas, his round sunglasses, and red bib shirt covering the sides of brick buildings and slapped onto street lamps. Under each the slogans "Defending the coach of America" or "Join the Shotgun ranks today, defend the coach!" commonly appeared referring to an old western tradition or myth, Jerry wasn't sure which, that placed hired men with real shotguns in the passenger seats of stagecoaches defending whatever was being transported within. Lately, Jerry hadn't thought much about the man himself, but this was the first time he had ever seen the Shotgun Relief Army in its full glory.

"Keep your eyes peeled." Marty said, "Near the back of the bunch is the head honcho's private ride." It's the fourth or fifth one from the rear, it looks just like the others, but it's the only one with blacked-out windows in the back. My fellow truckers on the CB said you'd know it's his because of the license plate. Missouri all the way." He took his left hand off the steering wheel to point out the license plate of the very bus he'd described as it passed by.

Hell, Jerry thought. *Raimes is probably too smart for that. I wouldn't be surprised if he isn't even on that bus.*

****

Simon sat among the rank and file volunteers that made the bulk of the Shotgun Relief Army in the second to last charter bus in the cavalcade. Like so many times since his childhood, he sat in silence, looking through a window to the world outside while waiting on someone else. He was entering his late forties, and it showed. He was in good physical shape, but deep lines had begun to form around his eyes and mouth, and gray hair had recently begun to invade his temples.

As his eyes scanned the horizon, he spotted a hawk flying in the distance. It circled once and then glided toward the highway to the west ahead of the bus he was riding in. Though it was more than a hundred yards away, his sharp natural vision could make out the largest feathers on its wings with ease. He looked in awe at the lone intrepid creature as it glided over the desolate and forgotten place. In his mind, it was a stoic and beautiful hunter, searching for any sustenance that might be scurrying under the ash laden fields and doing so without even once questioning its purpose or place in the tragic world in which it had been forced to live.

Having shifted his gaze in anticipation of the hawk's flight path, he saw something large and white coming down the other lane. An old gas operated tractor-trailer was passing by, pulling a large liquid container in the opposite direction. When it passed his window a few moments later, he saw that on its side painted in large red letters was the slogan, "Wholesome milk, we've got it!" The message was just one piece of a larger picture, as it was laid over the image of a long blue ribbon, behind which a caricature of an overly ecstatic farmer was depicted standing next to an equally excited cow. Both of the slightly disturbing looking characters stared outward with huge eyes and freakishly large teeth, daring anyone brave enough to glance in their direction and risk permanently imprinting the ridiculous depictions into their long term memory.

Simon smiled back at them. It had been a while since he'd seen anything other than a CAV on the road, and he certainly wasn't expecting to see an antique in pristine condition pulling a container of milk behind it during the long ride. Then it occurred to him that the truck must have been to Seattle already as it was heading away from the coast. Whoever the driver was, they must have just missed all of the excitement and was headed home. *Lucky dog.*He thought to himself.

The volunteers on that particular bus were wearing white bib shirts and he was no exception. White was the color that was used for the support and medical teams. At his feet was a small, dark blue duffle bag full of other neatly folded bib shirts, one for each team. He kept them so he could blend in with any portion of the Army at a moment's notice, should the need arise. He was its creator after all and had gone through the necessary training required for each position himself. How else could he expect the men and women he regularly led into danger to respect him, if he didn't know himself how to do their jobs implicitly.

There was a blue shirt for the communications and reconnaissance team, a black shirt for the special operations and advanced bomb removal teams, otherwise known together as the 'advance team' and a red shirt for the regular nonviolent defense, fire prevention, and survey teams. Buried beneath all of them, hidden from anyone who might be brave enough to open it were five rolled up pairs of socks, four neatly folded pairs of underwear, a pair of blue jeans, a pair of ear plugs, one bottle of mace, one taser dart wireless pistol with its charger and holster, a travel toothbrush with a small tube of toothpaste in a zip-lock bag, a few energy bars and a heavily earmarked hardcover copy of a book on Marine war fighting tactics that was written before the end of the last century.

The red shirt was his favorite and the one he was the most likely to wear when leading the relief army into a difficult area. To him, it truly represented what the Shotguns were all about. Unlike the other groups, the defense, fire prevention, and survey team was made of regular men and women who were trained to keep the peace without saying a word. They marched into the most dangerous situations without hesitation or much protection and made the majority of the Relief Army's forces. The newest redshirt recruits went through a brief training program that included a fire protection element with a volunteer firefighter certification. They also were required to complete a police styled self-defense and detainment course where they learned how to take hits without being reactionary as well as how to detain using hand to hand moves along with taser and mace safety procedures. Finally, they took a brief basic military tactics course where they learned how to give and follow orders with and without the assistance of technology and learned to work as a team in tense or even chaotic situations.

Each course was a week long, and after completing all three, redshirt members were added to their numbers in a pass or fail capacity. Any sign of unwarranted aggression or unprofessional behavior toward anyone that they engaged in any way during an excursion meant immediate dismissal. Every Shotgun had a camera attached to a button on their shirts, which, once activated and checked, would sound an alarm if the A.I. monitoring the action even suspected that unsanctioned activity was occurring. The micro-cameras gave Simon complete control not only of the redshirts but every individual under his command. Because of the constant surveillance that the cameras provided, deviation from Simon's rules was rare, and he was proud to see that the training programs he'd designed more often than not resulted with a majority of the recruits passing their examinations with flying colors.

The other teams went through similar programs but could only join them if they had previous experience in their respective medical, communications, law enforcement, or military fields. Utilizing the Relief Army in conjunction with the nonprofit organization he'd built, in Simon's estimation, he hadn't just brought peace to troubled American cities over the last few years, he had been raising-up an entire generation of future local community leaders, and true citizens. And that was just the beginning.

He leaned to one side, putting his head against the glass and looked forward into the distance at the Cascade mountain range, its looming evergreen peaks slowly growing larger as they drew closer to them. *This is it.* He thought. *The opportunity I've been waiting for. No room for error on this one, Simon.* His smile vanished and was replaced by a cold look of determination.

Robert Valley's tall and lanky form walked down the aisle toward him, holding an interactive tablet in his hands. The only person other than the driver who was wearing a different color, he sat down in the seat next to Simon. "At last count, we have enough water stashed under these buses for another two days. We completed the food check. Everyone brought their own as they were instructed. Now we just have to wait." he said.

"You know," Simon said. "We may not have enough money to get the latest tech out there, but I'm pretty sure we have enough in the budget to update that tablet of yours to something more modern."

"That's alright. I have everything I need loaded onto this baby. I've got it working just how I want it to, and it doesn't have a CPU that spies on me or that can be hacked through a hidden OS, unlike most of the other non-government stuff that's out there."

Simon nodded, "How much longer until we reach I-5?"

"Another hour, hour and a half depending on how bad it is, we should know soon. Reports coming in show a lot of smoke and fire on the highway. We'll need to break out the gas masks for the advance team."

"Add it to the list. How about the National Guard? Are they ready for us?"

"They've taken position at the 405 interchange. Their plan is to wait until we get there in case more protesters try to come in from Tacoma, Olympia, and further south. The local authorities in Olympia are sending us regular updates about a small protest that started there this morning outside of the statehouse. I've got Melissa keeping an eye on it. The National Guard has orders to move to the courthouse north of downtown Seattle when we arrive. That means everything on the highway between SeaTac airport and the police line to the north will be all ours once we get there."

"It's a shame the local authorities couldn't afford to let us borrow any of their riot control vehicles. Not that we could have refilled them with water on the highway anyway. Any news on the weather forecast?" Simon asked.

"It's still pretty dodgy. Right now, its blue skies over Seattle, but there may be some drizzle come sundown. The next real rain won't be coming until tomorrow night so it's going to be our responsibility to make sure all the fires are put out. There's a storm front coming in from the coast right now, but it looks like it's going north, over the city. That one's going to hit Spokane this afternoon."

"Didn't we just pass there?"

"Yeah, a couple of hours ago, which brings me to another issue. The Chief Federal Judge for the eastern side of the state called and asked me if we could spare anyone for Spokane today."

"Spokane? Why?"

"Apparently there's a dispute there about a gate being installed on the northern side of the city. It's gotten a lot of the locals upset and people are coming from as far as Missoula and Bute to protest. Some anarchists are among them and may be bringing weapons."

"Over a gate?" Simon grimaced at his subordinate before looking down at his duffle bag. "Nothing should surprise me anymore." he said. He waved a hand into the air, flippantly. "Let the locals deal with it for now. We have much bigger fish to fry in Seattle. Tell the judge to send us updates. Tell them..." He shook his head. "Tell them if it continues to be an issue we'll try to send some men over once I-5 is secure or we'll just hit it on the way home. And let me know when we're thirty minutes out from Seattle. I'm moving to the control center before we get into town. Make sure the other team leaders are there, I want to go over some details before I address everyone."

"There's a service station about thirty minutes out. I'll let the drivers know which buses are pulling over." Robert said. He looked around the bus. No one was speaking, and none of them were allowed to bring electronic devices. They simply looked straight ahead, through their own windows, or were fast asleep. "Some of the whiteshirts look a little nervous."

Simon looked around. "They have no reason to be. I'll be right there with them. That should make them feel a lot better. Just make sure the deployment goes smoothly, and the package is set up as soon as the buses are out of the way."

"You should see it," Robert replied. "They gave us an old one, ancient even, like Afghanistan ancient."

"I don't care how old it is, just make sure it's done."

"Will do. Hey, your brother called your personal line."

"Did someone die?"

"No, he just wanted to check on you to see how you were doing."

"Good for him." Simon looked out his window. A moment later, he noticed that Robert hadn't moved and was staring at him with a concerned look on his face. "Ahhh," Simon sighed and shook his head. "Call him back. Tell him that I'm fine and that I'll catch up with him when all this is over."

Robert smiled, "Will do boss."

"And Robert, please don't call me boss."

"Right, sorry." Robert walked to the front of the bus.

Simon shook his head again and turned his attention back to the scenery outside. They had finally come to the first of the new state of the art wind farms, something Simon had been looking forward to seeing in action since long before they'd left for the Pacific Northwest. As they came into view his eyes were drawn to the tightly spinning air catchers sitting atop their tall silver towers. It wasn't their aesthetics that drew his attention to them, however. It was the technology behind what made them so much more efficient than their predecessors that captured his imagination. *Outstanding.* He thought to himself. *So much from so little, but what happens when the winds stop blowing?*

*Can anyone hide himself in secret places so that I can't see him?" says Yahweh. "Don't I fill heaven and earth?" says Yahweh.-***Jeremiah, 23:24**

Chapter Nine

Interstate 90, Eastbound Lane
Ten minutes west of Spokane, WA
Friday, March 25th, 2:31PM PST

After another two hours of listening to Marty's strange but amusing stories, they approached the remote city. Rounding over a hill just east of the Spokane International Airport, its different districts sprawled out before them against the lush, picturesque countryside as one. A few taller brick and concrete buildings near the city center stood out against the otherwise rural motif, nestled comfortably within an expansive, almost tranquil valley. A flash of lightening to his left caused Jerry's head to turn sharply. He looked past Marty out of the driver's side window. To the north, he could see several large dark clouds gathering above an area just west of where they were headed.

"Which hospital was it?" Marty asked.

"What?" Jerry replied, half confused before remembering the story he'd told his ride at the truck stop. Not sure how to respond, words instinctively tumbled out of his mouth. "Uh, the big one...on the north end. You know what? You can just drop me off anywhere. I can get another CAV now that we're in town. I really appreciate the lift, Marty. I know picking up hitchhikers isn't exactly safe these days. I would've ended up waiting for hours at the service station if you hadn't given me a ride."

"You would have had to pay charging and mileage fees too, you know. They do that after the first hundred miles or so I've heard." Marty said. He reached out to an interactive media screen that was set into the dashboard to his right and touched it with his forefinger. A large map of the local area appeared on the windshield. "Show me the hospitals in the area." he said, raising his voice a bit.

Silently red dots representing possible points of interest appeared across the map. "Go up a little." The map scrolled slightly, revealing the northern part of Spokane and the surrounding areas. "Show me the names." The names of the hospitals currently in view appeared. He turned to Jerry. "Well, can't be the one furthest north, looks like that one is for emergency trauma only. How about that one, just south of it, the family hospital."

Jerry looked at the map closely and struggled to compare it in his mind with the holographic one he'd seen in Tom's office. *Maybe I've been relying on my Omni-Glass too much, geez.* He thought. Not far to the northwest of the data point that Marty had suggested he saw a topographic rise that closely resembled a hill where he recalled one part of the wall ending in the hologram. "Yeah, yeah, I think that's it." Jerry said.

"I'll tell you what, I'm in no hurry. I don't mind bringin' you all the way."

"Wow. Thanks, Marty, I really appreciate it. I'd give you some money but-"

Marty let out a laugh that was long and loud. "Don't you worry about that!" he said. "I do this kind of thing from time to time. I like to think I'm goin' to a good place when it comes time for me to leave all this behind, you know?" He pointed to the plastic statue on the dash and laughed a second time.

Marty took the Division Street exit, turned north, and drove to the first intersection. All around them, people could be seen walking along the sidewalks and getting in and out of their vehicles blissfully enjoying the crisp spring day seemingly oblivious to what Jerry had just come from on the other side of the state and the potential chaos that he was about to venture into. At first, as he watched them he wondered what kinds of lives they must have been living to be able to be so care free, then he remembered that he himself had walked through a similar park not two weeks earlier with Noel in Seattle and reminded himself not to presume too much about the comings and goings of those he did not know.

Going on a drive through southern Spokane was much like walking through a time machine. It was full of all manner of centuries-old brick and mortar structures and fixtures that stood side by side with a wide variety of haphazard twentieth century construction. Each building was a faithful representation of the period in which it was erected, together culminating into a record of sorts of architectural experimentation. Most were built in times and for purposes that were lost to history and to those who passed by them every day.

They drove past a large convention center and over the Spokane River before skirting along the side of a local University that contained on its property the largest church he'd ever seen in person, its two spires stretched into the milky blue sky like two great arms holding crosses in the air. After that, the view became less artistically inspired and more average residential suburb in its appearance. The traffic became more prevalent, and Jerry witnessed a CAV bus picking up and dropping off passengers as they drew nearer to the hospital.

A few minutes later, Marty drove into its parking lot, turned his big rig around and stopped. "Well, this is where you get off, my friend." he said, "Thanks for keeping me company for a little ways anyway. You're o' the good ones. I knew you were when I saw that you didn't have one of those augment thingies on ya'. You know the ones that do your thinking for ya'. I just don't trust anyone who's got one o' dose tings. Letting everyone know where you are and what yer doin' every minute of the day. No freedom in that, tied to what everyone wants from you, you know? Yeah, when I saw you didn't have one of 'dose on ya', I knew you were someone I could have a real conversation with." He reached out his hand toward Jerry. "Anyways, it was nice meetin' you, John."

Jerry ignored the kind gesture, fearful that he might catch something from the traveling nail biter if they shook hands. Instead, he raised his right hand a little and gave Marty a short nod. "Nice to meet you too, Marty. It's been a real pleasure." he said. He opened the passenger door and climbed out, careful not to touch more of the cab than he need to along the way. "Be safe!" Marty said and toot the horn on the rig twice as he drove the truck back onto the street. Jerry looked on as it drove off, a little amazed at the series of events that had led him to the place where he was now standing. He shook the feeling off and remembering the map, turned northwest toward the plateau and started to walk.

Jerry didn't know much about Spokane. What he did know, he had gleaned from news stories he'd read or watched that were published on the Introspector's website. He knew that it originated out of the mining and lumber industries that once covered the western United States, but over the years had turned into a college town. He also knew that a few large tech companies had moved in recently and that it was one of the last cities where American products, mainly tools and heavy equipment, were made by people instead of A.I. controlled robotics. The unique environment that existed somewhere between the present and the past attracted all kinds of people to the area, both those that wanted to "bring it into the new century" and those who liked it just the way it was. With its natural splendor and sense of community, the city had an excellent reputation as a place in which people would typically help one another out despite any ideological or social differences they might have.

Jerry heard the shouts of a bunch of teenagers who were headed north on four old scooters as they came up from behind him. One of them had a solar panel strapped tightly to the front of their scooter, tied beneath its headlight with a bungee cord. Two of the other scooters were almost completely covered with colorful stickers, some political, others carrying the names of lesser known local bands. He could hear their riders arguing with one another as they drew closer. They were fighting about which streets to take, and at one point, the bickering caused them to ignore a stop light entirely so that they drove dangerously into a four way intersection inspiring several drivers of other vehicles to express their dissatisfaction by laying on their horns. As they rode past, Jerry thought he heard one of them say the word 'gate'. He ran to the side of the street and yelled out after them, "You guys headed to the gate?"

The driver of the second scooter from the front stopped and turned his head around to look at him. His hair was dyed red, some of it sticking out from under a white bicycle helmet, which was also embellished with slogans and popular phrases of the day, the largest of which was almost as big as a bumper sticker. It covered nearly a third of the helmet's right side and stated in no uncertain terms in bold black letters, 'GRIEFERS GONNA GRIEF'. The thin red haired boy put his kick stand down and took a pair of yellow tinted augment-capable goggles, the kind that were typically used for social media gaming and interacting with friends, off of his face. The soft round features and inexperienced eyes that were revealed as he did so made Jerry smile at him even if the young man was looking him over with a dubious expression.

"Yeah, we're headed that way. You need a ride?"

Jerry nodded, still smiling and let out a small laugh. "Yeah, yeah, I do."

"You don't look like you're from around here. What's your 'sidge man? You a Uni? That why you don't got a ride? You don't look like one." the kid said.

"No, I don't live on universal income. My situation is that I'm a reporter from Seattle, and I've come here to get a story." Jerry replied. Now that he'd managed to arrive at his destination without being noticed by the authorities he decided it would be good to start sharing his true identity with some of the locals to make his alibi as convincing. "My name's Jerry, Jerry Farron."

The kid used his right index finger to motion Jerry closer to him. Jerry walked up to the scooter within a few feet. The kid leaned close to him and looked directly into his eyes as if looking for something. "Where's your Omni-Glass?" he asked. "Don't you use 'em to upload your vids? I thought all journos used those."

"I had to leave it at the office. I had a pair of ProtoMark sync compatible glasses too but...I lost those."

The boy's eyes grew wide. "Protos! Man, those are expensive! Sorry man."

Finally, the serious act dropped, and the kid gave Jerry a broad smile. "Name is Devon, man. Hey, maybe we'll see some action near the gate. Hey, I can send any vid I take anywhere you want if you give me your info. Can't get too close to the gate though, everything gets messed up if you get too close."

Jerry let out a relived sigh and nodded. "Thanks, that really helps me out. Whatever you get, send it to TomMerrick299@SLspector. It's a Skyway Network cloud account. My boss will know what to do with it." Devon put his single line sync visor back on. Examining it more closely, Jerry guessed that the cheap tech probably couldn't take more than QK10 quality videos, but it was good enough. As long as it could record a partial 3D Lidar scan of the area around the gate, so the viewers on the website had something to play with while reading or listening to his article.

"Got it." he said. "Get on normie, we goin' for a ride! HAHA!"

Knowing that any ride he was about to go on couldn't possibly be as bad as the one he'd endured earlier that day, Jerry walked to the back of the scooter. He thought about putting his jacket back on and noticed that he didn't have it with him. He looked back where he'd come from and remembered that he'd taken it off when he got into the cab of Marty's truck. *Damn! Must have left it behind without realizing it.* He thought. *Maybe I'm not as lucky as I thought I keep losing things that aren't mine. Hopefully I won't lose my shirt next.*

Forgetting whether or not he'd left the keys to Sarina in the jacket, for a second, he felt a wave of panic come over him until the memory of what the officers outside of the service center had said about the keys came back to him. *Sorry Perry, man, I suck. Hope he doesn't get into trouble. Oh who am I kidding, Tom would probably just bail him out if he did.* He climbed onto the back of the scooter, and they took off.

In the distance ahead, the dark clouds Jerry observed on the way into town took on a foreboding appearance, swirling into and around one another like an undersized cyclone. Violently they pushed against and through each other, all of them circling around a wide area in their center that his eyes could not penetrate as if a great battle were taking place in some unseen arena within. The flashes were more threatening in their appearance too, their brightness more intense than before, their shapes evolving into straighter, more well defined bolts. The loud claps of thunder that followed each one became shorter and shorter in the amount of time they took to reach their ears.

****

A few minutes later, Jerry saw a local CAV station where several wide rows of the big gel pills were dutifully lined up, awaiting future customers. They were red, black, or blue in color and were attached by cables to charging stations that could facilitate up to four vehicles at a time. A twenty-four hour kiosk stood next to a small maintenance shed behind them. Jerry made a mental note of the location. *If I can get my hands on a phone, maybe Brenda can order me a ride home from there.*

Devon flipped off at least three motorists and sped through two more red lights before they reached the gate. At first, Jerry thought the kid was just trying to catch up to the friends he had been riding with before he'd stopped for him, but the rebellious teen seemed to be getting off on the excitement of the moment, the protest at the gate probably being the most exciting thing that had happened in the area in years. Jerry figured the boy was hoping to see something violent or even participate in ripping one of the walls down based on the slogans he was yelling at the people who were walking on the sidewalks along the way like, "This ain't no border town! Walls don't belong here!" and "Bring down the illegal wall! They can't keep us out!"

When they arrived at the four-way intersection where the street they were on connected to one of the lesser used state routes in front of the main entrance to the enclosed territory, Jerry could see some of the same catch phrases Devon had been belting out in print. They, among many others, were plastered on picket signs throughout the ten or more groups that had gathered there to protest the wall's erection. He could hear some in attendance chanting the slogans openly toward the wall as they approached in an attempt to intimidate any inside who were within earshot.

Devon's voice joined theirs as he slowed down and pulled the scooter over to where his friends were waiting for him. A quick estimate brought the total number of protesters to just short of two hundred in Jerry's mind. Not as many as he had hoped, but still enough to make an interesting story. Along with the chanting, the occasional rude one-off comment was made mainly by a few individuals who had ventured closer to the wall than the others. Angrily, they shouted out obscenities and the occasional threat.

They also threw trash over the wall and from time to time at a line of men who were standing stoically behind two rows of concrete barriers near the wall's main entrance. The barriers they stood behind were set up in a semicircle in front of a large ditch that was dug into the street beneath a tall archway that stretched over the street. They insulted the men calling them names like, "backward rednecks" or "stupid cult crazies" before retreating back into the safety of their own respective parties.

From where Jerry was on the far side of the intersection, he could see that the gate had not yet been set into place. Its dark, monolith-like shape was suspended high above the giant concrete archway by a crane that was positioned on the far side of the wall. The team of a dozen or so unarmed volunteers were all that stood between it and those who opposed the project.

Jerry got off of Devon's scooter and reached into his back pocket to retrieve the notepad and pencil that Tom had given to him. He opened it and almost as if on queue, a single drop of rain landed on the first blank sheet of paper. He looked up at the clouds again. They had become terribly dark and were moving even faster than before, the flashes within them occurring more frequently. Devon tapped him on his shoulder.

"This is 'da man!" Devon said as Jerry turned around. Devon reached out his hands, palms upward, his friends standing behind him. "He's gonna blow this thing wide open!"

Jerry looked over the unsure faces of Devon's adolescent cohorts who had parked their own scooters and come over to discover who he had brought to the party. They looked genuinely excited to meet him, but Jerry could see that their eyes were shifting nervously back and forth from him to the storm that was forming above their heads.

"You know, they were secretly building the wall." One of Devon's friends said. She was a small girl, couldn't have been more than sixteen years old, braces and everything, and like Devon, her hair was bleached except hers was bright green. She wore a black tee shirt and denim overalls with a series of political buttons on them. One of the larger ones he saw said, 'BASED SPEECH IS NOT PROTECTED BY THE CONTSTITUTION'. "Each one worked on it in secret on their own property," She continued. "Crazy religious nuts built it right under everyone's noses and didn't even bring it to the city for a vote. They bought off or replaced the local politicians over the last few years and then BAM! They connected the walls last week and announced that it was their own little 'private community.' There was a ribbon cutting ceremony and everything! We couldn't believe it! They even have a name for it. They call it the 'Territory' or something."

There was a loud crash of thunder. Jerry turned back toward the wall and looked at the crowd. For a moment, there was an awkward silence as everyone took a second to look up at what was coming toward them. Jerry turned his attention back to Devon. "If you can, get some footage of this before the storm hits from the other side of the street and send it to my boss today, I'll give you credit as my camera man when I put out the article in a couple of days."

Devon gave him his biggest smile yet. Not only had Jerry made him feel important, but he'd asked him to be a part of his article right in front of the boy's friends who Jerry could tell were instantly impressed by the way they were looking at him after Jerry made the offer.

"HELL YEAH!" Devon yelled out.

"Good man," Jerry said. "What's your last name?"

"Fromeyer."

Jerry wrote it down on the notepad. "Devon Fromeyer, cameraman." he said and smiled at them. "I gotta go. I have to do some interviews now in case that storm decides to rain this out. Get them lowering the gate if you can so everyone in the world can see it happening." He tapped Devon on the side of his shoulder with the notepad.

"Rain don't scare us!" the girl shouted. Jerry smiled and nodded at her and ran back to the crowd of protesters. A bright flash from a lightning bolt that originated from somewhere deep within the storm clouds lit up the entire construction site, followed by another loud boom. Instead of dissuading those present from continuing their contrarian activity, however, the fit of nature only seemed to encourage the local activists, as they were hoping it might cause those beyond the wall, including the crane's operator, to abandon their posts, if only for a short time.

****

Jerry made his way cautiously through the protesters toward the entrance. The walls were just as Tom described. They looked to be made of slightly worn brick and concrete up to about eight feet, then, there were cinder blocks to the very top, not quite twenty feet up but definitely sixteen or seventeen at least. These had been placed perfectly, definitely by a large 3D printer or automated brick layer that was nowhere in sight. Around the top, Jerry could see metal bars jutting out every ten or twelve feet. Nothing was hanging from them, but they were a perfect support for barbed wire and may have even been part of the jamming system. As he examined the strange metal outcroppings, several men emerged from the far side of the wall and stood above the structure. They started patrolling along a walkway Jerry couldn't see from the ground while scanning those below with their eyes. *That means there must be a catwalk up there that's at least a few feet wide with stairs leading up to it from the inside near the entrance. This isn't a private community, it's a giant compound!*

The crane emitted a loud hum as it continued to lower the gate into place. Upon closer examination, the gate itself looked to be made out of welded black iron set in a carbon fiber frame. It was large and thick, about twenty feet in width and fifteen in its height, but definitely not solid, as one could easily see between its wide flat bars. It certainly was not made out of steel either, as Tom had told him in his office. Jerry wrote all of his observations down in the notebook. Looking under the archway, he could see several men busy at work behind the guards. They were yelling back to the crane operator, giving him directions as the gate slowly crept downward. A few of them appeared to be connecting electrical wiring to a spot just inside of the archway beyond his line of sight.

The pit below the gate where the sentries stood fast in the area between the gate and the concrete barriers was essentially a large bowl of loose dirt and rock. Jerry looked around for where the excavated spoils had been placed. He found what he was looking for piled high next to some trees about thirty or so yards north of the entrance behind a turn around on the side of the road. Satisfied, his curiosity quenched by the discovery, he began to turn back when his eyes caught something moving. In his hurry to continue his investigation, he almost missed an unassuming looking man who was watching the entire affair transpire from an unlikely spot, the top of the dirt pile itself. The strange observer was wearing a baseball cap, hiking boots, jeans, and a checkered long sleeve dress shirt with the sleeves rolled up. There was something else too that he had with him that Jerry couldn't quite make out, something small and black just sticking out of the man's shirt pocket. *Who would sit on a big mound of dirt when it was about to rain?* Jerry thought. *Hmm, maybe he hasn't noticed the thunder yet because he's deaf?* That's when his eyes were drawn to a sign standing next to the mound that said, 'Wall Street'.

Not sure what to think, with the multiple layers of irony and coincidence that came with seeing the sign in that moment, he snapped himself out of the odd trance the sight had put him in and forced himself to look in the opposite direction. Some sixty or seventy yards south of the archway, a moderately high hilltop loomed over the entire scene casting a shadow over the area surrounding the entrance. It ended suddenly against the west side of the street with a cliff face that ran alongside the road, the wall butting up against it, ending where the bottom of the hill met the pavement.

The most interesting thing about the rise to Jerry was the row of expensive homes that had been built atop the high plateau. The ones that he could see had large expansive windows that faced north, which gave whoever lived in them a perfect view of the entrance and the surrounding area. Some of them also had overhanging patios that didn't look cheap. It was Jerry's guess that he would find whoever was responsible for the wall's construction living there, far above the riff-raff. For a moment, he could even see a few people standing behind a railing on one of the patios looking down. One of the onlookers appeared to be a woman who was wearing purple and something big and metallic that hung around her neck, which Jerry couldn't make out.

Seeing the clouds above their heads again reminded him that he had a limited amount of time before all who were present could be forced to take a raincheck. He shifted his attention to the people who had showed up to share their dissatisfaction with those inside the newly established private community and worked the crowd. Several groups had gathered together for the protest. Some were animal activists, when he asked them why they were there, they said that they were concerned about the local wildlife and how the wall would affect them, their 'local migration patterns' and their accessibility to natural food supplies that may or may not be out of reach for both those that were trapped within the wall and those that could no longer pass through it.

There were the representatives of various immigrant and minority groups who felt that the predominantly but not completely white residents of that particular section of Northern Spokane were trying to make their own little isolated kingdom that did not want them, though they could not support this information with any solid examples. At one point, they even contradicted their own arguments, by conceding that living in the northeast section of the 'Territory', as they called it, was a small Korean community that was not affiliated with the prosperity church groups which made up the majority of the population. According to one of them, the immigrants had moved there only recently. Apparently, they were living in small, inexpensive apartments, and had very little if anything to do with the wall, but didn't seem to be against its existence either.

The same protester, a short, rotund middle-aged man with a long curly beard and wearing a tie-dyed tee shirt, told him that there were also still a few elderly hold outs inside, most of them Catholic if what he said was to be believed, who had not yet sold their property to their charismatic counterparts. Apparently, they were the ones who first sounded the alarms and contacted the media when they noticed that nearly all of their new neighbors along the edges of the territory had begun to build the foundations for what would later become the wall in their backyards. Many of them had lived in the suburb for decades and had no plans for moving any time soon, but there weren't many of them left, and because of their age and waning influence as their numbers dwindled, no one had bothered to listen to them until it was too late.

Another group that was present represented other citizens of northern Spokane who were concerned that the wall would affect the city's reputation. Many of the people in that crowd were an unlikely lot as they were mostly consisted of local small business owners, college students, and professors. There were also some students from one or two High Schools in the area chaperoned by a few teachers who had volunteered to go with them to the protest during school hours.

Some non-prosperity based Protestant and Baptist Christian groups had also showed up to represent their own versions of their faith, a few of them carrying their own less offensive signs with other slogans painted on them like, "We are meant to be in the world but not of it!" and "The Great Commission is out here!". Unfortunately, these were largely ignored, and when they did engage one of the other groups, they were told very clearly that they should leave and were even threatened with violence by some of the more aggressive members of the other groups on occasion. Jerry couldn't help but feel bad for them, not only for the fact that they believed in what he considered to be a fantasy, but because their stubborn unwillingness to give up on what they said they believed often left them out of any real decision making despite the fact that some of them genuinely seemed more intelligent than they were given credit for. In better, more reasonable times, a few of them might have made ideal mediators. Instead, they were marginalized by the majority and forced to watch from the sidelines.

The drizzle that had started when he began the interviews turned into a light shower and from behind the band of concerned citizens the final group arrived, the one he had been waiting for consisting of the local chapters of your run of the mill wannabe anarchists, all of them wearing something on their faces to mask their identities. Within seconds of their arrival, the police appeared seemingly out of nowhere and moved into the area between the protesters and the pit. Remembering what he had seen at the truck stop, Jerry could tell that some of them were Staties while others from the immediate area by their uniforms. About ten of them lined up between the volunteers and the most aggressive of the masked trouble makers before the anarchists reached the barriers, telling them to stay away from the entrance or face the consequences.

By the time Jerry finished his interviews, the rain was coming down in earnest. His notebook, despite doing his best to cover it by keeping it close to his person, began to get wet. Also by that time, the lightning had finally closed in, the flashes appearing a short distance to the West, forcing the authority figures that were there to use the loud speakers on one of their cruisers to address the crowd: "Due to dangerous weather conditions, the mayor will not be able to address the crowd's concerns at this location. He has asked that everyone who is interested in sharing their grievances about the gate go to the new High School gymnasium on Monroe Street. For your own safety, please disperse."

The crowd jeered loudly. The construction did not appear to be stopping, nor did the volunteer guards move no matter how loud the thunder was or how close the lightning came to the construction site. After a few warnings, Jerry looked to where the police vehicles were parked on the opposite side of the road and watched as one of the officers shrugged at another and pointed in the direction of the oncoming storm. The raindrops grew in size and gathered in Jerry's hair, making it fall over his eyes, and he found himself moving it aside almost constantly to keep it from obscuring his vision. A few people in the back of the crowd of protesters began to leave as did the police, turning their emergency lights on as they slowly drove off.

On their way out, Jerry was able to make out the voice of the officer again: "WE WILL NOT BE HELD RESPONSIBLE FOR PROTESTERS WHO ARE STRUCK BY LIGHTENING. PLEASE DISPERSE!" When the voice stopped, the last two remaining cops got into their cars and followed the others to the south no doubt so they could assist them with managing traffic and tempers at the High School. Another reporter that had been canvassing the protesters that Jerry hadn't seen before then ran to a news van that was parked a good way down the road to the south, likely concerned about the elevated equipment on the top of it. Many of the protesters remained, however. Some became even more aggressive, emboldened by the absence of the local peacekeepers. Jerry turned to see if Devon was still recording from across the street behind him. Instead, he saw a large group of the anarchists, dressed head to toe in black was marching toward the gate. *Maybe this will turn out to be a good story after all. Even the local news is in the wrong place. If Devon is getting all of this from somewhere...*Jerry thought. Then it truly began to pour, the water hit him in waves, the churning wind growing more powerful with each passing second.

In the midst of the increasingly loud peals of thunder and bright streaks of lightning, a few members of the black clad anarchists that had made it to the concrete barriers found their courage and charged at the men standing guard in front of the great archway. The rest began to throw smoke bombs, and one even threw a Molotov cocktail, which lit up a few of the barriers. Then the sentries, who before that moment had seemed fearless, finally flinched. Some of them began to retreat, ducking under the gate, which was still being lowered. A loud cheer could be heard coming from the remaining protesters as they ran to safety.

Jerry knew that he should have been looking for cover, but he didn't want to miss what was about to happen. Once again, he turned around to see if Devon was still where he had parked his scooter. After a moment of scanning the area across the street where Devon had dropped him off, Jerry began to lose hope. Then he saw that the boy was still there. His friends had moved on, but he had moved his scooter behind a parked car and was still capturing the entire thing using his yellow tinted glasses while keeping his head just over the hood of the vehicle, his helmet still on. He saw Jerry and flashed a giant smile while emphatically raising his thumbs in the air. Jerry gave him a firm thumb up in return, his lips pressed together, and his brow lowered in an expression of genuine pride.

Jerry looked back toward the entrance. Water from the surrounding area and the street was pouring into the ditch behind the barriers forming a large pool. The agitators had stopped moving forward, and began pelting the ground around the entrance with more Molotov cocktails. The sudden escalation prompted some of the nonviolent protesters to run to their cars so they could get themselves and their children in some cases away from the flames that prospered along the edges of the great ditch despite the extreme weather. Still, many others stayed to watch, like Jerry curious to see where the conflict would end. By that time, aside from the anarchists, there was no real opposition to speak of. Only pockets of protesters apart from the conflict stayed, those strong enough to brave the dangers that the storm posed. Most were recording the event with their own syncable devices and snap cameras streaming it out to god knew where, that is if they could even get a good enough signal to stream as they were in a storm just outside of an artificial dead zone. Meanwhile, the guards completed their retreat, going further inside and away from the fire below the gate which at that point was suspended only a few meters from the ground, and took positions on the top of the wall with those already there.

From the center of the commotion a large burly looking man, who Jerry hadn't remembered seeing earlier during his interviews, and who didn't appear to be in league with the anarchists, walked past him toward the gate as if hypnotized. He looked up at the men standing on the wall and yelled, "NO!" The man was tall, standing six and a half feet with arms as round as tree trunks. He was bald, wearing only a pair of dirty jeans and a dark leather vest and was covered in a variety of seemingly random tattoos on his chest, arms, and neck, none of which complimented him or each other particularly well. He was not what some might have called a handsome man, but he was certainly imposing, something that Jerry supposed was exactly the look the brutish looking fellow was going for.

The Anarchists moved aside to give him room. Some continued to throw rocks and other objects over the wall along with the occasional Cocktail, but overall they left it to their new friend to intimidate the volunteers on his own. Standing above the gate, those tasked with guarding the wall looked at one another with a degree of uncertainty, clearly not sure what to make of the new development.

Then the big man spoke, his voice was as broad and clear as the clouds that were bellowing out their cries above, only his came from below, "You freaks brainwashed my daughter! She's staying in there with a friend!" He made air quotes with his fingers as he said the last word and contorted his face, giving the guards a particularly nasty look. Jerry thought that he must have looked like a monster to the sentries in that moment, lowering his head and reaching up his hands in the air as if they were claws, flames burning around him while lightning flashed and thunder boomed from every direction. "I–WANT–HER–BACK!" the man screamed. The anarchists cheered and began to move in again.

Unexpectedly, more men began to appear behind the gate at ground level, Jerry counted a dozen, this time they were carrying white objects in their hands, some of which they started passing out to the others. They took positions around the crane and on either side of the archway. Jerry could hear orders being barked from behind the walls. A moment later, he saw some of the men on the wall turn around and reach down behind it. They lifted up a bundle of the same white objects that the others near the entrance had come with and began to distribute them among the rest. *Printed guns!* Jerry thought. *My god, it's going to be a massacre!*

In response, the large angry man walked over to two of the concrete barriers between himself and the entrance. Jerry and the others watched as he single-handedly pushed two of the heavy barriers with his bare hands and moved them apart so that there was enough room for a vehicle to get through. Then he marched back across the street to what must have been his car. It was an old gas powered two-seater, unusually small for someone of his size. He squeezed into it, started it up and put the gas pedal through the floor in an attempt to drive it under the gate before the crane operator could finish lowering it into place, but as soon as the car reached the muddy pit it bottomed out, and the tires began to spin moving the rear end of the car side to side and dousing everyone and everything that was standing behind it with a curtain of dirt and mud. Undeterred, the man continued pushing down on the accelerator until the car had slid sideways along the outside of the archway, blocking the way in but not breaching it. In his attempt to prevent the crane from completing its task, he had succeeded not only in putting out most of the flames that had been set outside of the entryway but had also added cover for those that he had sought to cause harm.

Flailing his arms like a giant bear escaping a well laid trap, the large man got out of his car in a rage, clearly dissatisfied with the result of the failed infiltration. So angry was he that he took ten steps back and charged at his own vehicle. As he collided with it, he gripped the undercarriage, and with a loud war cry, managed to flip it on its side. Jerry saw some of the anarchists inching their way closer to the wall again and noticed that some of them were using the distraction to slowly gain ground, approaching the first line of concrete barriers again. It was obvious to Jerry that they were preparing to sneak around the vehicle with the hope of surprising the men on the other side of the entrance. *They're gonna rush the crane.* Jerry thought. *They have to if they want to stop it.* It was then that Jerry realized that he was a little too close to the action and that he was still wearing the white dress shirt that Brenda had put on him. *A friggin' strobe light in a rainstorm! Damn, Brenda was right! I'm a human target out here!* Jerry heard the guards on the wall cocking their plastic pistols and loading rounds into carbon fiber rifle chambers. It was too late. Rather than attempt to sprint away from the action and risk getting shot in the back, he ran forward instead and crouched down behind one of the barriers sitting on the edge of the pit, getting as low to the ground as he could.

What was left of the crowd behind him let out several loud gasps, realizing too late what was about to happen but powerless to do anything about it. For a brief second, Jerry wondered if he was a coward, if he should have warned the others that the area was about to become a shooting gallery, that in their desire to get something memorable on video they had neglected to notice that they too were standing in the line of fire. *No, I'm not responsible for them.* His conscience argued against itself. It had been a while, but it was hardly the first time he'd found himself in a war zone, and he wasn't about to be stupid enough to run through the middle of one just as the shooting was about to start so he could warn people who should have been smart enough to look out for themselves.

When it came down to it, he supposed that no one could have predicted that what had begun as a simple protest would have turned out the way it did. Even he couldn't imagine that those calling themselves prosperity 'Christians' would be willing to lose everything they had by causing a massacre just so they could finish installing a barrier between themselves and the rest of the world, the same world that they derived their prosperity from. After all, the confrontation he was witnessing wasn't about national borders or the rule of law. It wasn't even about personal rights or land ownership like what had happened in Provo. Based on the design, the gate was made to open, and there were foreigners and others who likely weren't even part of the scheme still inside, meaning that at some point those who built it must have planned on allowing people to come and go. *These people are about to risk their lives to protect themselves and their families from something, but what?* Jerry asked himself. *Are they afraid of the Supreme Court? No, that can't be it. They started building the wall's foundations years ago. If they're so worried about the way the world is, why did they wait until now to finish the wall, and why do it in secret to begin with? Tom said they'd come from all over the country, why did they decide to come to Spokane of all places? Something about all of this just isn't right.*

Questions gnawing at his mind, Jerry's need for answers soon began to overrule his better instincts for safety and removed his fear, replacing it with strategies. If he was fast enough, he could get under the gate himself before the anarchists got there and the shooting started. He was close enough and was dressed more like those inside than out and could try to blend in. He psyched himself up and peeked over the barrier he was using as cover. Breathing heavily, he got ready to launch himself over it.

That's when he heard something strange. Somewhere along the wall to the north, someone cried out something that was not discernible through the heavy patter and splashes that were resonating all around him. What he did hear clearly was the faint cheer that followed. At first, Jerry thought the sounds were coming from the other side of the wall, but as the cheering began to grow as it came closer to the entrance, he noticed several heads looking over the edge of the wall in between the legs of those who were standing on it, each man trying to get in a good position so that they could see what was coming. Jerry squinted and placed a hand against his brow to shield his eyes from the rain. The rest of the onlookers shifted their attention to the northern side of the wall as well. Then the sound of the original voice began to cry out again. Unlike the large man who had entered the pit, the sound of the new voice was more even, more certain in its tone. Jerry's ears strained to make out what was being said.

It was in that moment that Jerry finally saw what those standing atop and behind the wall had been almost climbing over one another to get a look at. It was the man in the baseball cap, the same man he had seen earlier sitting on top of what by then must have by then been a pile of rock and mud. He was still there, standing on the top of the mound, yelling something out at the top of his lungs. As Jerry watched the strange observer stopped his sermon and ran down the side of the great mound of dirt and along the wall toward the pit. He took off his hat and shirt in mid stride and shouted something that sounded like, "Who is this uncircumcised Philistine!" Then Jerry lost sight of him behind a group of anarchists who had been amassing on the northern side of the archway. The giant man, still standing in the pit and desperately trying to wedge the back end of his car under where the gate was being lowered, looked curiously in the direction of the newcomer's voice and the cheers that seemed to follow each outcry. The big man stopped what he was doing, and arched his neck, looking for the source of the increasing roars that had become louder than the sounds of the storm itself and which seemed to be attracting more people from behind the wall, their faces popping up over its entire visible length despite the danger.

What Jerry saw next, he would remember to his dying day. The crowd of anarchists parted about twenty yards north of the giant man's position, allowing the much smaller contender to join him by jumping into the pit. He couldn't have stood more than five foot, five inches tall, but even from his hiding spot behind the row of concrete barriers, Jerry could see that this was no ordinary individual who was marching his way through the mud. He was stocky, with broad shoulders, and had a full head of curly brown hair. His face was round, giving him the appearance of being much younger than Jerry suspected he actually was, and he was in shape, unlike the giant who could easily have lost a few pounds around the waist. His powerful legs flung mud and water in every direction as he walked, an action that served to conceal the fact that his bright and piercing eyes were carefully scanning everything in sight. By the way the strange character was acting, an untrained eye might have thought he did not care about himself or his surroundings, but Jerry could tell he was actually paying close attention to both.

"What is he doing?" Jerry said to himself under his breath. The thought that passed through his mind next, he kept to himself. *I can see the headline now, 'Moron pummeled by tattooed brute'.* He looked around and could tell that others were experiencing similar sentiments in their own minds by the looks he saw on their faces. Looks of both surprise and pity directed toward someone so small about to go up against a man who had just flipped over a car on his own. *Anyone stupid enough to challenge this guy head-on must be the dumbest...*

While he was thinking this, Jerry watched the smaller man walk until he was less than ten yards away from his target. He then altered his course and walked to the western side of the trench where the big man's car still sat on its right side and with a bright and confident smile that caught Jerry off guard he tossed his bundled up shirt and baseball cap under the still hanging gate to the gang of armed sentries on the other side. From what Jerry could see, the guards seemed almost ecstatic to receive the pieces of clothing, cheering him on as one of them caught the small bundle. Then the new arrival turned to face his oversized adversary.

He must be out of his mind! Doesn't he know he can't win? Then through the thick sheets of falling water, two gray-blue eyes shot in his direction as they scanned the crowd, and Jerry froze. The odd arrival's confident and determined bearing made all who were there to see it to fall silent. His unanticipated entrance as an unknown quantity was both fascinating and bewildering for those on both sides, the mysterious party crasher seeming the least concerned for his own welfare out of all of them despite possibly having the most to lose if he was about to try what Jerry thought he was. For a brief trice the world seemed to pause, only the noise of the rain as it spattered and splashed over everything in sight gave away the passage of time, its constant sound reverberating through the ears of the onlookers as they in unison waited anxiously to see what would happen next.

The new contender moved toward the center of the trench, treading water up to his shins the entire way. He shifted his gaze from the crowd back to the skyscraper of muscle that stood in front of him. He looked his opponent squarely in the eye and spit on the ground. Jerry stood up, and slowly started moving closer to the pit. He wiped the rain off of his face and attempted to shield his eyes by placing his right hand over his brow again. Several anarchists had moved into position not far from where he'd sought shelter. They appeared to be just as dumbfounded by what was happening as he was and simply moved out of his way without giving him so much as a glance as he pushed his way through them so he could get a closer look. He stopped when he reached the edge of the pit within a stone's throw of the two titans.

The contender cracked his knuckles. Jerry could clearly see that the man wasn't just in good shape, but great shape, nor were there any markings on his body, not that he needed them. The sneer that overtook his face shortly after he squared off with his adversary was scary enough. Jerry heard each knuckle pop, then the soaking wet character in nothing but a pair of dirty jeans and hiking boots looked the big man up and down and said, "Time to bind the strongman." His calm baritone voice resonated so that though he didn't speak loudly, everyone could still hear what he was saying, even through the heavy rainfall.

The men standing on and behind the wall's entrance began to cheer again. The big man, looking as bewildered as the rest of the anarchist crowd, stopped pushing his car toward the gate and straightened up. Forced to divert his attention to someone half his size, the frustrated golem looked in the direction of his nemesis at first with an uneasy dismissiveness, followed by a forced and unsure grin. Jerry noticed that he was breathing a little too hard. It was obvious that he was trying to conceal the fact that moving the car and barriers had worn him out. He looked at the new arrival across the pit and, with some effort, said, "Look little man, you come any closer and I'm gonna use you like-"

The contender began to laugh. Not just any laugh, a great laugh. The sound was grand and deep like a great roar, like it originated from somewhere other than his small frame. It rang with a good sound too, as if tuned and was from a throat that could sing and sing well. A loud crash of thunder that made the ground shake immediately followed, making everyone look upward for a moment, astonished and afraid at the uncanny timing of the earth shattering sound. But the new contender was unphased. He looked up, raising his palms up to the sky for a moment. When he let his arms back down again, he leaned forward and bent his legs at the knees as if preparing to run. Then with his fists clenched so tightly that tendons could be seen protruding from his wrists and with eyes that blazed brightly in the failing light, through his teeth, the contender said two more words:

"Bring it."

David said to Saul, "Let no man's heart fail because of him. Your servant will go and fight with this Philistine." **-1 Samuel, 17:32**

Chapter Ten

Christian Territory, Main Gate
Spokane, WA
Friday, March 25th, 3:10PM PST

There was nothing pretty about what happened next. Both men were ready to mix it up, and neither seemed like they were open to changing their minds. Jerry half expected the smaller of the two to try to diffuse the situation with words or even back off when he'd gotten close enough to see just how formidable the other man actually was. But when he saw the grin and heard the laughing rebuke, Jerry knew he was about to witness a real one-on-one drag-out fight, something that rarely happened in his day and age. His body, aware of what was about to transpire before his mind was, reacted in a way that Jerry could not have anticipated. He felt something inside of himself rise up, an excitement that made his senses more alert. Despite his inability to recognize the feeling, he welcomed it all the same. It cut through his cynical nature, leaving a suspenseful hope in its wake, the kind that can only come when one roots for the underdog. Jerry looked at the others standing around him. Like him, everyone was trapped in a state of bridled anticipation. It was clear to see that the insane act of defiance playing out before their eyes was affecting them all in some unexpected way.

The fight began suddenly and with no small amount of awkwardness. The tattooed man kicked a swath of water and mud in the general direction of the new arrival. This strange act showed everyone that he had been more than a little rattled by the dramatic entrance of the challenger. The move appeared petty and was somewhat useless as neither the water nor the mud actually reached its intended target and would not have done much to help even if it did, with the rain coming down so hard. Not knowing what to do next, the large man glanced at the crowd, an unsure look on his face. Before he could make his move he needed to be sure that, should one of them record him beating someone up, someone that was half his size no less, the incident would be spun in his favor if and when it was posted online. To his dismay, the protesters and anarchists recording on the edge of the pit only provided him with blank stares in return. It was only fitting as no one there appeared to know him personally or the full extent of his motivations for being there.

Not having received the support he was looking for, the large man hesitated further and took a small step back. Then, as if to answer his uneasiness, one of the anarchists finally shouted out, "Get that crazy moron!" The rest of the anarchists joined in, each of them egging him into the confrontation, and it was on. The great behemoth smiled and charged forward. He let out a strained battle cry while the smaller man held his ground.

What is he waiting for? Get out of the way! Jerry thought. Then Jerry noticed that the contender was turning to his right and shifting his weight to one side. He lowered his chin to his chest, his eyes trained on the massive obstacle that was rushing toward him. Jerry didn't know much about fighting, but he did know a trap when he saw one. *Hook,* He thought to himself as the hulkish brute hurled through the wall of wet and muck that splashed up before him as he ran, his arms reaching forward in an attempt to catch his prey.

Fully leaning to one side by the time the giant reached his position, the smaller man jumped backward to one side just out of reach of the gargantuan appendages that were groping for him, his teeth and fists still clenched and looking as determined as ever. *Line...*Jerry's train of thought continued. The big man, seeing that his opponent was trying to escape, attempted to lunge sideways toward his enemy's new position but his feet, which due to his large size had sunk deeper into the mud with each colossal step as he crossed the center of the pit became caught in the sludge. He struggled to lift his left foot but couldn't,turning what should have been a minor adjustment of his trajectory, into a part stumbling, part falling scramble.

The attack did not go completely awry, though. The big man did manage to make contact, getting his left arm around his slippery foe and firmly placing his left shoulder into the contenders' stomach. The two of them, having collided in mid-air, flew as one toward the northern side of the trench toward the area where the contender had entered and where a few large, misshapen rocks were waiting for them, their hard edges forebodingly jutting out of the soft earth. The anarchists began to cheer again, believing that the fight was about to end before it had even begun. What they didn't catch in their excitement, but Jerry did, was how the small contender had leaned back before being hit as if anticipating the blow. Still airborne, he clasped his hands together, and after raising both of his arms into the air, brought his left elbow down on the back of the great man's head with the power of both.

The blow made a disconcerting noise, like something a large hollow log might make when hit with a stick. Then without warning, a bolt of lightning hit a nearby tree causing it to explode. It was the closest strike yet, the force of its impact casting fragments of wood in all directions. The blinding flash and rain of splinters that came with it startled the protesters and anarchists but not Jerry. He was unaffected, having become too invested in the fight to notice the intensity of the phenomena or the booming aftermath that hit him like a shockwave milliseconds later. Only shaken a little by the thunderous roar, Jerry allowed himself a brief moment to finish his train of thought,*Sinker.*

The fighters had vanished behind splashes of dark water that their collective fall sent up into the air as they landed, the bottom of the trench having by then become a pool nearly six inches deep. A piece of the northern edge of the pit collapsed and came down on both of them. Some of the anarchists that were shaken by the lightening strike, began to leave. They went a few at a time seeking shelter from what had become a life threatening storm, choosing their lives over their cause. A few of the sentries that were still on the wall retreated as well, but like Jerry, most of them continued to hold their ground, unable to take their eyes off of the action.

The two men began to emerge from where they had landed. They rose from the dark water, like two elemental beasts coming out from the earth itself. By then, the downpour was worse than any Jerry had ever witnessed in person, and it became difficult for him to make out either of them through the dense torrent. He decided to move closer, but as he did, he stepped on a weak layer of dirt on the southern edge and began to slide into the ditch. Since he considered himself to be an objective observer in the conflict, he reconsidered what he was doing and decided instead to keep his distance as he did not want to give anyone the impression that he was the kind of person who would interfere in the contest or by accident encourage others to do so.

Soon the smaller man was up and smiling again, the entire top half of his body covered in dark clinging chunks of topsoil. Combined with the increasing darkness caused by the heavy cloud cover, it somehow made his smile all the brighter. The giant was not smiling, however. He had tried to stand up but only managed to fall onto his knees, lifting a hand to his forehead which was bleeding profusely into his eyes. Looking back to the side of the pit, Jerry could see a large rock jutting out from the exact spot where the tattooed man's head had landed. He then moved his hand to the back of his head, where the smaller man had hit him on the way down.

Seeing an opportunity, the small contender took his turn. He walked a short distance toward the uplifted car, turned back around and ran swiftly toward the wounded Cyclops on his toes so that his feet did not have time to sink. As he approached, the tattooed man, barely able to see the threat heading in his direction through the rain and blood, began to stand back up on both feet, albeit still wavering, and prepared himself for the coming impact. He widened his stance a little and reached out his arms on either side, ready to grab the little annoyance so he could break him in two.

The contender mimicked the tattooed man on his approach, spreading his own arms out as if he intended to grapple with him. The fake-out confused the giant just long enough for the contender to nimbly hop once again to one side, that time just before reaching his target. Deftly he lunged for the big guys' left arm, embracing it with both of his own and swung, like a monkey on a vine, causing the foe to lose his balance. In the follow-through, the contender kicked his opponent's left shin, knocking a leg out from under him. Then he planted one of his own legs, this time pushing his right foot firmly into the ground and pulled down on the giant appendage with all his might, letting out a short but intense cry of his own. This made the large man spin around so that he lost his balance.

For a second time, they fell together, and the sentries on the wall began cheering once again, even more loudly than before, encouraged by the progress of their unlikely champion. Meanwhile, the anarchists who were still braving the storm began to say things like, "That's slammin'!" and "Damn!" Some of them had taken out their own sync devices in an attempt to record what was happening but were unable to use them, their devices having been affected by the jamming signal that, Jerry observed, seemed to start within twenty to twenty-five feet from the wall. Most of the remaining onlookers, though, were simply dumbstruck. The losing battle they were watching was not how their little get together was supposed to end.

Back in the pit, the smaller one had climbed onto the larger one's back, trying with all of his might to twist the bigger man's arm, but the tattooed man was not about to give up. He used the same arm to pull the contender off himself, and without being able to find any footing he could depend on, opted to simply crush his new wrestling buddy with his torso by throwing his entire body on top of him. The contender tried to get away from the unforeseen tactic, but to no avail. No longer able to fend him off, the big man grabbed at the contender's neck, and forced his head underwater.

Choking, and with the weight of what must have seemed like the world on top of him, Jerry could barely see the contender. He thought he was about to witness a murder and wondered if he should do something to stop the whole thing when he saw something beneath the tattooed man was still moving. With all of his strength, the contender, who was no longer smiling, flipped himself over so that he was facing the ground, and with what could only be described as a pushup to end all pushups, he managed to lift the tattooed brute into the air before leaning to one side until he fell off of him. The contender then emerged from the muddy water, his face bright red and eyes filled with rage.

Having risen from what should have been a watery grave, he managed to flip the tattooed man, who was visibly exhausted, onto his back and climbed onto his chest while one by one prying the five large fingers of his opponent off of his own neck. Grabbing one of the last, he twisted until it seemed as if the finger might break. Drained of energy and just keeping his own head above water, the brute let out a loud shriek and let go of what little grip he had left. He tried one more time to grab the contender with his legs, but the all too nimble opponent easily evaded the sluggish move.

The contender then jumped onto the giant's upper half, using his legs to pin down the arms of his would-be oppressor, a move that might not have been too much of a problem for the larger fighter in a regular match, but there, with no strength left and just inches from drowning, it made all the difference. *The car,* Jerry thought. *The little guy didn't get into the pit until after the guy pushed the barriers aside and turned the car over. He was tired before the fight even started.* His mission fulfilled, the proverbial David then grabbed one side of Goliath's vest and pulled so that the man, now blind and splashing in an attempt to keep his head up, could hear him.

"Give up!" the contender said, gasping for air as he spoke, his face still three shades of red darker than it should have been. The rain began to slow from a raging torrent back to a more tolerable shower, allowing the fallen man a moment to see the victor's face set against the clouds that were circling around his head above them. Then Jerry saw what looked like two small nods come from the beaten warrior.

"Good, good." said the contender, he opened his hand, releasing the hold he had on the vest and crawled off of the other man's chest. Then kneeling in the mud, he looked at the faces of the few who remained to witness the end of the battle. No one, not even Jerry, had noticed that the rain had slowed to almost nothing in the last few seconds of the fight. They were too enamored with what they had just seen to care. When it was over, the large man propped himself up on one side and started coughing up water. Soon after, the clouds began to dissipate, allowing for a few rays of light from the sun to shine down on them all. The champion, still kneeling in the water, lifted his hands toward the sky again but for a different reason.

"Thank you, Father." he said nearly out of breath, and then with a little less strength in his voice, "Thank you for this victory. And for what is to come." He let his hands splash back into the water almost lazily as if there were nothing left within them to hold them up with. He looked back at the few remaining dissenters, many of which had moved forward as the rain subsided and were standing around the edges of the pit. Some of the protesters that had previously gone to their vehicles for shelter opened their car doors and walked back across the street in silence as they wanted to know what the winner said when the fight had ended. They had no time to ask the others, however, as the champion saw them gathering and decided to address the growing crowd of awe-stricken onlookers.

"Hear this!" The champion proclaimed. For a moment it was as if his strength had miraculously returned to him, and he stood to his feet. "The God who is one with Christ, the Father of Moses and Abraham did this for you, so that you might come to know Him! Go back to your homes now and think on these things, so that you are not consumed by your hatred for those who you do not understand and condemned for your sin at the final judgment. Examine yourselves and search out the true intentions of your hearts! Know that He is a just God, who brings blessings to both the righteous and the wicked, but it will not always be so. The true believer gets their righteousness from the sacrifice Christ made for them, not from anything they have done on their own. That is the standard the Lord will use at the final judgment when He will come for all of us, the standard of the cross. When that time comes, where will He find you? With His Son fulfilling the purposes He made you, for or indulging in your own sinful desires?" Upon hearing the words, those standing outside of the wall groaned. Some waved their hands out of disbelief, and all of them slowly started to meander back to whence they came until none were left. A few others walked by saying things like, "Let's get away from the lightening." But the worst of the storm had ended, the rain having stopped completely by the time the victor had finished his little speech.

As they walked away, laughing and mocking him as they went, the champion turned his attention again to the man he had bested. The tired giant was sitting upright in a daze, recovering from the ordeal by simply trying to breathe. The champion placed a hand on the man's chest, looked him in the eye, and said something to him. The larger man nodded and said a word or two back. He then helped the humbled man get back onto his feet, and smiling again, patted him on the back. Then in a strange twist that made Jerry wonder if the whole thing had been staged, the big man turned and gave the underdog a hug, before placing a hand on his own forehead again and walking to the side of the trench, his legs making large rippling waves through the shallow water. Carefully, he climbed up and out of the pit on his own and started walking down the street.

Jerry remembered Devon again. He looked around for the kid but couldn't see him anywhere. *Makes sense,* He thought. *The storm did get a little hairy for a minute there.* He noticed that he wasn't completely alone, though. A few hippy-looking folk were still sitting along the side of the road across the street, motionless in their lawn chairs with umbrellas above their heads, their picket signs no longer held high but instead leaning on the arm rests of their owners, their painted slogans turned in so that the rain would not ruin them. Undaunted, he looked toward the gate to see if those within the walls had managed to complete their work. He saw that the gate was not yet fully in place and that there was still some room to pass underneath. He then watched as the champion walked around the abandoned overturned car and did just that.

The guards had come down from their posts to meet him, and after giving him back his shirt and hat, they lifted him up in the air, cheering "Praise Jesus!" As they passed the man over their heads, Jerry saw the crane operator. *He must have abandoned the crane when the lightning was too close for comfort.* He thought. But the operator had returned, and no longer worried about being encased in a giant lightening rod, was climbing back into it. That's when Jerry, still soaked and shaking from the cold rain, jumped into the mud filled pit and sprinted toward the gate.

They run like mighty men. They climb the wall like warriors. They each march in his line, and they don't swerve off course.One doesn't jostle another. They each march in their own path. They burst through the defenses and don't break ranks.-**Joel, 2:7-8**

Chapter Eleven

Interstate 405, Southbound Lane
Nineteen minutes north of the 405/I-5 Interchange
Friday, March 25[th,] 3:15PM PST

Simon Michael Raimes took off his sunglasses and walked up the six small steps of the Shotgun Relief Army's mobile control center, remembering to thank the driver as he passed by, addressing him by name. The driver closed the door behind him, and he proceeded down a narrow aisle that started just behind the driver's seat. Four communications specialists in blue bib shirts, two male and two female, sat on either side of the narrow passageway, carefully analyzing monitors that were embedded into the sides of the converted charter bus. On the monitors, live video feeds were displayed that divided each of them into twenty small squares. "Check red two-thirty-five, turn on camera two-three-five please." One of the female operators said. She followed up by tapping one of the squares. It reacted, enlarging so that it filled the entire screen. "Running spectral and audio checks...now recording...red two-three-five is good, accessing cam for red two-thirty-six..." When he walked by one of the operators, a gruff-looking volunteer in his twenties with a bad case of bedhead and five o'clock shadow on his cheeks, stopped what he was doing and stared at Simon with an irrepressible admiration. Simon put a hand on the young man's shoulder, and pointed to the screen he'd been watching before he was distracted. The specialist returned to his work, quickly giving orders and explanations to the Shotgun lieutenants who were waiting for them in the other transports.

Beyond the communications center, the rest of the bus was essentially one large operations room. A long wooden table made so that it rose from a space in the floor stood in the center. When elevated to its full height, up to twenty chairs could be unfolded from beneath it simply by pulling up and outward using handles that were set into panels along the table's sides. The convenience of having such a dynamic space being that it allowed for the planning of large scale operations while in transit. Wary of those who might want to retaliate against him, Simon rarely rode in the command center during long range interventions like the one they were headed to. As such, the operation in Seattle had been planned in advance, Simon having anticipated the eventuality of having to deal with a riot on a major highway in the area. There were details to be hammered out before boots hit the ground, however, and he was there to make sure everything was in order and to give a few last minute instructions before the final approach. The bus pulled back onto the road after some of the others that were behind it had already passed and gone ahead, and they picked up speed. Simon stopped, giving his inner ear a moment to adjust before entering the conference room.

Only a few seats were being used at the table's far end. Robert Valley, Simon's second in command and leader of the redshirts, sat one spot adjacent to the empty seat at its head, with Brent Warner, the blackshirt leader, and Melissa Okida leader of the blueshirts sitting to his right. Amanda Bennett, who led the whiteshirt support team, stood leaning against the side of the bus opposite the others, her arms crossed. She was the only one not in uniform, wearing a long white lab coat instead with her name printed on it over a white tee shirt and jeans. She preferred to look different than the others on her team so that they could easily locate her for guidance in emergency situations. When she joined the relief army, Simon had attempted to explain to her that wearing the same shirt as the others would conceal her from potential snipers in the field. "Just because guns are illegal now doesn't mean people won't have them and won't be gunning for us, especially where we're going." he'd said. She refused and threatened to leave if he didn't allow her the one exception to his very stringent rules. As she was the best out of the few ER doctors that had offered their services when the need arose, he'd reluctantly agreed.

Above them, at the rear of the vehicle, a large framed print of a famous painting had been hung that portrayed a stagecoach racing through a prairie in the old west. Sitting next to the driver of the coach, a man wearing a red bib shirt aimed a long shotgun at a group of bandits that were giving chase behind them. Simon adjusted to the movements the bus was making, and walked around Robert and the others to the head of the table. He carefully placed his sunglasses down on its smooth, lacquered surface and pulled open his seat before sitting down. Then he examined their faces.

Through the heavily tinted windows, a world of pine trees and the occasional residential neighborhood could be seen passing by and not much else. Aside from the hum of the engine and low monotone chatter coming from the communications specialists, the inside of the control center was quiet. The team leaders, having briefly looked at him when he'd entered, appeared uneasy as he joined them, casting their eyes downward when he'd moved to his seat.

"Did I interrupt something?" Simon asked the group, breaking the silence. They looked at one another and then at him.

Simon could tell by Amanda's body language that she was clearly more uncomfortable than the rest, her lips pressed together as if she were trying to hold her tongue. The other leaders slowly started turning their eyes in her direction. Simon's followed, until all in the room were staring at her. Finally, she spoke up.

"We were just discussing where all of this is headed now that we've been sanctioned by the new government." she said, "You know me, Simon, I've been here over a year now, and we've done a lot of great work together, but this..."

Simon picked up his glasses and nodded soberly. He looked at his own reflection in their gold tinted lenses. The two identical faces in them looked back at him, both from slightly different angles. He turned back to Amanda. "We're just here to keep the peace, that's all." he said. He looked over the faces of the others. "You all know me. I have no bias here. Let the government work out its own issues. Personally, I think that we, meaning each of us in this room were destined in some way to be here right now, to make sure that this country, and possibly the future of the free world, still exist after this crisis is over." He looked at Amanda again, "As always you don't have to worry about seeing me make any big public speeches or taking sides on any issues out there, but I will not stand by while a few misguided malcontents set fire to an entire city, leading others like them across the country to believe they are free to do the same. The National Guard is already dealing with smaller riots in twelve other cities. It's time a message is sent, that average law abiding people, who just want to get home from work safely like everyone else, aren't going to stand for this kind of self-destructive nonsense anymore, and the Supreme Court agrees. That's why they asked us to be here today. This isn't about social or economic disparity, and it certainly isn't about me. It's about stopping the spread of a disease that threatens our way of life, and in turn, the lives of others around the world that depend on this country every day for their own economic and political security.

"Maybe it *should* burn." Amanda said, her face turning red. "I mean, I don't know about you, but I never voted for a bunch of- old people in robes! They're deciding everything now and using the court system like it's some kind of, of, Gestapo!" She uncrossed her arms and raised them toward him, her palms facing up as if pleading. "Maybe we're on the wrong side here. Maybe we should be joining the protesters this time!" The other three, acting surprised at her outburst, raised their eyebrows and looked at Simon.

Simon furrowed his brow and looked Amanda in the eye. "And undo all of the humanitarian work we've accomplished? All of the dilapidated inner city areas that we've turned into prosperous communities aren't worth anything to you all of the sudden? You want all of the people we fought so hard to help, to live in a world where everything could just burn down around them without warning? You want to abandon them so that they have no one they can turn to when that happens?" He looked back at the doppelgangers in his glasses again and carefully placed them back onto the table. "Listen, Amanda. I'm in complete agreement with you that this nation is in dire need of reorganization, and if you want, we can talk about how to wield the influence of my nonprofit to instigate change at a later date, but now is not the time for that conversation."

"I just meant to say-"

Simon turned his head in her direction again, "What?" He interjected. "That you'd rather we just get out of the way? Let the government 'Gestapo' as you put it run these people over? The way we do things is accountable, and a hell of a lot safer than just going in shooting rubber bullets and unleashing fire hoses every time something happens. Do you really want to see what happens when they unleash their new 'nonlethal' armaments on people who pose a real threat? Robert and Brent can tell you the horrible things that they can do to people without killing them, and believe me, there are those in places of power who are itching to try them out. The people we've been sent to put down today got lucky when the Justices decided to send us!" He pushed his right index finger into the table to emphasize his point. "Even if the protesters never know, never learn what would have happened had we not answered the call, well I'm alright with that, because we will still have done the right thing, and that is all-that-matters."

Amanda nodded and placed a hand on her forehead. "I'm sorry, Simon. I guess I was just concerned that you wanted to...I don't know. Don't mind me, I'll get over it. Our teams are ready. What do you need us to do?"

"I need you all to be the steady people you've always been." he said. He leaned forward and looked at each of them as he spoke. "You are the foundation that this humanitarian organization stands on. We don't have the tech that the government does, but we've gotten this far without it, and the National Guard is backing us up this time. Today we're going to show the world what people can do when they work together even when they don't have expensive gear."

Simon took a deep breath. The others noticed a gleam appear in his eyes that only came when he was about to say something that truly mattered. "Amanda, as soon as the advance team and redshirts are ready to march, I want you to send your best runners in to get any protesters who have been hurt or incapacitated out of the way. Have them wait behind the redshirts until Robert signals them. That will give them an idea of how many we need so we don't have any unnecessary injuries."

"Robert," Robert straightened up in his seat as Simon continued. "Like I told you earlier, I'll be leading the redshirts in myself. Don't worry about the look-a-likes until we reach the other side of the first zone. I'm sure the smoke will conceal me enough while I'm in the thick of it so that it won't matter anyway."

He looked at Brent and Melissa. "The blackshirts need to make sure they have all of their equipment ready before they line up. Have everyone double check and give a signal when they are ready and in place. I want you right behind them watching that line. If it is broken anywhere during the mission, have one of your lieutenants fill in the breach themselves. Give the instructions to the communications specialists before we deploy. They can give the orders to the lieutenants directly through their earpieces and direct them to any gaps they see in the forward lines using the drone grid. Melissa, you will be in charge of making sure those drones are in the air and managing the buses. After everyone gets off, the drivers have orders to follow your instructions. If there are any changes to the plan, Robert or I will contact you through our two-way radios, in the meantime, I want you to do what we've already discussed, move up to one of the four northernmost buses when we stop and take your breathing mask with you. When Robert gives the signal, have the drivers put out the call to get the buses out of there. Have them go at least half a mile to the south. That should be plenty of room."

He motioned to Amanda with one hand. "Once they're out of range join Amanda in the support fleet and don't move them forward until the air above the highway is cleared out. Our goal is to get you two to the protester's support vehicles A.S.A.P. just in case they have people in them who need real medical attention so we can get them the assistance they need. The drone team won't need you by then, just make sure they've set up the grid, they can handle the rest on their own. This one could last a while. We need a clear support line not only back to the mobile hospitals but to the storage compartments of the other buses so that we can get water and other supplies to everyone out there. I'm putting you in charge of that too."

Melissa took a deep breath, "Got it." she said, nodding nervously.

"I know you're new, but you can do it, and all of us are here to support you. If you need anything, just ask." Then he addressed them all. "I'll be mixed in with the redshirts. Don't proceed until I've made myself visible. I want all eyes on me when the action starts. Even though they won't be sure if it's me or one of the doubles, I'm hoping my presence will distract them. They probably won't know which side of the conflict we plan on joining when we first arrive, so we'll have surprise on our side. You all know when to start moving forward. Wait for it to happen before doing anything else and stay behind the blackshirts, the shields the military gave us with the buses are last generation transparent aluminum. That means they don't have augmented tech in them, but they can stop a few bullets just in case any of the protesters are carrying and decide to take a shot at us. As usual, the redshirts will put out the fires and detain any and all protesters who don't retreat or refuse to go down easily just like we've practiced a million times back home." He leaned back in his chair and looked them over a final time, his eyes searching for any lack of resolve. He was pleased to see that every one of them looked as astute as ever, hanging on his every word.

"Make it so!" he said jokingly and slapped the surface of the table with both hands. Smiles appeared on each of their faces. Brent got up, his dark muscular form easily filling the space between his chair and the side of the bus and headed to the communications center. He knocked on the table with the knuckles of his left hand and looked back at Simon for a second, "If only the younger ones knew what a redshirt *really* was." he said. Everyone let out a hearty laugh except for Melissa, who was much younger than the rest of the group, only being in her mid-twenties.

Looking confused, she said, "What does a red shirt mean? Isn't it the guy in the painting?" She pointed up to the large framed display behind her.

Amanda, much more relaxed, her concerns alleviated for the time being, walked around the table, reached out to Melissa, and touched her on the shoulder. "Come on, Melissa," she said. "Let me show you what we have to do once you come to the light side. The support team could use you for a few things when the rescue part of the operation is in full swing, and I'll explain the redshirt reference." Amanda led Melissa to the other end of the table near the communications center. She touched the flat surface of the table with her right forefinger in a particular spot, and part of the table's surface faded and changed into a digital map of the I-5 corridor.

Simon turned in his seat to face Robert so that his back was partially turned toward the others who by then were out of ear shot. Then he leaned on the table with his left elbow and raised his left hand to his chin, covering the side of his mouth with two of his fingers. Robert looked back at him, raising an eyebrow.

"When this is over, she's out." Simon said.

Without missing a beat, Robert tilted his head and gave Simon a half smile. "Whatever you say, boss, them's the rules of Simon says."

"Please don't say 'Simon says' it's so incredibly cheesy. And you know what I'm going to say next." Simon said.

"Don't call you boss either, I know."

"I don't want anyone out there knowing who I am unless there is a *reason* I am letting them know, understand?"

"Gotcha," Robert said. "So that means I can finally call you 'El Capitan'? Oh, I know! 'El Maestro!'" He raised a fist into the air, briefly getting the attention of the others.

"You're a jerk." Simon said in a matter-of-fact manner.

"I aim to please." Robert stood and picked his tablet up from the table. "We've got it covered. They won't know what hit them." he said.

"I hope you're right," Simon said. "I hope you're right."

"By the way, we've only got about ten minutes left before we reach the Guard post. I think it's time for you to address the troops."

Simon looked at the two women standing at the far end of the table. "Melissa, take a break from that for a minute. I think it's time to tell our brave volunteers what's what."

"Yes, sir," Melissa said. "This will just take a moment, Amanda." She walked over to the communications section and spoke to one of the blueshirts. They pushed a command into one of the touch screens and raised a single thumb to Melissa. "You're good to go Simon."

Simon placed his own thumb on the table's surface in front of where he was sitting, unlocking a private interface. An interactive display materialized in front of him consisting of a desktop style operating system with several sub-screens, each containing a variety of digital maps that were lined up in a long column of thumbnail sized images just to the right of center. In the other charter buses, monitors set into the backs of each seat turned on, their blank screens replaced with a picture of the Shotgun logo, a red silhouette of the same stagecoach that was in the painting over a black background. Simon's voice came over the speakers. Each and every Shotgun riding on the highway that day sat up straight and opened their ears.

"Shotguns, this is Simon Raimes. First off, I want to thank all of you for coming with us on such short notice. As I'm sure you know by the briefings that your team leads gave you before we left, we are heading into a difficult situation. This is not a relief effort or an attempt to take back an inner city street from some gang or cartel. The Seattle spring riots are known to cause extensive damage to people and property every year. Some of those who participate have valid beefs against how the government has dealt with the A.I. job loss crisis. Others will be coming out to take advantage of the situation by causing anarchy. These latter groups may be armed and ready to fight. Our job will be to make all of them disperse by applying our own brand of nonlethal force and by detaining the worst offenders. Do not attack the protesters. Tase them or mace them, but do not attack. As in all of our operations, anyone that shows an unsanctioned use of force will be immediately discharged from our ranks, and charges will be brought against them. Remember, you are not the only one with a button camera on your uniform, and our drone grid will be in the air watching everything."

Simon selected one of the maps, his fingers sliding effortlessly over the table's surface. He dragged it to the center and tapped twice on the image. In the other buses, everyone saw a map of the greater Seattle area. "Those we will encounter today have two targets, the first being downtown district buildings consisting of first floor businesses which they will likely be looting and state and federal structures in and around the downtown area which they will try to vandalize in retaliation for the recent decision by Congress to temporarily grant governing powers to the judicial system. The other is Interstate five, between the city and the airport. This is where we will be going, north of the airport, but south of where route five ninety-nine breaks off to prevent being surprised by unexpected visitors who might try to blind side us from the industrial part of the city."

He placed his thumb and forefinger on the map and spread them apart, enlarging the image so that it zoomed into an area north of the airport. "Our job will be to take the highway back and keep it until this all blows over so that people can return to work after the weekend. The goal of the protesters will be to disrupt commerce and travel in order to get as much attention as they can from the media. Many of the protesting factions will be politically motivated."

He closed the map revealing the logo again. "When we arrive, we will relieve the National Guard and proceed north toward the riot on foot. We have practiced highway deployments before. Stay with your teams and check the charges on your tasers. For those who have never used them in a live situation before, just remember to fire the darts at your target while keeping the business end pointed at said target for several seconds, or until they fall, so that the darts can be utilized to their full effect. Don't tase anyone more than ten feet away, and don't worry about collecting the darts until the cleanup phase. Remember to have your earplugs at the ready in case we need to use the emitters as they can cause eye and eardrum damage, they will be used only as a last resort. I don't have to tell you how proud I am of all of you today or how important this is. Today protests are raging across this nation, and we are about to go into what may just be the worst of them. Today we are the stop-gap, the line that holds this country together, and the world will be watching. Get your things ready, and remember, I will be out there with you. Now let's get to work." Simon waved his fingers across his neck, indicating to Melissa that he was finished. Seeing his signal, she cut the feed, and the screens in front of every seat in the procession turned off.

****

Five minutes later, the long line of charter buses left 405 West and merged onto the I-5 northbound lane to meet the National Guard at the 405, I-5 Interchange. Just north of the interchange, two large Bentley tanks sat unmoving on either side of the highway, both of them facing north. Some twenty feet in front of them, concrete barriers crossed the entirety of the highway using a police turnaround that connected both sides. Behind the obvious display of force, a small contingent of Guardsmen had been deployed. Six of them stood just behind the barriers, three of which carried long barreled high impact sniper rifles. Next to them, spotters looked northward through augmented goggles that could see the hairs on the legs of a flea from three miles away.

Another guardsman was doing maintenance on one of the tanks, and two more sat near a portable satellite communications relay dish in the emergency lane. The rest were either on patrol or sat playing cards in the middle of the north bound lane using supply crates for chairs a short distance to the south. When they reached the top of the ramp where the two routes merged, the buses stopped. A Guardsman who had been waiting for them got into a barrier mover with the word 'ZIPPER' plastered on one side over its otherwise bright yellow paint job and turned it on. Using the machine, he moved several of them aside, allowing the buses to pass. The transports split up on the other side of the barriers and headed north up both sides of the highway, half of them crossing the median via the same turn around. When they were all past the checkpoint, they stopped. There were forty-two of them carrying more than eighteen hundred Shotguns, their drivers, volunteer doctors, and other support staff from Simon's 'New Hope for All' nonprofit.

Robert got out of the command bus and walked along its side, stopping halfway to the rear of the vehicle and opened one of the storage bays beneath the conference room. He reached in and pulled out a flat rectangular device that had been neatly tucked to one side next to several crates of bottled water. It was metallic blue in color and only a few feet long with two small wheels protruding from it on either end. Placing it on the ground, he closed the door. He flipped the device over so that the wheels sticking out of its featureless surface were touching the ground and pressed a small triangular-shaped sensory pad on one side. The object reacted to the electronic command by unfolding into a bicycle-like frame without pedals in the shape of the Roman numeral XI while pushing an expanding seat rest and a pair of handlebars up to meet him. When the frame and seat support had fully extended, the handlebars turned and locked themselves into place.

Robert then pressed another button on the left handlebar using five small taps to adjust the seat upward so that he could sit on it comfortably and climbed on. Even with the adjustment, an onlooker might have described the sight of him riding on the contraption as being akin to Bigfoot on a ten-speed bicycle. He twisted the grip on the right handlebar and the electric propelled scooter hummed as he skillfully guided it between and through the bus lines, from where the command center had been repositioned close to the center of the fleet to the rear, past the barriers where a National Guard representative was waiting for him.

As he zoomed in and out of the long rows, hundreds of redshirts sitting inside the buses turned their heads to watch the awkward yet amusing sight, many of them pointing him out to their fellow Shotgun volunteers and smiling. When he saw their reaction, Robert put on a large grin and began to wave at them like a queen might, lifting his right hand in the air and moving it side to side, turning it at the wrist. Along with his dedication and uncanny ability to handle people in a crisis, Robert was known for his antics and his strangely amusing manner, and this little stunt was no exception. Anticipating nerves to be on edge after such a long trip, the only exciting thing on the road being the tanks and other military hardware they had just witnessed, his little excursion on the undersized vehicular gadget had the exact effect that he'd intended it to, adding a small but vital amount of brevity to an increasingly tense situation. It was a morale tactic that came naturally to Robert and one that Simon had learned to appreciate in his second in command. It was also one of the main reasons he had made Robert the leader of the redshirt battalion.

Robert arrived at the barricades just as they were being moved back into place. He drove around the Zipper machine, almost hitting it, and stopped next to one of the tanks. Curious about the Guard operation he looked beyond the checkpoint to the patrols farther south and observed several transport trucks including one that looked like its only function was to carry potable water, three jeeps with M-60 machineguns attached to their roll bars likely set up to fire rubber baton rounds and two heavily armored riot vehicles. By the large sonic pads and water spouts that were attached to them, Robert could tell that they weren't fooling around.

Most of the vehicles were painted the same as the tanks with brown tones that matched the soldiers' uniforms save for the two riot vehicles, which were black with wide white horizontal stripes that stretched down the full length of their sides. When he saw the bright stripes, he couldn't help but think of the intimidating crowd pleasers as a large pair of skunks. Even farther in the distance near the southern side of the intersection, he could see several soldiers directing north bound traffic to Interstate 405. After stopping, a woman in full brown desert camouflage started walking toward him from the side of the highway and raised her left hand. She had auburn hair that was partially tucked under a half-helmet, and a dark complexion. She wasn't tall like him by any means, less than five and a half feet in height, but she exuded confidence in the way that she walked, and had a face that was stern and sure, giving her a presence that overcame her small stature. Supposing that she was the person he had come to see, Robert started the scooter up again and shot off in her direction, stopping short only a few seconds later directly in front of her. Gravel from the side of the road sprayed onto her feet. She looked down for a second and then up again toward him and smiled.

"Nice ride you've got there." she said, "A little small for you though, don't you think?"

Robert got off of the scooter and pushed down a tiny kick stand with his right foot. He whipped off his sunglasses in dramatic fashion, moving his head as he did, so that his hair swayed side to side before giving her a look of faux smugness that made her laugh out loud. "It does the job." he said snarkily. He cocked his head to one side. "Shakes a little when the wind is strong, but I manage." He raised an eyebrow and looked her up and down. "And who might you be?"

Seeing that he was taller and more handsome than she'd expected her smile got wider. "I, uh, I'm Corporal Marilyn Houghton. This rag-tag group of soldiers and misfits are my charge." She reached out her hand to Robert. He took it. "I'm sure they told you that we'll be heading downtown to protect the federal courthouse." she said.

"They let us know," Robert replied, more serious than before. Behind her he watched as several men began to move the supply crates, preparing to break down the small outpost in preparation for their next move. "How many people do you have Marilyn?"

"Sixty altogether, not a lot, I know. Most of the National Guard on this side of the state was sent to Olympia to protect the statehouse. They expect more protesters to come up from Oregon. Anyway, I take it you're Robert Valley?"

He returned her smile. "That would be me." he said.

"Good, then I have a few things for you to sign before I give up this part of the highway." She passed him a tablet. Using her right index finger, she pointed at its small screen. "Just sign here, here and...here. I'll submit it to my superiors immediately, and the highway will be yours."

Robert took a small stylus off the side of the thin, graphene tablet and began to sign. "We requested some support. From what I can see here, you aren't it."

"We received your request. A bird from McChord is in the air waiting for your coded instructions."

Robert finished signing the tablet and gave it back to her. "Just one, huh?"

"All we can spare. I also have to let you know that if things get hairy downtown tonight, we plan on calling most of the cops north of the riot area back to the city. We'll try not to, but if we need more help, we've been instructed to call them in to make sure the courthouse and the rest of downtown Seattle doesn't go up in flames."

"Great, I'll tell the boss man." Robert said. He leaned his head back and to the left. "What's it like up there?"

"From what we can tell, the protesters haven't abandoned their efforts to break the police line to the north. They've been focusing on it ever since it was reinforced this morning. They do this every time, trying any which way they can to shut down traffic between the airport and Seattle proper. At least that's what it looks like, anyway. Personally, I don't think the veterans in their ranks will ever forget the lesson they learned the last time they tried to head to the airport a couple of years ago. The baton rounds from our M-60s did a number on some of them. We'll keep the barriers up along with the detour signs so that you won't have to worry about anyone coming up from behind you uninvited. You should consider keeping a drone or a look out down here, though, just in case a few troublemakers actually make it through our guys in Olympia and try to join up with the others."

"Yeah, that's what the back end of our drone grid is for. We won't be setting it up until after we've established our presence on the highway though, do you mind waiting a little longer?"

"Alright, but don't take too long." She took the tablet back. "We're already getting reports of vandalism not far from the courthouse, and it's going to take a while for us to get there without access to the highway."

One of the other Guardsmen ran up to her. "Hey Corporal, Stevens found your necklace." He reached out his hand and gave her a silver chain with a small crucifix on it. Robert looked at it curiously.

"Oh, thank goodness," she said. She put it on and tucked it underneath her uniform. "My mother gave me this. Tell Stephens I owe him a drink after we finish here, whatever he wants."

"Sure thing," he said, and jogged back to his post.

"Well thanks," Robert said. "Maybe we'll see each other again on the other side of all this."

"Maybe," she said. "Good luck."

"You too," Robert got back on his scooter, retracted its stand, and headed back to the command bus letting the rear tire dig into the ground as he turned around. He looked over his shoulder to see Marilyn laughing to herself and shaking her head.

****

After returning to the command center, Robert ordered the buses to continue in formation northward, their four columns running parallel to one another. The buses filled all eight lanes of the highway, the command center moving in formation again, taking up the rear of the procession behind the medical transports. Within minutes, the first buses reached a virtual wall of dense smoke created by scores of decades old gas powered vehicles that had been parked across the lanes in a staggered pattern and set aflame. Melissa ordered two of the buses from the front row, those with plows attached to their forward sections, to drive ahead of the others. Their drivers carefully pushed the first group of destroyed vehicles to the sides of roadways, clearing enough of the smoldering chassis aside to allow the rest through before moving to the sides of the thoroughfare themselves.

Fifty or sixty yards from their positions, a few of the protesters who had been assigned as lookouts to watch for any changes in National Guard activity on the southern end of the conflict observed the unanticipated incursion into their section of the freeway. They immediately abandoned their positions and ran through the smoke toward their own support vehicles to warn the rest of what was coming. It wasn't long before the convoy came across a second group of abandoned vehicles that were still burning, and the buses made their final stop.

As soon as they came to a halt, the folding doors of the next eight transports opened. A single man in a blackshirt holding a riot shield and wearing a gas mask jumped out of the front door of each one and stood next to their respective bus exit at attention. From the backs of each bus, two more blackshirts emerged. These ran around their sides and opened the storage bays below the passenger compartments. This was followed by the sounds of hundreds of footfalls as the first blackshirt teams exited the vehicles and lined up between the rows ready to receive their equipment. From beneath the buses, riot shields were distributed along with remote tasers, their dart cartridges and charge packs, mace canisters, and expandable riot batons. Once a blackshirt had collected all of their equipment, they moved to their preassigned positions behind the lieutenants a few yards ahead of their respective vehicles to await further orders.

Those assigned to the forward most positions moved into the space between the burning vehicles and the buses, making a line across the entire highway, including the grassy median between them that was slightly lower than the paved lanes on either side. More blackshirts exited their transports and repeated the ritual until five hundred men and women with riot shields and wearing helmets they'd carried with them on the long ride to save space, spanned the highway. When all were in position, they were four rows deep, their ranks starting some twenty feet in front of the buses. Brent then appeared from one of the first buses and walked around the lines to the front. He gave a hand signal to his lieutenants, who then turned to face those in their charge. They made a slightly different hand gesture to their subordinates, who responded by raising their right arms to indicate that they were fully equipped and prepared to move forward. No vocal orders were given so that their positions and numbers would not be given away through the smoke.

With the main contingent of the blackshirts in place, a smaller group of twenty more stepped out of the same bus that Brent had, many of them tall with broad shoulders and faces that looked like they were carved from stone. They were equipped differently than the others as they were not burdened with shields, were allowed to use short knives for emergency situations, and carried several extinguisher grenades. Steely eyed without even a hint of fear in their eyes, they had an air of confidence about them that could only come from experience. These veterans made the advance team, an elite version of the blackshirts that performed high risk tasks and provided security for the rest of the command structure wherever it was needed. They split up, also ran around the rest of the blackshirt ranks and joined Brent so that there were ten of them on either side of the highway. The last of his men in place, Brent walked the full width of the lanes making sure that each and every hand was up. When he was certain they were ready for the next step of the deployment, he walked in front of the lieutenants again, that's when he noticed the first of hundreds of camera drones that had begun to swarm on their position.

"Just like the man said, damn, he's good!" Brent said to himself. He looked at the two advanced blackshirt groups that were standing at attention in front of the rest. All twenty of them were looking in his direction. Brent moved his right hand in a chopping motion toward a few of the burning vehicles. Several of the veteran advance team members unhooked a few small canisters that were attached to their belts. They pulled a pin from each one and threw them at the flames.

The small grenades exploded in quick succession next to the cars creating a large white cloud. After waiting a minute to verify that the fires had been extinguished, both groups ran into the smoke, splitting up into even smaller groups of five each. They then got to work disabling emergency brakes or getting those they could into neutral gear before pushing the extinguished vehicles off of the highway, four men per vehicle. Their first task accomplished, the advance team went back through the blackshirt lines and ran south to provide protection for the command center and support vehicles until needed.

The charter buses that had carried the blackshirts then moved into the emergency lanes, allowing the redshirt transports to move forward. When they had completed their advance, their passengers went through a similar ballet, but instead of riot shields, they were given several bottles of water that were placed in holsters they were already wearing around their waists and fire extinguishers that they strapped to one another's backs using a buddy system. They were also assigned their own tasers and smaller mace bottles and were given plastic masks that only provided minimal protection from tear gas and smoke. Unlike the blackshirts, they also carried with them thick plastic restraint ties that could be used for detaining protesters who proved less than cooperative so that they could be moved away from harm or kept from harming others. After detainment, those individuals would be relocated to the sides of the highway and kept under supervision until they could be moved to one of the prison buses or turned over to the local police.

Robert, along with several of his redshirt lieutenants, walked between the large vehicles making sure that everyone in his much larger group was properly equipped. When they were ready, ten more lines of men, women and a few that didn't consider themselves to be either from all walks of life and every cultural persuasion silently marched toward the front of the convoy where they formed up behind the blackshirt riot troops, twelve hundred strong in number. The main forces of the Shotgun Relief Army in place, Robert moved to the front of the buses and walked across the highway, giving a clear-out signal to the drivers by spinning his right index finger in the air.

The drivers in the front, having seen Robert's signal, sent instructions to the command center to let the rest of the drivers know it was time to back away from the action. The call went out, and row by row, they drove in reverse, backing away from the volunteers on the ground, allowing the support transports, converted mobile hospitals that housed the medical support teams and equipment, to replace them. When the new configuration had been achieved, ten small teams, each consisting of three or four members and all of them wearing white bib shirts, got out of the last group of vehicles and retrieved stretchers from their storage bays. They lined up last, standing almost a full twenty yards behind the rest. Finally, the blueshirts sprung into action, using a small, five man team to move some equipment that was appropriately concealed under a blue tarp, positioning it just behind the blackshirt lines in the far west CAV lane on the southbound side.

The smoke immediately ahead was beginning to clear when a group of protesters, fifteen or sixteen in number, came running out of it. As they did the entire first row of blackshirts, their shields already poised for action, simultaneously reached down for their tasers with their right hands. Only allowed to tase those who were likely to assault them directly, they waited until a few of the protesters ran right up to the line before firing the first volley of taser darts in their direction. After they fell, their limbs shaking violently as they collapsed to ground, the rest of the protesters quickly retreated but not before they noticed that every member of the Shotgun Army was armed with a bright yellow taser dart thrower which they were clearly not afraid to use.

The small threat abated, Robert moved to the front of the redshirts carrying several different colored flags in his left hand and a small walkie-talkie in his right. He lifted up a white flag and moved it side to side three times, indicating that three teams were needed from the support group. Three small whiteshirt teams of two people each jumped into action and sprinted down the median past the redshirts. There they waited behind the blackshirt lines for Brent to wave them through. He did, and they pushed themselves through the lines, tapping the blackshirts on their backs as they went as a signal for those in front of them to move out of their way. They picked up the three protesters who had been tased but hadn't yet recovered from the experience and hastily returned to their starting points where the unconscious detractor's vitals were checked so that it could be determined if they should be moved to one of the support stations or detained and moved to one of the prison buses.

By then, the air between the Shotgun Army and the smoke still yet ahead of them was filled with drones. They were competing for space, nudging each other aside so they could get a better angle or overall view of the operation. That was when Simon walked out from among the redshirt volunteers in the northbound lane, his signature round gold reflective sunglasses shining brightly in the sunlight. He walked past Robert and tapped his way through the lines ofblackshirts just as the whiteshirts had. The smoke had cleared away enough for him to see that the pink support vehicles manned by the True Bolsheviks were less than fifty yards ahead. Around them, at least four or five hundred riot participants had amassed to see what was going on. Every one of the drones tilted their cameras downward and focused on him, ready to stream his next move to a worldwide audience.

Simon stared defiantly at the protesters and then looked up at the drones. He took a small walkie-talkie from his right pants pocket and pressed the button on its side. "This is Simon," he said. "We are a 'go' for drop. Deploy the Laser Spot Tracker. I repeat, deploy the LST." Simon then lifted up his left hand so that the drones could see it. He made a thumb up gesture and then turned it so that his thumb pointed down. This was the last thing that the drones and most of the world would see of Interstate five on that day.

Behind the blackshirt line on the opposite side of the highway, the blueshirts quickly pulled the tarp off of their equipment, revealing it to be a compact lasing device commonly used by the military at the turn of the century for guiding air support to their targets during air-to-ground combat. One of the blue team members picked up the device and rested it on one shoulder. He pointed it at the protesters and flicked a large switch on one side while the rest of the blueshirts ran for cover. The blackshirts, having seen Simon move to the front, did as they were instructed and began to place their riot shields over their heads in order to protect themselves from what was to come.

A few of the drone operators or A.I. guidance systems noticed the strange behavior and attempted to flee, but it was too late, their frantic response only serving to cause several of them to collide against their neighbors. Likewise, the protesters, many of which at the sight of Simon on the highway, had begun to sprint down the northbound lanes in his direction, saw the unveiling of the strange device and slowed their advance unsure of what was being pointed at them. So distracted were they at the sight of the unfamiliar tech that they didn't hear the low hum of jet engines coming in from the south. It was in that moment of addled hesitation that the National Guard dropped thirty tons of fire retardant on the highway.

Starting only a few feet in front of Simon's position, the red substance covered everyone and everything in the northbound and part of the south bound lanes for the length of a football field. As the seven-sixty-seven jet that dropped the heavy viscous liquid roared overhead, protesters and drones alike, fell like rain onto the hard concrete. The former, completely unprepared for the onslaught, were forced to ground without warning but also without serious injury. The latter hit the pavement with a great roar, their fragile forms breaking into a million pieces, destroyed under the weight of the red curtain that had slammed into them like a great tidal wave from above. That's when the Shotguns, despite having been instructed not to so much as speak to one another during the initial phases of the mission found that they could not help themselves and cheered.

There Simon stood, between his followers and the protesters, the entire world confounded at what he had just done. Savoring the moment, he closed his eyes and took in the sounds of elated praise as they combined with the ear-splitting clamor of the shattering drones, the resulting chorus undoubtedly the most beautiful thing he had ever heard. But like so many beautiful things in life, the moment passed, and when the cheers ceased and the last drone had fallen from the sky, he raised his arm, waved it forward, and began to march. Behind him, the Shotgun Relief Army, his army, obediently followed in formation.

"Simon says." he said to himself.

Not that I speak because of lack, for I have learned in whatever state I am, to be content in it. I know how to be humbled, and I also know how to abound. In everything and in all things I have learned the secret both to be filled and to be hungry, both to abound and to be in need. I can do all things through Christ, who strengthens me. **-Philippians, 4:11-13**

Chapter Twelve

Christian Territory, Main Gate
Spokane, WA
Friday, March 25^{th,} 3:25PM PST

Using the car to conceal his approach, Jerry ran to the front end of the overturned vehicle and squeezed through the narrow space that was between the front of the car and the side of the archway. The sentries were distracted, busy welcoming their new hero into the compound on the opposite side. He ducked under the heavy obstruction that hung precariously just inside the wide entrance. As he crossed the threshold into the Territory, the gate started to move down again, the crane's operator having returned to the task of lowering it into place.

Safely on the other side, he turned around to look at the large black Iron bars sliding down along the side of the archway behind him. A feeling of claustrophobia came over him as it inched closer to the ground. *Now I'm a rat in a cage, and to think this was the plan.* I must be crazy. He thought. He turned toward the group of men standing on the other side of the entrance and saw that the one he was looking for had been set down beyond the crane only a few yards away from where he was standing. His legs and parts of his torso still covered in mud, the champion of the rumble at the gate shook hands with the others as he put his shirt back on.

One man shoved the cap back onto his head, rubbing it in playfully as he did. The champion, his wide smile revealing how pleased he was with the outcome of his tremendous effort, tried his best to oblige their expectations of him by being as positive and thankful for their assistance as he could. Occasionally he would glance in Jerry's direction, seeming to notice that someone in the small crowd was not like the others. *Damn, he remembers me from outside.* Jerry thought. Those surrounding the man completely ignored Jerry, only occasionally looking his way as he was dressed in a similar manner to most of those present. Since everyone there had the common bond of being completely wet, a simple smile and nod seemed enough for him to pass as one of them. A minute later, after asking the small man a few questions like his name, which was Mark Tunbridge, and where he was from, which apparently was somewhere 'back east', most of the others returned to their duties guarding the wall or fastening the gate into place. Some began gathering the 3D printed guns so that they could be returned to their hiding place.

Mark began to excuse himself, saying, "Thanks" or "I'll be fine, thank you." to the sentries that remained. As they dispersed, some of those that hadn't seen Jerry before that time began to look at him suspiciously and started asking one another about him. Not knowing what to do and afraid of being found out, Jerry began to walk around to the back of the crane, putting his hands in his pockets and looking over the large piece of equipment feigning interest in it. He tried to make his way without bringing too much attention to himself, but it had the opposite effect, and the crane operator who had seen him slip inside became nervous upon his approach and waved a few of the gate workers over before saying something to them and pointing in Jerry's direction. The three men walked briskly around the crane, one of them pointing at him.

"Excuse me, I'm not sure you belon-" the man said before being cut off.

"He's with me, we'll be staying here for a couple of days."

Jerry turned and saw that Mark had walked around and behind the crane and was standing just behind him, wiping clumps of mud and dirt off of his jeans. Mark looked up at the three men nonchalantly and waited. Afraid of giving himself away, Jerry looked back to the workers again. This time he forcibly turned up the sides of his mouth and pointed at Mark as if to indicate that they had come together and didn't say a word. Mark faced the crane and waved to the crane operator, who waved back and went back to finishing his work. The three men quickly apologized and walked back to the gate. Jerry looked down at Mark, an expression of confusion plastered across his face.

Mark, holding his cap in his left hand, punched the inside of it a few times with his right fist and placed it back onto his head. He straightened it out, moving the brim front and center and carefully positioned it, lifting the front end slightly until the hat sat on his head exactly as he wanted it to. When he was finished, he noticed out of the corner of his eye that Jerry was staring at him. A blue logo that said 'Mt. Washington Observatory' was stitched into the front of the grey cap, but Jerry didn't recall there being an observatory on Mount Washington, or Jefferson, or Adams for that matter.

Mark smiled at Jerry, and looked at him as if he were an old friend that he was happy to see after a long time apart. He looked so friendly in fact that Jerry could not help but to return the expression. Then a man standing near the crane cried out, "Dropping! Clear out!" Mark tapped Jerry on the arm and motioned for him to follow, and together they started to walk away from the gate. A loud clanging thud rang out, as the gate was released by the crane operator and fell the last few inches. The jarring noise was followed by the whirring of several bolt drivers as the workers furiously secured it to the guiding mechanism that would enable it to move. Jerry briefly looked back, arching his neck. Beyond the arm of the crane, he could see that the steel frame the gate had been lowered into was connected to a large chain operated motor on the eastern side. *Well, I'm in. Hopefully, I'll make it back out.* He thought.

Mark continued to pick off the small clumps of mud that still clung to his jeans as he walked. Some of them were only wet on the surface and as he tried to get them off, the dry dirt beneath smeared, often making the situation worse instead of better. "For crying out loud," he said. He looked at Jerry, "Oh, sorry." Jerry gave him a perplexed look, not sure what Mark was apologizing for. Mark stopped walking and kicked his toes into the ground, dislodging even more dirt from the treads of his hiking boots before continuing on. He looked up at Jerry. "I must look like crap...literally." he said, smiling again. He let out a small laugh and breathed in deeply before looking down at himself again. It was only then that Jerry noticed the sheer exhaustion that was hiding behind his eyes.

"Do you need to sit down for a minute? I mean, you've just been through hell." Jerry said.

"Ha!" Mark let out another short burst of laughter, this time followed by a hearty cough before speaking again. "It would have been a lot worse had I eaten something this morning, let me tell you!" He put two fingers in his mouth and bent over as if to indicate that he was about to puke but then stood upright again. Jerry noticed he was swaying a little and looked as if he were close to falling down. He reached out one of his arms to offer assistance.

"No, I'm good, thanks." Mark said, waving him off. He straightened up even more and started walking faster. Jerry kept pace, looking behind them from time to time to make sure none of the workers or sentry volunteers were following them.

"I'm Mark Tunbridge," he said. He wiped his right hand on his otherwise clean shirt and reached out to Jerry with it. "And I'm not the only one who isn't from around here, am I?"

"Uh, please excuse me if I don't shake your hand," Jerry said. "I take it you saw me outside of the gate earlier just like I saw you sitting on that dirt pile." He sighed a little as he spoke, a part of him relieved that he wasn't alone in his subterfuge.

"Yeah, I saw you. You were interviewing everyone using a pad and pencil. Who does that anymore? What, nothing to record with? I'm guessing you're a reporter but I'm not entirely sure though, I think it would be hard to publish an article these days without having at least some kind of unalterable recording to prove your quotes are legit."

"I'm kind of here...incognito...kind of." Jerry said.

"Are you now?" Mark let out yet another short but hearty laugh and slapped Jerry on the shoulder. "I take it I don't have to tell you that neither of us is really safe in here."

"Are you saying we're in some kind of mortal danger?"

"Mortal? No. If they catch on to us, they'll probably just throw us out...probably. Whatever you plan to do here, I wouldn't advise getting anyone angry at you though. The people here, well, let's just say they aren't exactly thinking clearly right now."

He's right, Jerry thought. *Those guys were about to kick me out of this place. It's only a matter of time before they approach me again and ask who I'm supposed to be staying with. Maybe he knows someone here.* "Yeah, I think you're right." he said. He followed Mark west down a street named Price Avenue. Mark stopped and kicked his toes against the ground again. Even more mud fell from his boots than the first time he'd done it.

"So, what do I call you?" he asked.

"Jerry, Jerry Farron. Tell me, how did you end up here, Mark, and where are we going anyway?"

Mark chuckled, still looking at his feet. Jerry looked down at him again. He was still getting used to the unavoidable fact that the odd acting man he was walking next to, someone who was at least a foot shorter than himself, had defeated one of the largest men Jerry had ever seen in person in hand to hand combat. The only real physical confrontation Jerry had ever really had with another person was the skinny teenager he'd knocked out earlier that same morning, and he was easily six inches shorter than Jerry with a thin frame. For him, the idea of physically taking on someone three times his size was too horrifying a prospect to think about, even if the other guy had just used up most of his strength, like the man Mark faced off with had.

Mark looked up at Jerry. "You'd think those would be such simple questions, wouldn't you? But they aren't." he said. "In fact, I wish you'd ask me just about anything else." He laughed again, this time more to himself.

"What do you mean?" Jerry said.

"Nothing," Mark said, "We're headed this way." He pointed straight ahead.

Jerry began to wonder if he'd made a mistake by following Mark's lead and was actually sharing the street with a madman. "So, you're saying you're from nowhere?" he asked.

"I'm from Kansas City. Before that, I lived on the east coast. I did live in Tacoma for a time though, a long time ago."

"I see, and what brings you here?"

Mark looked up. The clouds had finally passed completely and were heading eastward, carrying what was left of the storm with them. The sun shone down, its rays warming their wet frames.

"The storm is over," Mark said. He closed his eyes and enjoyed the sunlight on his face for a few seconds, then, he opened them and looked at Jerry again. "But there is always another one coming, isn't there?"

Jerry noticed that much like himself, Mark wasn't carrying anything at all. He was about to ask if he lived somewhere nearby, when Mark asked him a question.

"Are you tagged?"

"Tagged? You mean like an animal?"

"Not quite. I mean like, with an RF chip, the ones that track you."

"Oh, no. I don't like the idea of people knowing where I am all the time. I heard that Christians hate the idea. I take it you don't have one?"

"No, no way. They aren't worth the cost."

"They don't cost anything. The government offers them for free, even the company I used to work for ..."

"Not what I meant." Mark said.

They reached the end of the street. Before them, a three-way intersection gave them only two options, north and south. Mark stopped, looked up for an instant, and then began to look around. Jerry took the opportunity to observe their surroundings himself. They were in a residential area surrounded by several brand new McMansions with freshly laid grass and large garages, the occasional older ranch style home, or small cottage standing between them. Several lots were under construction, just dirt with heavy earth moving equipment parked nearby. It looked like the new Christians were changing the neighborhood drastically as they moved in, knocking down old homes and erecting new ones like Tom's holographic map and the protesters outside of the wall had indicated. Mark's footfalls suddenly stopped again, but Jerry didn't hear the sound of rubber pounding against pavement that usually followed. He turned around and saw that Mark was standing silently, looking toward a small group of trees to the southwestern side of the road between two small houses.

Mark crossed the street and walked toward the small stand of trees. Mark's sudden change in direction took Jerry off guard, and he hastily followed, looking down either side of the roadway to make sure no vehicles were coming toward them from either direction, before crossing it himself. Mark had spotted a young teenage boy sitting behind one of the trees. He had his arms crossed over his knees, and his head was down between them. He was sobbing. Mark approached the boy, and kneeled down next to him, careful not to sit too close.

"What's your name?" he said. The boy looked up, tears in his eyes.

"Eddie." the boy said.

"I'm Mark. This is Jerry, do you live around here?"

The boy shook his head and started to cry again. He was wearing a bright yellow Jersey, and long black basketball shorts. Jerry noticed that he had no socks, and his sneakers were particularly worn, the rubber soles fraying on their edges and several holes developing where his toes ended at their tips. "No. I don't know where I am," the boy said, "I don't..." The tears intensified until they became a small waterfall. The boy covered his eyes.

"Hey," Mark said to him. "Come with us. It's ok, maybe we can ask someone if we can use their phone."

"I don't know who to call!" the boy said, "She told me to stay here! She told me to stay! I don't go anywhere!" The boy was becoming upset. As he spoke it became clear to Jerry that his mental capacity was somewhat slower than that of the average teenager.

"Maybe we should bring him to a police station or something." Jerry said.

"There aren't any police in here right now." Mark said. His voice was soft and calming. "Who is she, Eddie? The woman you mentioned, who is she?"

"My aunt, she dropped me off down there and told me to go in." He lifted up a hand and pointed toward the gate. "She said people here would take care of me. She left me here! I don't know anyone here!"

"How long ago did she leave?" Jerry asked.

"Yesterday. I don't have nowhere to go." Eddie said, "Nowhere!" He began to sob again.

Jerry saw that the boy was wet, almost as wet as he and Mark were. He looked down at the deep depression in the pine needles that Eddie was sitting in, and realized that not only had he been sitting next to the tree since the previous day, but he must have been there during the storm that had raged through the area a short time earlier. He was completely alone through all of it, with nowhere to go for shelter, and was unsure of what would happen next the entire time. He had also positioned himself, out of embarrassment, so that he was facing away from the street. *It was lucky that we ran into him.* Jerry thought. *He may not have moved for days. He could have gotten sick or died from exposure.*

"It's ok Eddie," Mark said. "We're going to make sure you get some help. Come on, come with us." Mark stood up and reached out his hand to the boy. After a moment of looking up at Mark, Eddie grabbed it. Mark tried to pull him up but couldn't. Jerry, seeing that the small task was not easy for him in his current state, took Eddie's other hand and assisted with helping the boy get to his feet.

Eddie was almost as tall as Jerry but looked much younger. His features were smooth, his expression both lost and innocent. "How old are you Eddie?" Jerry asked him.

"Eighteen." Eddie said. "I'll be nineteen soon."

"Cool." Jerry said. He looked at Mark.

"Let's walk up the street a bit," Mark said. "It doesn't look like anyone is home on this block right now. Maybe we can find someone further down who will let us use a phone. It'll give the police a reason to come in here anyway. They'll be looking for one once they get wind of the make-shift rifles and pistols the men on the wall were carrying. That is, if someone hasn't already gone and told them about it already. 3D printed guns are illegal in this state, aren't they?" He looked to Jerry for an answer.

"Uh, yeah they are." Jerry said. *Who is this guy and whose side is he on?* Jerry asked himself. With every passing minute he became a little more intrigued with the man and more than a little confused by his words.

They walked a few more blocks. Jerry noticed that Eddie had calmed down some and was wiping the tears from his eyes. *Man, this kid is having a rough week.* He thought.

Eddie looked at both of them, and seeing that he wasn't the only one covered from head to toe in rain water, shouted, "Hey! You guys are wet too! And you're dirty!" He pointed to Mark's jeans and followed the observation up by wiping his nose with his right arm.

"Yeah," Mark said, "We got caught in front of the entrance when the rain was coming down, just like you did."

"Yeah?" Eddie said. His face lit up, his mouth breaking into a small smile. Jerry could see that his teeth were in pretty bad shape, jumbled together as if his molars had either not been removed fast enough, or at all. Realizing that Jerry was looking at them, Eddie pushed his lips together again, and momentarily raised a hand to his mouth.

Jerry listened as Mark asked Eddie several questions about his situation and where he was from. Eddie didn't seem to know the name of his aunt, or where he'd lived before she dropped him off. All he seemed to know was that they had driven for almost a full day before she had abandoned him, telling him along the way that the good Christian people would take care of him from then on. He also told Mark that his parents had died years earlier in a car crash, but the memory of it did not seem to upset him. Jerry guessed that it was because he was too young to know his parents when they died. He was amazed at how good Mark was with the boy. He seemed to know exactly what to say and how to say it, making Eddie more and more comfortable with both of them as they talked.

Up ahead, the road turned west. Jerry began to hear a faint flapping sound, and when he looked to find the source of it, saw that the soles of Eddie's shoes were beginning to break off, causing them to slap against the pavement as he walked. Seeing this, he couldn't help but feel even sorrier for the boy. Jerry hadn't had any family in his own life for years, but at least he had work and a place to call his own, not to mention plenty of shoes.

Just as Mark had said, no one seemed to be around, leaving Jerry to wonder if they would find anyone that could help them or if they would have to risk bringing Eddie back to the gate. Then Mark saw something ahead of them and spoke up. "There." he said. He lifted his right hand and pointed into the distance. Sitting in a lawn chair a few blocks to the north was an old man. He was wearing a bright orange tee shirt and blue jeans. There was almost nothing on the top of his head, but he made up for it by sporting a good amount of bright silvery white hair on either side of it. An equally impressive beard covered almost the entire bottom half of his face. A rake sat across his lap, and to his left was a tall paper bag, used for yard waste removal. He was looking up to his right at a large oak tree that towered over him as they approached, its enormous branches casting a shadow over a large section of the property the man was sitting on. Since it wasn't fall, and there didn't appear to be many leaves on the lawn, Jerry wondered why the man had the rake at all. As they drew nearer, the man spotted them on the road. He watched them closely as they approached, staring at them with a skeptical gaze, as if he were trying to make out who was walking toward him.

"Hi," Mark said to the man. He had begun to walk slightly faster than Jerry and Eddie, getting a little bit ahead of them. He stopped just short of the grass, on the side of what must have been the old man's front yard. Jerry looked at the beige house that stood behind them. It was two stories high, taller than all of the other older homes on the street, but definitely not new by any means, nor was it one of the much larger McMansions that they'd seen on the way there. A damp American flag that stuck out from the eave above the front doorway, fluttered in the breeze, and Jerry noticed a small white and red banner with a single gold star hanging in one of the first floor windows.

Overall, the property was well kept. A tall wooden fence separated the front yard and driveway from the back. Near the front of the driveway, a plain black mailbox stood alone, attached to the top of a large wooden post. Behind the mailbox, closer to the house, was the stump of a dead tree that looked like it had been cut down only recently. Parked in the driveway in front of a two car garage, a dark green Cadillac was parked with the word 'Fleetwood' on the side in silver lettering. The long car appeared to be in decent shape, save for a few spots on the hood and sides where the paint job had faded a bit. Parked next to it, sitting on a single axle trailer, was a fishing boat at least as old as the car and almost as long. It was white, and covered by a tarp that was held down by three ratchet straps. One of the straps looked like it was partially ripped, its metal clasp hanging open as if no one had touched it in years.

The man leaned forward and looked over Mark carefully, the chair he was sitting in only a few feet from the street, "Hello to you." he said. "Can I help you with something? What the hell happened to you?"

"Actually, we could use some help." Mark motioned to Jerry with one hand, "My friend and I were at the gate when it was being put in-"

"They finished it? I was hoping the storm would slow them down, I have to go shopping. No telling when I'll be able to get out now," the elderly man said. "They had no business putting that in. Seriously, I don't know who they think they are. This country is going down the tubes I'm telling you!"

"Well," Mark continued, "We found this boy on the side of the road not far from here after the storm stopped. It looks like he was abandoned near the gate. I was wondering if we could use your phone. I take it the landlines can still call out?"

The man turned his attention to Jerry and Eddie, "Yeah of course, they can't stop us from calling our families just because they want to live in their own private community. It's not like it's a border wall or something! Come over to the door on the side, I'll have to stretch the phone with the cord. A few weeks ago, my cordless phones stopped working. I stopped using my wall phone years ago, but I had to dig it out of my things and hook it back up again. I have no idea why the wireless ones don't work. The phone company keeps telling me they should be working fine." He got up.

Unable to control his natural curiosity, Jerry addressed the old man, asking him a question in as polite a manner as he could. "Excuse me sir, if you don't mind my asking, why do you have a rake? There aren't any leaves on your yard."

The man looked at him stunned, like he had just been slapped across the face. Mark looked at Jerry, his eyes widened in response as if to ask him, "What are you doing?" without using words.

"Sorry, I didn't mean..." Jerry said.

"It's no problem son," The man looked down at the ground at the base of the tree to his right, using the rake to move some of the grass. "I never got around to picking up all the acorns that came off this tree last fall. If I leave them, they'll start to make little trees all around this side of the lawn. I was also planning on raking up all of the dead grass and putting down some fertilizer and pesticide to keep the ants from taking over, but I just don't know if I can do it. I twisted my back, you see, and had to sit down for a minute." He looked at the giant tree again, "I hate that tree. Trouble is, I can't cut it down, it's not mine, it belongs to the city and it's right on the edge of my neighbors' property. It just dumps all of its leaves and acorns on my lawn in the fall and I have to clean it all up, been that way for years!" He stood there for a moment staring at the tree, his face twisting into a sneer. He looked back at Mark, "Wanted to take care of it this morning but that storm just came out of nowhere. Unfortunately, if I don't do it soon all the acorns will sink into the ground, then it'll be too late." He sighed.

"Well, in exchange for using the phone, maybe we could help you out." Mark said. "Eddie, do you think you could rake all of the acorns to the street? Jerry could hold the bag open for you, and you can just rake them in."

Eddie raised his shoulders, "Sure." he said. He stepped onto the lawn and reached out for the rake. The old man looked at Eddie suspiciously, unsure about the boy. Then, seeing how innocent Eddie looked upon closer inspection, his countenance changed. He nodded, and handed Eddie the rake. "It's plastic so don't press down too hard, just comb the grass with it. The acorns will roll through it on their own."

Eddie tried what the man told him, "Like this?" he asked.

"Yes, that's good!" the man said. "Just remember don't push down, you don't need to."

Mark stepped onto the lawn, grabbed the paper bag and handed it to Jerry. Jerry, annoyed, took it, realizing that he had just been suckered into doing yard work. He didn't complain though, as working in plain sight always made good cover while trying to figure out what to do next. Perhaps the old man had a landline and would let him use it to call Tom at the office, so he could find out if the authorities were looking for him yet. In the end, it was a good idea to just go along with the whole thing. He could head to the center of the territory to look for the jammer later, for the time being it was more important that he find a place to stay for the night, but even if he couldn't he wasn't too worried. He'd taken a survival course in college and had stayed outside overnight many times over the years in Glacier Park and while away on dangerous assignments, so he could sleep under the stars if he needed to, even if he did prefer more comfortable accommodations. Making sure his clothes were dry before nightfall would be the biggest challenge, and without his Omni-Glass there was no way for him to know if or when another storm could sweep through the area.

"That's no good." the old man said to Mark. He looked at Jerry. "I have a shovel over here you can use to pick them up. And yes, you can use the phone. My name's Levi." He shook Mark's hand and walked over to the side of his home. He grabbed a flat edged shovel that was leaning against the siding near the front steps, and brought it over. Then he handed it over to Jerry.

"Come on Mark, let's find out where your young friend, Eddie is it? Came from and how we can help." Levi said.

Mark walked with Levi to the garage. Along the way, Levi stopped next to the long car. He opened the driver's side door and reached inside.

"The garage door opener isn't working either!" Levi said. "Nothing works around here anymore!" Jerry guessed that the radio jammer was interfering with the door opener as well as the portable phones. *The controller couldn't be more than ten feet away from the opener in the garage. Either the jammer is extremely powerful or it isn't far.* Jerry thought. *Hell, I wouldn't be surprised if every security camera and alarm system in the area has been affected by it.*

"Hold on a minute." Levi said. He went through the front door of the house and reappeared a moment later, having opened the garage from the inside manually. He waved Mark in. Jerry noticed the garage was filled with old cardboard boxes and furniture. He then remembered Eddie, and looked over toward the tree. Eddie was silently and diligently using the rake to get each and every acorn he could see that was hiding in the grass. He had started to make a large pile of them along the edge of the property where the yard met the pavement. After a brief moment of hesitation, brought on by his general distaste for doing manual labor, Jerry got on with the chore of using the shovel to pick them up and putting them in the bag.

****

Almost twenty minutes passed before Mark and Levi returned. They emerged from the garage engaged in what sounded like a friendly argument about whether or not there was such a thing as purgatory. Levi insisted that some people who give their lives to Christ still require purification after death, while others who receive something called 'absolution' might have committed sins that were too serious to be forgiven simply through repentance and acceptance of Jesus alone. Mark responded to this by positing that the sacrifice of the Son of God in a process he called 'propitiation' was more than enough to cover even the worst sins a person could commit, as long as the heart of the person asking for forgiveness did so in a genuine way and turned away from their sins as Jesus instructed sinners that he'd encountered in the New Testament to do. Though Jerry was not familiar with the subject matter, it looked as if the topic could have been examined further except that Levi, after looking down and seeing the lighthearted expression that had appeared on Mark's face during his rebuttal, simply decided to end the conversation by waving an exasperated hand in Mark's general direction before breaking away from him to move a few things around in his garage.

Mark walked down the driveway a bit, and crossed the front yard to where Jerry and Eddie were working. "Levi had a few friends in the police department in downtown Spokane." he said. "They asked him if he could put Eddie up for the evening. I told him that we didn't have a place to stay either, and are stuck here without money until the gate reopens, and asked if there was anything else that we could do around the house that would allow us a night of room and board as well. He said he had a few things for us to do, starting with helping him straighten out his garage. We can't go into the house except to use the bathroom, but he has some cots and blankets that we can use."

Jerry looked at the garage. Levi had started to move several of the boxes and other assorted items in it to one side. "Are you saying we're supposed to spend the night in there?" He pointed at the garage, a degree of distaste in his voice.

"Better than sleeping outside," Mark said. Jerry frowned. "Oh, come on," Mark continued. "It's not that bad. It'll be fun!"

For the next two hours, the three of them followed Levi's instructions closely, moving previously stored furniture into the house and categorically stacking most of the boxes to the areas farthest from the door that connected the garage to the kitchen area of the house. When they had completely cleared out one of the two car bays, Levi asked for Eddie to help him with something inside the house and, after a few minutes came out with two cots and an inflatable bed. Mark told Eddie he could use the bed. When they were done setting up their provisional living space, Levi went into the house again and brought out robes for each of them, and one by one, they took turns using Levi's shower to clean themselves up. Levi threw their damp clothes in his dryer except for Mark's pants and socks, which had to be washed. While waiting for his clothes to dry, Jerry found himself constantly pulling down the right sleeve of his robe so that the others wouldn't see the long dark tattoo of a dragon that ran down his right arm. Though he didn't think they would care about the expensive marking, he wasn't taking any chances.

As the day progressed, Levi opened up to them more and more. He told them about his house, how he had built the entire second floor himself almost forty years earlier and how he'd added the garage not long after that. He was very proud of his work and his family, mentioning his son, who had died overseas while serving in the Army during the last war and his late wife, who had passed away only a few years earlier. He spent his days mostly with other men his own age or older that, like him, had lost loved ones over the years, from time to time, visiting his two daughters and his grandchildren who lived in northern California along the coast. He also kept busy locally by participating in a bowling league for seniors and helping to organize events for a men's group that met regularly at a Catholic church located outside of the Territory in downtown Spokane.

In regard to the wall, he said that the organization responsible for it had come by to reassure him and his neighbors that each of them would eventually be given a card that would allow them quick access in and out of the area at no cost to them. He also mentioned that some of his neighbors, though initially upset at the sudden erection of the structure, had begun to appreciate the added security that it provided them as they were growing older, and many, like him, essentially lived alone. It was the way that the project had been implemented without making sure every resident was onboard first that seriously rubbed Levi the wrong way, "Not that the government hasn't been doing that for years now anyway," he said, "But I just can't help but think that the wall wasn't built so much to keep people out as it was to keep people in. Not people like me mind you, but those that built it. Ah, I'm not making any sense now. They can do whatever they want. It's not like I'll be around forever anyway." He also couldn't stand the new McMansions the prosperity Christians were putting up all around the town, each one replacing the more quaint, aesthetically pleasing homes one by one as their original owners either moved or passed away, changing his neighborhood into something he could no longer recognize.

The three of them got comfortable, each setting up their own small area and started looking around for the blankets and pillows that Levi told them they could use if they could find them among the other things he had packed away. After finding what they needed and agreeing to who should have what in relation to the bedding, Levi came out of the kitchen to give Mark his clothes back. Jerry noticed that Levi was grinning. He could smell something amazing coming from inside the house, but didn't know what it was. Levi asked Mark to go into the kitchen and help him with something after he had changed. Mark agreed, and they both went inside, returning that time with three bowls of Ziti pasta covered in homemade marinara sauce and a large plate full of garlic bread along with a few forks and plenty of napkins. Eddie beamed, taking one of the bowls into his hands. He was about to start eating when Levi placed a hand on his, stopping Eddie's fork from reaching his mouth. Eddie looked up at Levi, confused.

"We have to remember to thank the Lord before we eat." Levi said. He took the garlic bread and gave a piece to each of them. Then he broke his piece in half with his hands and, with an expectant look, urged each of them to do the same. Mark did so immediately and looked at Jerry and Eddie, who followed suit even though neither of them knew what they were doing it for. Then Levi continued, "Father, thank you for this day, for this food and for the help you sent your servant. Bless them for their service and bless this food as it enters our bodies as we remember the sacrifice your Son made for us on the cross. Amen."

"Amen." Mark said. He turned to the others. "You can eat now."

Eddie immediately started chowing down like his life depended on it. Watching the boy wolf the food down, it occurred to Jerry that they hadn't asked Eddie how long it had been since he'd eaten a decent meal. Depending on how long the ride from his home had taken, it could have been several days.

Levi went back into the house. After they had all eaten, Mark gathered up the bowls and forks and brought them inside. Jerry could hear him thanking Levi for the food as he began to wash the dishes. When he came back to the garage, he had two books in his hands, one large and one small. They were both Christian Bibles. He gave the larger one to Eddie and the smaller one to Jerry. Eddie opened his right away, and started flipping through it.

Jerry looked at the small Bible Mark had given him. On the front it said:

The Bible
Old and New Testaments
New Kings James Version

"What am I supposed to do with this?" Jerry asked.

"Think of it as research." Mark said. "I'm guessing that despite your need to write everything down, like most people today, you've probably never actually taken the time to read the most influential book ever written."

Jerry hadn't and had never cared to. He looked at Mark as if he were a Chinese puzzle box that refused to give up its secret. "Who are you, and why are you here?" he asked him again.

"Like Levi, I'm a Christian." Mark said. "Levi is Catholic, so we have some differences in the interpretation of that book, just an FYI. I am nondenominational, but the core of what we believe is the same, that Jesus, the Son of God came to the earth in the form of a man, lived a perfect and sinless life, and allowed Himself to be killed by other men who wouldn't accept his message of love. Because of this perfect sacrifice that entailed His being punished harshly and nailed to a cross, all who believe in Him and that He rose again can ask God to be forgiven for their sins."

"No offense, but I don't believe in any of that rubbish." Jerry said.

Mark picked up a plastic milk crate that had been lying next to the pile of boxes they had reorganized for Levi. He sat down on it, facing Jerry and leaned forward, looking him in the eyes. "Do you read?" he asked him. Eddie, who had already started reading the Bible that had been given to him, stopped what he was doing and looked up at both of them. He waited patiently for Jerry's answer.

"Of course I do." Jerry replied.

"And you haven't even once read that book yourself?" Mark pointed to the small book in Jerry's hands. "You seem like a decent guy to me Jerry, one that looks for the truth and doesn't spend his life avoiding it. You seem like someone who can see through the bull in this world. Have you ever wondered why you've never read the most printed book in the history of the planet? I'm not asking you to accept my version of it, I'm just asking you to take a look at it. The book of John is a good place to start." He got up and helped move the pages for Eddie, pointing at a certain place indicating where he should start reading. "Feel free to ask Levi or myself any questions you might have."

"Listen, Mark," Jerry said. "I appreciate you helping me out. I don't know how you could tell I needed a place to stay tonight, but I do have to leave in the morning. I have important work to do."

Mark sat back down. "Let me guess, a strange and unlikely series of events that you shouldn't have been able to get through, brought you here today. You might have even dodged the law or almost died on your way here. Am I right?"

Jerry was earnestly surprised. He stared back at Mark without an answer. After a moment, he said, "You know, I think I saw a pack of tarot cards in one of the boxes over there..."

Mark gave him a disappointed look as if knowing that Jerry had just lied to him to make a joke out of the situation. "Listen, you can judge what is happening here from your own limited perspective, or you can try to understand what is really going on by taking my advice and reading that book. Even if you decide not to, though, you should stick around. I have some very important business here of my own, the kind I think that just might cut to the core of what this place is and the people who turned it into the joke that it has become. Come with me tomorrow morning, Levi said he's got some more work for Eddie to do in the backyard while he waits by the phone for the police to get back to him. If you come I promise you won't be disappointed. It's your choice, though. You have free will."

Mark got up again and lifted up the garage door by hand, as Levi had disabled the electric door opener while they were reorganizing the garage. Cool, clean air wafted through their little three-man camp. Mark then picked up the milk crate and set it down in front of the entrance to the garage. He sat back down and looked at the red and purple hues that lined the bottom of the clouds, searching the sky for the earliest appearing stars as the sun began to set.

Jerry considered Mark's words. He couldn't imagine any situation in which Mark could lead him to what he was looking for, but deep inside his instincts told him that wherever Mark would go next, there was sure to be something worth writing about especially after what had happened at the gate. Unfortunately, Jerry didn't have time to waste following what very well may have been a crazed homeless man around, no matter how interesting he may have seemed. For him, the assignment he had been given in Spokane was as much a mission that Tom might pay handsomely for, as it was a potentially good story in its own right. One he himself could capitalize on for years to come. Having achieved his first goal of establishing an alibi with some of the locals, it was time that he completed his work there by finding and disabling the signal jammer and heading home. After all, he couldn't risk his reputation as one of Seattle's best freelance investigative reporters on Mark's word alone, even if what he had said was true.

"Don't lay up treasures for yourselves on the earth, where moth and rust consume, and where thieves break through and steal; but lay up for yourselves treasures in heaven, where neither moth nor rust consume, and where thieves don't break through and steal; for where your treasure is there your heart will be also." **-Matthew, 6:19-21**

Chapter Thirteen

Christian Territory, Levi's Garage
Spokane, WA
Friday, March 25[th,] 8:32PM PST

Sitting in his less than comfortable cot, Jerry put a musty smelling pillow behind his back and propped himself up against the garage's back wall. He half-heartedly flipped through the pages of the small Bible, randomly reading snippets of verses here and there unable to make heads or tails out of any of them. Soon his eyelids grew heavy, and before he knew it, he was asleep, one of the most tumultuous and exhausting days of his life behind him.

Sometime later, his eyes opened into a much darker room, not so dark that he couldn't see at all, however. As his vision adjusted, he could see that he was no longer leaning against the wall but was in fact, lying flat on his back, twisted up in his blanket. An arm and one of his legs were entirely off of the cot so that he was teetering on its edge, about to fall onto the floor. Careful not to turn the cot over, he righted himself and sat up. His eyes opened wide, and he took in a deep breath through his nostrils.

Mark hadn't moved. He was still sitting on the plastic milk crate near the entrance, where he appeared to be listening to the crickets chirp in the still of the evening. His eyes were closed, his head tilted slightly upward. Eddie was also awake. He sat with his legs crossed on the air mattress next to a large pile of Levi's belongings, trying to read his Bible using the small amount of light that was coming in through the thin glass panes that were set into the door that joined the garage to Levi's kitchen. It was silent and peaceful, and Jerry didn't mind the silence, not after all he had gone through to get there.

Half awake, looking at Mark and Eddie, he realized that he also didn't mind being there. Despite the fact that he was surrounded by a bunch of religious nuts, he felt that the change of pace had been good for him, fun even. And though he knew nothing about the man, Mark seemed like a good guy, and the others, the old man and the kid, were good people too, different, but good.

The rain began to fall in the harmless form of a light, shower and the choir of crickets was replaced by a steady patter. Feeling the air as it began to push itself through and around the garage like a light breeze, Jerry noticed that it was unusually warm in the evening for that time of year. Mark opened his eyes and looked into the rain. As it fell, he focused his gaze on the street somewhere beyond the end of Levi's driveway. Looking out, Jerry could see the soft glow of old lamps coming through the windows of the homes of Levi's neighbors. Some of them, it seemed, had returned home from wherever they had been that day and were settling in for the night. A waning moon began to creep its way into view over their rooftops, spilling its cool pale luminescence over everything as it rose. Mark moved the milk crate into the garage just behind the door to get away from the rain, sat back down, and looked up at the stars. He was no longer radiating the natural gregarious nature that normally dominated his features, having exchanged it for something else, some distant dream or memory that made him seem aloof. Jerry decided it was best not to bother him.

He propped the pillow against the rear wall of the garage again and tried to move back into his former position, but noticed that he couldn't, as the blanket was wrapped around and between his limbs. The thin layer of fabric twisted its way around his left arm and leg in such a way that they could not be moved independently from one another. With an annoyed grunt, he used his free arm to untangle himself and threw the blanket onto the floor. He sat up against the wall and looked around for his Bible. Hearing a short giggling sound nearby, he looked in Eddie's direction. The boy was smiling up at him from the air bed, quite pleased by the night's entertainment that he had provided. Eddie lifted up a hand and pointed at the floor near the discarded blanket. A corner of the small book was peeking out from under it.

With another incoherent noise coming out of his mouth, Jerry got out of the cot and picked it up. He waved it at Eddie and said, "Thanks." As Eddie returned to his reading, Jerry saw that the kid was struggling to see the pages of his own Bible in the failing light. Wide awake, he took it upon himself to search out an old, funky looking sixty's style lamp that he'd seen earlier that day, while they were reorganizing Levi's things. After flailing through the darkest corner of the garage and tripping several times over items he could not identify, he was able to find the thin wavy-shaped pole that the lamp was attached to. He brought it back to his cot and plugged it into an outlet on the back wall. He turned the head of the lamp to direct its light up toward the ceiling so that it lit up the entirety of the small space without blinding anyone. Eddie turned toward him and smiled before moving himself into a more comfortable position on his air mattress and returning quietly to his reading.

Sitting back down on his cot, Jerry took the opportunity to examine some of the things he'd just stepped on or over. From what he could tell, most of Levi's possessions consisted of tools and trinkets from bygone eras of a consumerist culture that had desperately tried to look like it was anything but. Not seeing anything of interest, he looked down to the little Bible in his hands and attempted to continue the herculean task of trying to make some sense out of what was "really" happening inside the wall, but his eyes kept wandering back to the pile of junk. They had stacked it nearly all the way to the ceiling. Old books, toys, worn out clothes, even magazines which had no value whatsoever were, with his help stacked with care. Once a nice diversion for those who'd bought them so many decades before, the pile of obsolete items, out of fashion clothing, and assorted expired products existed in the present only as a fire hazard kept for the sake of nostalgia alone. But perhaps he was being too hard on Levi and others like him. The man had lost a good portion of his family. Memories and the belongings that were attached to them were all that was left of their time together. Something Jerry should have been able to relate to, even if he didn't.

Still, he genuinely couldn't see a reason for the old man to have *all* of it. Had it been his garage, he would have tossed most of the stuff out long ago. Then again, had the old man been more like him, the cots might have gone too, and the lamp, giving their little group nothing to lay their heads on and no light to read by. The last notion took on a strangely familiar ring as it echoed through his head. Jerry started flipping through the first pages of the Bible until he saw the first words in it that appeared in large print: 'Genesis'.

He was beginning to read the first chapter, when Mark said something to him. "The rain is a beautiful thing, don't you think?" he asked. Jerry put the Bible back down on the cot next to his leg. Mark was silent for almost a full minute before he continued. "Storms blow through the midwest pretty quickly, they don't last long, but they can be pretty rough, then there's the floods and tornadoes. In New England, storms can last for days because of the mountains." Mark continued, "They usually don't, but they can."

"I've heard that it can get pretty overcast up there, like it does in Seattle." Jerry said. He had misplaced his notepad and looked at the floor to see if he'd dropped it like he had with the little book. He picked the blanket up and threw it back onto the cot. As he did so, he spied a small orange container behind a large tackle box that Levi had placed in a corner near the entrance to the house. He got out of his cot again and picked it up to look at it.

"Overcast, yes, but not like Seattle." Mark said. He was speaking as if in a trance, reaching out of the garage with his right hand to feel the rain as he spoke. In the far distance, a thunderclap could be heard. The sound of it was so weak that it was almost indiscernible from the noise of the rain with no way to know from which direction it had come. "To me, the rain was always far more interesting than television ever was." Mark paused, a concerned and more focused look coming over his face. "I never understood why people kept watching. Especially when they knew that every word, every image, was a lie. The only time I kept looking at something that lied to me like that was when I was addicted to it....that must be it."

"But people here only watch Christian programming don't they?" Jerry said with a small amount of sarcasm. He opened the plastic container. Contained inside were a red flare gun and two cartridges. Wondering why Levi would need such a thing he shook his head, closed the box, and placed it back in the same place he'd found it.

"You would think". Mark stated simply. He looked distant, like someone who was lost in the raindrops of their past.

Jerry walked to the garage opening and joined Mark's storm watch. Not wanting to be drenched again for fear of getting a cold, he decided to take a raincheck on sneaking out and searching for the jammer that evening. He turned toward Mark and, with the intent of satisfying his increasing curiosity, seized the opportunity to find out more about the man. He posed Mark another question. "Did you say you were once addicted to something?" *Damn.* He thought. His tone was far too obvious.

"We all have our addictions, Jerry." Mark said without missing a beat. "Most of us just have trouble admitting it to ourselves, but the truth is our addictions originate from root sins, the symptoms of which destroy lives every day. But you don't need to be a Christian to know that." Mark took a deep breath and spun himself around on the milk crate to face Jerry.

"What was your sin, your addiction?" Jerry asked. Eddie stopped reading and carefully watched the two men in silence.

"Don't worry, it's nothing serious, at least not by your estimation I'm sure. Nothing that isn't common to man." Mark replied. With that he let out a small grunt of his own and stood up.

He folded his arms and leaned against the side of the garage doorframe.

Ok. Jerry thought. *He's not going to take the bait, but he's definitely game for a debate. Let's see what he thinks about this one,* "Couldn't god be considered an addiction?" Jerry said. "After all, an awful lot of time and money go into doing things for him, people even become fanatical about him enough to kill one another."

Marks' head lowered, then he said, "Is that what the rest of the world is saying about Christians these days?"

"Yeah, sort of,"

Slowly shaking his head Mark gave his answer, "I'll be the first to tell you that especially today, there are many sham Christians out there, but I can also tell you that there are many who have not only known God's presence but also felt His love as they followed Him and His wrath when they resisted Him. Because of this they have decided to live in obedience to His love instead of walking away from to live purposeless lives driven only by their own self-gratification."

"Felt his wrath?" Jerry asked.

"God disciplines His children. Those who are not being disciplined but still claim to be Christian are the ones you need to watch out for."

"So you're saying God hurts people for their own good?"

"I'm saying God can cut off the things in our lives that we think are most important, because we want *them* more than we want Him. Everything here is temporary, when we go to heaven we will be with Him forever. It's a painful process, but a necessary one. Losing what you desperately want always is. I'm saying in this way God helps us to rid ourselves of the self-serving destructive things we put in our lives so that we might give them up and just follow Him. Only then can a person find true peace. Christians who understand how to live as the Holy Spirit leads recognize the reality of what He is doing because His Word, that is the Bible, reveals it to them, and when it does, they are able to ask for His help so they can resist temptation the next time it comes. That way, they can avoid going through the pain brought on by their sinful tendencies." He paused and looked down for a moment deep in thought. "He does not enjoy doing this. God is spirit and Love according to that book you're holding, not some biological secretion or recurring promise of financial reward or recognition. He is a spirit that inspires us to be content in all things. He is not a system that we can manipulate. He does not give as the world gives, and because of this could never become an addiction, at least not in the way you might describe one. In fact, you could say that He is the only real cure for it. False Christian culture on the other hand..." His words faded.

Jerry said nothing. Not being a self-professed expert on anything 'spiritual' He couldn't think of anything to say. Besides, Mark's lengthy and unfamiliar explanation had caused him to lose interest in the topic. Instead, he responded by sitting back down on his cot. He placed the Bible on his lap and looked at it skeptically. Then he put a hand over his face and moved his fingers to his hairline. That's when he saw Eddie. The boy was looking at Mark with a reverence that Jerry had rarely witnessed. Eddie, who just a short time before Jerry would have thought incapable of following such a complex topic, had sat there attentively soaking it all in. Perhaps the boy wasn't as simple as he'd originally thought. Not having gotten the kind of answer from Mark he'd hoped for, Jerry rubbed his eyes, and opened his Bible again and tried to pull his mind out of the discussion that had just taken place.

Mark read the tired defeat in Jerry's body language and spoke again, "But you haven't even begun to read it yet." he said. "Like I said earlier, if you really want to understand what is happening here, you should. Go ahead, read, I won't bother you. I'm done talking now. We can talk more about it later if you want. Again, you should start with The Gospel of John. It's always a good place to start." But Jerry didn't want to start near the end. He wanted to start at the beginning. He didn't know why but in his mind he had already determined that he would read the book *his* way or not at all.

Mark turned back toward the street, not noticing Jerry's face as it slowly transformed into a twisted scowl at his last remark, and for the next two hours stood there motionless, his thoughts lost within the raindrops. Still restless, Jerry searched for his notepad until an old magazine caught his attention. It was partially sticking out of a stack that had been placed only a few feet from his cot. Its cover was a black and white picture of two men that looked strangely familiar to him. Next to them in an antiquated font, were the words 'Meet the Valiant Brothers'. The words reminded him of the ad he'd seen in the CAV that morning. He picked it up and read the article inside until he fell back to sleep.

So Joshua went up from Gilgal, he, and the whole army with him, including all the mighty men of valor. Yahweh said to Joshua, "Don't fear them, for I have delivered them into your hands. Not a man of them will stand before you."
-Joshua, 10:7-8

Chapter Fourteen

I-5 Corridor north of SEATAC International Airport
Seattle, Washington State
Friday, March 25th, 8:41PM PST

After the airstrike, the going was slow but easy. Simon moved into the grassy median and led the Shotgun Army north. Along with the torched vehicles, they encountered large burning piles of used furniture, bedding and a wide variety of other debris ranging from large stacks of broken-down building materials to giant heaps of worn and tattered clothing, all of which had to be extinguished and removed from the lanes as they progressed. Many of the items had been brought and placed in their path by the protesters to create a continual smoke screen so as to conceal their numbers and identities, but they weren't the only ones. A multitude of poorer local residents from around the city had come throughout the day, drawn out by news reports of the riots to get rid of their trash, as it was too expensive for them to dispose of in any normal fashion. The charred refuse obstructing their path was troublesome to be sure, but it was not something for which Simon and his crew were unprepared. Along with the riots, the burning of garbage on the highway during that time of year had become something of a tradition, those less fortunate taking advantage of the regular and predictable chaos even if they didn't participate in it themselves.

Occasionally a protester ran out of the smoke to attack the blackshirt line, but they were easily dispatched, hit almost immediately on sight by several high voltage taser darts. After the initial push, the blueshirts returned to the buses and deployed five hundred small but ruggedly built drones. When activated, each one traveled to a pre-designated area so that when in proper formation they created a grid the size of a football field about fifty feet above the highway, their purpose to monitor and record everything on the ground below by utilizing three miniature wide-angle cameras which were firmly fastened to their undersides.

Most of the protesters that were hit with the fire retardant managed to get back on their feet in short order. They retreated to an area between their own support vans and the police line farther to the north, which by then only consisted of close to three hundred officers, the rest having been reassigned to various other locations around Seattle where smaller riots, fires, and widespread looting had virtually taken over. Some protesters were sighted leaving the area altogether, coughing as they abandoned their positions. Simon estimated their remaining ranks to be somewhere between eight and fifteen hundred from what he could observe from afar.

Before Simon arrived on the scene, the protesters believed they were close to winning the engagement with the police. With the arrival of the relief army they were caught off guard. Not long after his dramatic entrance, their numbers became disheartened and began to scatter. The few union gangs determined enough to stay joined forces with what was left of the DSR and True Bolsheviks. Realizing they were soon to be outnumbered and facing enemies on two fronts while choking on the smoke from their own fires, many more of the protesters chose to join the rest in abandoning their latest effort. From Simon's perspective, the fight seemed like it was over before it had even begun.

As they advanced, the blackshirts stepped over any of the protesters that had been hit by the menacing wave of red liquid, macing any that still moved. The redshirts that followed bound the fallen rabble-rousers with the wide plastic ties they carried on their belts, attached by easily removable Velcro strips. No longer able to resist, two redshirts per agitator would leave their positions among the rest of their unit and move the detainees to the side of the road where they would pour water on their faces to reduce the effect of any mace that had been used during their capture, and stay with anyone who looked like they needed medical attention until the whiteshirts arrived to bring them to one of the mobile hospitals. When finished with their task, the redshirts returned to the rear most lines of their original formations to await their next turn in line, each individual position moving forward to replace the last.

Whenever a detained protester started acting particularly unruly, they would be brought to one of the prison buses where they would be handcuffed to a seat and watched by the driver and a supervisor, both of whom had previous prison transport experience. It was a full hour before they arrived at the pink support buses that were operated by the True Bolsheviks. When they finally got to where they were parked, Tammy Shelton, along with a small band of her followers jumped out of one of them and attempted to attack some of the blackshirts with a variety of blunt instruments. The transparent aluminum shields easily held against the blows, however, and a few taser shots later, they were reunited with those already taken into custody.

Simon walked ahead of the front line the entire time, using his two-way radio to communicate to Melissa. Any movement he could see on the ground ahead he reported, as the drones were at times unable to see through the dense smoke, so that she could send updated information to Robert, Brent, and the Shotgun lieutenants. Stoic and fearless, he wore no armor of any kind, nor did he wear a mask. Only his sunglasses covered his eyes as he marched into the gloom. He was confident that without independent drones in the air, he was relatively safe as long as he changed position from time to time. He was also sure that there wouldn't be any new drones joining the party, other than his own with the constant and unpredictable threat of another dousing by the National Guard still present.

The plan was to continue north and eventually meet up with the police line, effectively trapping the protesters between the two groups so they could be arrested or forced to leave the highway altogether, effectively ending the conflict in one fell swoop. After the pink support buses and most of the burning vehicles nearby were extinguished and moved by the redshirts to the side of the highway, Robert saw that Simon had ventured farther away from the blackshirt line than usual. He was trying to see through yet another thick wall of smoke about thirty yards ahead of his position, this one darker and denser than what they had managed through thus far. He walked up alongside Simon and attempted to look into the latest obstacle himself to no avail.

"Do you think we should request another drop?" Robert asked him.

"No." Simon said. "The police line is within a hundred yards of where that wall begins, we don't want to hit the men on the other side. We'll wait until the smoke gets to be too much for the protesters inside. They should disperse soon enough, they can't stay in there forever. Get the support staff up here. We'll bring the line as close as we can and offer assistance using the bull horns to anyone that comes out and is willing to give themselves up. If they don't resist we'll make sure their lungs check out and let them go home before putting out the fires and hunting down the rest."

"Sounds good to me," Robert said. He turned around, walked toward the blackshirt line, and raised a black flag. He waved it forward and the line started moving again. Brent paced back and forth behind them making sure the line was sound, pointing out to the whiteshirts which of his men hadn't eaten lunch yet. Since two o'clock in the afternoon the whiteshirts had been handing out sandwiches and extra water to anyone in the relief army who needed something to eat or drink. Though the blue and redshirts were allowed to sit on the sides of the highway while they ate, the blackshirts were not allowed to leave their lines for any reason unless they had to take a bathroom break or were injured. They ate quickly where they stood, never breaking from their formation.

****

The fires burned on into the evening. Protesters came out sporadically, one at a time or in pairs. Several of them responded to Simon's offer to let them go after a preliminary health examination, which one of the lieutenants proclaimed every thirty minutes via bull horn, but not as many took the bait as he had hoped. He'd begun to wonder if the remaining dissidents hiding in the smoke had made a suicide pact. The last thing he wanted to do was make martyrs of them. He attempted to use his walkie-talkie, but it was dead, the batteries having run out. *Too much time near the smoke,* He thought. *My solar unit didn't have enough to charge before the sun went down, damn!* He looked around for Robert, spotting him near the blackshirt line talking to Brent.

"Robert!" He walked up to his second in command. "This is taking too long. My battery is dry, I want you to get on your walkie-talkie and ask Melissa what she can see up north. Have her open the channel with our liaison up there. I want to know if the police have been arresting people. Maybe the air is clearer and that's where they're all going."

"On it," Robert said. "Blue team one, blue team one. Request status report for police line and protester activity to the north."

"This is blue team one." The sound of Melissa's warm and innocent voice came clearly from the speaker. "Our contact says no activity. I don't see anything on the drone cams either, not for the last few hours. We got most of those who came out. The ones that we were able to interview said there weren't many left inside, but that contradicts the previous numbers we saw when we arrived. Orders?"

"No orders. Out." Robert said. He looked at Simon, who was staring into the smoke again. "We knew they'd try to conceal their numbers using the fire. Some of them could be using oxygen masks..."

"No. Something's wrong," Simon said. He squinted, and a stern look crossed over his face. He looked at Robert. "They're waiting for something."

"Waiting? What could they be waiting fo-"

Then they heard it. Sounds of several gunshots came from the north and echoed across the landscape. Simon froze, his bones turning to ice as a feeling of shock came over him. He looked at Robert, who immediately used the walkie-talkie again. "Melissa? We heard gunshots to the north. Move the drones to the police line now!"

Melissa's voice returned. "I, I see them. Hundreds, no, over a thousand people coming out of the dark! More! The motion tracking software is identifying them. Hold on!"

"We don't have time to hold on!" Robert said. "How many people do you see and how many guns can be identified?"

"Uh, um, about thirty-five hundred protesters so far, they came from somewhere behind the police to the northwest using Route Five Ninety-Nine's southbound ramp. They went right through the fences that the police set up there, tore them down in a few seconds! Uh, the object identifiers show that only a few have guns, mostly pistols. They snuck up behind the police and just started shooting!" Several more gunshots rang out in the distance. "The police are firing back! They're shooting at everyone! I'm sorry, I didn't see them. I didn't..."

"It's not your fault." Robert said. "Hold on."

Hearing Melissa's voice, Brent ran over to join them. "Screw it, let's have the guard come in for another drop." he said.

"No." Robert said. "The plane was in the air too long, it would have returned to McChord by now. By the time they get the bird back in the air, it'll be over." They both looked at Simon.

Simon's face hardened. He looked back to the wall of smoke and the red glow of the fires within. His eyes caught sight of a single ember among the smoldering vapor and followed it upward. The dark cloud towered over him in the failing light, stretching over his head and into the sky until it was indiscernible from the blackness of the void between the stars. *No, it can't end this way, it won't!* He thought to himself. He closed his eyes for a second and concentrated, searching his mind for the answer. *You read that book over and over, you must have learned something! Come on, what did it say? Confound the enemy. Do something unexpected. Separate their main for-* The answers began to pour into his mind like water from a breached dam, ideas and connections spilling forth from his imagination in quick succession, taking form in a barrage of words and moving images.

Opening his eyes again, he turned to face the others. "We're moving in, now." he said. Robert and Brent's eyes became wide.

Brent's mouth fell open as if he were about to speak, but no words came out. Simon looked toward the wall of smoke and flames again but differently, as if to size them up. "We'll use the smoke for cover. Robert, tell Melissa to have the whiteshirts distribute all of the remaining masks. Have them pass them out to the redshirts first. We'll also need any rags or anything else that can be wrapped around our faces. Brent, it's time to bring in the advance team. Tell them to bring their riot gear. They have full permission to take out anyone they need to however they need to, using hand to hand. The riot shields can deflect a few bullets before they crack. Have the first line of the blackshirts follow behind them in a phalanx." He put his finger tips together to demonstrate a triangular shape.

"Robert, have the redshirts find their buddies and line up behind the blackshirts in four rows of two each, that's eight across. We'll have them follow using the median. It's a little lower than the rest of the highway, so the smoke shouldn't be as bad." He looked at Brent again. "The other two lines of blackshirts will line up on either side of the redshirts for protection. We're going to push through anyone hiding in that cloud, and we're going to rescue those cops so that they stop shooting people!"

Robert and Brent stared at him unmoving, paralyzed in a state of amazement. "NOW!" Simon said. The two men got on their walkie-talkies and got to work shouting out orders. Within minutes, Amanda was with them helping the red and blackshirts put on their masks. After distributing them, she went to the front line to give masks to the team leaders. She approached Simon with a relaxed swagger and a faint smirk on her lips. When she was only a few feet away, she averted her eyes from his, casting them downward and moved her hair to one side. Then she placed a hand behind her neck, caressing it. Reading her body language, he could tell that his next interaction with her would be far warmer than any of their previous encounters.

"I heard you're trying to save the protesters." She was smiling brightly. "Are you sure you want to do this?" she said.

Simon took off his glasses and looked down at her, a rare appreciation in his eyes. "Get back to your station. We're going to need you there now more than ever, and we need you to be safe."

Amanda nodded, still smiling. She quickly gathered her team and ran back with them to the hospital buses. During the hasty preparations, an occasional gunshot could be heard from the other side of the smoke, every one of them elevating the urgency of the moment in the minds of all who were present. Simon took Robert's walkie-talkie out of his hand. "Melissa, this is Simon. Amanda's coming back. I want you to head to the main control center. You'll be able to see more than you can from a tablet or a terminal on the hospital bus. Do it now. If anything changes, tell me. Don't wait for a response. Give us a play by play as we go."

"Yes, sir," Melissa responded. "You should know, I've lost contact with our police liaison. The mob pushed the police into the smoke from the northern side, after that, I don't know what happened."

"Just keep watching and give us an update if anything changes, Simon out."

Simon looked back to Robert and Brent who had put on their own breathing masks. The advance team ran around the rest of the relief army and joined them, head to toe in full riot gear. Behind them, the blackshirts formed into a large triangle and even further back, the redshirts completed their new formation, standing shoulder to shoulder in two long lines, each four men wide. Simon looked at the advance team. "Gentlemen, you are now the head of the spear. If you encounter any hostiles in that smoke, you take them out! We will not be stopping!"

Simon and Robert moved to the front. Brent went forward and gave each of them a riot shield and a helmet. He then rose his own in front of him. "I'm not missing this one!" he said.

"Give the order." Simon told him.

Brent smiled. He unhooked a miniature bull horn that was attached to his belt, lifted it up to his lips, and turned around. "Alright everyone, move out!"

Both companies of black and redshirt volunteers shot into the smoke like a righteous arrow. The advance team ran ahead of them all, unaffected by the smoke. Using only their fists, and knowledge of hand to hand combat, they easily dispatched one attacking protester after the next, despite the extreme lack of visibility. The blackshirts led by Simon, Robert, and Brent, came up behind them, the men on the left and right edges of the phalanx pushing away any who dared approach with their shields, while macing anyone they came across that they considered a threat. They moved swiftly and silently as one body. Only the sounds of their foot falls reverberated beneath their feet, as they made short order of the pitiful resistance, most of which fled before them as they sprinted around or pushed through the makeshift obstructions and barriers that had been placed in the center of the median. The worst resistance they encountered consisted of a few people who were throwing rocks and anything else they could find at them from a distance.

When they reached the opposite end of the noxious cloud, there were no police to be found. Only a large mob of men were present, the undulating flames surrounding them, illuminating the mysterious marauders, so that they appeared as a frightening visage to the Shotgun volunteers. Most of them had dark hair or none at all. Tattoos of every shape and color covered their arms and, in some cases, their faces. The only indication that the police had been there at all was the riot gear that could be seen strewn across the highway in every lane. Several bodies of the new round of protesters lay on the pavement as well. Some of them were surrounded by others who were kneeling next to their motionless forms, openly mourning them, using words that Simon could not recognize.

For a split second, Simon thought he saw a man in a uniform being carried off some distance behind the rest. The protesters had lifted him above the crowd and were moving him to the back of their group. Then the gunfire started. Brent ordered the advance team to throw both teargas and extinguisher canisters into the crowd, telling them to use everything they had. Screams and shouts followed from the protesters, and an opening in their center appeared. As the final redshirts caught up to the rest, their lines slowed and almost halted completely, the red and blackshirt lieutenants baffled by the confusing scene.

"Keep going!" Simon screamed, "Don't stop!" They continued right into the middle of the nearly four thousand as yet unidentified party crashers. Surprised by the move, the new arrivals gave little resistance to the maneuver. Simon led the charge through the center of the horde himself, pushing men away on either side of the column, the aggressors hitting their shields with an assortment of metal rods, two-by-fours, baseball bats, and other blunt instruments while screaming at them in what was clearly a foreign tongue. When they had broken through, again Simon found no signs of the police. Robert looked at Simon, not knowing what to do next.

"Brent, turn us around!" Simon cried out, "We're the northern line now!" Brent used his bull horn again. He ordered the blackshirts to line up across the highway behind the redshirt column. Meanwhile, Robert ordered the redshirts to reorganize back into their original formation behind the new blackshirt line facing south. Only when all of the redshirts had finished coming through the crowd did Simon see that a few members of both groups hadn't made it all the way through the violent crowd and were still in the midst of the mob being knocked to the ground or worse. "Advance team on me!" he screamed, and ran toward those who had fallen behind.

Using his shield, he hit a protester who was running at him with a brick in one hand under the chin, before using his vial of mace to force several others to back off. Together, mace canisters and tasers in hand, he and the advance team members that had rallied to his side were able to keep the mob away long enough to get most of those who had fallen behind on their feet and out of the fray. One overzealous disruptor managed to get around Simon's shield and slashed him with something like a machete on his left arm, and many in the insurgents seeing that he had been wounded became more daring, closing back in on them. Realizing they were out of time, Simon yelled, "Back to the lines!" and the advance team withdrew behind the newly established riot line.

Beaten, exhausted, and still wondering where hundreds of police could have disappeared to so quickly, Simon reviewed the redshirt ranks. He had lost almost twenty of the Shotgun volunteers going through the crowd and recovered only nine. Not long after, the new wave of protesters began to charge against the blackshirt's shields in groups of ten or more at a time, not caring about the tasers or mace that was being fired at them. Simon had never seen anything like it. He took a moment to look closer at the strange behaving reinforcements and observed that they had to be between the ages of eighteen and thirty-five, and almost all of them looked like they had at least one tattoo somewhere on their person. Most carried some kind of cheap, melee weapon that could have been taken from the side of the highway or stolen from someone's backyard. Bricks, wooden blocks, and tire irons seemed to be among the most common.

They let us through because they couldn't understand why we would just let them take the highway. They thought we were trying to get out of the smoke. Simon thought. *Now they're fighting back because they can see we have no intention of leaving.* The grown men in front of him were not at all like the college kids, hippies and political activists he'd faced off with a few hours before, they were hired thugs who were sent there for a purpose, one that they were determined to accomplish. He also observed that though the new arrivals were superior in number, they lacked two things that were far more important, organization and leadership.

Simon walked over to Robert, and seeing blood spattered across his forehead, began checking his face for wounds.

"It's not mine." Robert said. His face sober as ever, his eyes glued to the front line.

"Get on the radio again," Simon said. "Tell Amanda and Melissa to have the white and blueshirts to get out their stretchers and helmets and make a barrier on the southern side. It's time for them to put their defensive training to good use. And tell Melissa to have the plow buses move to the front and park across the lanes on either side. We're going to contain this no matter what it takes."

"And what about the guns?" Robert asked.

"Only a few of them took a shot at us, most of the weapons are gone. That means they've been taken to another location for some other purpose."

"And the police?"

"Hostages or killed by now. Either way, they aren't here. We won't know anything until morning." Simon started to walk away and kicked something. He looked down and saw an officer's badge lying next to his right foot. "Scratch that, have Brent get the advance team together. They're going hunting."

"And how are we going to manage...them?" Robert said. "They outnumber us!"

"One at a time," Simon said. "From here on out, only they lose people. Only they do!"

"Shouldn't we find out where they came from?" Robert asked.

"I can make a guess where they came from," Simon said. "But it doesn't matter. Whoever they are, this was their big play, they were supposed to surprise us, but we surprised them instead by taking them on! Now, let's use the shields to push them into that smoke until they can't breathe and start a few fires of our own!"

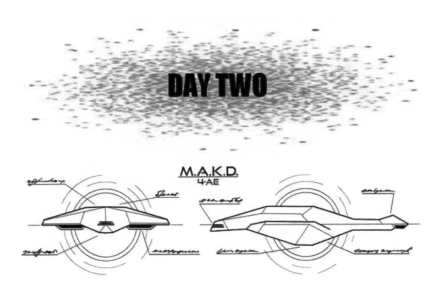

"The lamp of the body is the eye. If therefore your eye is sound, your whole body will be full of light. But if your eye is evil, your whole body will be full of darkness. If therefore the light that is in you is darkness, how great is the darkness!" **-Matthew, 6:22-23**

Chapter Fifteen

I-5 Corridor north of SEATAC International Airport
Seattle, Washington State
Saturday, March 26[th,] 12:10AM PST

During previous incursions to inner city districts, the Shotgun Relief Army worked in one accord, the team leaders using flags and hand signals to communicate with their lieutenants who, in turn, passed on their orders to the rank and file volunteers. The method came from Simon's original desire to be prepared for any situation that might arise in an urban environment. Fearing what could happen should an EMP or nuclear device be detonated in a city they were operating in, Simon chose a policy that involved avoiding dependency on the latest technological advancements as much as possible. Not taking on new tech also meant that his force could operate with a higher level of autonomy without appearing as if he and his people were trying to avoid prying eyes while protecting their internal communications from outside interference. In his experience any wireless device was hackable and thus a danger to their efforts, their own walkie-talkies and drones could be used to pass along misinformation at a crucial moment, be manipulated by unseen perpetrators to spy on them, or worse, be used against them in a more direct manner.

Though softened since the army's inception, the approach still forced them to limit the majority of their activities to daylight hours. That night on the highway, however, was a far cry from what they were used to. The headlights on the buses paired with the one hundred flood lamps they'd brought with them were simply not enough to pierce the thick pillar of smoke that separated the red and blackshirt ranks from their transports and supplies. On the other side of the great wall of smoke and flame and blocked by a hostile force, they were forced to depend on the dull glow of flames that flickered and danced around the dark rampaging forms before them, the street lamps that lined the highway having been knocked out by the first wave of protesters before the relief army had arrived. Even the pale light of the moon had been greatly diminished by encroaching cloud cover that had come in from the coast hours earlier.

The skirmish continued on into the night with little progress, each side crashing into the other every few minutes. Seeing that they were outnumbered and their flanks on either side of the highway were vulnerable, Robert discarded his flags, throwing them into the median and began yelling at the lieutenants by name. Together they organized four hundred redshirts that looked as if they were ready to take a break. The lieutenants took them away from the main group and split them in half so that two hundred stood on either side of the highway. Robert then returned to the forward line and told the redshirts there to lock arms behind the blackshirts so that they could not be pushed back any further than they had already. While there, he saw that some of the redshirts were passing their mace and tasers to the blackshirts in front of them as their own ran out of juice, and ordered the rest to do the same.

Robert also noticed that many in the blackshirt company were nearing a point of complete exhaustion. They were fighting back as best they could using their shields and batons, but the new wave of protesters were relentless and unforgiving when compared to their predecessors. Thankfully the insurgents hadn't attempted to push through the Shotguns as one mass as they had done, but they were comprised of able bodied men who were coming at them tirelessly. Their latest tactic was to try and hit the blackshirts on their heads with the blunt instruments they carried. Every now and then, one succeeded, forcing another blackshirt off of the front lines. The resulting losses prompted Robert to order the redshirts to collect any shields, helmets, or other armaments that the injured blackshirts still had on their persons when they were taken out of the action and replace them by filling in the gaps in the formation as they appeared. The strategy seemed to work, but he simply didn't know how long they could hold the position or if they would be able to move forward any more than a few steps an hour.

Behind the Shotgun lines, Brent was organizing another smaller group of redshirts. He directed the volunteers to take the injured to the western side of the highway and to provide them with medical attention as best they could by applying their training. The advance team members joined them, utilizing their first aid kits along with anything else they could find to patch up the more abused Shotguns. Some of the injured jumped back into the fight as soon as they were able and coherent, while others had acquired more serious wounds that had to be bandaged or had shown signs of smoke inhalation.

Checking in on their progress, Simon ran across the highway to join them. When he got there, Brent was walking around, looking in on the wounded men and women. He was full of energy, very lively for a man who was fifty-two years of age. When he saw Simon approaching, he raised his voice to match the war-like cries and violent noises originating only thirty feet from their position.

"I haven't seen action like this since I was swat chief in Oakland!" he said.

"Gather the advance team together," Simon replied. "The redshirts shouldn't need them anymore. They can handle this on their own. I have a new assignment for them."

Brent put a thumb and finger in his mouth and whistled loudly. The heads of the advance team members, who at that time were taking a few minutes to share a few medical field techniques with the redshirts, immediately stopped what they were doing and looked in their direction. Hurriedly, they finished instructing the others and ran over to meet Simon and Brent. They kneeled in silence in front of the two men in a semicircle and looked up at Simon as if he were the coach of a football team about to give a halftime speech. He didn't disappoint.

"You're here because you are the best." Simon said to them. "I know your backgrounds and your loyalty to your country." He pointed to the line. "I want you to know that the group we now face is NOT from that country!" Some on the advance team looked surprised at the revelation, a faint hint of anger appearing on a few of their faces. Most, though, were unaffected by his words and continued to give Simon the same straight-laced and emotionless expression he had become accustomed to when addressing them. "They have no conscience right now, no remorse. The only reason they stopped shooting at us is because they plan to use the bullets they've collected to either take SeaTac or kill police and National Guard troops that are stationed in the city. THAT IS NOT GOING TO HAPPEN!"

"HOOAH!!" the men shouted in unison.

Simon continued, "I want half of you to find out where they took the police and their firearms. Locate them and come back here, the drone feeds showed that they left by foot so they can't be far. Five of you will go west where the highway splits and five more to the north and east. Those are the two directions the drones caught them going in. Brent is staying with us. Decide who is best among you for recon duty. When you're finished, go. Don't wait for an order. The rest of you, I have a special mission for, that requires stealth. I need five of you to stay with Brent so that any drones flying in the vicinity, including our own, show evidence of your team here at the front lines while we make our move. The final five will meet with me, alone on the eastern side of the highway." Brent looked at Simon, not knowing what to think. It was the first time since he'd worked with him that he'd seen Simon tested in such a way, and he genuinely didn't know what the man was capable of. "You have two minutes to divide your team according to the parameters I've given you. Know that your actions tonight may very well save this country in the long term. I'll be waiting." Simon pointed to the eastern side of the highway behind the last of the redshirts.

What these most able of mighty men did next, surprised Simon. Instead of talking among one another, they closed their eyes and lowered their heads. One of them started mumbling. When he was finished, another spoke, picking up where the first had left off. Brent kneeled and followed suit along with them. With the sounds of clashing instruments mingling with the screams of the attackers behind him, Simon could hardly make out what they were saying. He leaned down toward Brent and asked, "What are they doing?"

"They're praying, and so am I." Brent said.

Simon's face twisted in the flickering glow of the flames. "We don't have time for this."

Brent stood up and placed a hand on Simon's left shoulder. "Simon, I have no doubt that you are a very capable man. I would follow you anywhere, and have. But sometimes I wonder why you're doing what you are. I fight with these men because we want our kids and grandkids to have the same freedoms that we do. That includes the freedom to openly have and share our faith. The same faith that stops them and me from doing terrible things that we might otherwise do without it. What are you fighting for?" He paused, but Simon only looked down, his expression turning to one of disgust. Brent finished, "Whatever you're planning to do tonight, know that you may be able to cover your tracks from the rest of us, but someone else is watching, someone who controls all of our fates. You might consider making Him an ally instead of an enemy. It couldn't hurt. "

Simon pushed Brent's hand away. "If Christians were half of what they claimed to be, the New Hope For All organization wouldn't need to exist, none of this would be happening, and I wouldn't have to be here to clean up this mess!"

"You know as well as I do, that one has nothing to do with the other!" Brent shot back.

Simon looked down at his own shadow, the dim wavering light from the fires burning behind him, pulling and twisting its dark form. He looked up at Brent again. "No, no I don't." he said. He walked to the east side of the highway, where he'd told the others to join him. Disappointed, Brent went back to kneeling with his men, making sure to add one more request to his prayers.

****

Simon leaned on the guardrail, and waited for the advance team to break up. As he'd instructed, five went northeast, five northwest and five ran in his direction. The rest stayed with Brent, who spoke to them for a moment before they sprang into action, pushing through the red and blackshirts. Working as one, they stood together in a half-circle just beyond the line. United in their movements and actions, they went east and west along the front, disarming any in the opposing force who were close enough to reach and threw the captured weapons over the heads of those who were standing their ground behind them. Their moves were swift and their fists sure, each man hitting their targets with near deadly accuracy. Any who dared approach, risked broken bones or other forms of severe trauma that often took them out of the fight entirely, forcing their comrades to carry them off into thesmoke. Some of the wounded redshirts behind the lines began to stand up and collect what was thrown back, tossing the items off of the highway and into the darkness beyond.

The five men that were assigned to Simon ran to his position and stood at attention. One of them spoke for the entire group, "Former Major Justin Anchorhead, United States Marine Corps. Ready to take orders for my team, SIR!" he said.

"Marine, I am not, nor have I ever been a member of the military. You do not need to salute me or call me 'sir'." Simon said.

"Yes, sir! I mean, sorry!" Justin said.

"No apologies. Just treat me like any other redshirt," Simon said. "I don't want to get sniped while giving orders. Now, I want you all to turn around for a moment." A little confused, the men lined up and turned to face the freeway. Simon reached into his left pants pocket and took out a small plastic sheet covered in small grey circular stickers. He placed his arms behind his back and peeled one of the stickers off of the sheet. Quickly, he slapped it over the tiny recording device that was located on the top left button of his shirt. He then reached around each of the men standing in front of him while they were facing in the opposite direction and covered each of their button cameras in the same way.

"You can turn around now," They turned to face him again. "The stickers I've placed over your recording devices are electromagnetic. They contain a small battery and a circuit designed to interfere with radio waves. Right now, they are scrambling your frequency, appearing on the monitors in the command center as normal interference. No one can hear or see us until they are taken off. Now, what I am going to tell you to do, you cannot repeat to anyone. Nor can you be seen doing it under any circumstances. Do you understand?" The men nodded in silence. "Good. Time to get to work, we're burning darkness, and darkness is what we need if we're going to do this right."

****

Less than thirty minutes later, the five men returned, carrying the spoils of their labor. Ten full gas cans, twenty road flares, and a roll of duct tape. Their mission, break into a few of their own transports to the south without being seen and bring the supplies north of the flames using a route far enough away from the highway so they would not be seen by the drone grid. Simon took a moment to look at his watch, impressed with the speed at which they had accomplished their goal. To his surprise, they had even requisitioned some used oil from one of the older vehicles that had been pushed off of the interstate, using it to cover both their faces and the red plastic tanks so they would be harder to see on the return trip.

He looked to the line where Robert was screaming for the red and blackshirts to push forward. Robert had updated him with the current state of affairs during the long wait. Almost all of the tasers had run out of juice, and it was only a matter of time before the last of the mace was also used up. They had succeeded in holding off the constant attacks, but at a cost. Many were injured on both sides, and the flames were beginning to die down. Their backs to the smoke, the marauding dissenters weren't at all interested in keeping the fires lit, and Melissa had reported that at least four or five hundred of the original protesters that had been hiding within the cloud were slowly trickling out of it by what she could see through the drone cams.

"This is the game plan." Simon told them. "I need three of you to smuggle five of these tanks to the other side of the highway. You're going to have to go around the northern edge of the surveillance grid so it might take some time. No one is to see you carrying anything, NO ONE. You'll also have to wait until the smoke gives you cover, depending on the wind. When the first tanks go up on this side, you will follow suit and throw your tanks at the insurgents. We're going to tape the flares to their sides, light 'em up, and toss them right onto their heads. I need to know you can do this." They nodded without hesitation. "Good. Three of you go. The rest of us will stay here. "

Justin immediately pointed to three of the others. They picked up five of the tanks, and disappeared into the night. Simon looked at the line again. The redshirts had become the majority of the front line and the predominant group using the shields, two roles they had not been trained for. Behind them, blackshirts littered the highway exhausted or wounded. The two advance team members still with him finished taping the flares to the sides of the remaining tanks, and they moved south along the eastern side of the northbound lane. Through the smoke, they could see hundreds of shadows of men advancing and retreating from the line. Simon spotted two men covered in tattoos and wearing black under shirts hanging over one of the guardrails. He stopped at the sight of them and raised a fist, signaling for the others to do the same. One of the two men was breathing heavily, and the other was completely motionless, blood from a gash on his head covering an entire side of his body. Another man came out of the smoke carrying a third who was coughing violently, clearly suffering from smoke inhalation. Simon could tell that he wouldn't last long if medical assistance wasn't given to him soon. Justin stood beside him, the sight not affecting him in the least. When they were within throwing distance, he looked at the three men and then to Simon.

"Are we a go, sir?" he asked.

Simon stared into the smoke. The wind had shifted direction several times in the last few minutes, and he didn't want to take any chances. He turned to face the failing Shotgun lines. *We can't lose the highway.* He thought. *No matter the cost. Right now they can't see enough to organize, but soon those flames will be out, and there will be nothing to stop them from getting together and mobbing us. If we hit them now...* He took a deep breath and turned back to face the men on the guardrail again, Brent's words echoing through his mind. Then he did something he had never done before, he hesitated. He looked at Justin and said, "Go to the men on the other side. Don't let them throw the tanks into the southbound lane, like I told them earlier. Tell them to meet up on Brent, behind the line instead. Just you, go!"

Justin took off like a rocket. Simon led the other men with their gas tanks back to the north behind the line. Within moments all ten of the remaining members of the advance team were with them along with Brent. Simon waved Brent aside, and when he was within an arm's reach slapped one of the jamming stickers on his button camera. Brent looked up at him, surprised, not sure how to respond. Simon put a hand on his shoulder. "Brent, I need your help. We've got ten containers of gasoline here that we can use to force them to disperse, but no way to do so in a manner that won't seriously burn some of them. The fires are dying down, we need to get them off the highway before that smoke clears, or they will overrun us. I need options."

Brent gave Simon a look of renewed confidence. He looked down, his mind concentrating at the problem at hand. A moment later, he snapped his fingers and pointed north. "While you were gone, Melissa notified us that the recon team that went northeast contacted her using a police radio from one of two abandoned squad cars they'd found. They were already broken into, and their shotguns removed, but we should be able to hotwire them and bring them here. If we put a couple of gas tanks in the back of each one and throw in a third with one of those flares attached as we drive them into the smoke. I think it will give you the effect you're looking for. If we can get them both going we can do it on both sides of the highway. There will be a lot of glass and a concussive blast for each one we send in, that should separate them into two groups. Then, once the center lanes are clear, we'll send the men down the center median again. We can throw the rest of the tanks behind us as we head to the southern line. The median is lower and the grass will catch on fire. The blaze should separate the groups east and west with minimal collateral damage. Then we only need to turn around again. The support team can take the shields and join us. We should be able to rout whoever's left one side of the highway at a time, especially since it looks as if they are already looking for an excuse to get out of that smoke."

Simon smiled, "Have you done this before?"

"No," Brent said. "But I've had a lot of experience on the receiving end of stuff like this. And don't worry. The smoke will cover up what's happening in the median. We will have to make sure that we put the gas cans in the back seats of the cars while they're still outside of the drone grid, though. What Amanda doesn't know, won't hurt her."

"Do it." Simon said. "Take Justin and his team. Remove the sticker off of your body cam after you've given the orders. I'll stay here and organize the wounded so they'll be ready to move."

Brent led Justin and the other nine advance team members north, and it wasn't long before the police cars were up and running on either side of the highway. Simon told Robert to be ready to let them through. When the moment came, Robert and Brent yelled to their men on the line to move out of the way. As they did, the advance team turned on the cruiser's lights and sirens. They lit flares and threw them into the back seats of the cars, closing their locked doors as they did, having doused the interiors with the highly flammable liquid and having placed two full cans in the back seats of each one. Ready to go, they put the cruisers in neutral and pushed them past the line into the crowds on both sides of the highway.

Some of the brighter members of the opposing force knew what was headed their way and ran off of the freeway, while others appeared confused as no one was driving the vehicles. A few even tried to open their driver's side doors in an attempt to hijack them, but to no avail. The cruiser in the northbound lane exploded first, followed by the southbound car a few seconds later. The explosions were loud and deafening, blowing out the windows just as Brent had predicted. Glass shot in every direction, but it was the sudden and powerful booming sounds that came from them that seemed to rattle the second wave of protesters the most. They immediately began to separate, retreating to the far sides of the interstate.

As soon as the cars exploded, hundreds of red and blackshirts, holding their shields and wielding batons, let out a loud and piercing war cry and ran into the smoke and down the center median, deflecting any protesters in their path. The ten remaining members of the advance team followed, carrying what was left of the blacked-out gas cans. The two foremost of the group quickly moved aside any enemy wounded that were in the median, so they would not be harmed by what was coming next. The rest poured out two lines of gasoline on the ground, and threw the tanks behind them every twenty yards, causing smaller explosions in their wake and leaving much of the center median in flames. They continued the routine until they reached the end of the smoke, but stopped twenty yards short of the southern edge, so that what they were doing would not be seen by the support and communication teams.

On the way back, Justin, who Brent had given his walkie-talkie to, informed Robert that the center of the highway was clear. Robert screamed, "LET'S GO!" at the top of his lungs. Brent gave a similar order, and the rest of their ranks began to press onward to the support line to the south. Separated and no longer sure of what the Shotguns might be willing to do next, the second wave protesters simply got out of their way, disappearing into the night ,and leaving many of their wounded behind. A closer examination revealed that the protesters had been affected by the dense smoke and were coughing constantly, and with the fires burning anew, for the time being, seemed to have given up. Despite the positive development Simon had the feeling that the confrontation was far from over, however.

Simon used his walkie-talkie. "Melissa," he said, "Move the men and buses forward along the sides of the highway using the emergency lane on the east side, and the CAV lane. Have the plow buses move up first. Once we push the remaining cars into the center median, move the support buses and the control center north. We've won, for now."

"Will do!" she said cheerfully, "What were those explosions? The drones showed your men throwing something into the back of those police cruisers, but we couldn't see what happened to them after they entered the smoke. Oh, and we're having some trouble getting a good signal from some of the members of the advance team."

"It was Just road flares." Simon answered. "We planned on setting a couple of more fires, hoping to use the continued smoke to our own advantage, but I guess the gas tanks went up faster and bigger than we'd anticipated. It's possible that the concussion force of the explosions messed up some of the cameras. Send someone out here with a list of their names, and I'll check them out myself."

"I see," she said, sounding doubtful. "I'll tell Amanda what happened, and one of the blueshirts will have that list for you ASAP."

A few minutes later, the buses arrived, lining both sides of the highway. The support and medical teams followed and began giving medical attention to any and all that were injured. Many of the second wave of protesters and a few more from the first that had been in the smoke for several hours were taken to the hospital buses for treatment. Robert led the Shotgun army north again to the center of the smoke-filled area and ordered any redshirts that were still standing to put out the flames.

Amanda arrived on the scene and walked up to Simon. "That was some show." she said. "Melissa and I were watching from the drones. Looks like your little trick with the police cars worked out. The late arrivals separated into three or more groups and scattered after they left the highway."

"How bad is it?" Simon said.

"We've got some people with minor burns, and a few with tiny pieces of glass stuck all over them, but nothing too serious. The worst ones are the members of the original groups who spent too long inhaling smoke, we're doing everything we can for them right now, but how they will turn out is anybody's guess. I'm more concerned about the ones that left the area. The drones caught more than a few who were carried out by their friends that are probably in need of attention."

Simon looked around at his exhausted and battered men. "Sorry Amanda, there's no way..."

"I know." she said. "You did your best."

"Well, you still might get your chance anyway." he said.

"What do you mean?"

"I mean in a few hours it will be daylight, they might be coming back. Come on. Let's get to the command center. It's time to talk to the local authorities and the press. We need to get the word out about the missing police in case our guys can't find them."

Amanda saw that there was blood on Simon's head and left arm where he had rolled up his sleeve to his elbow. "Simon, you're hurt. Let me look at-"

"It's OK." Simon said. "I'll have one of your people look at it in a few minutes at one of the care stations." He saw two whiteshirts run by. They were carrying one of the injured attackers on a stretcher. "You two, hold up!" he said. He walked over to them with Amanda and looked at the man they were carrying.

"He's dead. Shot in the chest." One of the whiteshirts pointed out two small bullet holes among the collage of tattoos that covered the man's upper body. He wasn't wearing a shirt, only jeans and a pair of worn black boots. He also appeared to be wearing an old Rolex watch. Among the skulls and animals that covered his body was some kind of writing that Simon didn't recognize. It looked a little like Spanish but not quite.

"Portuguese, maybe?" Amanda said. She had been looking at the words as well.

"I have no idea." Simon said, "How many have they found so far?"

"Four or five I think, that didn't make it," the other whiteshirt said. "We did find a few that were still alive. They had smoke inhalation. We found them hanging on a guardrail on the eastern side of the highway. They were brought to bus...ten, I think. A few blackshirts have been posted there in case they wake up."

"Take me." Simon said.

Simon and Amanda followed the whiteshirts to the hospital bus. Three blackshirts were standing at the door on the far end. They were covered in soot and dirt from head to toe, like they had just come out of a fox hole, and were just as shaken up. Occasionally one of them peered into the back of the bus to make sure everything was alright inside, while the others coughed. One of them looked like he was about to hack up a lung and spit on the ground. The whiteshirts Simon was following, pointed in their direction and left them carrying the dead body to another location. Simon thanked them and continued on to bus ten.

"Brent told you guys to cover this bus?" Simon was walking in their direction briskly with Amanda at his heels.

The three men quickly lined up beside the bus and stood at attention. "Y-Yes." One of them said.

"Have any of them woken up yet?"

"Uh, no sir, uh, I mean, I don't think so." He looked at the others.

"Oh, for crying out loud," Simon said. "Amanda, do you have smelling salts on this bus?"

"I have some with me," she said.

"OK then, let's get some answers."

They climbed into the back of the bus. Inside, several protesters from the second wave lay on thin bed stands, none of them conscious. Amanda checked the vitals of the ones that appeared to be in the best condition, and looked at their charts. They had tanned skin that was slightly burned as if they had spent a lot of time in the sun recently, not something that could have happened in Seattle during that time. All three of them looked to be in decent physical shape. They were not kids, nor were they the average migrant looking for work or higher pay, and just like the rest, they were covered in tattoos.

"Here, this one's vitals are the best." Amanda said.

"Let's sit him up then." Simon said. Amanda waved one of the other attending whiteshirts in the bus over, and together the three of them carefully moved the man into an upright position, so that his back was propped up on the inside wall of the vehicle. Amanda took off the oxygen mask the man was breathing through, and used some of her smelling salts on him. He awoke almost instantly. The mask removed, Simon recognized him as the first man he had seen draped over the guardrail a short time earlier. The realization brought a wave of relief over him that he did not expect. Pushing back the feeling, he pulled himself together and began to interrogate him. "Where are you from?" he asked. Fearful, the man looked around at the unfamiliar surroundings he awoke in, and tried to pull away from them, but he was hand cuffed by one of the plastic ties to the bed, which in turn, was attached to the wall behind him and couldn't move.

Amanda put a hand on his shoulder and tried to calm him. "Ok," she said. "It's ok." She was an attractive woman who was used to tense situations, and her sudden intervention using the universal word seemed to work in calming the man down.

Simon started again. "Donde esta? Where are you from? Hablo Espanol?" Again, the man only stared at them.

Amanda looked at the attending whiteshirt and said, "Get a digital translator wand for me, will you?"

Then Simon saw something on the man's left shoulder. It was surrounded by what looked like a colorful ornamental skull on one side, and some kind of sea-serpent on the other. The serpent was concealing a part of it, but it was undeniable. What he saw was a small picture of a green flag, with a blue circle in its center. Recognizing the symbol, he said, "Brazil." The man looked at him, his eyes screaming as if frightened of the word, then, he looked down at his shoulder.

"No, no!" the man said, becoming increasingly upset as he spoke.

Simon looked at Amanda "I have all I need. Make sure he doesn't go anywhere. Call Melissa and tell her that we have illegal aliens here. Have her contact the FBI as soon as possible. We'll hand him over to them, but she'll need to let them know that they're going to have to bring a Portuguese translator along with them." He walked to the rear entrance of the bus.

"Where are you going?" Amanda asked.

"To the prison transports. It's time to visit an old friend, who I've never actually met." Simon said.

****

Simon ripped off the magnetic sticker he had placed over his body cam, and walked to the prison bus placements farther south. He stepped up to the first one he saw, and pounded on the retractable door with his fist. The door opened and he asked the bus warden inside, where he could find Tammy Shelton.

"You're Simon, aren't you? I'm right here, you son of a bitch!" Simon leaned in and looked down the aisle. Tammy was sitting in the second row from the front on the passenger side. "You're people assaulted me, my lawyers will-"

Simon cut her off with a loud rebuke. "WHAT?" He walked up and into the forward section, his eyes focusing on her with the intensity of an animal that hadn't eaten for days and had finally cornered its prey. As they moved in her direction, she recoiled in her seat. He stopped just behind where the driver was sitting and leaned forward, placing his left hand over his ear and tilting his head as he yelled out again like someone who was hard of hearing, "THEY'LL WHAT?!"

She stared at him, sheepishly stung by the sharp reply. Rarely did anyone in her inner circle dare cut her off when she spoke, and what little Tammy had gleaned about Raimes from the media over the years had never indicated that he would act in such a disrespectful manner to anyone. In that moment, she realized that when it came to Simon Raimes, neither had done her any favors.

"I want to know who your backup is, and where they came from." He continued.

"I have no idea what you're talking about." Tammy's face became defiant, contorting at the suggestion that she would give information to an enemy so easily. "But I can tell you that since it looks like you don't have any troops with you, it'll only be a matter of time before I get broken out of here, and you are just another stain on the pavement outside." She spat at his feet.

"Really," He leaned in closer, and spoke with a softer tone that was filled with contempt. "I know you're bringing people in from Brazil, Tammy, who organized it? Who is the middle man? You couldn't have done this on your own. Who helped you, and how did they get this far north?"

That's when Tammy gave herself away by accidentally showing her surprise at the mention of the country where the latest wave of protesters had come from. "LIAR! There's no way you could-"

Simon straightened up and pointed at his left shoulder. "One of them was wearing it, right on his arm."

She looked at him a bit more defeated than before. "Well, you're sure as hell not getting anything out of me!"

"Fine, I'll just submit a request to the human rights commission asking them to recognize the True Bolsheviks as a terrorist organization, one that attempted to bring an invading force into the US, circumventing its borders. Then you won't be able to operate anywhere."

She laughed at him heartily. "We're *already* everywhere, you can't stop us! After we prove we can take western Washington on our own, our people in all of the other cities we own will rise up! The National Guard won't be a match for them. We'll have dozens of state capitols under our control in a matter of days."

"Hmm," Simon raised his left hand to his chin and responded to her threat in a sarcastic tone. "You know what? On second thought, it might be easier to contact the Justices right now to let them know that you and your group are implementing an attempted coup, and suggest that you all should be hunted down and arrested for further questioning until we get the information we need."

His tone turned serious again. "You haven't won here yet, Ms. Shelton. We've already pushed your reinforcements back once, and I'm guessing it will be a while before the next group can get here, if there even is one. It's not easy these days to conceal thousands of people on the march. Come on, Tammy, who are you working with? It must be one of your crazy 'One World' buddies in southern California, am I right?"

Tammy Shelton's whole body began to shake, her face became a vision of anger and frustration, "So, the great Simon Raimes has finally revealed his true colors!" she said. "I should have known. After all of your good will and great deeds, you're just another lackey of a corrupt government." Simon began to turn back to the exit. "Well, let ME tell you something, mister!" She twisted in her seat to face him, pulling on the metal hand cuffs on her wrists, as if she were trying to lunge in Simon's direction. Then she screamed at the top of her lungs, "This isn't your country! It doesn't belong to you or a bunch of unelected judges who were appointed to uphold their worthless Constitution, only to break it by taking power for themselves anyway! It belongs to the world! The only reason it's here is because it kept other nations poor, after killing its original inhabitants! We're coming to take it back for the people, and there is nothing you can do about it! I've seen your face! I've seen-"

Unmoved by the outburst, Simon stepped forward and leaned in her direction so that his face was suddenly only a few inches away from her own. He then looked her directly in the eyes, "You sure about that? Because you'd better be." he said angrily, showing his teeth. Then, returning to the better known and more controlled version of himself, he stepped back and stood next to the driver's seat, making sure to stand on the far side of a yellow line on the floor that was meant to separate the driver's area from the passenger seats.

Remembering what the National Guard had done to the highway when he'd first arrived, Tammy began to realize the amount of influence that Simon held in the world at that moment. He had positioned himself to be a force of order amidst the chaos, the answer to the countries' inevitable destruction, and he was making his own play, just at the right time. She compared his progress on the great chess board that resided in her mind's eye to the unfortunate place she'd found herself in. A look of doubt and fear began to creep over her face, and she fell silent. Simon pulled down the bottom edges of his shirt, and brushed it off with his hands. "By the way," he said, "The rank-and-file Shotguns aren't the only ones that carry video recorders on their uniforms." He pointed to the top left button of his bib. Then he turned to the warden. "If she screams again, feel free to gag her." Then he walked down the steps and out of the bus.

"But woe to you, scribes and Pharisees, hypocrites! Because you shut up the Kingdom of Heaven against men; for you don't enter in yourselves, neither do you allow those who are entering in to enter."-**Matthew, 23:14**

Chapter Sixteen

Christian Territory, Levi's Garage
Spokane, WA
Saturday, March 26^{th,} 7:04AM PST

Mark Tunbridge woke up with the sun. Trying his best not to make a sound, he climbed out of his cot and picked up Jerry's small Bible, then read for the next half hour. When he was finished, he placed the little book back where he'd found it next to Jerry's shoes and looked at his new found friends. He stared at their peaceful faces as they slept and thought about all of the other good and decent people the Lord put in his life over the years. Those he came to know and who had come to know him, those he'd wanted to know more but just ran out of time with and those that had already gone to be with their Father. The pitter-pattering noise of a squirrel as it ran along the roof of the garage stopped him from dwelling on the subject.

Slowly, he opened the garage door as high as his waist and ducked under it, lowering it back down even slower until he was sure it was closed all the way. He thought of Jerry and Eddie, two young men who like him had probably been through a lot to get where they were, the difference between them being that they were merely at the start of their long journeys. Across the street, a few houses to the north, he saw Levi. He was already wide awake and talking to one of the neighbors as he'd told them about as he did every morning. When the man Levi was speaking to pointed in Mark's direction, he waved to them. Levi watched him for a moment, waved back, and went back to talking, likely gabbing about the wall, yard work, or catching up with stories about absent family members.

Mark walked toward the street. He stopped to look up at the great oak tree that had given Levi so much trouble over the years. It was old and twisted, with several power lines resting on one of its wide branches. He raised a hand toward it and closed his eyes. After a few seconds, he continued walking, heading in the direction of the gate. Noticing that it was warm and he couldn't see his breath, he looked up at the sky. "It's going to be a beautiful day today, thank you." he said.

When he arrived at the entrance, he saw a few men taking what little dirt they could find on the inside and shoveling it into the pit. Overnight they had installed a slotted rail beneath the great arch that was meant to guide the gate when it opened and closed. The rail was embedded into the ground to prevent unwanted visitors from squeezing underneath. One of the men working on the project was leaning against the crane that still stood several yards behind the entrance. Another worker was walking around the crane, checking for something. They appeared to be preparing the crane for its removal. Mark walked up to them. "Good morning!" he said.

The man investigating the area around the crane looked up, uninterested. "Good morning." he replied and got back to his inspection.

The one that was taking a break smiled at him. "Morning to you too," he said. Then a spark of recognition spilled across his features. "Hey, you're the guy who-"

"Yeah, that was me," Mark said. "It's amazing what God can do when you ask Him for strength. You guys, uh, getting ready to open the gate yet?"

"No, not yet. I mean, we should have been done with all of this yesterday but with the storm, and well everything that happened. We were told to just leave the gate where it was and wait for the water to drain. We took out part of a culvert on the other side to do this, we're gonna have to put it back, or the city will have our butts."

"You don't work for the city?" Mark asked.

"Me? No, none of us here do. I used to run a contracting company outside of Detroit, moved my whole family here. Best thing I ever did."

"So, how long do you figure before it's open?"

The man let out a deep sigh. "Well, the darned thing works just fine. We've put in the rail to stop it from swinging, now we just have to put the dirt back in. We have a little on this side, but most of it is in a big pile outside of the wall. We could move it, but we were told not to until around ten or ten-thirty."

"Why's that?"

The man leaned toward Mark. "A federal judge is on their way. Apparently, they call the shots now, at least for a little while. Anyway, we're supposed to tell them the gate isn't working until we know what their intentions are. Hey, you should come by. A lot of people would feel better with you here. What God did with you yesterday, I mean, I've never seen anything like it."

"It was *all* God, believe me." Mark said, letting out a small sigh. "Thank you, though, I'll be here. I'm curious about what a judge would have to say about all of this. It's been nice talking to you..."

"Louis." he said and shook Mark's hand. "Hey, what kind of ministry do you do anyway?"

"Missionary work mostly."

"Really?In what country?"

Mark looked at him, plainly. "This one," he said in a nonchalant manner.

Louis' lower lip rose, and his brow lowered. He nodded. "Yeah, I could see that." he said. "Hey, you should come to the gate celebration picnic at the Temple Foundation site afterward. It's not that far, just head north up Cedar and turn west onto Strong. It's a little ways up on the right. I think they're gonna start serving the food at eleven. Well, it's back to work for me, nice to meet you, Mark."

Mark walked to the southern side of the entrance and kept walking until he reached a steep cliff where the wall suddenly stopped alongside a sharp outcropping of rock and slate. He climbed it, pulling himself up by grasping the branches of several small trees that grew at sharp angles out of the cliff's edge. He continued to climb until he reached a small precipice that overlooked the entire site and the city of Spokane to the southeast. Looking down, he could see that the dangerous climb he had just completed would have been impossible had it been attempted from the other side of the wall since the tree line stopped just short of it, and the cliff became concave where it met the roadway. The rock face reached out over the street, jutting out of the hillside for nearly a hundred yards to the south along Wall Street before the wall began again. Turning to look far above his head, he could see the patios that precariously hung over the edge of the cliff, like they were waiting to fall on top of him. Confident that he had found the perfect spot, he knelt there and prayed.

"Lord my God, King of Kings, Creator of all that is, was and ever will be. Please forgive me of my sins. Please soften my heart for others and increase my faith. Grant me your wisdom, guide me, and show me how I need to change. Please reveal to me the path you would have me follow and give me the grace to let go of the things in this world and in my heart that would hinder me from following it and accomplishing your purposes for my life. Please guide and protect those you have put in my path in this place. Reveal yourself to them and comfort them in their times of need. Lord, please answer their prayers, forgive them of their sins as you have forgiven me and lead them to you. Please give me the words to speak to them and help me be more like your Son when I am around them. Also, please forgive those who might try to come against me as I do your will."

He looked down at the gate. A police car drove up and parked next to the dirt mound on the far side. He looked up at the sky and spoke again. "You brought me here Lord. Your will be done. I'll try to do my best, but I really don't know about these people. But if you want me to witness to them even if they refuse to hear, I'll do it. I know your Word. Thank you for this life and for using such a wretch as myself." He closed his eyes. "In the name of Jesus Christ, I pray for these things. Amen."

When he'd finished praying, Mark sat unmoving. After a minute, he opened his eyes again. He watched as the sun rose above the city and listened to the exquisite chirping of the birds that lived there, the cool air embracing him.

Taking in the moment, he meditated on all of the things he had been privileged enough to see His Father in heaven do while on he was on the earth, and day dreamed about the true promises in His word that spoke of the life that was to come for those who were obedient, those who were doers and not only hearers. A world taken out of darkness transformed and renewed, a King to serve that was worth serving forever, a Love that was greater than all loves combined and peace, peace everlasting. He had seen the evidence of these promises, more than he deserved to see, evidence that so many others had not. But there was still time for the faithful to do what they were sent to. He heard a vehicle driving toward the gate on the street below. It was black, and was followed by something that would strike fear into the core of any other man. His mind now returned to him, Mark climbed down from the secret place and made the short trek back to Levi's.

"But God said to him, 'You foolish one, tonight your soul is required of you. The things which you have prepared--whose will they be?' So is he who lays up treasure for himself, and is not rich toward God."-**Luke, 12:20-21**

Chapter Seventeen

Christian Territory, Levi's Garage
Spokane, WA
Saturday, March 26^{th,} 8:55AM PST

Vague impressions of human voices howling with despair echoed through Jerry's unconscious mind as he slept. There was a crowd there, a terrified mass running toward him through the black. They were neither near nor far, but he did know that they were too far away for him to help, as the feeling that the distance which separated him from their cries grew exponentially with each passing second. A rumbling sound followed. It came from the same general direction, and changed into more of a churn as it drew closer. Then it became louder and louder, until it overtook the horrifying choir. He was not safe, and he was not alone, he could feel that others were with him. "Jerry! Jerry!" Someone called to him through the void. A bright light, in the likeness of a man, appeared before him as the soft daylight penetrated his eyelids. He began to open them.

"Jerry! Levi made us breakfast! Get up!"

Eddie was standing over him, smiling. He was holding on to Jerry's shoulders and shaking him. Jerry forgot where he was for a few seconds. He was groggy and not at all amused by the fact that his sleep had been interrupted, even if he was having a nightmare. Eddie's disfigured smile sparked his memory, and he sat up in his cot.

"Got it, I got it!" he said. As lovable as Eddie could be, he was really beginning to grate on Jerry's nerves. He always knew about people who were mentally disabled or just slower than other people, but they were few and far between, most never given a chance to live after they were identified as such in the womb. Jerry told himself that interacting with Eddie was not only a learning experience, but also an opportunity to practice patience. That, and he would only have to be around the boy for another few hours if everything went according to plan.

He got up and followed the boy into the house. Levi was leaning over his stove cooking pancakes. On the kitchen table, four plates were neatly laid out with silverware and napkins, with a small plate of butter, and a container of syrup in the middle between them. He walked only as far as the closest chair was to the door, and sat down. He noticed that two Bibles were also on the table, both of them opened to the first page of the Book of John. One sat next to Eddie's setting, where he sat down near the head of the table on the opposite side, and the other one was at the head of the table itself on the side, closest to the cooking area, a seat which Jerry deduced was Levi's spot.

Looking around, Jerry saw that the kitchen walls were filled with pictures of Levi's friends and family, each one framed and hanging in no particular order on every side, sparing only a little room for a cork board to which a few to-do lists, utility bills, and a variety of Catholic themed Christmas cards and church notices were pinned. Hanging next to the board was a calendar with several events written on it in permanent marker and an ancient landline phone, with a cord that was so long it almost touched the floor.

Sliding glass doors on one side of the room allowed for sunlight to come in. Through them, Jerry could see the backyard, where several faded statues of what he could only assume were Catholic religious figures stood among the finely trimmed bushes, which had been planted on the inside of a tall picket fence that surrounded the property behind the house. On a counter that started next to the doors and stretched to the burners on which Levi was cooking, several tall stacks of old magazines had been placed, waiting for a new home. Jerry guessed that Levi must have brought them in from the garage the previous day.

As a cloud passed, allowing the rays of the early morning sun to enter the room, they caught something on the counter that shone so brightly, it made Jerry wince. Squinting through his eyelids, he saw the source of the illumination. Something gold and shiny was there, sticking out from between two of the magazines. He couldn't see exactly what was reflecting the incoming light, but whatever it was, it did so well enough to almost blind him.

Levi came over to the table, a pan in one hand and a spatula in the other, singing and swaying as he moved around the kitchen. Jerry couldn't make out all of the lyrics of the song he was singing, but he was able to gather that it had something to do with a well running dry and walking. He sang in a high pitched voice, as he used the spatula to slide two pancakes onto Eddie's plate. Eddie had been waiting eagerly for his food from the second he sat down, holding his utensils upright with both hands. When he got his pancakes, Eddie started chowing down on them immediately.

"Eddie." Levi said. Eddie looked up at him. Levi tapped the syrup and butter with the spatula. Eddie nodded, his mouth already full. "And pray before you eat like we practiced." Levi said. Eddie nodded again. He bowed his head for a moment and went for the syrup first. Levi looked at Jerry. "Yours will be up in a second, Jerry. You're quite the sleeper, you know." He walked back to the stove.

Jerry looked around for a clock and found one hanging next to the door to the garage. It said that it was nine in the morning. "Nine AM is sleeping in for you?" Jerry asked.

Levi turned around for a moment. "Are you kidding? Half the day's over by eight!" He turned back to the stove and continued making Jerry's pancakes. "Don't worry, I've put some coffee on. Unfortunately, I don't have any milk or orange juice right now. I do have some prune juice, though. Do you want some prune juice? It's good for you, you know."

Jerry raised one hand as if to say no, while shielding his eyes with the other. *Old people.* He thought. Levi returned with two pancakes for him. "Thank you, Levi," he said. "What brings on this hospitality if you don't mind my asking?"

"Oh, well, you boys didn't tell me the reason Mark was covered in mud yesterday. He's a local celebrity! Like I said, I'm not too keen on that wall, but kicking that brute's butt and sending off those anarchist cowards with their tails between their legs, well that is something. This morning, a couple of my new neighbors told me who was staying in my garage when I went to check the mail. Not that there was any mail of course," He face-palmed himself. "Old habits, you know?"

"Where's Mark?" Jerry asked, his mind beginning to break out of its usual morning fog.

"He left earlier. I think he went to pray somewhere." Levi poured a cup of coffee for Jerry, and brought it to the table. "I'm sure he'll be back around soon. Eddie and I were just discussing what we're going to do today in the backyard, right Eddie?"

"Uhmhm!Right!" Eddie said through his latest mouthful.

"Mark said you two had plans and asked for another night. You're welcome to stay one more night if you'd like to. Not like there's anywhere to go while the gate is closed anyway." Then Levi gave Jerry a curious look. "I get the feeling you two haven't known each other for very long." he said.

"You'd be right on that one." Jerry said. "Hopefully I'll be moving on sooner rather than later, I have to get back home." He reached for the syrup and looked at Eddie again. "What about Eddie? Any news from the Spokane police?"

"They said they planned to come by today to get a statement and possibly bring him in, but they were told there's been a malfunction with the gate and apparently they still have to remove a car and fill in the trench near the entrance before any vehicles can safely come through." Levi went to the cork board and took something off of it. He dropped a bright yellow flyer in front of Jerry. It was a notice from a group called the 'Temple Foundation' concerning something called the 'Christian Territory Project'. It showed a detailed timeline of the gate's construction, which revealed that they had originally planned the gate's completion for Friday afternoon. At the bottom was a number that residents could call if they had any questions, or needed a card pass that would allow them in or out of the area after the construction was finished.

"I just hope they open it soon so I can get my mail and do some shopping, there's a market in here, but it doesn't have what I need." Levi said. His eyes became wide as if he'd remembered something important, and he walked over to the calendar. "They'd better be finished with that gate by Monday, I have bowling league, and I don't intend to miss it!"

"So, they weren't planning on sealing the place up indefinitely?" Jerry asked.

"Oh, I think they would have eventually, but in the short term? Nah, they're still prospecting. There's a lot of money floating around Spokane for them to nab before they would close up for good. Haven't been any real con men around here for a long time. This city is ripe for the picking, and they still need to buy up a lot more property around here to complete their little project. No, they're just getting started. My guess is the government's sudden change in management made them nervous, and they jumped the gun on completing the wall."

Jerry was surprised to hear a believer in God call other believers 'conmen,' but he supposed from Levi and Mark's perspectives, that's exactly what the Temple Foundation was, a con. Neither of them had asked him for money in the name of their Jesus since he'd arrived, and he doubted that they ever would, from what he could tell of their characters. He picked up the flyer. "Can I keep this?"

"Sure, I guess. I don't need it."

Jerry looked at the old corded phone on the wall again. It was a black, roundish thing, that had a cradle of the same form and color. "Hey, Levi," he said, "Mind if I borrow your phone for a minute? I have to let someone know where I am."

Levi nodded. "Ok, it don't work on apps, though. You have to press in the number you're looking for. If you don't know it, just dial four-one-one, and tell the person on the other end the name and place you're calling."

"Thanks," Jerry said. "I appreciate the help."

Jerry picked it up, and dialed as Levi had instructed. He heard a low fluctuating hum that seemed out of place. When the automated operator came on the line, he asked it for the number to the Seattle Introspector. The robotic voice connected him, and a few seconds later, he was talking to Marcy, the receptionist. "Hey Marcy, this is Jerry Farron. I need to speak to Tom right away."

A moment later and he was on the line with Tom. "Jerry! Where you? Are you in the compound? What is that annoying sound in the background?"

"Yeah I'm here," Jerry said. He walked out of the kitchen into a nearby hallway, stretching the phone cord, and turning his back to Levi and Eddie. "I'm still working on finding that thing we talked about. It could be causing the interference on this line. You should check your personal drop box. Some stuff went down at the gate yesterday while they were lowering it into place. In it, you'll see that some of the Christians here have enough 3D printed guns for a small army, and an attack by some local anarchists."

"Were any of them shot? Where were the police?" Tom said.

"No, no one was shot. Something more interesting happened than that. It should all be in the video. If you plan on posting it I get Investigating Reporter credit, and the camera man is uh," He reached into his back pocket and took out the notebook. "Devon...Fromeyer, just like it sounds." He looked at the flyer again. "Have Perry look up the 'Christian Territory Project ' and the 'Temple Foundation'. See if he can get any leads. They have a number, its 555-2329."

Jerry could hear Tom writing the information down. "Alright, I'll put him right on it. I have the video up. It's over thirty minutes long. I'll have Brenda look at it and cut it down. Can't wait to see what you're talking about. I take it you've found somewhere to stay, since you're still there?"

"Yeah, for now. Right now the gate's closed, I don't think anyone will be going in or out for at least another day."

"That's not all." Tom said. "We've got word that the Chief Justice for that side of the state is on the move, headed in your direction. Now I think we know why."

"That means they'll be at the gate, I'll need to head back there." Jerry said, half to himself.

"You should know that things aren't going well here. I made it into the office, but I gave most of the staff the day off. Fires are burning all over the city, and people are openly looting. Everywhere you go, most of the public facial identity scanners and security cams have been smashed, but that's nothing compared to what's happening on the highway."

"Why? What's happening on I-5?"

"Simon Raimes, that's what. He came in yesterday and painted the town red, literally. He had the National Guard cover the lanes in flame retardant. Took out all the drones except for his, and knocked a bunch of the protesters on their collective asses. The jet buzzed right by the building. Scared the crap out of me! Then last night, just when it seemed like they had everything under control, more people started swarming onto the highway. No one knows who they are, or how they got north of the airport. They took down the police line on the north end, no one even knows what happened to the cops who were there."

"I saw Raimes' charter buses on the way to Spokane. What's going on now?"

"Well, the National Guard is defending an empty federal courthouse, while the rest of the police and fire brigades deal with the smaller riots downtown. There's a lot going on in Olympia too. Our people on the ground there are reporting that another riot near the Statehouse has gotten more serious since yesterday. A large group came up from Portland, and is causing a ruckus. Personally, I think SeaTac is their main target though. If Raimes and the National Guard in Olympia lose the highway, and the protesters manage to take the airport, business in the Tri-City area could come to a standstill. Who the hell knows what will happen if they manage to do that."

"It's a flagship play..." Jerry said.

"A what?" Tom asked.

"They're trying to set an example. They want to prove that they can take and keep the Tri-City area, so that other groups around the country will be emboldened and try to do the same. Look at the video Brenda recorded through my Omni-Glass yesterday. Tell her to show you the part where I was talking to Tammy Shelton. She said something about a takeover. It makes sense. The only ways out of the western side of the state are the airport and the highway. It might not be a protest at all. It could be a precursor to an all-out invasion, with the goal of controlling the entire western side of the state. That would explain why all those extra protesters showed up all of the sudden. Have someone check the Sound around the west side of the industrial area, I'd bet good money they came in by boat last night, and aren't even from Washington State. If they take out Raimes' forces and kick out the Guard, more will come. They'll be going after the wealthiest people and anyone that's associated with the media first, to shut them down. Tom, you need to make sure you have an exit strategy in case things go south."

"But wouldn't the Coast Guard stop them if they came by boat?" Tom asked.

"Not if they were paid off, or thought they were just letting a bunch of migrants through on their way to Canada. Remember Carol's article last year about human trafficking along the coast? She never did find out how they were getting so far north."

The line went silent, save for the strange undulating hum. "You might be right." Upon returning from the short pause, Jerry noticed that Tom's voice had changed. He now sounded solemn and distant. Jerry could hear shuffling papers, and drawers being opened and closed on the other end of the line. "I'll do that Jerry, I mean, I'll send someone to check on your hunch about the boats, and see what I can do to get everyone out of here and up to the border if I need to." Silence came over the line again.

Jerry broke it with an apology, "Tell Perry I'm sorry about his motorcycle. I never meant for the cops to pick it up."

Tom's voice returned to its usual tone. "Sarina? You lost it? That thing didn't come back here, we never heard about any police report either. Maybe Perry made it so that it couldn't be traced back to him. I'll tell him what happened. Wherever it is, he should be able to reach it. Heck, he probably taught it to break itself out of the impound lot on its own. Don't worry about that. Be safe Jerry, hopefully all this will calm down in the next couple of days."

"Hopefully," Jerry said, "You too Tom. Tell Brenda I said hi." Jerry hung up the phone. He entered 411 again and called Noel. After a few rings, her familiar message came on the line. "Noel, it's Jerry," he said into the phone. "I know we're not on good terms right now, but you need to pack a bag and prepare to leave the city. If you can't get out, make sure you have enough food and water to last a couple of weeks. I'll come and find you. Needless to say, I think the latest round of protests might be more than what they seem. Be safe." Jerry walked back into the kitchen and tried to hang the phone back onto the wall, but couldn't put it back in its cradle without it falling back out again. Exasperated after a few tries, he passed it to Levi, who had stood up, seeing what he was trying to do. Levi hung it up.

"You ok, son? You don't look so good. Before you left the room, you said something about finding something here. You aren't a drug smuggler, or something are you?" Levi asked.

Jerry had to think fast, "Uh, I was sent here by the phone company to locate a device that's been jamming all cell phones in the area, along with other radio signals, like your garage door operator, for example. They sent me in to find it, so that they can find a way to counter the signal it's putting out or to shut it down. It's not legal, wherever it is."

"You work for the phone company, but can't hang a phone up on the wall?"

Caught in his lie, Jerry froze, not knowing how to respond. Then Levi smiled and hit him in the stomach playfully. "I'm just joking with ya'. I know that even at the phone company people don't use these anymore! Well, if it gets my door opener working again, I'm all for it!"

Jerry sat back down and ate his breakfast. When they were finished, he volunteered to wash the dishes, and recruited Eddie to help dry them. Then he watched and listened as Levi read and began to explain to Eddie what prophecy was, and how Jesus had fulfilled the prophecies that were made about the coming messiah in the Old Testament. He decided to wait for Mark before heading out, so he could thank him for helping him find a place to stay. To pass the time, he decided to go back in the garage, and retrieve the small Bible that Levi had given to him. *Just to be polite, I'll at least look like I'm interested while I wait.* He thought. Seeing that it was still under his cot right where he'd left it, he picked it up, went back into the kitchen, and sat at the table again, opening it to the part in Genesis where he'd stopped reading the night before.

He read through the story of Noah, which he had heard of before, but while examining the pages, he noticed that the stories he had learned about the man when he was a child were noticeably different from the one in the actual book. Most notably, he never knew that God was the one who led the animals into the Ark according to the tale, and not Noah himself. He also didn't know that again, according to the story, it was supposedly God himself who had shut the door to the Ark, and not Noah, when the rain came and the great flood began.

The inconsistencies with how non-Christian sources of information represented the character of Noah in the legend confused him, especially since he saw no reason for the discrepancy. If nonbelievers didn't like God and how He judged things, wouldn't it make more sense to disparage His character by simply stating what was in the Bible as it was written? After all, tons of people died in the flood either way. For that matter, why even sully the character of the one man who was intelligent enough to save himself and his family, by following the will of a God that he *knew* was speaking to him? If God was indeed speaking to him directly, wouldn't it have been stupid not to listen? Could such an act of survival be considered a kind of natural selection?

He looked ahead a few pages and saw that the story of someone he knew even less about was next, Abraham. He was wondering if he would notice differences in interpretations of his story as well, when Mark interrupted his train of thought by walking in through the door to the garage. "Hey." Mark said. He kicked his feet against the steps as he came into the house. Jerry surmised that he was either still worried that some of the dirt from the pit was still sticking to his shoes, or he had recently been walking somewhere that was muddy.

Jerry yawned and asked, "Where have you been? Do you want some pancakes? Levi made them."

Mark answered with a bright and pleasant smile. "No thanks. I've already eaten."

Jerry nodded and turned back to the others. Both of them seemed confused, and a bit concerned by Mark's answer. Mark sat down next to him.

"Are you ready to head out, Jerry?" He asked.

Levi looked at the clock on the wall and Jerry's gaze followed. An entire hour had gone by since he had started reading. "I think we can get going on that yard work." Levi said to Eddie. Then he looked at Mark. "Eddie's going to help me rake up the dead grass in the backyard, and bag it. Then we're going to see about putting down some insecticide on the front lawn, too many ants."

Jerry looked at Mark. "Where are *we* going?" he asked.

"You and I are headed back to the gate. I was just down there, and noticed something was going on that you might be interested in. After that, we're going for a walk."

"Where to?"

"A picnic. Apparently, there is going to be a celebration in an area northwest of the gate that's starting in a few hours. I have a feeling what you're looking for won't be too far from where the picnic will be."

"Why do you say that?"

"Because," Mark said. "They're celebrating the completion of the wall and the installation of the gate. That means at least some of those responsible for planning all of this should be there. But first, I have to take a piss."

"You mean leave a piss in my bathroom, don't you?" Levi asked.

Mark and Jerry looked at him and then at each other. Mark shrugged, "Leave a piss." he said. He took off his cap and put it on the kitchen table before getting up to go to the bathroom.

"And don't put your hat on the table, its' bad luck!" Levi said, clearly agitated.

"Sorry." Mark said, taking his hat and putting it on again. He left the room.

Jerry looked at Levi. "Bad luck?" he asked. Like a superstition? Is that in the Bible or something?"

"No, it's not in the Bible." Levi said."Nothing that you would call superstitious is, it's just disrespectful, and I don't like it. My parents thought that putting your hat down on a table was an omen that someone is going to die. They were from Sicily, you know. Call it a family tradition if you want."

Jerry nodded. In the corner of his eye, he noticed the sunlight was hitting the glint of gold between the magazines again. He got up to see what it was. Between copies of 'Bold Gardens' and 'The Scientific American,' he found a thin and delicate white cloth, with gold-laced embroidery. The gold areas in the center took on the shapes of a variety of animals, including a deer, a bear, an elk, and many others. Around its edges in an elaborate pattern, was an intricate border that looked like some type of Irish weave. Jerry took it from its hiding place and unfolded it on the table so that he could see it in its entirety.

Levi saw what he was doing. "So, that's where that went." he said.

"What is it?" Jerry asked. "It's beautiful." Levi moved a little to his right, so that the sunlight caught every part of the golden embroidery, and it began to sparkle. As soon as Eddie saw it, his eyes became transfixed.

"My wife made it. It's a representation of a vision that Saint Peter had. You see, he was a Jewish man, and shortly after Jesus died and was resurrected, Peter was still not fully convinced that God wanted him to go to the gentiles to preach the Gospel. The gentiles are those who weren't Jewish and didn't practice the Jewish religion. So God gave him a vision. In it, Peter saw a great tapestry, all of the wild animals were woven into it or painted on it, I can't remember which. Anyway, the point is, through the vision God showed Peter that anyone He wanted to have in His kingdom could be brought into it. Peter then went out to the gentiles and brought many of them into the church. We Catholics believe that this is one of the things that God did that made Peter the first Pope."

"I wonder what Mark thinks about that." Jerry said.

"Mark doesn't really believe in taking orders from a Pope." Levi said. "He told me that he believes the Pope is just a leader of a large church and not God's sole authority on earth. He said he goes to God directly for his walking orders."

"And what do you think about that?"

"Well, all Christians are supposed to learn to walk in the spirit. That's what leaders of the church are for, to teach the rest of us how to do just that. On the other hand, I still think God definitely chose each Pope for his time. Much like He chooses political leaders. That *is* in the Bible. For a while the Popes chose the kings in Europe, and those choices shaped the modern world so..." Jerry nodded. It sounded to him like Catholics, and other Christian groups had just as many things in common as they had differences.

"Believing in Christ is the most important part though." Mark said as he came back into the room. "It's what's in the heart that matters. Paul wrote about the heart many times in his letters in the New Testament. Every church gets some things wrong and some things right, no one is perfect under Christ, as we are all sinful and fall short of Jesus' example, and no one who thinks Jesus was just a prophet or a man is really a Christian."

"That's right!" Levi said.

"So, how do you know your hearts are in the right place?" Jerry asked.

"Because we spend time with our Lord in prayer, and we read His word." Mark pointed at Eddie's Bible. "And then we try our best to do what it says."

"John uh," Eddie turned the pages of his Bible frantically. "F-Fourteen...verse... fifteen!" He looked around for approval.

Mark and Levi looked at each other with pride. "That's right!" Levi said again. "You've got it, Eddie!" He rubbed Eddie's hair. Eddie beamed, showing a wide smile.

"Come on," Mark said to Jerry, elbowing him while looking at the clock. "We don't want to miss the grand reception at the gate."

****

Mark and Jerry got on their way. Levi gave each of them a bottle of water before they left, so they could stay hydrated. Stepping out into the rural suburb, the air felt crisp and clean as it moved in and out of Jerry's lungs. The experience brought forth memories of the time he and Noel had hiked through Glacier Park. For a few minutes he let his mind wander while he reminisced, recalling her smiling face looking up at his as they stood under the branches of a sequoia tree, during a brief downpour. How they'd laughed while attempting to start a fire using the wet undergrowth, something neither of them had done before. He pictured her walking over boulders and looking into the horizon, her long dark hair rippling around her shoulders while flirting with him in her smart, subtle way. He glanced over to his right, and saw that Mark was looking up at him, an odd expression on his face.

"Oh, sorry," Jerry said. "I zoned out for a minute there. It's such a beautiful morning!" He lifted up his arms and stretched them outward.

Mark looked up at the sky, it was deep and blue. The clouds had vanished completely, allowing the sun to shine brightly as the birds sang melodies that were like new songs to their ears. "It always is, Jerry," he said. "We just have to remember to recognize them as such."

"So, why are we headed to the gate?" Jerry asked.

"I walked down there to see if it was open yet when I got up this morning, and talked to someone there who was part of the construction crew. They moved the crane, but can't get it out of the area until they fill in the ditch on either side of the structure."

"And?"

"And they're filling in the part that is on the inside of the gate, but not the outside." Mark said.

"Because there's a 'malfunction' with the gate, right?" Jerry said.

"Not quite," Mark said. "A federal judge is on their way, I don't think having to actually deal with the new government hierarchy was a scenario that they'd anticipated when they were setting up their end game here."

"They who?" Jerry asked.

"The church leaders that brought their people here."

"So I take it both you and Levi don't like prosperity Christians that much."

"We like them just fine. It's their leaders we don't like. Those who followed them here don't know they're being duped, and the sad part is, if they just read their Bibles instead of shoveling their money and time into the swindler's pockets, they might learn that being 'content in all things' is really what the Bible teaches us to do. God can make people wealthy, especially if they are good stewards of their possessions like He wants all of us to be, but if it's not His plan for someone, or the right time, because He wants a person to learn a lesson or do something else for a while, a person who wants money more than God in their life will only get angry at Him in the end, for never having gotten enough of it. This principle extends beyond just the pursuit of money too. Plead enough to God, and He may make an exception, and even change a believer's path, but when we make idols out of blessings, most of the time, His answer is just an emphatic no. He may even stop speaking to someone who has abandoned Him in their heart for other things, and won't do anything for them until they've repented and come back to Him."

"So you think if they spent more time reading the Bible, they'd figure this out on their own." Jerry said.

"I've seen it happen too many times to count," Mark said. "There are plenty of verses in the Bible in the Old and New Testaments that warn against pursuing wealth, but they are never mentioned in prosperity churches. You have to ignore them completely, and really twist other things in the Bible to even understand where these people are coming from with their false doctrine. The truth is God wants us to be a spiritual people, not materialists who store up worthless things that rust away or vanish when bad times inevitably come. He wants us to be salt and light in the world."

"Salt, you mean, like, bitter?"

Mark chuckled. "No, not bitter. Salt was once used to stave off infection, clean wounds, and preserve food. You know, before refrigeration."

Jerry thought of Levi's garage. "So, why do you think people follow them?"

"Most of them learned to be like the rest of the world when they were young. They just agree with the current leadership in whatever groups they find themselves in, so they can fit in out of fear of being ostracized from the rest of the community. Also, like the rest of the world, most don't even know that they aren't really thinking for themselves. Others were so poor when they were young it traumatized them, and they can't imagine a God who would allow anyone to live in what they think is an intolerable situation, even though most people never had what they did when things were at their worst for them. Jesus said, 'The poor will always be with you'. Prosperity preachers, whether they believe in what they do for the same reasons or not, take advantage of their congregant's fears, and profit from them. The real problem, though, is that when they do this, they deprive their followers of the true spiritual growth that can come from completely relying on God for things, and the rest of the world sees right through it. Nonbelievers often hate Christians all the more as a result. In the end, they do more harm to the Kingdom of God than good."

"So, how do you know you're the one who is right?" Jerry asked.

Mark didn't miss a beat, "Because I believe in the Bible as God meant it to be presented, in its full context. I don't cherry-pick verses out of it to support my position, and I don't add to it, like many do both in and out of the church, in order to confuse or take advantage of others. That, and I've seen and experienced the true fruit of the Spirit, and the inevitable persecution that comes with it. I've also been humbled, and had to give up many things that I wanted in order to follow my Lord. You might not know what I mean by this right now, but one day when you get to the end of the Bible we gave you, you will understand more. Stick around a little longer with me, and you might see some of what I am describing in action. That's not pride speaking, it's fact."

Jerry was astonished by Mark's last claim. *Speaking about spiritual things as if they were as provable as scientific facts?* He thought. *He must be crazy.* Ahead of them, a disheveled, average looking woman wearing a red robe, walked out of one of the McMansion style residences that lined the street they were heading down, and walked to the edge of her driveway. She stood there, staring at them with dark circles under her eyes, her auburn hair sticking out in every which way, until they passed by. Jerry gave her a smile as they got closer, but her gaze was upon Mark the entire time. He was about to wave his hand in front of her face in an attempt to wake her up from whatever trance she was under, when she opened her mouth.

"You know these people chose to come here, don't you? You shouldn't be here." she said. Mark didn't even look upon the woman, instead choosing to observe a few birds that were flying overhead. Snubbed, the strange woman turned around, and started walking back to her house.

"What the hell was that about?" Jerry asked Mark. After they'd passed the edge of her property, he looked back over his shoulder. She was standing on her porch staring at the front door, a confused look was on her face, as if she'd been sleepwalking and had just woken up to find herself outside.

"Just ignore her," Mark said. "It can't hurt us."

"It?"

"Don't worry about it, Jerry. She's probably just having a bad hangover."

A hangover? Here? Jerry thought to himself. *Sure, why not? It's not like they're not allowed to drink...or are they?*

****

When they arrived at the gate, Mark and Jerry were greeted with smiles and handshakes. As they neared the archway, several people surrounded them. Some patted Mark on the back while others, clearly glad that he was in attendance, introduced themselves. These were part of a small, unassuming group of around twenty that had gathered on the inside of the wall, near a set of steps that led to the top just south of the entrance. *These must be the leaders, or at the very least some of their immediate subordinates.* Jerry thought. *No wait, no one really sticks out, they all look kind of average. Hmm, must be middle management then.*

The pit was still in the process of being filled by a few workers. Jerry remembered the large mound of dirt that Mark had been sitting on when he'd first seen him on the other side of the wall. He hadn't seen anything like it on the inside, only a small pile of gravel not far from the crane. They would have to open the gate if they wanted to completely fill in the trench, or get the earth needed to finish the job from somewhere else. Until then, the rail they had installed remained, sticking out of the ground enough so that it could stop most vehicles from entering, even if someone were able to knock the gate off of its mechanical hinges.

Soon the hand shaking and patting moved from Mark to him. Jerry forced a smile and went along with it, even if it did make him feel a bit uncomfortable. It wasn't long though, before he realized that they were actually mildly pushing both he and Mark toward the steps that were embedded into the side of the wall. Following Mark's lead, Jerry didn't resist. They went up the steps, ascending to the narrow walkway at the top. Though the catwalk there stopped just before the archway on either side, they could still see over it. Three others were already standing beyond the arch on the northern side. Nearest to them was a middle-aged woman in a bright red dress, who was wearing an awful lot of jewelry. The tacky display reflected the rays of the sun so effectively, that it almost blinded them when she turned in their direction to see who was coming up on the other side of the entrance. Beside her stood a man in an expensive suit and tie, with classic good looks, a tan, and hair that was styled a little too perfect. A third man stood behind the other two. He was taller than they were, and wore a long dark sport jacket that partially covered up his girth. He was wearing glasses, had a full head of white hair, and a giant, well groomed, and equally white beard that seemed to shine in a strange way when the sun hit it, as if it were absorbing the light as much as it was reflecting it. In his right hand, he held a large cane, made out of darkened wood with a gold handle. *These must be the ring leaders.* Jerry thought. *I wish I had my lens. Guess I'll have to find out who they are some other way. At least I know what they look like.*

The three of them were conversing with someone outside of the gate when they arrived. The first two, upon hearing their foot falls as they reached the top, looked in Mark and Jerry's direction with great confusion. They looked down and behind themselves at their own people as if seeking an explanation from them, one that never came. When the third man, the one with the beard, saw Mark standing on the wall, his face became pale, and his eyes so wide that Jerry wondered for a moment if he was having a heart attack.

Mark didn't give them any of his attention, not even looking in their direction as he found his footing, and instead helped Jerry to steady himself, as there weren't any rails on top of the wall for either of them to hold on to. Feeling stable, Jerry turned east, carefully controlling his balance. He stood straight up, and looked cautiously down over the gate to see just what was going on that had brought everyone out. An unexpected spell of vertigo came over him as he glanced downward, but it only lasted for a few seconds. From where he stood, he could see that the car that had been overturned in front of the gate the day before was no longer in sight. The only evidence that remained of its presence was two long and muddy tracks that marked the ground just outside of the pit. When they reached the adjacent street, they vanished.

Beyond the remaining concrete barriers on the other side of the street, were two police cruisers and a long dark CAV. Five police officers and a rotund man in a dark brown suit, stood in front of the ominous vehicle as if waiting for something. Jerry recognized the face of the man in the cheap suit from an article a fellow journalist had written about the city a few years earlier, identifying him as the mayor of Spokane. Walking up to the mayor at that moment, however, was a much more interesting looking fellow. He was dressed to kill, wearing a sleek pitch-black outfit, complete with a blackshirt, tie, and an equally dark pair of augmented sunglasses, the likes of which Jerry had never seen before. In stark contrast to the black hole of a man who had captured his attention, another figure then appeared in Jerry's vision, one that he'd almost overlooked.

The slender form of an incredibly tall and stone faced woman stood next to, and slightly in front of, the stylish man in black. Where his suave attire made him stand out from the others, she almost completely blended in with the street itself, covered from the neck down in a grey buttoned-up overcoat, its collar turned upward. Her long dark hair was pulled tightly behind her head, and try as he might, Jerry could not determine her age from where he stood. She was like a sculpture, her perfectly proportioned facial features, long neck, and unmoving frame fooling Jerry's senses. As the sun rose behind her, she took on an almost timeless appearance, all the while casting a long shadow that went clear across the street, ending somewhere far below his feet at the wall's base. In one of her hands, she held a thin white tablet, and in the other, a stylus.

Biding her time, she looked at the tablet, which she held away from her face at eye level, an aura of cold, calculating confidence emanating from her statuesque form. It was clear that she was trying to make an impression on all of them, one that clearly conveyed the idea that she was not someone to be messed with. As amazing and impressive as lady justice appeared on that stirring morning though, all of her splendor paled in comparison to the terrible marvel of engineering that began to materialize above her head almost immediately after he and Mark had found their footing.

Floating in near perfect silence about twenty feet above the visitors, and at eye level with those standing on top of the wall, was a Palmer three-eighty-two tactical smart drone, otherwise known as a Military grade Autonomous Kill Drone or M.A.K.D. for short. Covered with materials that had light bending capability, it revealed itself in bits and pieces at first, revealing only small sections of its surface to them in quick succession before completing its de-cloaking routine, in response no doubt to their arrival on the top of the wall. The drone was similar in appearance to that of a great manta ray, with a wing span that was nearly eight feet across. It was almost completely flat in its design, only ten inches at its thickest point with two fully articulated gyroscopic turbines set into its fin-like wings for maneuverability. But it was the two fully automatic machine guns attached to its undercarriage that made Jerry nervous. The weapons that were pointing directly at him were capable of firing explosive smart rounds, the kind that could fly around corners, and turn the wall they were standing on into so much dust and rubble. He knew as much, because he had witnessed a M.A.K.D. in action once while on assignment two years earlier during the Cartel war in Mexico. In his wildest dreams, he never thought that the government would dare deploy one domestically though.

Within the thinking weapon was a semi-autonomous task oriented A.I. that was capable of choosing what targets to fire at, and when to fire at them, completely on its own. Like Perry's motorcycle, it was a type of A.I. that was illegal for American civilians to create or own, the only difference being that the one observing every move he was making in that moment was not designed to get a person from point A to point B. It was designed to kill with extreme prejudice, and with absolute efficiency. Chills went up his spine, as he remembered how easily the M.A.K.D. he'd seen had rid the world of over thirty cartel members in under a minute. After Mexico, he promised himself that he'd never end up on the wrong side of any conflict that involved one of the monstrosities, and had he known the government would be showing such force, he never would have agreed to go to Spokane to begin with.

Standing there afraid to move, he realized it was likely that the synthetic brain inside the drone had targeted both he and Mark the moment their heads had begun to appear over the edge of the catwalk. The realization made him feel a sudden urge to be anywhere but in the killer machine's line of sight, an urge he had to force himself to resist. He started shaking a little, a sudden weakness seizing his knees, but he knew that turning back might only make matters worse. Gathering his courage, he gulped and stood his ground, the sun lighting up his white dress shirt like a torch for everyone to see.

The woman had already begun to address the others that were present. It wasn't until Jerry was able to rip his attention away from the heavy dose of overkill she'd brought along with her, that his ears began to catch up with what she was saying, "...You may think you are in control here because of your local influence, but you have no right to restrict access to this area or to keep people hostage inside who do not share your beliefs, and know that until this gate opens, I will hold you three responsible for anything-" She leered at Mark and Jerry, not at all impressed by the interruption created by their unexpected entrance. "More leaders?" she asked. "I know that there are some..." She looked at her tablet. "Twenty-three churches that are participating in this little project. Which ones are the two of you representing today?"

"We aren't associated with any church here your honor," Mark said. "I *am* here to represent someone, though. A private benefactor, who cares for and actively looks after all of them." The three across from them looked at him amazed by the proclamation, the mouths of all three visibly agape in disbelief.

"And you are?" the judge asked.

"My name is Mark Tunbridge." he said.

"And your friend?" She looked at Jerry.

"Just that, a friend. He is not a leader, and is only here to assist me with a few personal matters during my stay."

"Just a moment." She said to them. Jerry saw her look straight ahead at the wall for a moment, and then at Mark again. *She's looking at something through an Omni-Glass.* He thought.

"Looks like you've been getting around quite a bit recently, Mr. Tunbridge," she said. She turned her attention to Jerry, "And you keep very interesting company."

The man with the beard lifted up his cane and pointed it at Mark, almost knocking the other two standing next to him off of the catwalk on their side. "HE does not represent us!" he said. "He shouldn't even be here!" The M.A.K.D. made a whirring sound and aimed its guns in his direction, prompting him to quickly lower the cane. The others, taken aback by his crass gesture, turned to him, a new look, one of sheer terror overtaking their faces.

One of the local police officers walked up behind the judge and spoke into her ear. "You sir," She raised her voice again, still looking at Mark. "This officer says that you match the description of the man who fought off the driver of the car that was towed away from here a few minutes ago. Was that you?"

"It was." Mark said.

"Well, from the commotion I could hear on the other side of the wall while you were climbing up there, you obviously have a few supporters inside, and from what I can see in the video that's going around, many of them look to you for leadership. You may stay. By the way, your little wrestling match may have saved several foolhardy young people from being killed, and almost everyone in this community from prosecution. Thank you for preventing what could have been a blood bath." The three leaders looked back to Mark obstinately. The man with the beard looked especially enraged, his features quickly changing from pale white, to a deep unnerving red. Jerry noted that Mark still hadn't so much as looked in their direction since they'd arrived.

"As I was saying before..." The slender woman looked at her tablet again. "3D printed weaponry is illegal in the state of Washington. Failure to turn over the weapons that appeared in the video within the next forty-eight hours, will result in an immediate forced confiscation period." She looked up from the tablet, and motioned to the man in black standing next to her. "Believe me when I say that we reserve the right to use bulldozers if we need to. We will search each and every home in your little sanctuary, until we are satisfied that we have found every weapon in the aforementioned video."

The three leaders huddled together. They were arguing in hushed voices, trying not to let their voices carry. This continued on for about thirty seconds. Mark finally looked in their direction and turned back, shaking his head. He then yelled down to the woman. "We will turn them over." he said. The three stopped their bickering. Then all of them looked at Mark with angered stares that could shatter steel. "We have one concession. That after the gate has...started working again, no one in this community will be harassed or questioned, and that it will be treated as any other community in Spokane. That includes immediate police assistance, should any..." He looked fearlessly back at the others, fixing his eyes on theirs. "Accidents occur here."

She nodded. "You have my word, and the word of the Supreme Court Justices of the United States." she said. "And when can we expect the gate to be um, fixed?"

The bearded man and the woman in red began to argue with the tanned man again. That time, he was the one who ended the squabble. "We will have it open tomorrow, along with your weapons. Please know that the church leaders did not sanction the construction or proliferation of any 3D printed weapons. We'll make sure they are safely in your hands as soon as possible."

The Judge looked from him to Mark. "Good." she said. "I'm glad all of this has been settled. For a moment I was concerned that this might turn into another Provo, but I'm pleased that it hasn't." She looked at the leaders. "You might want to consider letting your people choose their own negotiators more often." She turned around, and walked to the CAV. One of the police officers opened a door for her, and she got in. As she left, the police followed, giving her an escort through the city. Less than a minute later, the judge and her entourage were gone, except for the armored drone. Then, as if to demonstrate its capabilities, the M.A.K.D. shot straight up into the sky without a sound, and vanished into the clouds. A purposeful tactic no doubt, meant to make them wonder where it was going, if anywhere at all. The mayor, whose presence had hardly been felt throughout the entire meeting, looked up at the three church leaders. "I'll call you tonight!" He then looked around to see if anyone was left outside of the wall that may have witnessed the brief interaction, and walked a short distance down the street to another vehicle that was waiting for him.

The three leaders turned their eyes once again toward Jerry and Mark, and started to walk down the steps on the north side of the gate. Mark motioned for Jerry to go back down the same way they had gone up. When they reached ground level, the tan man walked around the partially filled pit to meet them, the twenty or so men and women that had almost pushed them up the stairs still very much on their side by the smiles and encouraging words that they gave to Mark upon their return.

Walking right up to Mark, the well-dressed leader pushed out his chest, and talked down to him. "My name is Edwin Alstead. I don't know who you think you are, but you had no right to give up our defenses-"

Mark butted in, "Are you saying you don't have any 3D printers here? Or that you can't simply have more made out there, that you can bring in later?" He pointed at the gate. "She gave you a break just now! She could have come in here today and taken everything you have! Give her the guns, and make more if you're so worried about losing your precious lives!"

Alstead, who upon closer examination was wearing the most expensive suit Jerry had ever seen in person, stood dumbstruck at Mark's astute observation. He looked at Mark with no small amount of astonishment, as did the rest of the crowd, though for completely different reasons. Mark stormed off, leaving those behind to wonder why he was angry, while Alstead contemplated why a lowly person of such short stature would ever want to interrupt anything someone like himself would have to say. Guessing that no one there had ever seen someone speak to one of their leaders in such a manner, Jerry, not knowing what else to do, turned to the crowd and said, "We won!" The people started to cheer, their smiles, and the pats returning. In the ensuing commotion, Jerry then turned to face the three leaders, who by then were looking at him with no small amount of disdain. He gave them a quick bow and ran to catch up with Mark.

*For if I do this of my own will, I have a reward. But if not of my own will, I have
a stewardship entrusted to me. What then is my reward? That when I preach the
Good News, I may present the Good News of Christ without charge, so as not to
abuse my authority in the Good News.***-1 Corinthians, 9:17-18**

Chapter Eighteen

Christian Territory, North of the Main Gate
Spokane, WA
Saturday, March 26[th,] 9:43AM PST

W hen Jerry reached Mark he'd half expected him to still be
angry, but he wasn't. In fact he appeared perfectly calm, tranquil
even. He was walking slowly, taking in the natural sights and
sounds that were all around them, and breathing in the cool
morning air. Together, they headed along the side of a street that
ran up a hill in the opposite direction of Levi's place. Without his
Omni-Glass to guide him, Jerry wasn't sure exactly which direction
they were going in, but supposed that it must have been the way to
the picnic that Mark had mentioned earlier.

"Interesting group of people," Jerry said, his jog turning to a
walk as he caught up to Mark. There was a small amount of
sarcasm in his voice. "That judge, she seemed *really* nice."

Mark looked at Jerry briefly then shifted his attention to the
tree branches that hung over the sides of the street they were on. A
look of concentration was on his face, as if he were quietly
contemplating something. Still walking, he turned to Jerry. "Tell
me about yourself, Jerry." he said, "I'd like to know more about
you. Where are you from?"

"So now you're asking me the same questions you've been
dodging since yesterday? I asked you first."

Mark looked forward, pressed his lips together and nodded,
"Fair enough. Not much to tell though."

"Why's that?" Jerry asked.

Mark took a deep breath. "Well, I'm originally from Missouri. I got married down there a long time ago to a great woman. We did a lot of ministry, some of it in Seattle, some as far away as New York. We even spent a few years doing missionary work overseas." He looked at Jerry. "Then, she died of cancer." Jerry raised his eyebrows. Seeing that Jerry was looking at him from the corner of his eye, he looked back, "No, it was nothing like that," Mark said. "We believed God made doctors for a reason. No, it was a rare form of lymphoma. The kind they haven't been able to find a cure for yet. It was brought on by a genetic defect she'd had issues with her whole life. We thought the worst was over, but it wasn't. We tried everything..." His face became solemn for a moment, then the smile returned, but not as easily. "I'm sorry. I meant to say that the Lord took her home."

Jerry forced himself to put on a more serious face. "I'm sorry," he said. "What was her name?"

"Angela, Angie, we called her, and there's no need to be sorry, she's in a much better place than we are."

"Did you have any kids?"

"Kids? No. After she passed, I moved to the northeast to be closer to family for a while. My sisters both moved there when I was young. I went because I was trying to find out what God wanted me to do next."

"And?" Jerry asked.

"He led me many places. To others, I suppose the path I took after that might look jagged and haphazard, but to me, it was very straight and narrow. Eventually, it led me to that gate behind us."

"Sounds to me like your life is a lot more interesting than you're letting on. I got the feeling you knew that guy at the gate, the one with the cane I mean."

"Who? Oh him, yeah, he looked pretty angry, didn't he?" Mark looked at the ground and put his hands in his pockets. In front of his path, a rock was sitting on the pavement. He kicked it to the side of the road, reuniting it with the rest of the gravel. "What about you? You've heard my story, what about yours? Let's hear it."

Jerry pressed his own lips together and let out a deep breath through his nose. "Well, I grew up near Puyallup, south of the city."

"Oh," Mark said. "Who did you lose?"

"My folks," Jerry said. He nodded. "I was an only child. It happened as we were leaving school. Going home on the bus."

"But you made it out."

"Just barely, some of us got to the Sound, and we thought that one of the ferries was gonna pick us up, but..."

"The tsunami came into the sound."

Jerry nodded. "A rescue helicopter had just arrived. We were the only ones it picked up, just before the wave hit, left a lot of people behind. Excuse me if all of this God stuff doesn't excite me too much."

"I get it," Mark said. "You should know that I was an atheist before I was a Christian. There are times I still don't understand God myself. Do you miss them? Your parents, I mean."

"Not really to be honest. My mother was a lawyer who worked out of a firm on the northern end of Tacoma, my dad was an executive for a telecommunications corporation with offices in Fife. They were always working. A housekeeper took care of me until I was in seventh grade. I found out later that both of them were less than a mile away from me in my mom's car when they were swept out to sea. The only good times I remember having with them are from a few vacations we took in Florida in the winter during the holidays. We spent a lot of time on the beach looking for sand dollars and shark teeth for fun. When I was home, I spent a lot of time playing games online with friends from school, all of that ended too. After everything happened, I was adopted by a foster family in Bellevue. They were pretty well off, nice people. They helped me with college even after I moved out when I turned eighteen a few years later. Been on my own ever since, now I do freelance work for an online newspaper and some smaller organizations around the city."

"So, you're a writer," Mark said. "So you never got married then?"

Jerry's face twisted, giving Mark a clear indication of what he thought about the idea. "No one gets married anymore, Mark. It's stupid to be married these days, no offense."

"None taken," Mark said.

"There is a girl, her name's Noel. Sometimes we get along, sometimes we don't. Even though I don't believe in marriage per se, I am a one woman guy most of the time. I'm not into the screw everything and everyone you see scene. Unfortunately, she is. She wasn't always that way, but she is now."

"That sucks." Mark said.

"I broke up with her Thursday night. Both of us were probably a little drunk at the time, though. I'm not sure what to do about it right now, if anything. I don't want to go back to her..."

"But, you love her."

"Yeah," Jerry said, "Yeah."

"Even though we may not be surrounded by friends right now, there is a reason that you are here, Jerry. There's a reason for everything." Mark said.

"Normally, I'd talk to her several times a day using my Omni-Glass. I miss my Omni-Glass."

"Why don't you have it with you now?"

"I uh, forgot it at home."

"Back in Seattle?"

"Yeah."

"I've never used one of those things. I saw the glasses once. I've always wondered, how can you hear what someone is saying through something that you put in your eye?"

"Well," Jerry said. "They have a few different options. It can sync to your glasses, which have speakers in their arms, or you can sync it to an earpiece. I chose option three, though."

"What's that?"

"I have a chip attached to my skull behind my right eye. It uses my head as a speaker and takes customized commands, so long as I focus my thoughts well enough. It works by monitoring my brain functions and predicting what I want by...well, you get the idea."

"Sounds expensive."

"It was. But with it, I can store what I capture with the lens locally without having to depend on a network or some company's server. It comes in handy when I'm doing work off the grid. I still need the lens to record with though, and when I'm on the grid signals from the lens can sometimes be traced, even if hacks are employed to conceal the user's identity."

"Do you ever pick up any other signals?" Mark said. "Like hear extra stuff in your head because of the chip?"

"Nope, no voices in my head yet. Speaking of voices, does God ever talk to you that way?"

"Ha!" Mark let out one of his boisterous laughs. He was back to his normal self again. "No. Not in my head anyway. I have felt His presence in my spirit, though." He hit his chest with his right fist. "Right here. It's almost exactly like words, no, more than that, like knowledge and purpose mixed with a compassionate urgency that's hard to describe, yet it's also peaceful, warm, and reassuring all at the same time. It usually comes to me while I am praying or reading His Word like a still, quiet voice. It comes at other times too, when my heart is intent on doing His will. With experience and understanding it can be quite specific, especially when certain spiritual gifts are operating. I've heard of Christians who say they hear a literal voice, but I've never heard one myself, at least not yet. I'm glad for it, though."

"Why?" Jerry said.

"When the Holy Spirit speaks to me, it not only brings peace, but a kind of personal instruction that is hard to put into words, and it comes with perfect timing, timing that matches what God is doing in the world around me even when I don't fully know or understand the bigger picture in a given situation. That part is really important, because moving in obedience in God's timing and not your own can determine how successful a ministry is. I'd rather have all of that, than someone calmly telling me about those things in my head. It's like I *experience* Him instead. Anyway, I don't need tech to get through my day. I have the Holy Spirit and my Father's Word. They sustain and guide me." He paused, and looked down at the ground for a moment. "In a way, it's better than any tech I could have on my person to tell you the truth. He tells me everything I need to know, right when I need it most. God is good."

"So, that's how God speaks to you." Jerry said.

"There are a few other ways too, signs that have Biblical meaning and show up in my path as I follow Him sometimes. There are also some ways that He uses to speak to everyone, including unbelievers, but most of them are just too blind to see them or just chalk them up to coincidence, even when they start piling up to the point where they shouldn't be ignored. There are also visions and dreams, but I've only had a couple of those in my life that were from God, at least in retrospect it seems like they were anyway."

"Has he spoken to you recently? Has he told you anything about me?"

"I am not some lab rat to be poked and prodded Jerry. Nor am I a medium or soothsayer that can read your fortune by communicating with demons who, posing as spirit guides that speak to dead loved ones, conveniently confirm people's biases in an attempt to manipulate them to their own destruction. If you want to know what I am experiencing, keep reading the Bible, and pray for God to reveal it to you. I can say that God usually only tells me enough to fulfill the latest mission He has for me before guiding me to the next one. Sometimes, He gives me a word or two to speak to others while witnessing or ministering to them for confirmation or encouragement, and over the years I've had a few visions of things to come, or of the Kingdom that I will one day live in under my Lord, but that's all, no great new revelations for anyone, just the work He has made for me to do, always with the same goal, leading others to His Word and to relationship with Him."

"How can you be sure it's not a relationship with you that you're promoting?"

"That's easy. I'm never around long enough to enjoy such a thing. God is always moving me to the next place just as the fruit is coming. To be honest, I don't think I would even know what that would look like, at least for me."

A bike trail crossed the road in front of them marked by a large bright orange sign. Mark walked onto it, to the west. "Come on," he said, "Let's take a detour."

They walked up the trail for a while. Many of the trees there were just starting to bud, a reminder that the local flora were in their season of renewal. A few were already covered in growth, while others had nothing on them at all. Jerry wondered if a few of those trees were dead. Squirrels and field mice that were almost too fast for Jerry to spot, scurried through and around them. One ran across Jerry's path, almost causing him to accidentally step on it.

"Little devils," Mark said.

After a few minutes of enjoying the sounds of spring birds and the crackling of leaves underfoot, Jerry broke the silence. "So, you're not much for new technology then."

"I don't think of myself as a Luddite, but I do believe there is more meaning to words and actions when they are experienced more directly, sometimes the most meaningful human exchanges happen without any words at all. People can see if a person genuinely cares about them, if they're able to interact with them in person. I've lived in the digital age for a while now, it's almost like people who partake in it are participating in the deconstruction of their own hearts, while presuming the worst of others."

"Well, I'm not sure what a 'Luddite' is, but are you sure you're not just overreacting? Maybe even being a little paranoid?" Jerry asked. "I mean yeah, we're always being spied on through technology, and it is pretty impersonal, but who cares? I think it's all about how you decide to use it."

"True enough..." Mark said, "I do think that today's technology really has separated people from one another, though. Meaningful relationships simply cannot be made through technology alone, they just can't. You only truly know someone after spending time with them face to face, kind of like we are doing now. This is how God works. We are meant to seek His face in a personal relationship. It's how He meant for us to work with each other too."

"Even with all of the diseases going around these days?"

"Well, when something breaks out, of course, people should hold off visiting one another for a while, but sickness and disease shouldn't be used as an excuse to separate ourselves from the rest of the world indefinitely."

"You're crazy." Jerry said.

Mark didn't miss a beat with his response, "The Bible says that's what you'd call me."

They chuckled again as Jerry shook his head. "So you're not Catholic, and you're not one of these prosperity Christians. You haven't told me which group you belong to yet."

"Well," Mark said. "I was saved, or I should say I had an experience with God, when I was in my early twenties in a nondenominational Christian church. The Christians there basically believed that God's people live under a covenant of grace. They focused on the New Testament, and worked hard to understand Christ's teachings and to follow them. They didn't believe in what's called 'works righteousness,' that is the idea that doing things a certain way can give someone more favor with God than the next guy. They believed in the power of the Holy Spirit, and that God forgives, and does not take away His plans for us just because we stumble and fall or screw up sometimes. In regard to wealth, that means if He wants us to be wealthy, He will direct us that way, and give us those opportunities. If He doesn't, then there is a reason for it, like missionary work, humbly serving in a specific church in some capacity, or maybe just witnessing to those who don't have much, and refuse to listen to those who do."

He put his hands on his hips as they continued. "We *don't* believe that Christians can buy their way into favor with God, or twist God's arm to get what they want, when they want it. Paul teaches us to be content in all things, and Christ said more than once not to pursue or worry about such things. God isn't a fast food joint that gives you what you want right then and there, at least not most of the time anyway. Sometimes, maybe in an emergency when we pray for something according to His will, but usually, He uses our needs and wants to pull us closer to Him. As a wise pastor once told me, the Lord never does anything without having a multitude of reasons for it, and immediate gratification is never one of them."

Jerry pointed at Mark with his right index finger. His next words were sharp and pithy. "That's *your* truth."

"The same pastor told me that 'truth comes to its own conclusions' Jerry. When Jesus comes back, He'll be coming back for all of us. Then He will be everyone's truth, and everything that comes with Him."

"This pastor sounds like an interesting guy. What's his name?"

"Sebastian. He does homeless ministry out of the Bronx in New York City, or at least he used to. I haven't spoken to him in years. He was the one who taught me about spiritual gifts. If you're interested in seeing God do some truly amazing things, he might be someone to seek out. But before you go down that road though, you should know that God wants *you*, not what you think you can offer Him. That and...well, be prepared."

"What do you mean?"

"Well, Sebastian...he isn't exactly the easiest guy to get along with."

"I thought the more spiritual Christians were supposed to be kind hearted and patient with people and all that."

"Oh he is, he really does care about people, and can be a very tender guy when doing ministry. He just dwells on things, negative things he sees in the world a little too much sometimes. You see, it's the fact that he cares *so* much, that makes him hard to deal with or even talk to. Some Christians are like that. They are in God's will, but when they see evil in the world, a righteous anger can come over them, one that they have to learn to control, just as the rest of us have to learn to control our vices. In Sebastian's case, it might be *that* very thing that keeps him going. He is always praying for the needs of others and for God to fix His church. Heck, I wouldn't be surprised if God were using me to answer some of his prayers. Sorry, I shouldn't be talking about him like this, especially to you. He really is a man of God. My wife and I learned a lot about doing ministry from him."

The trail reached the other side of the patch of woods they had been walking through, and came out along the side of another street. Up ahead, they saw a large parking lot next to a large white dome-shaped structure, and two smaller rectangular buildings, one of which was clearly reserved for office space, and the other for maintenance by the industrial sized lawnmower and other lawn maintenance equipment that could be seen strewn across the turf in front of it. Several people were milling around the entrance to the dome. The building looked relatively new, and had several banners hanging on and around its exterior. A large sign near the road read 'Victory Center'.

"Huh." Mark said.

"What is it?" Jerry asked.

Mark looked at him again. "Follow me. Don't talk to anyone, just watch and listen."

They walked toward the parking lot, the smell of freshly laid tar filling the air around them. It was as wide as a football field, and there weren't any parking pylons in the section that they crossed, as they were yet to be painted. Turning toward the building, they passed a group of teenagers that were huddled together in a circle. As they walked by, Jerry noticed that each of them was holding some kind of device that was the size of a smart-ID card and just as thin. They appeared to be playing a game together, the cards connected by a wireless signal. None of them even seemed aware of the jamming signal that should have been interrupting their gaming session. One of them looked up at Jerry's inquisitive stare and nodded. Jerry nodded back with a perplexed look on his face.

Near the entrance, Jerry noticed that upon the banners were pictures of a couple. The man they had kind of met at the gate, with the overly expensive suit was depicted on each one, standing next to a beautiful blonde woman with the name of the church printed vertically in large purple letters to one side. Both of them were smiling wide, and were so happy and larger than life, that Jerry found the whole display both extremely obnoxious and more than a little intimidating at the same time. *Is this supposed to be a church, or some kind of personality cult?* Jerry asked himself. They walked in through the main entrance and into a tall and rounded hall that must have been thirty yards across. In the center was an unmanned, circular information desk. A kiosk, specifically meant for giving donations, stood to one side of it. On the right side of the hall were three doors for the bathroomsa and another with a plaque on it that said 'Maintenance'. On the left side were two small meeting rooms, and straight ahead, two open double doors led into a dark auditorium.

As they approached the open doorway, an attractive young woman came out, wearing a dark green pantsuit and high heels. She seemed agitated and was walking with a purpose, looking past the two of them as if they weren't even there, while she talked to someone through yet another strange device Jerry had never seen before. It consisted of a single orange lens that covered her left eye, and seemed to be attached somehow to her left temple. It was obviously some kind of augmented reality headset. As she drew closer on her way out of the building, Jerry caught some of what she was saying. "Yeah, show me- right, that's the one, let's get those printed out right away- No, what are you- well, we need them by tomorrow, Rick!"

Mark didn't look at her, nor did he stop walking, or even slow down. He led Jerry through the doors and into a grand sanctuary that was capable of accommodating up to ten thousand people. What shocked Jerry the most however, was the color scheme that they had chosen to go with, the entire space was painted in black. Black seats, ceilings, floor, even the stage was dark as night with a pitch backdrop. *Kind of odd for people who promote life, or are they all former theatre majors putting on a show?* Mark turned right as soon as they went in, staying close to the wall at the back of the auditorium. He continued at the same pace around its edge, toward another set of open doors on the far side of the enormous space. On the stage, a group of well-lit young people were standing and playing music that didn't actually sound that bad to Jerry's ears. The song they were practicing had a warm melody and a good beat. It was a hopeful kind of tune, a type of music that was uncommon in the popular culture of his day.

"STOP!" Jerry heard a shrill cry from the right side of the stage. The woman from the banner was standing there live and in person, wearing an all-white outfit that looked like it was entirely made out of leather. She walked out from behind a dark curtain, and placed two angry fists on her hips. "You're screwing it up!" she yelled. "At our last show, we didn't get enough people coming to the altar!" She motioned to the seats with her left hand, shaking it as she yelled, "How are they supposed to come down when they can't stand the sound!" She turned around and looked at a man who was standing just off stage behind her. "Joe, it's your job to make sure we get enough people coming down to the front, and I don't care if some of them are confused as to whether or not they are coming up for salvation or just for prayer, we need all of them to go to the meeting rooms out front, so they look like they are getting saved, understand? Once we're up and running, we're going to be on every screen in this city, and we need to get as many people as we can to come here. This isn't cheap! I want you all to participate in passing around the collection buckets during the service too. There's no reason to be lazy, we have plenty of them. We'll do one before the service begins, one after the worship, and one when my husband asks for other offerings. Same as in Seattle, got it?" Like a small collection of bobblehead dolls, everyone on the stage nodded repeatedly in her direction, and she stormed off the stage in a huff as if she were hurrying off to somewhere more important.

The strange display didn't make Mark so much as even flinch, or cause him to stray even an inch from the track he had set them on. A moment later, and they were back out of the dark room and in another reception area in the eastern wing of the building. To their right was a small book store, Jerry could see someone inside, putting on the shelves what looked like several different types of Bibles and other Christian books. In front of it was a giant cut out of the same man he saw on the gate, and on the banners at the entrance, this time he was holding a book in his hands. The title: 'Well, excuse me for wanting more! Ten tips on how God can help you transform your finances and make your name known by Edwin Alstead'. *Alstead,* Jerry thought. *Must be Henry's son. So the whole family is corrupt, go figure.*

Next to the exit on their left was another open entrance. As they walked by that one, Jerry saw two young men just inside, shoving what looked like a bunch of fake play money into a black duffle bag. "We have to make it so that it opens when you pull the fishing line, that way, it will drop on the kids when we explain that God *can* be like an ATM machine sometimes, get it?" The other boy nodded. Hearing their footsteps, the boys stopped what they were doing and looked up at Jerry and Mark as they went by and smiled. Jerry gave another silent nod, and continued to follow Mark through a final set of double doors that led into a different section of the parking lot, on the opposite end of the building from where they'd entered.

"So, the guy on the wall was Henry Alstead's son?" Jerry sped up a little, and moved next to Mark as they left the parking lot and stepped onto an adjacent street heading north. "I didn't see a cross. Isn't there supposed to be a cross somewhere to remind people of how the Christian God sacrificed His Son for the world or something? What the hell did I just see in there?"

"Exactly what God wanted to show you," Mark said. "The Lord knows I got tired of being around places like that years ago." He looked ahead again, and pointed north. "I think the park where the picnic is happening is this way." He started crossing the street, Jerry followed.

"Do you know those people?"

"Know them? No, not really. My wife and I did have an unfortunate run in with members of his father's church when we worked with a homeless ministry in Seattle. They tried to discourage us from helping out a group of homeless people that had set up tents not far from their building there. They said that we were only facilitating their poverty, and encouraging bad behavior or something like that. In the end, we did our best to avoid them altogether."

"Are most churches like that one?"

"That?" Mark said, "Lord, no. Praise be to God!" Most churches are genuinely full of good, decent, and forgiving people. They've learned their lessons from the self-serving materialistic ways of the past that always lead to jealousy and division. There are some, though, that are still too judgmental or fearful, and some that think they are better than others, but such places are few and far between. Most churches have humble people in them, who want to know God personally and live to serve and love others. Unfortunately, you do have to be careful when picking a church these days. Churches, just like people, can go through seasons of good and bad times. It can take some serious resilience to go through the bad if God has called for someone to stay in such a place. You also have to watch out for churches that compromise the Bible to get people in the seats."

"How could they have such a lack of self-awareness?" Jerry asked. "Even I know the Bible isn't a self-help book for making money."

"Some of them think it is," Mark said, "Prosperity Christianity shouldn't be a surprise to anyone living under a Capitalist system. Capitalism itself is not at fault. Having traveled to other countries, I've seen firsthand how it's brought millions out of extreme poverty. But it's common for people to come to church with all kinds of ideas from whatever system they live in day to day, that can twist the Word of God into something other than it was meant to be." Mark walked to the edge of the street and stopped. He knelt down and picked up a handful of small rocks.

"For example," he said, "Some people think the Bible is a Socialist book, or that Christians are all meant to be poor, but God's plan does not follow human constructs and ideals like these. He doesn't think like us according to Isaiah fifty-five, and he doesn't give as we give according to John, chapter fourteen." He let the stones fall through his fingers until only one remained. "His plans for us are individual plans that are greater than any we could come up with without Him. We are witnesses who partake in His Spirit, and God adds or removes material things from us based on *His* plans, not ours. Christians can and should ask Him for help when they have specific needs, but they should also be ready for any circumstance." He dropped the stone and started to walk again, more briskly, brushing the dirt off on his jeans as he went. Jerry kept pace.

"Paul wrote to the Philippians that when the Spirit of God is with us, we can learn to live in any situation, finding contentment in the peace of God both in times of prosperity *and* poverty. You see, having Christ in one's heart means that a person can transcend the wants and needs of this physical existence and all of the worries and concerns that go along with it, while still participating in it as God wills for us to. Many people ignore this though, because walking such a path is not natural to their flesh. Our tendencies differ, depending on the culture in which we are raised. Unfortunately, many believers assume God wants to give them the same things He has given others around them. Believers who think this way are drawn to churches like that one. They often end up proudly wasting their lives on their own desires, only to discover too late that God really wanted them to focus on Him, and Him alone. That He wanted their hearts, so that they could have been free to follow Him where He wanted them to go, to accomplish the work He specifically made for them to do. They head down the wider path, eventually ending up in places they shouldn't be, where people tickle their ears, only telling them the easy things, what they want to hear. In the end, they simply suffer from a case of just wanting to fit in."

"I think that happens to non-Christians as well." Jerry said.

Mark looked down and thought for a moment. "Of course, it does." he said. "But not in the same way. Going down the wide path after knowing God's grace can be a dangerous thing to one's soul, a very dangerous thing. God can allow people's minds to become deluded according to scripture, or to even become strongholds for the enemy in the midst of a congregation. Like a social time bomb waiting to go off, so that it destroys the faith of others. That's how the enemy can destroy a good church if people are not diligent in their prayer lives."

"So you're saying that God's ways are not like the ways of men and women, and it can take a lifetime to figure this out even for those who do their best to follow God?"

"Yes, exactly, especially when one's identity or measure of self-importance comes from what they do with their flesh, or how they feel they need to be seen by others."

"Ok. One thing, though."

"What's that?"

"You said it's alright to ask for things when you need them, and God will give them to you *if* you really do, not just because you want something really bad, at least that's what I think you meant."

"Well, He can do that too, but sometimes the answer is no, especially when the thing we want is not in His will, or is asked for with the wrong intentions or for reasons that are ungodly."

"So that means you are serving a God, for your whole life that is basically using you to accomplish *His* goals. I understand that it's easier to do when you have His Spirit with you, but why would you do such a thing in the first place? Why go through so much trouble for a God who doesn't give you what you want most of the time?"

"Because He is real, He's God, and one day He's coming back. Those who do their best to serve and obey His commandments, no matter what they went through while they were here, will be rewarded greatly in the everlasting Kingdom that is coming, and they will be with Him in that perfect Kingdom forever. That is the true hope and the true reward, not the junk we pile up while we're here. By *not* choosing to follow God, and instead attaching ourselves to things, experiences, and ideas here that are temporary, humans actually hurt themselves in the end. Our pain is not God's fault. It is our own, because most people refuse to see the truth behind the world that they are living in. Those who have exchanged the truth for a sad counterfeit will eventually be let down by it, no matter how much they try to avoid or ignore it."

Jerry became quiet. He thought about Noel, and all of the things he wanted to do and see when he was younger that never came to pass. He thought about how angry he was for never having gotten a chance to know his parents as he grew older, remembering the times when he blamed a God he claimed to not even believe in for their loss. "Maybe you're right." he said to Mark. "It would certainly explain a lot in my life, who knows?"

Mark laughed. "I do," he said. "And I thank God every day for it, because He didn't need to show such things to a wretch like me."

Jerry smiled at this. He enjoyed listening to Mark. There was an unusual juxtaposition in how he spoke, like he was a bit of a know-it-all, but at the same time was humble in his own way.

Mark looked off into the distance again. Jerry had begun to recognize the look Mark had in his eyes whenever he'd found something he was searching for. He looked in the same direction, and saw a large sign near a clearing. Not far behind it, hundreds of people were walking around what appeared to be a giant cross that stood next to a large bouncy house that was moving slightly from side to side.

"That's it." They both said.

****

After walking another quarter of a mile down the road, they reached the clearing. The giant cross they had seen in the distance turned out to be something entirely different than what they had assumed it to be, the automated brick layer. Essentially it was a 3D printer on eighteen wheels, each one taller than the average man in height. It was the largest industrial replicator Jerry had ever seen up close, its two long distribution arms stretched out on either side, as if it had been intentionally left in the pose while awaiting a new set of instructions now that the wall had been completed.

At first, Jerry thought the grassy area surrounding the great machine was part of a park that had been established long before the new inhabitants had moved in, but then he saw a random collection of tree stumps scattered along a small forested area that was behind it. A newly laid gravel path also came into focus, starting from the side of the road they were on and winding like a snake toward the center of the area. On their way toward the path's entrance, they passed by five large white cargo containers. One of them was open, and a group of men were taking what looked like solar panels out of it, still in their packaging. *I'd be willing to bet they've got an AIR-LEV solid state battery in one of those containers to store excess energy too.* Jerry thought. Looking down at the spot where the path met the sidewalk, Jerry noticed that hundreds of little orange flags lined both sides of the windy pathway. He guessed it was because those responsible for its creation were close to covering it with tar or concrete.

Beside the path's entrance were two signs, one large and one small that had been placed parallel to the street, so that they hadn't been able to see what was on them during their approach. The larger of the two was held up by four large wooden posts, and showed a picture of a modern building with sleek lines and large windows. It reminded him more of an airport terminal than a spiritual center. It was tall too, if the trees on either side of the portrayal were any indication of size. Beneath the image in large white letters, the sign read 'Foundation Temple Site' at the top, and 'A congregating place for all who live in the New Christian Territory'. At the very bottom of the sign, Jerry saw what appeared to be the names of the Foundation leaders who were a part of the project. Mark had already started down the path on his own, giving Jerry a moment to take out his notebook so that he could jot the names down without being noticed.

The smaller sign was held up by a thin wire frame, causing it to sway slightly in the wind. It said, 'Celebrate the completion of our walls! All are welcome, bring your kids!' Jerry took a moment to look around after reading it. He saw lots of children running around the bouncy house enjoying themselves, and some teenagers playing Frisbee football in the nearby field. There looked to be a garden area and a small greenhouse, where some people were walking around and looking at the different plants that were being grown there. In the middle distance, a large crowd of people stood near some tables that were set up in front of a small, single level structure, and on the other end of the clearing, he could see a smaller group looking down at some formation on the ground that Jerry supposed was the spot where the foundation for the Temple had been laid.

After recording the names, Jerry returned the notebook to his back pocket, and walked swiftly down the unfinished pathway. A few seconds later he was at Mark's side again, some twenty or so yards in from the street. Farther in, bright and beautiful flowers of all types lined the path on either side of the rocky walkway several rows deep, their brilliant colors were hard to ignore, as all of them were fully open, welcoming the sun. Eventually, they reached a circular causeway in the center. It was surrounded by thick grass and even more flowers. They walked through the large crowd of people there. Jerry was surprised to see how diverse it was. Every nationality and class, judging by their clothing, were represented. A few of the more well to do looking people there recognized Mark from the gate. They pointed at him and started talking to others nearby, spreading the news that he was among them. The talk made Jerry nervous, as he still didn't know exactly what the average Territory resident was capable of should they suddenly find themselves unwelcome. *They don't seem to be afraid of getting germs from one another here that's for sure, not one mask or pair of slap-goggles in sight.* He thought.

On their way by one of the tables, the smells of freshly cooked bar-b-q ribs, spicy wings, and hot dogs entered Jerry's nostrils, smells he hadn't experienced for years. He looked at the table closest to him. On it, a massive amount of well prepared food had been put out for any who wanted it. Distracted, he lost his train of thought and made a b-line to the table. As thankful as he was for the two pancakes that Levi had made him that morning, all of the walking had made him hungry again. He grabbed a plate and some napkins, and was loading up with a little of everything when he accidentally bumped into someone.

He turned around to apologize, only to see that it was a stunningly beautiful woman who was about his own age. She was also about the same height as he was, had bright, naturally curling red hair that just covered her shoulders, and was wearing a light blue and white summer dress. Freckles adorned her face, and there was a sultry manner in the way that she moved, that when combined with the sly smile she gave him, almost caused Jerry to spill his food onto the ground.

"Himph," Jerry realized he had half of a chicken wing in his mouth. He took it out without missing a beat, "Hi!" he said. He hadn't felt so nervous around someone since before he'd graduated high school. "Uh, sorry, I-I wasn't..."

She opened her mouth part way, ready to speak as Jerry fumbled with his plate, still smiling. "That's ok." She finally let out. She had a cute southern drawl that made Jerry feel even more uncomfortable than he already did. She straightened up and put out her right hand, fast and sure. "I'm Maribelle." she said.

After a bit of fumbling, Jerry put his plate down on the table and quickly used one of the napkins to wipe off the bar-b-q sauce that was on his right hand. At first, he resisted the idea of shaking her hand as was his normal reaction with everyone else, but seeing how attractive she was, he decided to make an exception and reciprocated the gesture, grasping her fingers in a confident grip. "Uh, Jerry," he said, "Maribelle, huh? I've never heard that one."

"My parents are a little old fashioned I guess." she said. She let go of his hand, placed her arms behind her back, and started to twist from her hips up, so that her torso moved side to side, one shoulder moving forward and then the other, her pale green eyes gazing unabashedly straight into his own. Jerry was nearly hypnotized by the sight.

"Uh yeah, it, well, I think it's a nice name." he said. "Um, so are you new here? Did you move here with your family?"

"Me?" she said. "No. I mean, I know some people here from my old church, but I'm just checking the place out right now. Thinking about renting a room from some folks for a while."

"So, you're not from one of the churches that set up this whole thing?"

"No." She giggled a little and shook her head. "To tell the truth, I'm just lookin' for somewhere to get closer to Lord while I write. I write Christian short stories and make materials for churches around the country. I can work from just about anywhere."

"That's great." Jerry said. "I'm a writer too. So uh, why did you choose this place?"

"Oh," She tried to look serious for a moment, but Jerry could tell that serious for her was a foreign concept, a thought that made him like her even more. "I used to live in Atlanta, I loved being in the city. I was raised in the countryside, you see. Couldn't get off the farm fast enough, let me tell you! But a few years ago, things started changing down there."

"You mean the tax riots? Didn't they up the price of food imports and stop people from buying from the piers or something?"

"Yes, but that wasn't it. It was those miniature drones, you know the ones that look kind of like insects, and are almost as small. A couple of years ago, I noticed they were following me around. I thought I was going crazy!" She reached out and hit Jerry's left shoulder with her right hand playfully, startling him. He returned the odd gesture with a nervous smile, unsure what to expect from her next. "But then they started showing up at my house and at work just outside my window! Finally, I was eating breakfast one morning, and I noticed what looked like a fly on my kitchen table, so I hit it. It wasn't a fly! Turns out somebody was streaming me all over the internet for a couple of days!" Her voice hit a high pitch as she said the last part. "Well, at the time, I was thinking about starting my own business anyway, and a friend from another church told me about this place. They said when everything is set up, no drones would be able to fly anywhere inside the walls. So I decided to check it out."

Another person wearing an orange lens over one eye passed them on their way to get some food. "Hey," Jerry said. "I'm new here too. Maybe you can help me with something, what's with the cards and the orange...uh," Jerry used his hand to mime a patch over his left eye. She gave him a confused look, and then looked around at the others so she could see what he was talking about.

Almost immediately, her eyes widened. "OH! You mean the Elisha monocles."

"Elisha?" he asked.

"Yeah, you know..." She looked at him expectantly, waiting for the name to ring a bell, raising her eyebrows in anticipation. Not getting a response other than Jerry's blank stare, she continued slowly, "The prophet in the Old Testament that saw chariots take Elijah, his mentor to heaven..."

Remembering how Levi had responded to his own forgetfulness earlier that morning, Jerry smacked himself on the forehead. "Duh, of course." he said to her. "I've never seen anything like them. It looks like they're using them to communicate, how does that work with the jamming signal?"

"My friend told me they work on a different kind of signal, one that they used to use in really old submarines or something." she said. An entire side of her face curled upward, revealing how unsure she was about the subject. "You can stick the monocles right to the side of your head, they use the same micro-cling stuff that they have for those new pierceless earrings, the ones they based on gecko fingers." She leaned back, comically raised her hands up, and moved her fingers wildly before lowering them again. "The card looking thingies are just like the old smartphones, just smaller and made of that clear aluminum stuff. They print them out right here in the Territory. I know they can use them to talk, message, and vid-chat each other, but they told me they won't work outside the area, and can't pick up normal signals from out there either. I don't mind, I don't even want one. I had enough of that stuff in Atlanta. I think I was an addict." She giggled. "I'm going to quit cold turkey." She looked upward, crinkled her nose and raised a finger to her chin, "What do you think that means, 'cold turkey'?"

Not sure how to respond, Jerry just smiled in her direction and took in the moment. She reached down, grabbed a celery stick from Jerry's plate, and took a bite. His eyes became transfixed on her as she did this, that is until she had moved just enough for him to notice the large number of people that were sitting down in the grass behind her in a semicircle. One man was sitting in front of them slightly above the rest. He was perched on the edge of a concrete foundation that stood a few feet off of the ground, it was Mark. Past him, on the far side of the foundation blocks, Jerry could see a small group of serious looking men beginning to gather near the tree line. They were clearly unhappy, and were looking in the direction of the growing crowd. One of them was a man in a pinstriped suit. Some of the others were talking to him, and pointing in Mark's direction. "Um, I'm sorry. What was your last name?" Jerry said to Maribelle.

"Swanson." she said.

"Uh, I would love to talk more sometime, Maribelle. Unfortunately, I have to go right now." She frowned at him, placed her hands behind her back, and started to sway from side to side again. "Maybe I'll contact you...through your website?"

"It's called Maribelle's merry posters, cards, and brochures." she said.

"Thank you, excuse me." He put down his plate and moved in Mark's direction, stopping short just behind those who were sitting down, and kept a wary eye on the men who were standing on the far side of the clearing. A few of them took notice of him, and they stopped talking to each other for a moment. Jerry then heard Mark's voice. He was in the middle of explaining something.

Keeping his eyes trained on the men near the tree line, he attempted to multitask and listen to what Mark was saying.

"It is true that like Barnabas, many in the church are meant to have wealth and be managers of it. But even his wealth had a specific purpose for the church that God used at the appropriate time." Mark said. "That was part of his role in God's plan. Christ in the New Testament tells us how the Holy Spirit will send many out as missionaries and apostles who will need to live by faith alone at times, and Paul wrote that every believer should strive to be content, no matter what situation we find ourselves in. In light of these things, to teach that all should strive to be wealthy all the time is not only irresponsible, it is dangerous. God cannot always use wealthy people to witness to the lost. They often have too many other responsibilities. Paul knew this, and he urged us to be as he was, living a simple and quiet life in pursuit of the Kingdom of God that is coming, not in pursuit of our own kingdoms. The world teaches people to live for today, Christ taught us in Matthew Six not to store up wealth on earth, because it would rust and be destroyed. He told us to store up treasure in heaven."

He pointed a finger toward the sky.

Jerry saw that some of the people sitting nearby were wearing their own monocles, or had card devices. A few were also wearing an odd kind of wrist band that projected a screen onto their hands. Many were attempting to find the information Mark was sharing with them using the devices, but none looked satisfied. A few even appeared confused, or frustrated in their search. The rest just sat there, blank stares on their faces, waiting for Mark to continue. *The signal jammer should be blocking them from accessing the internet and other systems.* Jerry thought again. *Unless they have their own signal that isn't being blocked. But how could that be? Tom said the jammer was blocking everything from coming in. Radio, LiFi, everything.* He looked around again, and noticed that others had brought physical Bibles with them and were flipping through the pages, sharing what they had found with those around them. Side conversations started, as it seemed like a few of these had noticed that what Mark was saying was indeed accurate.

Mark leaned forward, and put his hand on the shoulder of a man that was sitting close to him on his right. "God wants a personal relationship with each and every one of us. He does not want us to be consumed by the worries of this world while we are here, but to focus on spreading His love. He will take care of you as you honor and obey His will. He did not save you from your sin so that you could win a rat race. When Paul wrote about running the race for God, he wrote that it was *your* race you should be running, a spiritual race. That is why you should not compare your race to those of others around you! Everyone's race is different and is meant to be."

He stood and raised his voice so that all could hear him. "In John Fourteen, Jesus said, He knows we love Him when we do what He asks us to do. He asked us to follow Him no matter the cost, and to love one another and our enemies. Find out what He wants *you* to do. Make sure you know it's from God, and not just from a man or woman who *claims* they are from God. Confirmation in church is good, but God is also able, and willing, to confirm things with us directly."

One man yelled out, "You said not all were meant to be rich! What about Malachi, chapter three, where it says store up your wealth in the store house?"

"One verse in the Old Testament taken out of its original context, does not discount several of them in both Testaments warning about the dangers of allowing money to have a place in your heart." Mark hit his heart with a closed fist. "In Malachi's day, very few people were tithing. They were robbing from God! When your leaders take tithes from you, are you financially blessed to overflowing as they promise? Most are not. This is not God's failure, nor is it yours. It is theirs. They constantly imply without telling you directly, that you must not be giving enough, and leave you in guilt and confusion, and others in great poverty, knowing that all of you will return to buy more of their books and trinkets, looking for clues on how to have more like they do instead of going to God to find out what your real purpose is in this world, which is what they *should* have been teaching you all along! There are so many believers who have been misled in this way when they should have been learning about their spiritual gifts, so that they could serve where they were meant to serve, or go where they were meant to go, into the world to save souls!" He began to walk toward the middle of the crowd, his voice getting louder. He raised his hands as if to plead with them. "You all know that Christ said that money is the 'root of all kinds of evil' but do you also know that in Proverbs twenty-three, Solomon wrote not to weary yourself in order to gain wealth, and that Christ himself said 'you cannot serve both God and wealth' in Matthew Six? And what about the young rich man?"

The heckler yelled again. "I don't think you know what you are talking about. You talk as if you know better than everyone. Where is your fruit? I don't see a church, or even a family! Do you have one, or did God curse you for the things you say? Everyone knows that Jesus wasn't testing the young rich man, He didn't actually *want* him to give away everything he owned!" Several people started to speak up in Mark's defense. Some said that the things the man mentioned did not qualify as real blessings. Others jeered, and began to correct the heckler in regard to this 'rich young' person Mark had brought up. But it was when a few men that Jerry recognized as being some of the workers from the gate arrived, that things began to get hairy. Having heard the arguments while getting their lunch, one of them felt compelled to stand up for Mark by telling everyone about how he had miraculously defeated a man 'as big as a tree' at the gate the previous day. Yet another then went on to describe how he'd also bested the judge with his wits, potentially saving them all from a desperate situation.

Upon hearing about the judge, the arguing ceased. Those who had gathered to hear Mark speak, began looking around for their own church leaders in an effort to find out what had happened at the gate less than an hour earlier. Seeing them frantically talking among themselves, it became obvious that most of those attending the picnic had not been made privy to the Chief Justice's visit, and were not exactly pleased about how they were only then learning about what had occurred.

Not ready to give up however, Mark lifted his right hand, causing a silence to wash over the crowd. He spoke again, his voice sterner than before, "I wasn't aware that you were an Old Testament Jew tasked with setting up the stage that was Israel, on which Christ would be crucified. I thought you were a Christian, one with the Holy Spirit dwelling within him, greater than all that came before Christ's sacrifice, even greater than John the Baptist. Isn't that what Jesus said about us? All that is in the Old Testament is good for teaching like Paul said, it is true. But we are under a new covenant, one of Grace. We are not under the law, nor do we live by works alone. If we do, Christ died for nothing! We, each of us, have direct access to God through his Holy Spirit if we choose to go to Him and not to men, to see His face and hear His voice. We do not need to be slaves, giving more than our tithes to others who wear soft clothing and store up wealth for themselves in the name of Christ, who will vanish like the wind when they inevitably die or fall. What I am saying is that one cannot come into God's presence by trying to get close to someone who is only driven to make money, and does not live in God's power! To have the truly abundant life that Christ offers us, we must get close to God and God alone, through His Son who died for us. We must seek to know Him more. Good pastors are here to help us do this. Paul said, 'I have nothing, but having nothing I have everything.' Tell me brother, what do you have?"

The rebuked heckler got up and walked away. As he did, several others stood up and followed. One of them said, "This is ridiculous, you can't do anything for God if you don't have any money, everyone knows this." Another said, "I'm sorry, I didn't move all the way here to listen to this, I have a family to provide for, I'm sorry."

That's when Jerry saw that the small crowd of men on the other side of the foundation had begun to walk around it in their direction. "Hey Mark," he said, "I think it's time we get going." Mark nodded and started walking to Jerry, not realizing what was happening behind him. Several people thanked him, many of them standing up at the same time so they could shake his hand, but Jerry's eyes were only focused on the angry faces that were headed their way. He could tell by their expressions that at least a few of them had temporarily lost Mark in the crowd, as he was shorter than everyone else there. He seized the opportunity, taking Mark's hat off of his head, and grabbing for his left arm. Then, he started to lead him back in the direction they had come from toward the street. Mark gave him a slightly confused and agitated look, but played along. "Back there." Jerry said to him, looking past the people surrounding them. Mark looked back for a moment and saw the group of men who were searching for him. He shook his arm loose and followed Jerry out of the clearing, snatching his hat back out of Jerry's hand in the process.

Halfway down the gravel path, a woman who was being pushed in a wheelchair motioned to Mark with her hands saying, "Please, please sir, pray for me." A sad and defeated looking man was standing behind her. He was hunched over, breathing hard, and holding on to one of the wheelchair's handles. Mark walked over to them and kneeled next to the woman.

"Isn't there anyone at church who prays for you?" he asked.

"No." the woman said.

"Then why are you here?" He looked at them both.

"Please, just pray for me." she said again.

Mark put his hands on both of them and asked God to increase their faith, and for guidance in their lives. He prayed for their eyes to be opened and for healing to come, but nothing happened, at least not in that moment.

"Thank you," she said, grasping his hand, "I knew coming here would be a good thing, I knew it." Mark frowned and looked up to her husband, who had a look of desperation on his face. Mark hugged the man and walked away.

"Come on Jerry," he said. "Nothing more can be accomplished here today."

When they reached the street again, Mark put his hat back on. "You didn't have to do that." he said, clearly not happy with how Jerry had dragged him away from what might have escalated into a very unpleasant situation.

"I didn't do it just for you," Jerry said, still looking toward the crowd behind them to see if they had been spotted yet. He looked at the temporary meeting house, which wasn't far from where the men he was looking for had stood when he'd first seen them. He hadn't noticed it before because the bouncy house had obscured the view when they'd first arrived. As they left, it was being deflated.

"They might have kicked us both out of here, and I'm close to figuring out-" As the bouncy house continued to decrease in size, he saw a thin metal pipe, like those used to shield electrical wiring, leading from the side of the small building to an even smaller shed that stood a few yards inside the trees behind it. The shed was covered in camouflage netting and had no windows or door that Jerry could see.

"Figure out what?" Mark asked.

Jerry stopped dead in his tracks. He looked above the shed to the tree tops looming over its position. A moment later, he could see it, hidden near the top of one of the tallest pine trees. Something was there that looked like an old cell phone antenna, with diffracting pads all around it, completely surrounded by a thick layer of fir branches. There was also a long, black cable that went from tree to tree until it reached the road, finally ending at one of the telephone poles. He looked at Mark.

"That's why the satellites didn't catch it." he said. "They're using the phone lines somehow, and the trees."

"Shall the plunder be taken from the mighty, or the lawful captives be delivered? But Yahweh says, "Even the captives of the mighty shall be taken away, and the plunder retrieved from the fierce, for I will contend with him who contends with you and I will save your children." -**Isaiah, 49:24-26**

Chapter Nineteen

Denny Triangle, Downtown Area
Seattle, Washington State
Saturday, March 26[th,] 11:02AM PST

Perry stood in front of Tom's interactive table, two full holographic displays open before him as he simultaneously controlled a pair of drones over different parts of the city. He waved his hands forward and back for propulsion, turned his wrists up and down, or left and right for movement, and by using his fingers to gesture as if he were opening a jar,he was able to turn their cameras. Stopping for a moment, he opened one of his palms, and spread his fingers wide. He pushed the open hand forward and one of the displays zoomed in on a warehouse on the western side of the industrial district. Behind him, Tom sat at his desk looking into a monitor. "Thanks for coming in, Perry, this helps a lot. I've gotten pretty good at using that thing, but I could never do what you're doing."

Perry turned around for a moment. "No problem." he said. "Any chance to work with tech like this is worth risking a beating on Third Avenue. You know, you could control a fleet of drones through this interface. I could set it up for you. You could be collecting news from all over the city!"

"That would be great, but there's only room for two in the budget, the traffic drone and the one we use for weather and local events. These days it would be tough to convince the board to give us a fleet of them just to cover news for Seattle, especially with all of the drone hunters out there that don't like being recorded, and after the little stunt Simon Raimes pulled on the highway yesterday, well let's just say we're lucky we pulled ours out when Jerry came in."

"That's only because between his Omni-Glass and the remote footage, we already had enough." Perry said. "Are you sure you don't want me to send one of these over to I-5 to take a peek at what's happening there now?"

"No." Tom said. "As far as we know, Raimes has a localized EMP device. That, or he'll just order someone to shoot the damn thing down. I'm not wasting any more money than I need to on a story everyone else is already reporting on. Just keep your eyes peeled. If Jerry was right, any one of those boats to the west of the industrial area could have been used to bring in the second wave of protesters. Tell me if you see anything suspicious, Perry. We need to know where they came from, that's the more profitable side of the story now. It's our edge."

Tom turned to face the window behind him. The highway was visible from his office and he could even see a small line of vehicles far to the south with his naked eye, but he hadn't been able to get any solid information about what was going on there since the fires were extinguished. He turned back to his desk, and pointed his right index finger at his monitor. Waving the finger toward the window, the images on it moved, sliding magically through the air and onto one of the large glass panes. He placed his hands near its center, and spread his arms wide. The implanted image followed his movements, making the picture on the window larger, revealing it to be a live satellite feed of the greater Seattle area. Next to it, a social media livestream appeared, along with a chat box with real time comments actively being written by several freelance correspondents, who were reporting from the ongoing riots in Olympia.

Perry turned around again, when he noticed that the digital projection in the window had changed the light level in the room. "What's going on in Olympia?" he asked.

Tom looked over at Perry. "Oh," he said. "A group of about a thousand came up from Portland and joined the others. They tried to force their way into the statehouse, but the local cops and National Guard were able to push them back. I'm beginning to think the original plan was to overwhelm them where the police are usually at their weakest near SeaTac and surprise everyone by sending up the group from Portland later, but they weren't counting on Raimes showing up when he did, allowing the Guard to protect the seat of government there."

Tom used his right middle finger to bring a menu up over the live feed. He selected a 'close' option from the menu, and the feed vanished, revealing the rest of the map. He centered it over the highway. When he saw the small lines of buses on either side just north of the SeaTac exit, he tapped on the glass, and the satellite camera zoomed in. He watched as several people milled around, carrying what looked like large sheets of something slightly reflective, and placing them along the gaps between the buses on the outside, as if they were using them to set up their own little protected compound right there on the highway. The protesters were nowhere to be seen.

Something is going on down there. He thought. *But what? Why are you still there, Simon? The protesters are gone, scattered just like you planned. Or do you think they're coming back?* Brenda walked into the room with two cups of coffee in her hands. "Hey, Perry," she said as she walked by the table. "I got some coffee for you. I'll leave it on Tom's desk." She walked over to it. Tom was still looking at the windowed display, his left hand lifted up to his chin. He reached out and tapped his wedding ring on the glass. "Here's your coffee, Tom." Brenda placed the cups on his desk, and moved over to the other side to join him in his search for answers. She looked at him with more than a little adoration on her face, and then to the window. "I've provided the others with the escape plan. They all know how to get out of the city if things get worse." she said. "What are you doing?"

Tom, his concentration broken by her inquiry, looked at her frazzled. "I don't know what Simon is up to this morning. Nor do any of the other news outlets. It...it looks like he's building something out there."

Brenda looked at the satellite footage for a moment. "Oh, he's putting up The Barn." she said.

"The what?" Tom looked at her, surprised. "What do you mean?"

Brenda stretched out her right arm, and, with a long and elegant finger, drew a line along the western side of the Shotgun transports. "I read about it in an article a few weeks ago." she said. "They did this in Miami. They carry heavy metal sheeting with them, bolted to the sides of their buses. Whenever they go into a high resistance area or need to set up a field hospital, they take the sheets off and rearrange them, using them to connect the buses front to back. It makes a perimeter, so that the gaps in between them are covered. Then all they need to do, is just sit and wait for reinforcements. I don't think they've ever done it with this many vehicles, though."

"And if there aren't any?" Tom said. Brenda looked at him, quizzically. "Reinforcements, I mean." he said.

"Oh," she said. "Well, I don't think they've done this on a highway before, plus it doesn't look like they're bringing out any of their supplies. The whole point of The Barn is to make a defensible base of operations." She used her finger again, this time pointing out the area between the two lines of buses where nothing and no one appeared to be. "They must be using it to do something else this time." She raised her eyebrows and shrugged.

"Bingo!" Perry yelled out behind them. They walked over to the table.

"What do you have, Perry?" Tom asked. The left holographic display showed a boardwalk with a pier, west of the Interstate and just north of a small building that wasn't far from the industrial district. Next to several red-tinged derelict crane barges were two thirty or forty-foot long boats with Chinese writing on their sides. Several men stood near their bows and on land nearby. Those standing on the boats were wearing black, while the others appeared to be patrolling the area in police uniforms or riot gear. "Chinese?" Tom said. "What are we looking at?"

"Chinese, but not Chinese." Perry said. "What you're looking at is gibberish."

Brenda gave him a strange look. "What?" she asked.

"I took a course in college. Everyone was doing it." He nodded toward the display. "Can you see the difference in the shades of white being used?"

"You mean in the area around where the characters for the ship numbers start!" Brenda said, excited that she was there to share in the discovery.

"Yup, and if I change the camera settings to infrared, which restoration experts use to see through layers of paint if I'm not mistaken..." Perry reached down and touched a digital panel on the tabletop, bringing up a light spectrum selection display. He used his left forefinger to slide a bar on it, and used another interface option to change the contrast slightly. "...We can see what was originally there before the new paint job."

Beneath several Chinese characters were the words 'La Madre De Los Mares'. "Mother of the Seas," Perry said. "And there's the original registration number. Now we just have to find out where she birthed out of last."

"Excellent work Perry." Tom said. He gave Perry a pat on the back, and looked at Brenda. "We have to notify the authorities. Some of the police that disappeared last night on the highway might be there." Brenda nodded.

"No so fast!" Perry said. They looked at the display again. "Looks like we have some visitors," He brought up the light spectrum tool again and changed it back to the standard setting. "The A.I. in the drone is identifying twelve of them. Two are sitting back behind that warehouse near the pier, see it? The rest are sneaking up from the south through the water. They're all wearing black, and they definitely aren't the police *or* the National Guard. The guys in the water don't even have diving suits on!"

Tom ran back to the display on his window and yelled out a command to his computer. "My active desktop, start 'Show-Me' app," he said. A small message appeared at the top of the image, indicating that the program had been activated. "Identify all people in Barnum Satellite Live Feed wearing black." Small green boxes appeared over the blackshirts in the image, and a simple computerized voice came from his desk, "Five hundred and six targets identified." it said. There weren't enough. "Raimes, you sly dog," Tom said to himself. "You're on a rescue mission!" He looked at Brenda. "Brenda, I think it's time to update the main page again. Perry, capture the rescue on video. It doesn't matter to me if he succeeds or not, I'm putting it up on the site immediately after it happens. And if he's there, make sure you get a close-up of his face."

****

Brent and Simon kneeled behind a dumpster next to an empty warehouse. From their hiding place, they observed the ten members of the advance team that had been sent out the night before, as they slowly and quietly swam through the frigid water of the sound to the first of two small cargo ships with Chinese lettering on their hulls. Both boats were freshly painted white and black, and had three decks, all of which were covered in a patchwork of green and blue tarps of varying sizes, so that the windows and entrances could not be seen. They were moored on either side of a short metal dock that extended out about ten feet from a wide wooden boardwalk, which ran along a concrete wall at the water's edge. The dock and boardwalk were newly built, as they were clearly constructed with fresh materials, proving that preparations for their arrival had been made in advance.

Brent peeked around the corner of the dumpster, and watched as two men with pistols stood on the boardwalk looking inland. He also saw two more on the main deck of the closest boat. They were carrying pump-action shotguns. For a moment, he thought he caught a glimpse of one of the three men that the advance team had reported as being on the top deck of the second ship, but he wasn't sure.

"You didn't have to come with us, you know," Brent said. "Me and my guys could have handled this."

"The protesters didn't show up at first light like I thought they would," Simon replied. Brent could hear a hint of disappointment in his voice. "That means they're regrouping somewhere. If the rest of them were here, I would have brought the entire Shotgun Army down on them, but they're not. Robert can handle setting up The Barn. In the meantime, I'll be damned before I lose any more men. The ones that died this morning because of that mess last night...that's on me. I'm also here to take responsibility should anything go wrong. No one goes to jail but me. It's my cardinal rule."

Brent grabbed Simon's arm. "You did the right thing, Simon. Trying to get to the cops before they were taken, and stopping them from shooting at those protesters, that was the right thing to do."

"Yeah, only now we know they aren't exactly protesting anything, don't we. They came to claim territory." Simon took a taser from his belt, and checked its charge. It was at half strength. "Good for a few more hits anyway." he said to himself.

"Should we let Robert know where we're at?" Brent asked.

"No, I want radio silence until we know for sure that the cops and their weapons are here." Simon clipped the taser back onto his belt and lifted up a baton. "Have they made it around the first one yet?"

"Yeah, looks like we should have our answer in a few minutes."

"Just let me know when we're up."

"I want to make sure the two guys with the shotguns on the deck are taken out first. Looks like they're police issue, they must have taken them from the squad cars we used last night."

A few moments later, Brent saw the dark form of one of his team moving up the rear port side of the first ship. Two more appeared beneath the dock, quietly moving through the dark water below two of the sentries there. When they were in position, they removed their tasers from their holsters, and pointed them upward, aiming between the boards and waited.

Brent raised his left hand, silently signaling Simon to be on the ready. When the advance team took out the men on the dock, it was their job to get in there and disarm them before they could get back up. They had twenty yards to cover and would be out in the open for a few minutes, an intended distraction while the others took down the rest of the lookouts on the second vessel. It was a risky play, but one Simon was confident would work, as long as they both kept their heads down and Brent was able to keep his riot shield up.

Another advance team member climbed up an anchor that had been cast from the stern of the ship that was nearest to them, and joined the first. After walking forward for a short distance along the starboard side, the experienced infiltrator jumped up and grabbed a railing that ran along the deck of the second level. Pulling himself up without making a sound, he then proceeded to sneak up behind one of the sentries, who had just sat down on the roof of the ship's bridge and was dangling his legs over its covered forward windows. The tired, gruff looking insurgent, placed the shotgun he'd been carrying across his lap, and had started to roll a cigarette. The other team member, careful not to be seen by the sentry on the roof, moved in as close as he could to another sentry who was patrolling the main deck without being noticed. The second sentry was located just short of the bow, looking down at the boardwalk. The rest of the advance team was in the process of boarding the second ship, of which Brent was only able to see a small part of its forward section.

The sentry standing on the main deck of the first ship began to walk around the bridge, prompting the team member on the roof to give a hand signal to his teammate to let him know that a target was headed his way. When the sentry on the roof finished rolling his cig and was attempting to light it, a taser dart hit him from behind. As the smoker began to fall forward, his assailant grabbed the back of the man's shirt in one hand, and the shotgun's barrel in the other, before pulling both back onto the roof. In one silent sweeping motion, he swiftly moved the body, hiding it under a section of tarp he'd requisitioned while he was waiting, that had previously been draped over a nearby window. The second team member then tased the other watchman as he rounded the corner from the bow toward him. He one didn't go down as easily though, and a trigger was pulled as he fell on the deck, the sound of the gunshot a clear sign to everyone present that the advance team had been discovered.

Brent opened his fist and moved his hand forward. He and Simon were on the dock before the two men on the boardwalk had time to react. The team members that were still in the water below the dock fired their taser darts upward, and the pistol wielding sentries fell like rag dolls on the wooden planks, just as one of them had started to look in their direction. Simon crouched down behind Brent as they ran, depending on the safety that Brent's shield provided for them. They heard yelling from the second boat, and by the time they got to the first of the two downed men on the dock, three different shooters had already begun to open fire on them.

Brent stopped just in front of the first incapacitated man on the dock, and Simon got to work. He picked up the man's pistol, and put it under his belt behind his back. Then he used plastic ties to bind the man's hands, followed by his ankles. He heard at least six shots as he did this, only one of which deflected off of the riot shield before the firing stopped. Simon tapped Brent on his right shoulder, and they ran to the second man. The farther ship now fully in view, Brent could see the rest of the team tying up the remaining sentries there. The distraction had worked. Then, without warning, he took a bullet in his left shoulder, causing him to cry out, and drop his shield.

Another invader they'd missed had climbed out of a small hatch on the bow of the first boat, after their men had gone below deck to look for hostages. Simon was in the process of tying up the second man on the dock when he heard the shot, turning just in time to see the shield land on the boardwalk, leaving both of them defenseless. Brent looked up helplessly as the assassin took a second pistol out of his waist, and trained both of his weapons on him and Simon. Then a single shot rang out, and they watched as he fell to the deck. Simon and Brent looked to the second ship where the final shot had originated. One of the advance team members stood there, pistol in hand. He gave them a quick wave and disappeared through a door in one of the ship's bulkheads.

Brent grabbed his bicep and sat down on the boardwalk, letting out a deep sigh. "Been a while," he said, looking at Simon.

Simon moved Brent's hand, and ripped off the left sleeve of his shirt. He twisted it in his hands, and tied it above the spot where Brent had been shot just above his elbow. "Don't need me, huh?" he said. Brent smiled back at him.

Simon then ripped the sleeves off of his own shirt, and used them to make a sling. He placed it around Brent's shoulders, and helped him to stand up. As they stood, they heard a whistle from the second ship. Another team member stood there, waving two more pistols in the air. They heard a noise from the boat closest to them, and saw several police officers climb up and out from its bowels, using the same hatch their unfortunate attacker had. Some of them were wearing uniforms, and some had been stripped down to their underwear. Another team member was with them. He held up a helmet with one hand, and a riot shield with the other.

Brent looked at Simon. "Now *that* is a real victory, Simon." he said. "Even if I had to take a bullet to get it."

Simon looked at Brent. "I know it's not your first time getting shot, but this one doesn't look good. Let's get you back to Amanda, and get this looked-" He looked at the ships.

"And what?" Brent said.

"Do any of these guys know how to sabotage ships like these?"

"You mean blow them up?"

"No, not exactly." Simon said. "I want to make sure the rest that aren't here have no means of escape, but it might be advantageous to us if they still think they can leave instead of seeing them burning from a distance, do you know what I mean?"

Brent put two fingers in his mouth and whistled. Three men on the second ship, who had just finished lowering an emergency ladder, ran over to meet them. "I'll see what I can do." Brent said.

He stood up and walked in their direction. Simon saw that the men on the ship closest to him were attempting to let down their own ladders, and started off to help, when the feeling that he was being watched suddenly came over him. He turned around and scanned the horizon. At first glance he didn't see anything, thenhe noticed something, a small object moving slightly from side to side in the distance. Something was hovering over a hundred yards to the south, using the corner of a building to partially mask its presence. *Perfect.* He thought. *Couldn't have planned it better myself.*

Your word is a lamp to my feet, and a light for my path.I have sworn, and have confirmed it, that I will obey your righteous ordinances.-**Psalms, 119:105-112**

For whom he foreknew, he also predestined to be conformed to the image of his Son, that he might be the firstborn among many brothers. -**Romans, 8:29**

Chapter Twenty

Christian Territory, North of the Main Gate
Spokane, WA
Saturday, March 26th, 12:25PM PST

Mark turned at the intersection in front of the self-proclaimed 'Victory Center' and headed east. He walked briskly for a while without saying a word, his hands in his pockets. Jerry followed, not sure of where Mark was going or what he was doing. They went over a low rolling hill and into a small residential area. The larger homes that had stood safely behind their white picket fences on Levi's side of town were behind them, only rundown, single-story ranch houses and low income apartments taking their place. On the other side of the hill the land leveled out. Another intersection was not far ahead, one with a street light. Allowing his eyes to wander as he walked, Jerry thought that he could see another part of the wall behind some of the buildings to the north.

Jerry was deep in thought, his mind occupied with how he could get into the shack behind the meeting house without being seen. It was obvious that he wouldn't be able to return to the foundation site anytime soon, which meant he might have to stay another night, something he hadn't planned on. He had discovered the most likely location of the jammer, though. All he had to do was verify that it was indeed in the shack, and figure out a way to shut it down so Tom could hire someone to send in a drone. After that it was easy, all he would have to do was get out of town and write a short article about his experience in the Territory.

Mark slowed down his pace, allowing Jerry to catch up. "What do you think about divine appointments?" Mark asked him.

"You mean like the Judge? The Pope? People who are appointed by God or something?"

Jerry did his best to answer the bizarre question that seemed to have come out of the blue.

"No, I'm talking about meetings and encounters. Being in the right place at the right time, that kind of thing."

"You mean destiny."

"Not exactly, no."

"Fate, then?"

"Hmm, no, not that either. What I'm asking you is, have you ever encountered someone or something just at the right moment in your life? An encounter or relationship that affected you deeply, but maybe didn't plan on or expect?"

"Well, if that's what you mean, I guess I could say there have been several, yeah."

"Christians believe that God puts people around us for a reason when we follow Him, and sometimes even when we're not. Some of us call these encounters divine appointments. When I saw you at the gate, I knew you didn't belong here. I could see it on your face. I also knew in my spirit that you had a greater purpose for being here than you were letting on. You do a good job of concealing your true intentions and blending into the background, but you're here for a specific reason, aren't you?"

"I'm a reporter," Jerry said. "I was sent here to find out what's going on. Do me a favor and don't tell anyone. At first, I thought it would be ok to tell people here who I am, since I got here though I'm not so sure."

Mark moved his right index finger and thumb over his mouth, as if to show that he was buttoning it up. "Don't have to worry about me," he said. "I'm glad you're here...for a lot of reasons."

Jerry smiled, remembering their previous conversation. "You don't seem to be planning on living here, and you obviously don't have a car or any belongings that I've seen, besides what you're wearing. I'm curious, Mark, how is it that you manage to 'get around' so much like the Chief Justice said at the gate?"

"How?" Mark pondered the question for a moment. "Well, these days, I kind of walk, like little lamps were attached to my feet, one step at a time." He smiled at the thought. "Actually, if I knew this time what I was walking into, I might not have come to begin with. But I prayed to be useful so..."

This confused Jerry greatly. *Is he saying he just goes wherever he feels like? How does that even work?* He thought to himself. "So, do you know where we're going now?"

"I have an idea," Mark looked up at him and pointed in the direction they were heading. "Shouldn't be far now."

When they reached the intersection, Mark turned south. Then without warning, he started walking faster and crossed the street again. Just trying to keep up, Jerry had forgotten to look at the street signs as they went by. In the direction they were headed, there were several small businesses on either side of the road, as well as a few restaurants. They passed a gas station and a small outlet mall before Mark finally found what he was looking for. "There, that's it." he said.

Directly ahead of them was a parking lot with a small white sign near the throughway, that contained a message in large, black removable letters. As they walked past the gas station, Jerry looked around it to his right. The cracked and rundown parking lot was full of used vehicles, almost all of which must have been old enough to run solely on gasoline. Behind them, he saw what looked like a large warehouse. On one side, in what looked like an area that had previously been used as an office for the building, he saw a lit neon light hanging in a window that simply said, 'CHURCH IN SERVICE'. Mark turned yet again, that time in the direction of the same building, when Jerry decided to stop and read what was on the sign at the side of the road:

Korean Family Of The Redeemer Church
Intercessory Prayer Saturdays at noon, Services 10AM Sundays
Youth Group 7PM Friday Night
ALL ARE WELCOME IN THE HOUSE OF THE LORD
Mark 8:37 'For what will a man give in exchange for his soul?'

Mark stopped when he could no longer hear Jerry's footsteps coming up behind him. "Come on," he said, gesturing with his hand for Jerry to follow. "I think we'll find what we're looking for here."

Jerry gave Mark a dissatisfied look, "How do you know you're not just making all this up in your mind?"

"Because when I am obedient to His Word and follow Him, Jesus is lifted up in ways that I could never accomplish on my own, and more often than not, I am humbled, that's how I know." They began to walk toward the building together. "He is glorified, not me...and sometimes other things happen too."

"What kinds of things?" Jerry asked.

"Things that can't just be explained away as coincidences, He only reveals them to those that He wants to, when He wants to, though. We'll just have to wait and see."

As Mark spoke, Jerry looked over the building, searching for any signs that it was not structurally sound before going in, a habit he had picked up from near constant use of his Omni-Glass. Of course, without its help, he saw nothing that would indicate the place was unsafe. The church was in a small office space on the first floor. On one side of it was a chiropractor clinic, and on the other, a small law office. The deteriorating red brick walls were right at home with the peeling white paint on the trim, a thin glass door it's only entrance. The partition had only one window as well. On it, the words KOREAN FAMILY OF THE REDEEMER CHURCH had been placed in the form of an arc, each letter a different color in a rainbow of bright stick-on letters. Under these and on nearby windows, crayon pictures of Jesus hung joyfully. Each one was attached with tape at different angles, as if to give visitors the impression that the children who had made them had also stuck them there.

Walking across the parking lot, it was obvious that it was in desperate need of repaving as it was full of potholes and rubble. Jerry nearly tripped at least once on his way to the front door, where several cars were parked right up to the face of the building, some of their bumpers dangerously close to the entrance. As they neared the door, they found themselves squeezing between a rusted pickup truck and some ancient utility vehicle.

Mark reached out for the door handle with his left hand, and was about to open it, when Jerry grabbed his arm. "How can you tell the difference between the good Christians and the bad ones who are only out for themselves?"

"You can't, at least not at first anyway. You have to wait patiently to see the spiritual fruit that comes from their lives, not just material fruit mind you, spiritual fruit. Hopefully, they aren't trying to fool you by showing you a façade. Either way, God is the judge. Eventually, everything that is hidden is revealed." Mark looked at Jerry's hand on his arm, a little surprised that he'd had grabbed him. He looked at Jerry's face thoughtfully, "Even then, it's important to remember not to judge them too harshly because they might be going through a tough period in their lives, or a test. God gave Job the right to judge his friends when they wrongfully assumed his lack of fruit was due to him having secret sin, when it was really just God testing his spirit, so that others in the future would understand that men cannot see or know all of God's mechanizations." Jerry was saddened by Mark's response, looking down on him depressed, as if he had not given him the answer he was hoping for.

Mark continued, "A believer knows when the Lord has sent them to the right people at the right time. But even then, some of them will inevitably mess up, so the believer must be ready and willing to forgive because it's likely that they too will eventually do something that requires forgiveness at some point. Jesus said, 'do not judge so that you will not be judged.' but he also said that in time, 'you will know them by their fruit'." Mark calmly removed Jerry's hand from his arm and began to open the door. As he did, Jerry noticed that Mark's countenance began to change. He looked as if something unseen had come through the door and hit him like a wave. He hadn't budged, only stopped for a moment. "Oh yeah, this is the place." he said, and they went in.

****

The inside of the church was nothing like Jerry had expected. It was completely different than anything he had seen in news vids online that were related to church services, and nothing at all like what they'd witnessed at the Victory Center. The interior had been completely opened up to take full advantage of the miniscule amount of floor space that was available. Lines could be seen under the spackled sheetrock on either side of the room, marking where the original walls of the office stood before they were knocked down. The place couldn't have been more than thirty-five or forty feet in length, and possibly only twenty feet wide, but that didn't seem small enough to stop people from crowding into the place.

On the floor tiles just in front of the door, and all the way to a small stage at the back of the room, some two hundred or more people were either standing or were down on their knees in prayer. Many of them had placed their heads on the floor, while others were stretching their hands upward, their eyes closed. A few were swaying from side to side, their lips moving with little sound escaping them, as if mumbling to themselves. Those who were too old to kneel kept their own hands in the air while sitting in their chairs. All in attendance appeared to be Korean in ethnicity, and only a few were wearing any kind of masks to protect themselves from infectious disease. *This is crazy! Don't they know they could catch something with so many people in such a small space?* Jerry thought. He crossed his arms, and was careful not to touch anything as they entered.

On a tiny stage at the far end of the room, a man sat in a padded chair next to a dark stained wooden podium with a cross nailed to its front. He was wearing a neatly pressed navy blue suit and a slightly worn blue and black striped tie, which looked like it had been put through the wash a few too many times. The man's head was lowered and his eyes closed, his right hand lifted in agreement with the rest, while his other hand lightly covered a large black Bible that sat on his lap.

On the other side of the stage, a young woman who must have been in her twenties, played an electric piano. She had long black hair and pale skin. Like the others, she swayed ever so slightly side to side, as she manipulated the keys. Her thin and delicate frame was covered by a long, flowing garment made of a material that was an even darker shade of blue than what the man was wearing, with a deep and velvety purple hue to it. The dress complimented her light complexion, allowing her other features to stand out. Her eyes were mostly closed, opening only slightly from time to time to look at her finger placements on the instrument, which she handled with incredible skill. The music that she produced was both haunting and beautiful to Jerry. Above them and behind the stage, a flat-screen monitor that must have been at least ten years old, showed a beautiful moving composition of a waterfall at sunset, with white Korean Hangul text suspended over it.

An older gentleman who had been kneeling on the floor to their right when they'd entered stood up, and walked to the right side of the room where a few unused chairs leaned against the wall. He took two of them, and passed one to Mark and one to Jerry, unfolding them as he did. Then, using his hands, he gestured for them to sit down. "Kamshamnida," Mark said to the man. Jerry looked at him, a little shocked. "Sit down, Jerry." Mark said in a low voice.

Jerry sat and watched the people pray. He was earnestly amazed at how long they were able to keep their arms in the air. Even those who were older didn't seem to mind keeping their arms up for extended periods of time, and Jerry began to wonder if he could do the same. Mark joined them. He didn't have enough space in front of him to kneel on the ground like the others without bumping into the last row of chairs, so instead he simply leaned back in his chair and raised his hands, his lips moving now and then. Jerry thought he heard Mark say a few prayers for those who had set up the wall and for the "lost" in and around Spokane, but he was unable to make out exactly what he was saying most of the time, as he mostly sounded like he was just talking to himself under his breath like all of the others.

After twenty minutes had passed, Jerry began to feel alone, and a bit claustrophobic. *What am I even doing here anyway?* He asked himself. *Sure, this place could make an interesting addition to my story, but I don't need to sit through an entire meeting, do I? Maybe Mark won't mind if I wait outside.* He leaned over to Mark, "I don't like it in here." he whispered.

Mark sat forward, opened his eyes, and looked at Jerry thoughtfully. "Hmm," he said. "I wonder why that is..." One side of his mouth turned up, forming a playful smirk. "Don't worry, it's almost over."

A few minutes later, the man who was sitting on the stage stood and walked to the podium. He looked up at the group of people before him. Some of them stopped praying and looked back, others continued in their prayers. He looked at Jerry and Mark for a moment, but did not seem affected by their presence. Then he briefly said something in Korean and walked back to his seat. Another moment went by, and an old woman who was already close to the stage began to stand up. The young piano player stopped playing, jumped out of her seat, and ran to help her. It didn't take much for Jerry to see that the old woman was at least partially, if not completely blind, her arms flailing slightly around at her sides. Her eyelids were clenched tight as she made her way to the front.

The young woman in the deep purple dress took one of the older woman's arms, and led her up a small set of steps to the podium, before adjusting the microphone on it so that her elder could be heard. Mark leaned forward so he could hear what the woman had to say. Holding onto the younger woman who was now helping her to stand, the old Korean woman spoke slowly and deliberately into the microphone for about a minute in Korean. When she was finished, the pastor leaned forward in his chair, and said something to the pianist. She looked at him with confusion, and he pointed at Jerry and Mark. The young woman looked in their direction and nodded. Then, still holding onto one of the blind woman's arms, she moved the microphone to her own mouth and spoke in English.

"She say that God give her a vision, she sees walls fall like Jericho. She say these not walls of a country, but walls of a people that lost their way. People that God wants to use. She say God brings brothers, righteous, um no." She looked at the man in the chair again, "Uh...hully-unhan?" He nodded, and she began speaking again, "Valiant brothers in her vision. Men that will bring the walls down. Um, not real walls, but walls in people's hearts so the people can see what they did wrong and repent." Hearing this, Jerry looked on in disbelief. *How...* He thought to himself. *This doesn't make sense.* The young woman looked back at the man in the chair again. The man nodded with approval. She led the older woman back to her seat. The man, who Jerry had guessed was the pastor of the church, stood up again, and walked back to the podium. He closed his eyes and said a prayer in Korean. When he was finished, he said, 'Amen.' Everyone in the room, including Mark, repeated the word back to him. Before long, most of the congregants were standing up and gathering their things. The service was over.

A few seconds later, the place was bustling with activity. Some of those who had attended the service began to pick up the chairs, folding them and moving them to one side of the room, while others took brooms out of a back room and began to sweep the floor. A few of the older women disappeared into the back, emerging a few minutes later with platters full of Korean style food, which they placed on tables that some of the men had brought out for that very purpose. A few people left but not many, nodding and smiling at Mark and Jerry as they passed by them. Jerry was impressed by the amount of cooperation and selflessness he witnessed. Never before had he seen people work together in such a way without complaint, without so much as a sound, other than the occasional helpful word of direction or instruction. For a moment he thought he was seeing the inner workings of a cult, but quickly noticed that neither the pastor nor anyone else was getting or looking to get attention from the others. No one seemed to be giving out orders or advice either, and people were coming in and going as they pleased without fear.

Jerry also didn't notice any containers for collecting money. All he could see that might have served such a purpose, was a small box that was attached to the wall next to the main entrance. A small sign was attached to it in Korean and English, which said 'Give as God wills.' A message that certainly did not fit the preconceived notions and assumptions that Jerry had been force fed since birth about churches in general. Overall, the church and the people in it were a welcome surprise, even if he still did not feel completely comfortable among them. When everything had calmed down a bit, the pastor walked over to the young pianist, who was rolling up a cord and getting ready to put the piano away. He spoke to her for a moment, then both of them began to make their way off of the stage, and across the room.

When they reached Jerry and Mark, Mark reached out his right hand and said, "Anyoung-haseo."

The pastor shook his hand. "You speak Korean?" he asked, with a somewhat broken sounding accent.

"A little," Mark replied.

"Jerry." Jerry pointed at himself with his left index finger as he spoke, his arms still crossed.

The pastor looked at the young woman standing next to him. She looked back at him and then looked at the pair. "My father wants to speak to you. Will you come to his office?" she said.

Mark turned to Jerry, a knowing look on his face, then back to the pastor's daughter. "Yes, we would like that." He then looked at the pastor again and nodded. They led Mark and Jerry through a small kitchen area that was hidden off to the side of the stage where three women dutifully cleaned and prepared even more food. Unfamiliar yet tantalizing smells caught Jerry's attention as they passed through. The aroma, a mixture of several spices he had never encountered before, floated through the air and filled his nostrils. He tried to catch a glimpse at what was being prepared, but only saw a collection of small bowls filled with things he could not identify and some type of food wraps that were covered in tinfoil. Having had nothing more to eat, other than half a chicken wing since they'd left Levi's, he was famished.

Behind the kitchen next to a tiny bathroom was a small office, just large enough for an undersized desk and a few folding chairs. The pastor walked around the desk, and sat down. The young pianist followed, and stood dutifully at her father's side, as Mark and Jerry did the same. Able to observe her more closely, it was obvious to Jerry that the young woman was nothing like the attractive redhead he had met at the picnic. Something was different about her, something Jerry had not encountered in a woman before. There was an air of peacefulness about her. She had a steady, graceful beauty that did not manifest in how she looked alone, though she was indeed pleasant to look upon. But there was something more, a confidence in her shyness that was hard to pin down. Her eyes were kind and calm, not mischievous or suggestive in any way. She seemed innocent and kind, something that was rare in the world in which he knew.

Taking his eyes off of her took some effort for Jerry, as it always did with attractive women, but he managed and joined Mark in facing the pastor. The man gave them an intense stare as they sat, and then said something in Korean. His daughter translated for him. "He is Pastor Goo. He wants to know if God sent you here, and if there is anything the church can do for you."

Jerry looked at Mark, raising an eyebrow. Mark responded, "The Lord sent us here, yes. But we are not from the Territory. We came only for the weekend. The Lord has something good for us to share with the Christians here, and work to do. No, we do not need anything. God is taking care of us. We only need prayer for protection. Please pray that the enemy will be prevented from stopping us, and that Holy Spirit will be with us until we leave."

The pastor's daughter conveyed the message. He nodded and spoke again. When he was finished, she looked back to them. "He say, we serve here for God. These people come when we come, same time. They build the wall, but they also give us work. God use us to witness to them through our work, through our good example of service in humility. We go into their homes and fix things. We serve them in the community at jobs, we pray for them as we do these things. Most times, they do not hear us though, they will not listen, they just want more things, and people in the city hate all Christians because of them. We pray for people like you to come, talk to them. Is that why you are here?"

Mark looked at Jerry again before turning back to face the pastor. "Yes, yes I think it is."

The pastor spoke once more, and his daughter continued to interpret his words. "We have another prayer meeting this evening. We will pray for you."

"It is all we need, that and...lunch?" Mark looked at the pastor's daughter and then back at the pastor.

Pastor Goo seemed to understand the last part of Mark's sentence. A great smile appeared on his face, and he stood to his feet. "Yes, lunch! Let us feed you!" he said. He walked around the desk and led them back out through the kitchen. When they returned to the sanctuary, all of the remaining chairs had been folded and lined up neatly against the walls. The tile floor was spotless, shining as if the entire place had been mopped in the few short minutes they'd been away. Several mats lay flat in the middle of the sanctuary in the shape of a long, open rectangle. Fifteen or sixteen members of the congregation sat around its edges, passing food around in small bowls, using chopsticks to pick up the large variety of spicy vegetables and fruit, moving a small amount of each one to their own plates.

The pastor's daughter led them to two open spaces near the stage, and they sat down with the others. She walked into the center of the rectangle and got them two pairs of the metallic chopsticks and two plates, retrieved another set for herself, and sat down next to Jerry. Pastor Goo sat on the other side of Mark. They were greeted with smiles by everyone that was sitting around the rectangle, followed by a series of the small bowls that were passed in their direction in quick succession, one after the next.

The food may have been unrecognizable to Jerry, but it smelled fantastic to his roaring stomach. He tried everything, starting things off with some kind of spicy cabbage, then moving onto a sweet yellow fruit that had been cut into small cubes. Struggling to pick these up with his chopsticks, he finally stabbed one of them. Several people looked his way and began to giggle. Without missing a beat, Pastor Goo's daughter took hold of his left hand gently with her soft fingers, and positioned the chopsticks in the correct configuration, pushing his thumb, index, and ring fingers together and apart, to demonstrate how they worked. Before then, Jerry had never bothered to learn how to eat with chopsticks, despite having been to more than his share of Asian style restaurants over the years, and was a little embarrassed as he had always meant to. He looked to see if Mark had noticed his error, but he was deep in conversation with the pastor, and appeared to be making out with his own set of chopsticks just fine.

Jerry looked at the pastor's daughter again. "What is your name?" he asked.

She motioned her freehand at herself and smiled, "Me?"

"Yes, you," Jerry smiled back. The interaction seemed to please her greatly.

"Min-Seo," she said. "You are Jerry?" she asked.

"Yes, that's me." he said, puffing his chest out a little. A piece of the yellow fruit slipped from his chopsticks and fell onto the mat.

Min-Seo started to giggle, covering her mouth with her hand. "You from here?" she asked.

"Me? No. I'm from Seattle."

"Oh." Her smile began to disappear. "I been to Seattle, when we first come over. I like it there, so much to see and do."

"Yes, there is." Jerry said. She grinned and continued eating. Then, putting down her chopsticks for a moment, she accepted a large plate from an elderly man who sat to her left. She placed it on the mat in front of them and from it, gave Jerry some kind of wrap full of rice, chicken, and several other tasty elements that he'd never seen before, but still enjoyed the taste of all the same.

Sitting next to the man that had given her the platter, was the old woman who had spoken before the end of the service. The man was helping her with her food, guiding her hands to one of the smaller bowls that contained some of the same yellow fruit he'd tried earlier. Her eyes still almost completely closed, she smiled as he helped her position her chopsticks so that she could pick one of the fruit cubes up.

"Who is she?" Jerry asked Min-Seo.

"She's my grandmother." She answered.

"The pastor's mother?" Jerry pointed his chopsticks at the pastor to his right. Several people stopped eating and looked at him.

Min-Seo smiled and calmly reached over again, that time to place her hand on his arm, lowering it.

"Oh, sorry," Jerry said.

Another man on the other end of the mats, said something in Korean, and several people laughed.

"Yes," she said, retracting her arm. "The pastor's mother."

"Did you bring her to the wall? It was only finished a couple of days ago, did you explain to her what it is? How big it is?"

She let out a small laugh. "No." she said. "She stays indoors most of the time. Sometimes she likes to sit on the patio outside our apartment though."

"You mean you didn't tell her about the wall?"

"We do not need to. The Lord tells her many things. Things happening now and that happen later. He told her that soon we will be able to go into Spokane again, we are not worried." She looked earnestly puzzled about the nature of Jerry's questions. "Does your friend want some?" Jerry picked up the platter, and tapped Mark on the shoulder. Mark took it from him, but was more involved in his conversation with the pastor than anything else. Jerry looked at Min-Seo again. She had resumed eating and looked back at him. Her eyes were bereft of guile, more so than anyone he had ever met, and even though he doubted what she had said, part of him believed her, or at least wanted to.

****

After they finished eating, Pastor Goo asked the entire group to pray for them. Several people stood up and walked around them, and placed their hands on their backs and shoulders. A few of the older members scooted across the floor, and placed their hands on Mark and Jerry's legs. Pastor Goo led them in the prayer in Korean and then said in English, "We will continue pray for you both. That God will protect you, and lead you home safely. Come back any time. Thank you for coming." Jerry could tell that it was important to the man that he wish them farewell on his own.

They thanked them in return, and waved as they walked out the door and into the parking lot. When they reached the sidewalk in front of the sign, Jerry asked Mark, "What did you two talk about?"

"He told me how they came to be here. It was quite an interesting story. Apparently, his family was among several in their church in Seoul that felt that God was leading them into the mission field, but they had no idea where God wanted them to start a church. Then one day, about five years ago, a Christian who had come from a large underground church in China came to theirs, and one night, when he was filled with the Holy Spirit, he instructed each family to go to different nations around the world to do ministry. Of course, it was only a confirmation of what they had already been planning to do, but the Chinese man had never met any of them before that night. He asked me if I thought this was what it was like in America many years ago when people here sent out missionaries, before we became one of the places that needed them. I said it probably was."

"So, you would consider this church to be a good one, then?" Jerry asked.

"Oh, of course." Mark said. "God led us there. There is always a place of refuge, a remnant, a place where the Holy Spirit still resides and even thrives in every dark valley. We were here to encourage them as well, and all we had to do was show up. Imagine that."

"How do you know Korean?"

"My wife and I spent a couple of years over there ministering in a church, and working with an orphanage just outside of Seoul.

We taught English for our Visas. God did a lot, it was a wonderful experience." Jerry could see that Mark's mind had started to wander again, noting that the small lines in his face, the only evidence that he was older than he looked at first glance, seemed to disappear when he became lost in thoughts of the past. He could have asked Mark a million more questions about the things he claimed to have seen his God do, but a more pressing one was on his mind.

"Do you think we are the 'Valiant brothers' that woman spoke about?"

Mark looked up at him, bemused by the notion, "Why do you ask? Is God telling you something? Telling you to get a sledge hammer and knock down some metaphorical walls is He?" He reached out and slapped Jerry's arm as they passed the gas station and approached the intersection where Mark had previously crossed the street. Jerry became quiet and didn't answer. Mark smiled at him and crossed the road again, heading back in the direction they had originally come from. After crossing behind him, Jerry took a deep breath and ran a hand through his hair, as he always did when he encountered something that proved too much for his rational mind to deal with.

A short while later, the wind began to pick up. It was blowing against them to the east, and the further they walked, the stronger it seemed to get. The harder the air pushed against them though, the more determined Mark was to walk into it. It wasn't too much of a challenge, the day having warmed up substantially since that morning, so Jerry followed, and soon they were both trudging along again at a decent clip.

They reached Levi's place just before three in the afternoon. Several people, most of them with grey hair, were standing around or sitting on Levi's lawn when they got there. Near the mailbox, a turf spreader sat, full of white granules. Next to it was a small pile of insecticide, the sure sign of an accidental spill. Eddie walked out of the garage with a large trash bag that he was carrying to the curb. As they approached, some of the people from the small group walked over to Mark and began to introduce themselves. Jerry walked over to Eddie as he was placing the trash into a hard plastic drop-off container that was next to the sidewalk.

"What's going on?" he asked Eddie.

"Huh?" Eddie said. "Oh, they showed up a couple of hours ago. They're some of Levi's neighbors, I think, and their friends. I was going to use the spreader, but I spilled it. Then they showed up. Levi told me I could take a break after I took out the trash." Eddie turned and stared at the people for a second. He looked back at Jerry. "Did you guys eat something?"

"Uh, yeah, yeah." Jerry said. He looked over the faces of each and every one of the visitors closely, to see if he could discern any indication of malice or negativity among them. Instinctively, he reached into his right pants pocket for his Omni-Glass case before remembering once again that it wasn't with him.

"Really?" Eddie asked. "What did you have?"

"Huh?" Eddie broke Jerry's train of thought. He looked down at the boy again. "Uh, some kind of Korean food. You know, rice, fish, chicken, some spicy cabbage that was pretty good."

"Wow," Eddie said. "I'll have to try it sometime. Where did you get it?"

"At a church on the other side of the Territory," Jerry said. "They gave it to us after the service."

"You went to church?"

"I think it was just a prayer meeting, but yeah." Jerry had gone back to analyzing the group. He counted maybe twelve people altogether.

"Cool. Maybe we can go sometime together."

Jerry's face became solemn. "Sorry man, I probably won't be here after tonight." he said.

"Oh," Eddie said. He looked down at his shoes for a moment. Then he looked back up with a smile. "Well, maybe Levi will bring me! Or Mark!"

"Sure thing, kid. You should ask them later. You got anything else you're doing?"

"No, just have to pray for some things. Then I'm gonna play another game in the garage. It's not so windy in there. It's warmer in the garage, you know, even with the door open."

"Game?"

"Yeah, I found this old handheld game thing in one of the boxes and a bunch of games! Levi said I could keep it for all the work I've been doing."

"Sounds good," Jerry said. "I think I'm going to stay out here a little longer, though."

"Ok," Eddie said. "I need to use the bathroom." Eddie walked into the house through the garage. As he neared the door, Levi came out, wiping his hands with an old face cloth. He stuffed the cloth into his back pocket and walked over to the group, stopping just outside of the small circle of people that were standing around Mark, and crossed his arms. Jerry decided to join him. By the time he reached the spot where Levi was standing, Mark had already begun praying over one of the visitors. He leaned over to Levi and asked, "So, where did these folks come from?"

Levi was focused, listening to Mark pray when Jerry spoke to him. He looked at Jerry somewhat dismissively. "Oh, hey, they're my neighbors mostly. Some of them have been here for years. A few of them are from some of the newer churches that set up the wall too, I think. I'm sure you saw all of the newer homes while you were walking down Strong Road."

"The main street through town, you mean? Yeah, lots of construction going on. Nice places."

"Yeah, well, there used to be smaller, less conspicuous homes in those places, small cottages and ranch houses mostly. Mine used to be the biggest one around. These people with all their money...some of them are nice people, good kids too, but it's obvious they don't know what the word 'contentment' means, you know? Ah, but who cares what I think, I'm just an old guy. I used to be young once, you know." He smiled sarcastically at Jerry, waiting for a response.

"You don't say," Jerry said, smiling back. "Never would have believed it."

"Heh, you're a good egg, Jerry." Levi said. They both looked back at Mark. His hands were on the shoulders of an older gentleman who was having trouble standing up straight, and was encouraging others to join him. He prayed a prayer of healing for the man's arthritis and wisdom for his doctors. The man began to cry and grasped Mark's hand with a firm handshake before walking away with his wife, admittedly a little more upright than he had been before.

The impromptu prayer meeting on Levi's lawn continued for another hour. Even more people began to show up, a few arriving in expensive cars, both young and old. Some asked Mark to pray for family members that didn't know God personally, others for health related issues for themselves or their loved ones. Several of them offered Mark money, but he declined, usually responding by saying that the Lord was providing for him, but thanking them all the same. Levi joined in a couple of times when his closest neighbors asked for him to. When he was finished, Levi went into the garage and returned with his folding chair. He set it up, and sat down near the front of his lawn in the same spot where they had first seen him the day before. As he sat down in it, a small, withered branch that had broken off of the great oak, fell and bounced off of his left shoulder. He looked up and spoke to it softly, trying not to make too much noise. "Oh, do I hate that tree!"

Eddie reappeared a short while later, walking back into the garage from the house, the game system he had found in his hands. He sat on Mark's cot, which was closest to the entrance, and started playing it. Jerry decided to head over and sit next to him, while they waited for Mark to finish. The temperature was indeed a bit higher in the garage, despite it being in the shade, and Jerry was quite comfortable looking out over the neighborhood on such a beautiful and peaceful afternoon. The wind continued to blow as time went on however, changing from a stiff breeze to the occasional strong gust. Over time, the gusts became powerful enough to move the ornaments that adorned the neighbors' yards, and threatened to knock over the turf spreader and the containers of trash at the end of Levi's driveway. Seeing the spreader almost tip over, and not wanting to be blamed for another spill, Eddie paused the game he was playing and ran to its rescue. Avoiding its spilled contents, he grabbed the handlebars of the spreader and wheeled it into the garage.

A few times, the sudden blasts of air caught the tarp that covered Levi's boat, so that it lifted one end up like a sail before settling down again. Jerry noticed that one of the straps that had held down the front end of the tarp, the one that was so frayed that it looked like it might break and fall off, was missing. The absent strap left the large piece of woven plastic to flap around violently whenever the air picked up speed, the sudden motion tempting Jerry's reflexes every time the wind blew. After a while, it made him want to look for something in the garage that he could use to tie it down with.

One by one, Mark prayed for those who remained, each thanking him before they left, having gotten what they'd come for. When most of the prayer seekers had gone, Jerry saw something big moving in the distance out of the corner of his eye. He looked away from Eddie's game, and watched as a large black SUV rounded the corner from the direction of the gate. It approached slowly, driving in the opposite lane of traffic from where Levi's place was situated. It stopped about half a block away, and four men simultaneously opened its doors and stepped out onto the pavement. The two that got out of the front end of the vehicle were dark skinned, one of them wore several gold rings on his fingers and looked like he was up there in years. The other was as tall as a skyscraper, and wore large, dark sunglasses. Both men wore giant trench coats, with black suits and ties underneath.

The other two men who got out of the rear seats were nothing like the first in appearance, but were no less imposing. Though not nearly as tall as the first two, both men were still tall, their complexions white as snow. One walked with a slight limp, and carried a long wooden cane with a golden handle. He had white hair and a beard of the same color and texture. Something about his face made Jerry squint when the sun shone directly on him, like something was odd about the way he looked in the sunlight, which by then was much lower, and hitting the man's face through the trees. When he was able to see him clearly, Jerry recognized him as one of the leaders from the wall. *The angry one.* He was dressed in a robin blue dress shirt, and black slacks. Behind him from the other side of the car, a burly looking man came around to join him.

He was much bulkier than the others, with wild curly red hair, and arms as round as cannon barrels. He walked with his chest pushed outward, in a manner that Jerry could tell was meant to be threatening.

When they began to cross the street toward Levi's property, Levi stood up and jogged to his house, entering through the front door, instead of going through the garage as he usually did, without saying a word. By the time the men had reached his yard, Levi had reemerged, a worn grey winter jacket covering his right arm. He looked at Jerry from the doorway, and then at Eddie.

Jerry looked at Eddie, who up until that time hadn't noticed what was going on and was still playing his game intently, his tongue sticking out from one corner of his mouth. "Hey." Jerry said. "I think it's time to have a snack. Are you hungry, Eddie?"

Eddie paused his game again, and looked around until he saw Levi. "Levi, can Jerry and I have some pretzels or one of the ice cream sandwiches you gave me yesterday?" he asked.

Levi was now walking toward Mark and the brutish looking men, who were only a few yards away from his property. He answered Eddie without turning around, his eyes fixed on the four men approaching them. "Sure thing Eddie, you can have both. Go inside and get one for each of us, but don't come back out. Go ahead and eat yours at the table, we'll be there in a minute."

Without needing to be told twice, Eddie got up and ran inside. As the men stepped up to the infamous oak and the property line, Levi calmly addressed them. "That's far enough, gentlemen." he said. "I have a rule here, no vampires allowed." The men noticed the jacket wrapped around his arm, and stopped short. "You see, if you invite a vampire onto your property, they can do whatever they want. But if you don't, well, they have no power over you where you live. Of course, sometimes you have to put a stake in their hearts to get rid of 'em either way. Got it?"

"We are not here for you, sir." The older man with a dark complexion said. "We have come to talk to him." He pointed to Mark, who was finishing his final prayer for a small, frail woman.

Mark finished praying and looked at her. "Go in peace." he said. The petite woman looked at the men standing behind him and said, "And may the Lord protect you." She turned and walked across Levi's driveway toward her own home, which Jerry speculated could not have been far.

"Hello, I am pastor Obobwey from Our Bountiful Savior church." The man announced himself. There was a long moment of silence as Mark, who was still facing the woman as she made her way to safety, picked up his chin and looked toward the sky above them. Having removed his hat while praying, he placed it firmly back onto his head. Then he turned around and looked at the new arrivals indiscriminately.

"And?" Mark said in a dull, tired tone.

"And this is Pastor George Harmin." Obobwey continued, "We are here to ask you to stop praying for the Holy Spirit over these people. Some of them are from our churches or know people from them, and you are confusing them."

Jerry walked over to Mark. Mark gave Jerry a look of agitated confusion. He turned his attention to the others again. "You don't want me to pray for the Holy Spirit to come to them for wisdom and healing? I don't get it."

"You are confusing them!" Obobwey said. "Even our elders do not pray for the Holy Spirit to come upon people. That is up to God."

Levi spoke, "You mean up to you." he said.

George walked up to where the grass met the street, his toes crossing over the line. He had a look of utter defiance on his face. "Look," he said. "You have no right-"

"I HAVE EVERY RIGHT!" Mark yelled. His voice boomed like a fog horn, bellowing down the street. "You have no right to deny these people what is theirs!"

Harmin's face turned red at the rebuke. He stepped into Levi's yard toward Mark. "You don't tell me-"

'Click – Click'.

A sound came from under the coat that Levi was carrying. He gave Harmin a searing stare, stopping the man in his tracks. The tall and silent man in sunglasses that was standing behind Obobwey, reached into the breast pocket of his jacket. Harmin, on the other hand, took a step back.

"Paul wrote that we would know false prophets and trouble makers by their fruit," Harmin said. "And from what we heard about your teachings in the park yesterday, you are already disturbing members of our churches with your barbs!"

Mark looked Harmin directly in the eyes. "So you think Christ didn't ruffle the feathers of the Pharisees when he challenged their wrong beliefs? Or do you even speak of the Pharisees in your churches, since they are so much like yourselves?" A look of disgust came across his face. "You call me a false prophet because I follow God so I can waste my time speaking to the likes of you? Believe me, if I had my druthers I wouldn't even be here! So here is a prophecy for you, this place will not be here for long. God wants his people out in the world living by the power of the Holy Spirit, ministering to the lost in these last days. Not cowering behind walls, giving their money and time to gangsters who promise to protect them, but will not be able to when the time comes. Mark my words. You are hired shepherds and nothing more!"

For the next few seconds, no one moved. The wind began to pick up again, blowing fresh leaves and acorns to the ground. Eddie, having heard the commotion outside, walked up behind Jerry, standing just inside the garage.

Finally Mark broke the silence. His voice was loud and clear, his words enveloping the entire street, as if he were addressing a much larger audience than the four men standing before him. "Nice cane!" he said, his eyes locked on Harmin. "You know Jerry, I knew a man once who had a cane that was a lot like that one. For years, he let people think the top of it was made of solid gold. Turned out that the handle was gold plated, though, and he added this...stuff to his hair and beard, to make it look better." He looked at Jerry for a moment, motioning the shape of a beard with his right hand, while cracking a somewhat playful smile. "Like it was glowing, it was his way of tricking weak minded people into thinking he'd been in the presence of God or something. You ever seen anything like that? You ever even hear of someone so ridiculous in your life?" He looked back to Harmin.

Harmin's face began to contort into something that almost didn't look human. To Jerry, it looked like he was transforming into some kind of comic book monster that was about to rip the oak tree standing next to him out of the ground, so that he could launch it like a missile in Mark's general direction. After a deep breath, and a few questionable looks from the others he had come with however, Harmin was able to calm himself. "I think it's time that you leave, you and your friend, whoever he is." Harmin said. The tall man that looked like he was Obobwey's bodyguard and the redhead walked around their masters onto Levi's yard, and headed toward Mark.

"This is my property! You can't..." Levi said, but the men were not persuaded, walking by him and whatever he was carrying under his coat, without fear.

"Do you mean to say you didn't pray for God to send me here?" Mark asked them.

The two pastors shared a glance, and for a brief moment a look of doubt appeared on both of their faces.

"So you did then. Tell me, what else did you pray for?"

Then, when the two juggernauts were only a few yards away from where Mark was holding his ground, Jerry witnessed something truly amazing. The wind began to pick up again, but something about it was different. Then, a single, extremely powerful gust of cool air blew down the entire street, turning it into something that could have been likened to a wind tunnel. It knocked over gas grills, shook power lines, and tossed around lawn furniture on both sides of the street, so much so that a chair hit the SUV the four men had arrived in, one of its legs breaking clean through the windshield. The powerful blast of wind was so strong that it pushed the men back slightly, ripping the sunglasses off of the bodyguard's face, immediately causing him to turn around in an attempt to retrieve them. He ended up running down the street, as the expensive shades hit the concrete and slid several meters down the road. The other, undaunted, continued forward until a cloud of insecticide from the pile Eddie had left on the lawn blew up in front of him, leaving him coughing and temporarily blinded in a toxic cloud of white smoke.

The wave of air pushing against him, Levi fell down on one knee. He unfurled the jacket, and used it to protect himself from the cloud. More of the insecticide blew over the yard with another gust of wind that followed immediately after the first, and was just as powerful, covering the majority of the front lawn in a white haze. Harmin limped over to the oak tree, and grabbed onto it to steady himself. He raised an arm over his eyes to protect them from the dangerous chemicals. Jerry found himself slipping on the grass until he finally gave up and knelt down as well, raising his own arm up, and turned his face away from the direction of the pile, while Mark simply leaned into the wind, closing his eyes and holding his breath as best he could. Eddie looked on from the garage, his eyes wide in utter horror, as he saw the waste container he'd placed the trash bag in, turn over, spilling its contents out onto the street.

When the wind stopped, everyone looked at Mark. Just as he had been when the men first arrived, he was facing the other direction and looking up at the sky. When he turned around that time though, he looked at each one of the aggressors, his face like flint, his jaw clenched.

"Come!" Obobwey said. "The lord of the air has come! He is of the devil! Come!"

The tall man retrieved his glasses, and walked back to the SUV, looking a little confused. He opened the passenger door for Pastor Obobwey, and took the lawn chair off of the vehicle, throwing it on the lawn across the street next to where the SUV was parked. The red haired man helped Harmin back to the car. He continued to cough, and was still brushing the insecticide off of his shirt, when he stumbled back around the vehicle and got in himself.

Kneeling on the ground and covered in poison, Jerry opened his eyes to check on Levi, who he had seen when he'd hit the ground. "You okay, Levi?" he asked.

"No worse for wear," Levi said, standing up. Jerry noticed the jacket Levi was carrying was sitting on the ground next to him, but there was no gun inside, only a long handled ice scraper with the frayed utility strap from the boat wrapped around it. When Levi noticed that Jerry had seen through his deception, he squeezed the metal ratchet-like fastener that was used to tighten the strap, causing it to make a clicking sound. He raised his eyebrows, "Better than nothing." he said. He groaned as he stood up, "Oh cold air, I hate the cold, hurts my joints." He straightened out his back. "Never seen nothing like that before, I mean it gets windy here, but not *that* windy. Well, not usually anyway. Oh, come on! My flag got all tangled up again! Eddie! Use the shovel to pick up the rest of that pesticide and put it back in the bag, then go get my stepladder. Remember, don't breathe any of that stuff in!" Levi started to walk back inside the house through the front door again. "You two had better change in the garage. You're gonna have to take showers again too. I don't want that stuff in my house."

Jerry shook his head and stood up. He attempted to brush the insecticide off of his shirt and pants, before walking over to Mark. Together, they both looked at the SUV as it turned around in one of the neighbor's driveways and headed down the street, seeing only their own reflections in the dark tinted glass as it drove off.

"Did...did you do that?" Jerry asked.

Mark looked at Jerry, raising an eyebrow. "HA, of course not! Come on, let's eat." Mark turned toward the garage.

"Why are you doing this? Standing up to these people? The government's probably going to come in here and take this whole thing down anyway, who cares about a couple of corrupt preachers?"

Mark stopped for a moment, and turned to face Jerry. "You make it sound like I'm the one who is doing something, and the preachers are the only ones I'm trying to reach. Truth be told, I'm just doing what I was asked to do by my Father. There's really no way for me to know all of the reasons why He wants me to do it, I'm just doing the best I can with what He gives me. As for why, well that's simple. I'm doing it because the God that made everything, and who loves everyone, had a Son once. A Son that was supposed to be the first of many. Now come on, I want an ice cream sandwich." Mark went into the garage. Jerry took a moment to digest Mark's answer and followed, stealing a brief glance at the sky as he closed the garage door behind them.

But godliness with contentment is great gain. For we brought nothing into the world, and we certainly can't carry anything out. But having food and clothing, we will be content with that.But those who are determined to be rich fall into a temptation, a snare, and many foolish and harmful lusts, such as drown men in ruin and destruction.For the love of money is a root of all kinds of evil. Some have been led astray from the faith in their greed, and have pierced themselves through with many sorrows. **-1 Timothy, 6:6-10**

Chapter Twenty-One

Christian Territory, Victory Center Meeting Room
Spokane, WA
Saturday, March 26[th,] 6:15PM PST

"He was out there telling our church members that prosperity is bad! He is only here to spread around his barbs and his discontent!" Pastor Harmin was livid. He raised his cane up with his right arm, shaking it in the air. After their confrontation with Mark, he and Pastor Obobwey had driven directly to the Victory Center and to Edwin Alstead's office, telling the receptionist that they weren't leaving until they had spoken to him in person. When Edwin arrived, he agreed to contact pastors Greeley, Branson, and Favorton for an emergency meeting in one of his own meeting rooms.

The room they used was much smaller than that of the temporary building near the Foundation Temple site. The chairs were all made of leather, and the smooth and shining metallic table in its center had its own built-in holographic system that could work in conjunction with the three sixty-inch flat-screen Q12 monitors that hung on the walls around them. Edwin had once called it their 'war room'. The most important leaders involved with setting up the territory often met there in secret, usually after the gatherings at the meeting house took place to decide what would *really* happen, as opposed to what they had allowed others to think, they along with the other less impressive pastors and church leaders had agreed upon.

"No, I was there," Obobwey said. "I heard what he said. He did not say that prosperity was bad, or that tithing was bad. He said that giving money to people like *us* was bad. That buying *our* products was bad, that being here was bad because he thinks it is not God's will. He even said that we make slaves out of our congregations!" He pounded the table with his fist. "He does not know who God is! If he did, he would be on our side. He was sent here by the enemy to confuse our people, to divide us!"

Pastor Favorton chimed in, "I understand what happened at the picnic. What I want to know is what happened when you two went to see him at the house where he is staying? One of my members was there. They ran to my home, screaming about how God had protected him from *you*."

Pastor Harmin looked at Pastor Obobwey, "He got away from us again." He said. Harmin bowed his head and peered down at the table ashamed, unable to look into the eyes of the others.

Pastor Favorton leaned over the table and looked directly at Harmin. "George, what happened?"

"We..." Harmin lifted his arms up again, that time more out of exasperation than anger. "We missed our opportunity. He eluded us."

"Eluded you? How? Don't you know where he is right now?" She looked around the table. "One man could destroy everything we have been trying to build here! You said you were going to take care of him! What are you going to do now?"

Pastor Branson had been listening intently, withholding his thoughts until all of the available facts had come out. He hadn't seen Mark in person up to that point, and was secretly interested in meeting the man based on what others were saying about him. "Do not assume he is the enemy." he said, responding to Favorton's words. "He may be from God. He could become a problem, but only if he has come here to stay. He might just be passing through." He stopped for a moment, pressing his lips together while using the thumb on his left hand to twirl a ring on his middle finger. "We need someone to go and to test his spirit." He closed his right fist, and softly lowered it down onto the table's surface. "To simply talk to him! Perhaps he can be convinced to come here to explain himself, and why he feels he needs to do what he is doing. Why would he be here if he did not think that God had led him here? Let us hear his story. I want to know how he even came to know about this place, so that he was in front of that gate just as things were getting squirrely out there. And don't forget," He looked at Edwin. "From what the three of you told me earlier, he did a much better job dissuading that judge from trying to force her way in here than you did! Perhaps he has been sent here to protect us for a short time while we get things set up. Let us not forget that God can move in such ways."

"It's true," Edwin said. "He was right when he confronted me this morning. We can replace the weapons quickly, and store them in a place that the authorities won't be able to find until they are needed. Those men at the gate jumped the gun and almost got us into a mess of trouble. It was a smart move on his part, and it looks like we now have more time to let things cool down with the new power structure." Edwin placed both of his hands flat on the table in front of him, giving him an air of control over the room. "I haven't seen it yet, but if there *is* a video out there that shows our men with weapons on the wall yesterday, our meeting this morning could have gone in a very different direction had he not been there." He took his right index finger and tapped it twice on the table top. "But if he wants to disrupt our ministries, there is little we can do in the short term. Once the gate is open again, we can toss him out, but there is nothing stopping him right now from climbing the wall, or one of the steeper hills they run up to, if he wants to get back in. The plan was to only put electric fencing and barbed wire along those areas when things started to get dicey down the road. But we do have another option. Before our corrupt government sent my father to jail, I saw how he dealt with people like Mr. Tunbridge first hand. We need only deny him access to our churches, while warning our members about him. We can use our messages and sermons to dissuade our congregations from engaging anyone who looks or acts like him in a subtle, indirect way, until he gives up and moves on."

Pastor Favorton turned her head to look at the last member of their core group. Pastor Greeley sat a few seats away from the others unmoving, his hands clasped in front of him. He had been looking down at them the entire time as they spoke, and hadn't said a word. "Pastor Greeley, Greg. You haven't said anything. What do you think?"

Greeley looked up at her with tired eyes. "I will meet with him," he said, nodding. "I was at the picnic, and heard what he said there. I wish to know what else he has to say. I'll find out how long he plans to stay, and I'll try to convince him not to interrupt what God is doing here anymore. He has very strong convictions, but I think he may be a reasonable man. He did not seem to be a nutcase or someone who wanted chaos." He looked back at his hands. His knuckles began to turn white as he spoke. "If he is willing to come and talk to the rest of you, I will invite him."

"We can do it here," Harmin said. "Tomorrow, after our morning services are finished." They looked around at one another for a moment to see if any one of them disagreed with the arrangement. The silence in the room that followed indicated that none of them did.

"Very well, go speak to him," Edwin said. "Tell him we would like to hear his message for us as the God chosen leaders of this place." He raised his eyebrows at Greeley as he said this. "Tell him after he has talked to us though, he has to go. We need all of this to blow over before we open ourselves up and allow the good people of Spokane to come in, so we can increase our revenue until people get used to us, and we are accepted as just another part of the community here. That, and we need to be sure that the people from out there who visit our churches are the kind we want. Recent events have been a stark reminder of that. When things eventually go down, as we all know they will, we don't want anyone like him stuck in here with us. We can't afford for that to happen. Now, if all of you don't mind, I have another meeting that I'm already late for. Greeley, please call each of us on our landlines tonight with his answer. Oh, and find out which church he is affiliated with. If he isn't one of those Catholics, maybe we can contact his pastor and convince them to do something about him for us." He stood up, straightened his suit, and walked out of the room.

The others followed one by one. Pastor Branson briefly put a reassuring hand on Pastor Greeley's shoulder as he walked by him. A few seconds later, Pastor Greeley, looking down again at his fiercely clasped hands, was the only one left. He looked to the ceiling. "Please, Lord, let your wisdom and love win out in this. I've done nothing other than what I thought you wanted me to do, but I have to confess I have never been completely sure that coming here was the true path you wanted us to follow. Please, Lord..." After another moment, he stood up and left, following the others out of the church.

"What was sown among the thorns, this is he who hears the word, but the cares of this age and the deceitfulness of riches choke the word, and he becomes unfruitful." **-Matthew, 13:22**

Chapter Twenty-Two

Christian Territory, Levi's Kitchen
Spokane, WA
Saturday, March 26th, 8:21PM PST

After they had cleaned themselves up for the second time since they'd arrived, Mark and Jerry joined the others in the kitchen. Levi put a frozen pizza in the oven and rummaged through a closet in his front hallway for a few minutes, before emerging with an old board game and a pair of slightly used sneakers. He gave the sneakers to Eddie. "Here," he said. "These were my son Johnny's. See if they fit you, Eddie, they look about the same size as yours. I'm surprised you don't have blisters on your feet wearing those old things." While Eddie tried on the shoes, Levi set up the board and began sorting out the pieces.

The game involved making words out of small wooden tiles for points. Jerry sat next to Eddie, and occasionally leaned in his direction to give him hints from time to time, while the others placed their pieces on the board, and argued over whether or not what they were spelling out were actual words. Every now and then, Mark would look up from the board and glance at the two, a degree of thoughtful pride in his eyes. Between turns, Levi would lean back in his chair look down through a well-aged pair of trifocals at his letter tiles, and think about the next step in his strategy, determined to best the others. Mark, on the other hand, didn't seem to care about winning, so much as making sure that everyone was being fair and following the rules. As the game went on, Levi, surprised at Jerry's ability to quickly organize and place long and complex words onto the board, began to watch him very closely, often saying things like, "Hmmm...you should be a writer." or "Are you sure you didn't choose the wrong profession, Jerry?" Jerry got the message.

"I read a lot." he eventually responded. "I've always had a big vocabulary." He thought about sharing his true vocation with the man, but decided it might be better if Levi wasn't aware of it for his own safety. At the very next opportunity, Jerry started to place smaller and simpler words onto the game board to throw him off, focusing instead on helping Eddie to stay in the game. Between slices of pepperoni and cheese, and wiping tomato sauce off of his mouth with a napkin, Mark told Levi and Eddie what had happened earlier that day while they were walking around town. He left out a few of the more exciting details, including the near physical altercation at the picnic and the prophetic woman at the church, not wanting to worry or confuse them.

Eddie placed 'OX' on the board, winning himself a triple score without Jerry's help. "Wow, that's a good spot for the 'X' piece Eddie!" Levi said. "You get a lot of points for that one." Eddie beamed, his smile infecting the others one by one. After he had doled out the points for the latest round, Levi got up, and walked over to a drawer below the kitchen counter next to the stove. Out of it, he took what looked like an old, and very well used portable media device, and some type of speaker that he plugged into it. "I usually just turn on the satellite radio service, but it's just not working. You have to find that jammer for the phone company Jerry." Understandably confused by the comment, Mark shot Jerry an odd look from across the table. Jerry put up his right hand and waved it from side to side, shaking his head while Levi's back was turned, as if to signal Mark not to worry.

Levi turned the device on and pressed play. For the next half hour, the sounds of old pre-twenty-first century music filled the house. According to Levi, the songs ranged from what Levi called Motown oldies, to 'original' Country, to popular power ballads from the nineteen-eighties. Most of it was relaxing, at least somewhat interesting, and incredibly dynamic, each one different than the last in almost every way. Every once in a while, Mark would say something like, "That was a good one." or "Oh man! Who was that?" Levi always knew the name of the artist and year that the song was released. The two of them talked about their different tastes in music as they continued to play. Before his next turn, Eddie asked for Jerry's help, and Jerry obliged. As he assisted the boy, he could sense that something had changed. Any tension that might have been left between any of them had melted away with the music. They were no longer a group of strangers, but were just some guys sitting around, enjoying each other's company. They were like a group of unwanted residents in that place, and as such, were dependent on one another. Like a group of soldiers behind enemy lines who had just only met, but had learned to tolerate one another just the same, in order to survive.

Jerry allowed the warm feeling of camaraderie wash over him as he studied Eddie's letters, looking for a good word that he could use in the next round. He liked these guys. He had almost nothing in common with them, but he enjoyed their company just the same, and despite the uncertainty of their situation, and the fact that he would likely be leaving soon, he was actually having a good time. Then a piece of music started that grabbed his attention. Two baritone voices began to sing a beautiful love song that stood out from the others. At one point, one of them hit a high note that seemed almost impossible without the help of digital manipulation, but of course, the song was recorded before digital voice alteration software had even existed.

"What song is that?" Jerry asked.

"That's 'Untamed Harmony' by the Valiant Brothers." Levi looked up at the ceiling for a moment. "That one came out in nineteen sixty...five, yeah nineteen sixty-five. I know all this stuff." He said. Jerry froze in his seat, paralyzed by the beautiful tune. He listened intently.

Suddenly, a knocking sound came from the front door. All of them stopped what they were doing, and turned their heads toward the front hallway at the same time. As his back was to the door, Jerry's body turned as well, and he almost slid out of his seat. The men who had come to Levi's house that afternoon had spooked him a little. It didn't help that before he'd come to the Territory, he'd spent little to no time around any Christians and only knew of them from what he'd heard through the grapevine or seen in the news feeds. He was smart enough to know that much of what was said about them in the press, like so many other groups, were one-off situations or exaggerations, but there was still the occasional story that was followed up by a court case. What came next often revealed how ruthless and inhumane the more zealous of those who claimed to belong to the "Christian" faith could be, and though Tom and the others at the office knew where he was, the group he'd fallen in with weren't exactly popular in the Territory. With the gate still closed and no easy way to escape, the simple truth was that if they wanted to, the leaders of the Territory could take them all out into the woods in the middle of the night and burn them at the stake, and no one would ever know what had happened to them.

After a second knock came, everyone looked at Levi. Levi looked back at each of them. Seeing the concern, on Jerry's face in particular, he stood up. "It's probably just one of my neighbors," he said. "I'll take care of it, don't worry." He took off his glasses, placed them on the table, and walked down the short hallway to the front end of the house. Jerry looked at Mark, who was looking in the direction of the front door with a modicum of interest, but did not appear to be nervous in any way. As if to show his lack of concern, Mark lifted his arms up, and rested his elbows on the table. He folded his hands together and yawned, looking back at the game board. Eddie turned back to the table and sat in silence, looking at his letters. His mind was completely focused on the game, and the last piece of pizza he was holding in his left hand. As the sound of the front door opening reached their ears, and the murmur of voices began to carry into the kitchen, Eddie started taking small bites of his slice while quietly deliberating which combination of letters he should use next. Slowly, he sounded out words to himself, while trying to take advantage of the extra time the visitor at the door had given him. Jerry on the other hand, was almost completely in fight or flight mode, and was on the edge of his seat, readying himself to get up at the first sign of trouble.

Not long after, Levi walked back into the kitchen, and looked at Mark. "It's for you." he said, and sat back down in his chair. From behind him, a middle-aged man appeared in a plaid shirt and jeans. He had gray hair, and was wearing his own pair of glasses, with lenses that were much thicker than Levi's. He walked around Mark, and pulled out a chair for himself, to Mark's left. Then he hesitated, and looked up for a moment at Levi.

"May I?" he asked.

"Feel free," Levi said, "Don't have any pizza left, but I can offer you some prune juice if you'd like some."

"It's good for you." Eddie said, still chewing on his pizza. He hadn't even so much as looked up from his tiles to see who had come in.

"Uh, no, thanks." the man said. "So, you're playing my favorite game!" He sat down and leaned toward the board, looking over his glasses at the words they had placed on it. "You can tell a lot about someone by the kinds of words they can come up with in a game like this, you know." he said. "Their level of education, how they think..."

"No offense, but who are you, and what do you want?" Jerry asked him. The man, slightly taken aback by Jerry's forwardness, leaned back in his chair. Sensing something serious in Jerry's voice, Eddie finally glanced up at the man who had joined them, before looking down at his letters again. Mark and Levi kept their eyes on the oddly dressed man, allowing Jerry to speak for them, waiting for an answer to his query in silence. Jerry looked at Levi. "Levi, I thought you said you don't invite vampires into your house." He looked at the visitor again. "Something about giving them power over you?"

Levi let out a small laugh. "He's not a vampire Jerry," He looked back at the man. "You aren't, are you?" Levi raised his eyebrows.

"Actually, I was going to ask you all if you would like to come to my place for dinner, but it looks like you've already eaten." the man in plaid said. "My name is Pastor Gregory Greeley. You can call me Greg if you want. Some of the young people in my church call me 'Double G'." He smiled, and looked around the table for some sign that he was making headway with them. His attempt at brevity was met with blank stares. "I'm with Abundant Grace Fellowship. It's one of the smaller churches that moved into the area. Many of the pastors that represent the smaller congregations which have come here look up to me, because I'm not afraid to challenge the bigwigs when I think they aren't doing the right thing. That means I have some pull with the Temple Foundation committee. The senior members are often willing to listen to what I have to say, and even take my advice from time to time. We had a meeting earlier today, and I volunteered to come and visit you all this evening, and to speak on their behalf." He looked at Jerry. "And I assure you, I am not a vampire."

Pastor Greeley looked around the table. "You may not have seen me there this morning, but I was at the picnic." He looked at Mark. "I saw you speak Mark, interesting stuff." Mark leaned back again, and crossed his arms. Greeley looked at Jerry. "I didn't catch *your* name, though." he said.

"Oh, of course," Jerry responded. "Arnold, Benedict Arnold. My friends just call me Benny, though." he said. Pastor Greeley gave him a strange look. Jerry noticed that everyone else was looking at him strangely as well after using the title. Greeley shook it off though, and moved on to Eddie. "And who might you be, young man?" he asked.

Eddie stopped chewing and looked up from his letters, which he had started moving around. "Eddie." he said, his mouth partially full.

Levi spoke up, "He's my ward for the moment, an orphan. His aunt felt like she couldn't take care of him, and decided that the nice Christian people here would do it for her. She dropped him off, just inside the gate the day before it was finished. He spent outside, with nowhere to go. Mark and uh...Mr. Arnold, here, found him before they showed up at my place. Tomorrow, when the gate opens again, I'll be taking him to the police station downtown. They asked me to look after him until then. The gate *is* still opening tomorrow, isn't it?"

Upon hearing Eddie's story, a look of shock came across Greeley's face. "Uh, yes, yes, of course. The um, malfunction is almost fixed. They should have it open by early tomorrow morning." He looked down as he said this, placing his hands flat on his thighs, "Well, how about that wind this afternoon!" His voice shook a little. "Caused quite a mess for everyone, didn't it? My wife and I live on one of the highest hilltops in the area. It knocked one of our patio tables over, and carried it clear off a cliff. Took me a while to find it..." He let out a nervous laugh that created a disquieting air in the room. "Uh, stopped now though, it's pretty quiet outside."

Mark began to slowly shake his head, and looked at Levi. Levi shrugged his shoulders. Mark turned to look at Pastor Greeley again. "What can I do for you?" he asked, finally breaking his silence. Greeley looked at the others sitting at the table. "They are friends," Mark said. "All of them are supposed to be here. You can cut to the chase if you want, you don't have to be polite."

Greeley's brow wrinkled. He looked down at the table's surface in front of him, as if contemplating his next move. Then he looked up at Mark again, and said, "I take it you are here to talk to those who followed God to this place, or to give a prophetic word to us? What message do you think you were told to give us?"

"I have no message, only myself." Mark said plainly.

"Then why are you still here? What is your role in the Church? What is your calling?"

"I've been a missionary, of one kind or another, most of my Christian life. Over the years, the Lord has taught me to operate in many of the spiritual gifts that are in Paul's letters, though rarely in the open. Usually, He leads me to use them to witness to, or help the lost outside of the church, or the neglected people in it. Only a few times has He asked me to step out and be seen like I have been here." Jerry attempted to follow the conversation, but found it difficult to do so, without the proper context. Still, he listened closely to what they were saying, and tried his best to remember every word.

"So God told you to come here and do these things, why?" Greeley asked.

"I haven't done anything but show up and follow His directions," Mark said. He paused for a moment, carefully deciding what to say next. "All I can say is that whatever happens from my being here, will not have happened because of me, but because of what the Holy Spirit did around me. I am not here because I want to be among the people here. I am here because my Father told me to come, and I want to do the will of my Father. He only gives me limited knowledge and instruction, and I follow Him wherever He wants me to go. Now let me ask you a question, what is this place?

Why are all of these people here? I hadn't even heard of it before I was led here. This can't be Biblical. This is out of the world completely, not 'In the world but not of it'."

Greeley wrapped his right fist in the fingers of his left hand. He looked around the table again, taking in the faces of the four men that God had thrown into his life. He began to nod. "Right," he said, "If you come with me to my home, I think I can help you with your questions. There's something there I'd like to show you, that might help to illustrate what we are trying to do here much better than any explanation I could give with mere words. Then maybe you can tell me what you plan to do with the answers."

"HA!" Levi let out a crass, rebuking laugh, "You expect them to go with you, after the lackeys that were sent here this afternoon? Were they sent to kick them out, or just rough 'em up a little?"

"I had nothing to do with that. If I wanted any of you hurt or tossed out of the Territory, I would have brought men of my own. The gate is opening tomorrow, anyway."

"Yeah, for now," Jerry said.

"Listen," Greeley attempted to regain control of the conversation. "I was put in charge of helping to organize where and how this place would be laid out. I also had some input into emergency planning. I have everything you need to know about this place at my home. If you don't want to take my word for it-"

"Ok, we'll go." Jerry interjected. Mark and Levi turned to look at him so fast, the sudden movement made Levi's neck crack. Both of them gave him surprised looks, stunned by his sudden turnaround. Mark's gaze moved from Jerry's face to the game board in front of him. Jerry had placed an unusual word on the board earlier that evening when the game had first started, 'Valiant'. Mark remembered the song, and the words the old woman used at the Korean church.

"Listen, kid," Levi said, holding his neck, as if it were in pain. "You don't have to go with this-"

"We'll go." Mark said, still looking at the tiles on the board. He lifted his head, and turned to Levi. "Jerry and I will go, we'll be alright. We won't be long. It shouldn't take more than an hour or so.

****

Pastor Greeley drove a large utility vehicle that looked like it could climb over the Himalayas without much trouble. It was a great green monster, new and shining, even in the dim light of the waning moon. "This is only for emergencies, of course," he said. "After tomorrow, the CAVs should be working again, and I'll have to put this baby back in storage. What do you think?" Jerry and

Mark shared a glance, and got in the passenger side doors without saying a word.

At first, they drove in the direction of the Temple Foundation site, but Greeley turned off onto another road before reaching it. The road was steep but well paved, making for an exceptionally smooth ride to the top of what turned out to be a high hillside with a tremendous view. When the street leveled off, Jerry could see all of northern Spokane and the surrounding area from the vehicle, the lights from thousands of homes in and around the Territory stretching into the dark, all the way into the center of the city and beyond. It didn't take long for him to realize that they were driving on the very hill he had seen just south and west of the gate when he'd first arrived.

They passed one mini-mansion after another. The homes there were different from the sprawling McMansions below, as they were far larger in size, and had much more property on either side. They also looked like they were made more out of stone and brick, than wood or prefabricated materials. All of them were well lit, and some were surrounded by small walls of their own, with steel or iron gates at the ends of their driveways. They passed a total of three black SUVs along the way that were parked on the sides of the street, before reaching Greeley's home. Each had dark tinted windows, and flood lamps attached to their driver's side rear view mirrors, and none of them had visible license plates.

After they passed the last SUV, Greeley slowed down and stopped his at the gate to a property with a frontal exterior that faced southwest. Greeley opened his window, and looked at a facial scanner that stood next to it. The gate opened, and they pulled into a long driveway that led to a large home, with stone surfacing at its base, and a white façade. The house had two garages and four floors, and must have been two hundred feet in length. Three of the windows on the southern end of the house were made of stained glass. They were thin in shape, each one only about a foot wide, and coming to sharp points at their full height. Greeley noticed that Jerry was looking at the strange windows from the passenger seat. "That's our sanctuary for now, where my church meets." he said. The driveway ended in a cul-de-sac. He parked on the far side, next to a small, illuminated path that led across a thin patch of grass to the front door.

They got out of the vehicle, waited for the Pastor to walk around the car to meet them, and followed him along the thin winding pathway. Greeley walked up to the large, red front door, which had a Christmas wreath with the words 'Merry Christmas' still hanging on it, and pressed a button, there next to an oversized handle on the right side. Above the button was a small camera. A woman's voice came from it. "I see you, honey. Are those the men you talked about?"

"They are, Diane." he said. "Boogaloo."

The woman giggled, and the door opened. "That's my wife. She's already in bed, probably reading. I can get you tea or something else to drink once we get to the den, this way, guys." He led them inside. "Please, take your shoes off in the vestibule. You can put them on the rack with ours, right over there." Jerry and Mark obliged, and took off their shoes. The entryway to the home was a sight to see. The white tiles that made the flooring stopped, quickly turning into a wide hardwood surface only a few feet inside. Two spiral stairways, one on the north end of the entryway and the other on the south, also made of hardwood, reached up to the third and fourth floors. Behind them, four large rectangular windows revealed a small in-ground pool on the other side of the house, and the lights of the city beyond.

His shoes removed, Jerry walked the ten meters across the large open space, and looked out through the windows on the other side. The hall and pool area were full of light, illuminated by a large, crystalline chandelier that hung from the high ceiling. As he approached the glass, Jerry found that he could look over the edge, past a railing that was suspended over a sharp cliff face. Far below to the north, he could see the gate itself, illuminated by street lamps, but it was what he remembered of the dirt mound that verified the location in his mind. *This can't be far from where I saw those people standing when I first got here.* He thought. *What's that?* Behind the mound of earth where he'd first set eyes on Mark north of the gate, he thought he saw something moving that was yellow in color, or was it orange? He couldn't tell.

"Uh, this way please." Greeley said. Both he and Mark were waiting at the southern side of the room, near an entrance to another area.

"Oh, of course," Jerry said. "Sorry, I just really like your view."

They went into the next room, where their feet met soft carpeting that was wall to wall. The room was twenty feet long at its widest point. On the far side, two leather chairs were placed with care in front of a wide, red brick fireplace, above which hung a gigantic mantle piece. On the chairs were several small pillows, covered with homemade crocheted images of crosses and angels. The mantle was covered as well, but not in Christian imagery. On, above, and around it, were a series of large printed photos that Jerry had a hard time making out, as the fireplace was not lit, and no lights were on nearby. A small coffee table sat in the middle between them, several books stacked on it, along with a chess set. A game was taking place, and it looked like the black pieces were winning. Along the walls of the rest of the room, were shelves full of books and mementosthat gave the space the appearance of an open library. Against the wall to Jerry's right, was a long leather couch, with a long metallic table in front of it. On his left, a wide set of carpeted steps led through a tall archway into some kind of den, where the soft lights of several lamps shone over a table with something displayed on it, and a nearby desk.

As the Pastor led them through the parlor-like area, he explained how the hardwood floor they had walked across near the entrance to the house had been moved from his old home in Kentucky. On their way by the fire place, the objects that were in the pictures became clearer. They were not of the Pastor's congregation, nor were they a record of his accomplishments, as Jerry had thought when he'd first entered the room. Instead, they appeared to be a historical record of sorts. In each photo, one of three children was doing some kind of activity, like swimming or horseback riding. Two of them were boys, and one was a girl. The photos were separated into three groups, and increased in size on either side above the mantle, until they met on its surface. The three largest pictures sat in the middle of the wide shelf, which was made of a thick hardwood, a quick examination revealing that they were photorealistic,semi-three dimensional images. They were also about twenty inches by thirty inches in size, the kind of specialty portraits that cost a small fortune to commission.

Standing in front of and around them, were smaller pictures of the same individuals, grown and with their own families. Aside from how expensive the presentation must have been to create the whole thing, it looked to Jerry less like a family photo gallery, and more like the type of shrine a serial killer might make for his victims. The eerie display was made even worse by the darkened room itself, as the three overly happy faces in the lifelike portraits seemed to follow them, their incredibly white eyes and teeth standing out, as Jerry continued across the carpet and up the small steps into the next room.

At the top of the steps, their feet hit hardwood again. Another set of large windows that looked over the cityscape, stretched from floor to ceiling on the far side of the den. These were built with a more modern, angular design, than the more traditional style that encompassed the rest of the house. A laptop sat on a small desk set against the northern wall, a mug half-full of cold coffee beside it. Nearby, an open Bible sat on a large lined notepad. Directly in front of the windows, several large pieces of paper were pinned to a drafting table, next to which was a small trash bin full of crumpled sheets of paper. In the center of the room, a large table stood with a cloth lying over an oddly shaped object that could only have been one thing, what Greeley had brought them there to see. "Here," Greeley said. He pulled the sheet off of the table, revealing a complete miniature of the entire New Christian Territory area. It was impressive, and incredibly detailed. Not only did it appear to have every building represented at scale, but it also included objects as small as individual trees, cars and even people, all of which appeared lifelike, having been 3D printed with great precision.

"So, you're an architect, then?" Jerry asked. He leaned over the extensively thorough mockup, and found the Temple Foundation Site. Noticing that the shack he had seen was the only thing not present, his eyes moved onto the gate. Seeing the archway, he searched for Levi's house, and then Greeley's home. When he looked up to Greeley for a response, he noticed that Mark was standing on the opposite side of the table doing the same.

"Yes," Greeley answered. He was standing at the far end of the table with his arms crossed, looking quite satisfied with his work. "Well, I *was* an architect before I became a pastor full time. After we joined with the other churches, Alstead himself approached me, and asked if I could put together this model and some other future plans. We've had some very productive meetings here. Through these windows, you can see most of the northeastern end of the Territory. We can walk out to the patio next to the pool to see the rest. This wasn't an easy job, either. When we decided to make the wall, we had to place families that were willing to be in charge of their own sections in certain properties. At times, the churches chipped in to help them buy the land. It was only after the Supreme Court took over, that Alstead and Harmin convinced the others we should complete it earlier than we originally planned.

"Where is the wall?" Jerry asked. "I don't see it, only the arch."

"OH!" Pastor Greeley said with some excitement. "Here, here." He turned around, and opened a door that led into a thin but deep closet. Inside, Jerry could see shelves full of artistic drafting supplies and instruments. Greeley came back out, carrying two separate foam carved structures. "I haven't covered or painted them yet. The walls weren't completed when I last worked on them." He placed the foam pieces on top of the model.

"Originally, the walls were to be completed as a last resort, part of an emergency plan, should some big calamity happen. We could weather the storm, and take in some of the local population if they needed our help. Otherwise, we were always supposed to be just another town that just so happened to be full of a certain...type of born again Christians."

"Huh," Jerry said. "Creepy."

Mark looked up at Jerry, smiled sarcastically, and shook his head. Greeley looked at both of them, confused. "Uh, well, you can see that the Temple Foundation building is complete here. That's where we planned for all of the churches to converge, so they can work together on things. It's like a great meeting hall, where everyone will be able to hold events and congregate, much like the picnic we held this morning. We were even going to invite members of other churches in the greater Spokane area to our events, including the Catholics. That probably won't happen now, though." He reached across the table, and using a finger, tapped what looked like some kind of odd looking structure, with a round, red ball on top. It stood in a small clearing, not far from the Temple Foundation building. "We even plan to put in a Tesla tower so we can generate electricity without depending solely on the wind turbines and solar panels that are being set up now. The plan is to put in a series of batteries that can store excess energy underground, so that we won't have to rely on the city's power grid. That was my idea."

"So why a physical model, though?" Jerry asked.

"I work best with these materials. Also, we didn't want anyone to know what we were up to before we had set anything in motion, should someone find a way to hack into one of our networks."

"What about the radio interference? How did you intend to communicate quickly over such a large area without the ability to use synced devices, or walkie-talkies for that matter?"

"You mean the signal jammer," Greeley said. "That's only a temporary stop-gap measure. We promised our people that when they came to live here, they wouldn't have to worry about drones intruding on their privacy from the outside. When we began to finalize the wall, we also realized that we didn't want anyone to know exactly what we were up to, or for anyone coming in to be able to communicate with one another in case any authorities decided to enter our sanctuary. So, in order to give ourselves time to react in an emergency, we set up the jammer. Now that the wall is up though, an electro-magnetic deflection ring is being built along the top. That will stop any drones from coming in, and will block any specific signal or signals we decide to set it to. In a few days, the jammer will no longer be necessary. Everyone will be able to use their regular devices again, and CAVs will be able to come in and out of the area. No one really has a CAV here, though, even those who were here before we came. They're much more popular in the big cities. In the meantime, we use landline phones to communicate, and speak in a code of sorts to arrange meetings."

"That's not all you use," Jerry said. "What about those monocles and cards I saw at the picnic today? How do they work while the jammer is still active?"

"You mean the Elisha tech. That's nothing special, really. It works on an extremely low frequency that no one uses anymore. It looks new, but it's really just old technology that the government made for submarine communication last century. It takes a ton of energy to use over long distances, but for a place like the Territory it's ideal. I know the signal uses the regular telephone lines in the area like a big antenna, that it took a lot of work to get it up to a bandwidth speed that was practical enough to use, and that the devices can be custom printed and connect to an intranet system somewhere nearby. Anyone living inside the wall can use it to communicate. The system is regulated by an A.I. that monitors everything that goes through it, and will immediately shut down any device interfaced with it that isn't following the rules. It's still in its Beta form. Every pastor was allowed to put in their two cents when they first decided to build it, but I was never on that project. That one is handled by Alstead's people." He pointed to the laptop on his desk. "They gave me an Extremely Low Frequency adapter for my old computer, but I haven't gotten around to hooking it up. To be honest, I'm just not interested. Amazingly enough, this house still had a landline phone when we moved in, and I think I like it better, even if the E.L.F. interferes with the sound a little when you're talking to someone on it. A lot of us came here, in part at least, to get away from the six G towers, and all of the unnecessary drama that comes with them.

"Is that how they got the word out, to bring the printed guns to the gate during the storm?" Mark asked.

"No," Greeley said. "The guns were stored at a private residence not far from the gate. The owner of the home was supposed to contact us in the event of an emergency before passing them out but panicked and started to do it without permission. His stupidity almost got us all arrested and could have cost us everything, had that Chief Justice decided to come in here for a closer look. That's one of the reasons I'm willing to tell you all of this. The others aren't sure if you are from God, but from what I've seen and heard about the both of you so far, I believe you might be. If God has something to tell us, I want to know what it is, and I'm beginning to wonder if- perhaps He sent you to set some things straight here before they get out of control."

Mark stood up straight, and looked the Pastor in the eye. "I told you, I don't have a specific message. I will say, though, from what I've seen so far, I don't approve. Nor would God, I think."

"Then at least tell me where you're from." Greeley said. "Are you affiliated with a church in the area? With some other church? What denomination are you? Are you Catholic?" His voice lowered, "You're not a Baptist, are you?"

"My last church was nondenominational, as was the one where I first encountered the Holy Spirit," Mark said. "It was in Kansas City. You may have heard of it. 'Worship and the Word', Andrew Stephen's ministry."

"You were part of 'Worship and the Word' ministries? That's amazing. But they broke up, what, five years ago?"

"Has it been that long?" Mark reached over and touched one of the little people on the model with his forefinger. "I hadn't noticed, I've attended several churches since and helped some smaller ministries here and there as God led me, nothing big." He looked up and smiled at the Pastor before looking down at the model again.

"What happened there? No one really knows why the ministry broke up. They were heavily involved in inner city outreach, right?"

"Nationwide street ministry, yes.Very organized, very Spirit-filled.Saw God do a lot in those days. My job was starting programs with the homeless, mostly on the east coast, but also throughout the midwest." He sighed. "Of course we were opposed by secular groups who didn't like what we were doing, but that wasn't what did the program in. People within the church, who had other plans for the ministry started grumbling, started saying we weren't really who we claimed to be. From the shadows, they slandered us, said we were doing things we weren't, so that they could step up and take positions of power in the church for themselves. They came up with their own ideas that had nothing to do with what God had spoken over the church and tried to gain control. When that happened, the more spiritual members, and those who actually served, started to pray. One day most of them simply moved on, going to other churches or ministries, taking their gifts with them. Myself, and my wife included. The Lord had answered our prayers and called us to do other things. We took it as a sign that a season of ministry had ended, and another one was beginning. A few months later, I heard from some old friends who were still attending the services there. They said that infighting had broken out. Those who remained began blaming one another for the exodus. Not long after, the church folded."

Jerry listened to the conversation like an astute student. Hearing Mark describe his past spurred something inside him. He joined him in looking down at the model again, taking a step backward, so he could see it in its entirety. Small blue signs had been placed at most of the intersections. They started somewhere around the middle of the area, and went north along two streets, meeting up again before heading off of the edges of the model completely. They reminded him of the emergency signs in Puyallup that had been meant to help people escape the area in case of an eruption on Mt. Rainier, a precaution that had proven to be less than effective in that instance. He put voice to what he was thinking, "I see markers for escape routes to the north on different streets. The blue signs next to the stop lights at the intersections.

Those signs haven't been put up yet." He looked at the Pastor. "You're not just hiding from the world, you're preparing for something, aren't you? Protecting yourselves and your families, even people from churches like yours wouldn't abandon all of the work you've done, all the progress you've made in your cities of origin, not without a good reason."

Greeley became uncomfortable at the suggestion. He picked up the cover, and began to place it over the model again. "Like I said, I was put in charge of contingency plans should a calamity occur. The signs lead to a back way to Canada, we-"

"Why Canada?" Jerry asked, "Why not Missoula or Boise? Come to think of it, Spokane wouldn't be a nuclear target. You're outside of Yosemite's secondary ash zone. I can't see why you'd need an escape route like this, it's not like you're close to a mountain like Rainier, and there is no strategic-" He grabbed the cover and looked closer. On the far northern end of the model, he saw what looked like a pair of large oil containers. They were similar to the old abandoned oil storage units that were common in Seattle's industrial district. "Wait," Jerry turned to face Pastor Greeley, a shocked look appearing on his face.

"We are following what we believe the Lord is telling us to do. We have to be ready for anything." Greeley said. "The others who have followed us here...are just...getting out of the way."

"Out of the way of what?" Jerry demanded an answer. "What is really going on here?"

Pastor Greeley looked at Jerry, "And who are you again? I know where he is from, but I know nothing about you-"

"I told you he's a friend of mine." Mark stated plainly. "Look, at this point you are only drawing attention to yourselves. He's right, why corner yourselves like this? What do you think is coming?"

Greeley gave Jerry an untrusting stare. "We didn't mean to cause a ruckus. It was supposed to go more smoothly than this. That's why, when it all started, we worked hard to get the correct people elected and used money to influence the rest."

"You mean bribe." Jerry said.

"I mean influence. We donated to their campaigns through people who already lived in the area. It was all perfectly legal. But then, some discontented folks that left our churches for...different reasons, began to ring some bells, and we ended up with a mob outside of the gate just as it was being completed."

"You didn't actually think that you could get away with this without anyone noticing, did you?"

"With the riots happening everywhere, we really didn't think anyone would care about us claiming a small part of a city on the edge of nowhere. Thankfully, the riots happening in Seattle and elsewhere distracted most of the country from what happened here and continue to."

"Thankfully?"

Mark tried to calm Jerry down by motioning to him with one hand, before speaking himself. "So, what are you saying? That something is coming? A war? Do you think the tribulation is near or something?"

Pastor Greeley scanned the faces of his visitors once more, before lifting his hands in the air as if surrendering, "I didn't tell you this." He looked at Jerry. "This is not on the record. We, we have sources that indicate that a change in management is coming. That is all I am going to say."

"What, like a coup?" Jerry asked.

Mark raised his hand toward Jerry again, this time motioning for him to stop. "Why did you come here?" he asked. "I've told you why I moved on from my old ministry, what made you abandon yours? Was it something similar? Tell me, what happened that caused you to think the Lord was telling you to come here?"

"You know what it's like out there!" Greeley's voice took on a defensive tone. "Everyone knows! Ninety percent atheist, no morals, trouble coming in from every which way! They've forgotten that this country was once a peaceful place. They take what they want from those God has blessed, and squander it amongst themselves! In some cities they're having sex in public, and no one even cares! It's chaos!" He raised his voice and pointed a finger down at the model. "How are we to live in such a world? They sacrifice their own children *after* they're born, like they were a bunch of ancient pagan tribes! During the last service we held at my old church, people were waiting outside to physically attack my congregation and even attempted to sexually assault some of them! Not because of anything we did to them, but because of what the Satanic system is programming them to believe about us!" He locked eyes with Mark, "All of us. It's more like Sodom and Gomorrah out there than ever before, to say nothing about all of the new diseases going around! We aren't safe out there!" He waved a hand in the air, exasperated. "They're even trying to force us to give them our children so they can be indoctrinated with complete nonsense, and be turned against us! They've taken away our ability to defend ourselves in our own homes! This is the only way we could think of to protect ourselves, our families! Here they at least have a fighting chance! The people who have come here have given all that they had to be safe, to protect their children. How can they go back into that mess of a world when they have given so much, and when their leaders have told them it is the will of God? And with what's coming next-" He looked down and became silent.

Jerry and Mark looked at one another. Mark shrugged. "What, what's coming next?" Jerry asked calmer this time. For the first time, he found himself able to sympathize with the man. He knew full well the wonton state of the country he had been born into, and though he never had agreed with everything people did, he'd just figured it was none of his business. Then again, he'd never even considered bringing children into the world.

Mark gave Pastor Greeley a moment to calm down. He crossed his arms, and looked at the floor. Then, using a softer tone, he asked again in a low voice, "What is coming next? Please tell us so we can understand Pastor."

Greeley looked up, raising his hands again in defeat. He walked over to his desk, pulled out his chair, and sat down, before attempting to speak again. "We don't know exactly. All we know is that five or six years ago, those in our churches that were on the-" He pointed a finger at his head and twirled it. "You know the doomsday preppers and survivalists? Well, a few of them started coming to church talking about revolution. They started telling us that someone behind the scenes, someone without a name, was organizing something. Then at one of our conferences," He looked at Jerry, "Events where we would meet and preach to one another's congregations, a pastor brought it up in an off-hand kind of way. We started comparing notes, and noticed many similarities in what these people were telling us, like someone was crossing the country, every part of it, and influencing our people, preparing them for something, a civil war against the government. They were recruiting you see, even some of the pastors were approached by people who wanted to know if we would like to participate. Of course, no one did."

Jerry walked around the model, leaned on the table it sat upon, and crossed his arms. He had found the story he was searching for, but there was more, there had to be. Pastor Greeley wasn't finished yet. He was still holding something back, Jerry could tell by the look on his face. He wanted to get something off of his chest, something he hadn't been able to tell anyone, or couldn't. "And?" Jerry asked. "What happened next?" Mark looked at Jerry, and back to Pastor Greeley. Both of them stood in silence, awaiting an answer.

Greeley sat back, took a deep breath, and sighed. "Then one year Edwin Alstead held a private meeting at one of the conferences. He invited only the pastors he'd worked with in the past. You should have seen his presentation for the New Christian Territory. He had it all worked out, revenue streams, projections, everything we would need to establish ourselves here. He had his people do public works research, and had lawyers to look into Washington State tax laws. He had plans of how to get into the area's politics, ideas about how to get the local community leaders on our side. He even had a strategy for bringing in families that had their own businesses first, guaranteeing them a permanent customer base and workforce that would do what they were told, a hard proposition to resist when A.I. jobs were taking work away from everyone hand over fist everywhere you looked. He said God had come to him, claiming that it was part of how He would save us from trouble like it says in Second Thessalonians. The idea of setting up the wall like Nehemiah came soon after, and everyone started to act like we were the new nation of Israel. That's when I first started doubting what we were doing, but by then, I was already in over my head. My congregation was all in, and I had led them here. God wasn't stopping us, so I just kept going along with it. We needed a place that could be closed off and protected. We needed a place where our children and grandchildren could be safe. Don't you understand?"

Jerry was confused. He shook his head slowly. "No," he said, "I don't understand. Aren't you supposed to reach people who don't know your God? How can you do that from here?"

"Clearly, you do not understand." Greeley said. "We are only doing what we need to in order to protect what God has given us! We're just trying to be good stewards!"

"But you must know this can only end badly for *all* of you if you think you can take U.S. territory without a fight, I mean, you've got a good amount of people here, but you're no Provo."

"I understand completely." Mark said. "You chose to abandon the great commission. To leave the lost to their fate, so that you could keep and protect what God has only entrusted you with for a moment." Pastor Greeley bowed his head in shame. His hands came up to meet it. Mark continued. "I just hope you haven't lost your souls in the process." He looked at Jerry. "This place is a refuge for those who spent too many years, allowing others to tickle their ears. They were used to being told that the world would get better for them and their children, only to find that it was slowly becoming more hostile and wicked instead. Without really understanding the Bible, and being led astray by false teachers, they ended up here. They just didn't know where else to go. They fear the world, and most of all, they fear for their children's futures, futures that were never guaranteed to be rosy, or even safe, in this fallen world. It was the Pastor who did not understand, Jerry, he and the other leaders that walked away from the path God set before them, long ago."

Pastor Greeley sunk into his chair. His head remained bowed as Mark spoke. At first, the expression on his face was one of disgust and anger. As the Pastor began to cry however, it became one of pity, and sadness. "Of course, you are right." the Pastor said. "I tried to warn them. I've gone to God so many times, asking for Him to help them to see." He looked at Jerry. "For years, I preached the Gospel of Christ. I thought that being blessed with money and fellowship with other Christians were the most important parts, the only real signs of true fruit in an obedient Christian's life. I told them that God wanted to bless them, and it was their duty to accept the blessing so they could give back to the ministry, to God. If they didn't, something was wrong with them." He looked down at his feet. A shadow of remembrance passed over his face, and he became quiet and took a breath. "Then, one day just before we started moving here, I heard that a young woman in my church had hung herself because of how the others had been treating her at church. Some had been telling her that the lack of blessings in her life must have been from unrepented sin and laziness, and ostracized her. I had no idea what was going on, I was too busy getting all of this ready, and had left the more troubled members of the congregation for the elders to deal with by then anyway." He waved his hands at the table. "She was one of the most virtuous and loving young women I had ever met, so giving. She had wanted a husband, but couldn't find one. The lack of love in her personal life, combined with the treatment she got at church, just became too much for her to bear."

Upon hearing the sad story, Jerry lowered his own head. The suicide crisis wasn't isolated to church life, he had lost three of his own friends to overwhelming bouts of depression and hopelessness over the years, and he was only twenty-seven. It was something that society in general had given up on, seeing it as a logical option, a choice to leave a desperate world in the hopes of finding a new one on the other side. Apparently, some churches had taken after the rest of the world, deciding to ignore the problem altogether, instead of taking a closer look at themselves and how they handled the issue when it appeared in their midst.

Greeley continued, "Next to her bed they found a Bible. It was open, the only scripture marked on the page was Acts, chapter five, verses forty and forty-one: 'They took his advice; and after calling the apostles in, they flogged them and ordered them not to speak in the name of Jesus, and *then* released them. So they went on their way from the presence of the council, rejoicing that they had been considered worthy to suffer shame for *His* name.' When I heard of this, I realized I had been wrong, wrong all this time. The gift that God gives us, is the ability through the Holy Spirit to embrace our persecution for the glory of God, not run away from it and expect Him to take care of us in our running. But it was too late. My congregation had been led astray....by me, and I've been living a lie ever since." Tears continued to roll down his face. Jerry, seeing a box of tissues on the Pastor's desk, walked around the table and took one out to give to the humbled man.

Mark knelt down in front of the Pastor. He looked up at him and, in his soft but sure voice, said, "There may come a time when the Lord asks for His people to leave their lives behind as we get closer to the Tribulation, but for now we are still able to bring God's light into this world. The world still needs men like you."

Greeley shook his head. "You don't understand, I can tell you've never been a pastor, Mark. I can't leave my flock, not now. Not after what I've done. All I can do is try to be better, maybe later I...I don't know."

Then Mark did something that surprised Jerry. He reached out, put his hand on the Pastor's shoulder, and said a prayer for his soul. When he was finished, he said, "God has sent me to answer the prayers of one of His true children. You are part of the reason I am here." Greeley looked up, hopeful. It was strange for Jerry to see a man of such strength and dignity who, having suddenly collapsed into the depths of despair, come back out so quickly, as if he knew all along there was a way out of his private struggle, he just hadn't seen the shape of it until that moment. Mark went on, "When it happens, whatever God does here, do not stop it. Do not get in the way, because you will be getting in God's way. Afterward, you will know what to do. He will show you what to do."

Mark stood up, and walked to the other side of the room, placing his hands on his hips. He turned around. "I would like to speak to them, to the other leaders. Perhaps God has something to say, after all. Perhaps He led me here because He knew that I would. Can you call them and arrange a meeting?"

Greeley wiped the tears from his eyes. "They have already instructed me to invite you to a meeting tomorrow at the Victory Center across from the Temple Foundation site, after the first services are finished. I don't think they would enjoy having someone they don't know or trust coming in to tell them what to do, though."

"Go ahead and tell them I have something to say. Tell them that I will leave the Territory when I have spoken my peace. Tell them after the meeting I won't bother them again. But I won't speak to them in some back room. No, we'll meet at that meeting house I saw near the Temple site, and we'll be there at noon."

Melchizedek king of Salem brought out bread and wine. He was priest of God Most High.He blessed him, and said, "Blessed be Abram of God Most High, possessor of heaven and earth.Blessed be God Most High, who has delivered your enemies into your hand." Abram gave him a tenth of all.
-Genesis, 14:18-20

Yahweh has sworn, and will not change his mind: "You are a priest forever in the order of Melchizedek." **-Psalms, 110:4**

Chapter Twenty-Three

Christian Territory, Levi's Place
Spokane, WA
Saturday, March 26[th,] 9:58PM PST

P astor Greeley drove them back to Levi's. No one was waiting for them when they got there, but that didn't stop Jerry from taking a quick look around, to see if anyone threatening was lurking somewhere in the shadows. He looked up and down the street, straining his eyes as much as he could in the dimly lit driveway. When he was satisfied that none of the shady looking SUVs were parked nearby, he peered over the fence and into the backyard. Then to Mark's surprise, he got down on his knees to see if anyone was hiding under Levi's car, and finished his search by lifting up one end of the tarp that was still draped over the boat.

"A little paranoid aren't you?" Mark asked, amused by the strange analogy. "Don't worry, they won't try anything tonight. They need Pastor Greeley on their side to make this place work. They wouldn't ask him to invite us to meet them, only to jump us in the middle of the night."

"You would think," Jerry said. "But I've learned over the years not to trust anyone when in a strange and unfamiliar place. Especially one that has a bunch of religious nuts with access to 3D printed guns, no offence." He walked to the front of the garage, and turned to look down both sides of the street one last time. "Just to be clear, as far as I'm concerned, just about everyone here is crazy, and in my experience, crazy people are not exactly consistent in their ability to follow through with their plans, or their promises."

Mark let out a small chuckle. "Are you sure you're not talking about people in Seattle?"

Jerry gave him a knowing look. "I get why the crazy people there are off their rockers. Not here, though, these people fell off an entirely different kind of furniture. The kind I wouldn't want in my house, if you catch my drift."

"Furniture?" Mark asked.

"Yeah, you know, like falling off the sofa...at the therapist."

"Oh, Understood." Mark grinned wide and nodded, trying to hold back another laugh.

Levi had left the garage door partially open using the milk crate Mark had sat on the night before, propping it up a few feet off the ground so they could get back in. Mark reached down, and pulled the door up so that it retracted the rest of the way. Sleeping on his inflatable mattress under a thick and comfortable looking quilt was Eddie, his arms pulled up close to his face. In one hand he held the portable game system, and in the other, his new pair of sneakers. He was breathing deeply. Jerry wondered if anything could wake the boy while he slept. Mark and Jerry looked at one another and then moved to their cots.

Both of them sat down and took off their shoes. Mark took off his socks as well, and stuffed them into his hiking boots. Jerry rubbed his aching feet for a few minutes, before mimicking him and doing the same. *How long has it been since I walked this much in one day?* He asked himself. *Man! I really need to get out of the apartment more often.* When he'd finished massaging his toes, he saw that Mark was already lying down. He was looking up at the ceiling of the garage with his hands clasped behind his head, and appeared to be listening to the sounds of the evening again. Taking a second to listen himself, Jerry only heard the sounds of crickets outside, and the occasional rustling of leaves.

Jerry puffed up his pillow, and put it up against the wall behind his cot again. He turned on the lamp next to it, and took out his little Bible. He opened it to where he had earmarked one of the pages and tried to read, but couldn't. Something in the back of his mind was bothering him. A question he'd already asked, but hadn't been answered to his satisfaction. "I still don't get it, Mark," he said. "What do you care about what happens here? You aren't part of any of this, why not just go to a church somewhere else and forget about these people?"

"God sent me here," Mark replied. "He calls, and I obey. They are His sheep. They are supposed to be His representatives to a lost and fallen world, while taking care of their own flocks. They're not doing either, they're fleecing them. No one ever came closer to

God because they got a shiny new CAV or a house in the hills, Jerry. Believers get closer to Him when they overcome adversity *with* Him. When things like this happen, when He is misrepresented, people can get confused or hurt, or even end up harming themselves, people like the young woman Pastor Greeley told us about. Even more can end up losing their faith, or may never find it to begin with, because of the poor example they and others like them have made. God isn't good because of what He can give us. He is good because goodness is what He *is*. No matter what happens to us in this world, He is still good, all the time. It is we that have fallen away from His goodness. God is about helping those in need, not ignoring or abandoning those who don't measure up to worldly non-Christian standards that Jesus never intended to be a part of His teachings. Jesus promised His followers that the poor would always be with them, as would those who would seek to persecute them. These people have rejected those parts of scripture and many others, and traded them for their own made-up theology.

"What do you mean? What kind of theology? How is it different than yours?"

Mark rubbed his eyes and let out a yawn before continuing. "They are obsessed with works, with making themselves 'better' in ways that have nothing to do with Christ. They even have a saying for it, something about being too spiritual to be any good, or something like that. As if Jesus ever told his followers that it was better to be less Christian in certain areas of life. Anyway, we Christians are called to live by grace, in the world but not of the world. We are to lead by example, to love and to live by the Holy Spirit. We do not love as the world loves, in sensuality or perversion, but altruistically, without expecting anything back. Without God's spirit dwelling within us this is impossible, but with it, nothing is impossible. This doesn't mean we allow lawless people to run over us and take what God has entrusted us with, but it also doesn't mean that one can simply run away from those that God has called them to minister to. He gives us the gift of His Spirit freely, and we are meant to give it to others by praying for God's intervention in their lives, and teaching them about what is in His Word. The people here refuse to understand these things, not realizing that if they continue down the path they are on, one day, God will make them understand, by forcing them to make a choice between Him and their money and possessions. Personally, I just think it's sad that they never understood what Paul wrote in his letters, or they do, and have just decided to ignore it."

"Why, what did he write?"

"That living a peaceful and quiet life of service to others while waiting on God's call, is not only not a bad thing, but is the best way to show nonbelievers that God is real. Sometimes the only way. The meek are the ones who will inherit the earth. Those who understand what Paul meant when he wrote, 'having nothing yet possessing all things' understand those words because they have God in their hearts, and know where they are going. The great irony in all of this, is that the people here claim they are doing great things for God, but God more often than not uses the lowly and humble to confound those who think that they are wise or powerful, because doing so brings glory to His Son. He does not use those who are proud, or are in constant need of recognition."

"Was he from your old church?" Jerry asked.

"Who?"

"The guy with the cane."

"Oh. Yeah, I've been dodging that one haven't I, I suppose you deserve an explanation." Mark looked somewhat exhausted. He pushed himself up, and planted his feet on the cold concrete floor, groaning a little as he moved. Then he stretched his arms out and yawned as quietly as he could, so as not to wake Eddie.

Wondering if his stretch was yet another attempt to dodge the question, as Mark himself had put it, Jerry tactfully continued his inquiry, "I figured it was a touchy subject for you, but after what happened on the lawn today-"

"Yeah," Mark interjected. "He was from that church, taught me a lot about how to minister to people." He looked down at the floor. "Most of what he taught me wasn't very effective, now that I think about it. I ended up using methods of other mentors I met later instead."

"What happened, a falling out?"

"Yeah, you could call it that. He was...a friend. At least I thought he was. In the end, he stood on one side of things, and I was on the other. Except I didn't resort to lies and slander, he did. Yeah, he created a real mess of things in that place, but he had been there longer than anyone, and everybody trusted him. Then, just when people in the leadership began to figure out that he was the source of so much junk that the church had been going through, he took his family and disappeared."

"Sounds like a real loser to me."

"He was under a lot of pressure at the time." Mark began to tap his right temple with his index finger. "Sometimes...sometimes Christians get it into their heads that God is going to do a certain thing for them, and when He doesn't, well if that thing has become more important in a man's mind than God, his true enemy, Satan, can really mess with him and everyone he comes into contact with. That's what the 'S' man does, after all, kill and destroy. People, relationships, ministries, you name it. That's why it's important for real Christians to keep their eyes on God and to focus on His purposes for their lives. The Bible says He made us each for specific reasons. We, all of us, have specific assignments to accomplish while we are here, but we need real faith to complete it, not a fake version that gives the appearance of faith but accomplishes nothing in the end. We have a tendency to let ourselves get distracted, desiring, or going after other things. What most people don't know is that claiming to live for God while chasing after other things, is like putting a neon sign on your back that says shoot me here."

"Wouldn't God protect you through something like that?"

"He does for a time, waiting patiently sometimes for years for a person to genuinely repent, and turn away from their sins. But sometimes that person has to be humbled before they understand what they were doing wrong, and learning from our mistakes is one of the main reasons God allows the enemy to mess with us in the first place. He does things that way so His people will realize how good it was when they were closer to Him and get back with Him, and like a good shepherd, when this happens, God puts them back to work again doing what He sent them here to do in the first place, but even more full of His Spirit, more thankful and more ready for the next attack when the stakes are higher. Do you understand?"

"I think so," Jerry said. "So I take it that what he did to you was pretty bad."

"Yeah, but it didn't bother me as much as it did my wife. She was strong though, and we got through it. Like so many other things..." Mark looked at Levi's boxes. They were stacked high, full of things that once seemed so important, but were no longer needed. He looked back at Jerry. "How is your reading coming?"

Jerry looked down at his Bible. "Oh, man!" he said. He sat up straight and crossed his legs, placing the small Bible on the cot before stretching out himself. "I just don't know, Mark. I was making some good headway, until I reached this lineage thing after the Noah story. After that, my attention span started to peter off. Why would any god write a book like this?"

"Not all of the Bible is laws and lineages, but it can be confusing for someone who isn't used to understanding things from a spiritual perspective." Mark said. "God wants us to spend time with His word so that we can get to know Him, not alone either, but with others, so that we can grow in the love that He is over time, while the Bible reveals itself to us. If He made it like a simple children's book, most people might easily discard it after one read through. When we spend time with it, and pray for the Holy Spirit to reveal to us what God wants to show us in it, we are building a relationship with Him. As we begin to act on what we've learned, He helps us to understand even more, entrusting us with more knowledge, blessings, and other opportunities to serve in the name of His Son. That, and He uses it as a way to weed out those who don't really love Him. The Bible confuses, or is just too much work for them, and they often give up before understanding the importance of spending time with God or building that relationship. I told you to start at the beginning of John in the New Testament, didn't I?"

"I started from the beginning. I want to have the full context in order. I don't just want to jump into the most interesting parts without fully understanding what the people in those parts are saying."

"That's good," Mark said. "It's a good approach, when we have the full context, it's difficult to stray from the true meaning. It helps us have a more accurate interpretation, but you have to be willing to get through the tough stuff first, while also understanding that a lot of the things God wanted people to do back then, before His Son was sacrificed for our sins was part of a larger plan, not only for the Jewish people, but for the rest of humanity as well."

"Didn't you say at the picnic that today's Christians aren't Old Testament Jewish people? That we're under a different covenant than they were?"

"Exactly my point," Mark said. "*Some* of the things God has for us today are not the same as those that were promised to His people back then, and serve different purposes under the new covenant that started when Christ died on the cross and was resurrected. Paul, the apostle and Jesus Himself, explain some of these things in great detail in the New Testament."

"Well," Jerry said. "I'd still like to read it from the beginning, like most people probably do. It is definitely difficult, though. Here, look at this, for example." Jerry moved to the foot of his cot, and sat on its edge closer to Mark. "How am I supposed to remember some of these names?" He picked up his Bible and turned it so that Mark could see what he'd been reading. Mark took the book out of his hands. "Who is this Mel-hiz-a-lek guy? How am I supposed to remember his name anyway? He's only in the book for, like a second."

"Melchizedek was a king and high priest of the Lord back in Abraham's day. Abraham gave him ten percent of what he owned to honor God. It's where Christians get the concept of what is called the tithe today. That is, how Christians traditionally give to their churches so that the needs of others in the congregation can be met, as well as many of the lost, those who don't know God. Unfortunately, the pastors I will be going to see tomorrow no longer believe in this manner of giving, not really anyway. They rightfully tell their congregations that all of their wealth belongs to

God, while wrongfully placing themselves and their ministries in His place. They heavily imply with their false words that giving to them is better than going directly to God to ask how they should give, and more often than not, they have their own twisted versions of how the money they take in should be spent."

"Yeah," Jerry said. "That I noticed."

"When it comes to Melchizedek and his role in the Bible, there's more than just the right way to tithe, though," Mark said, "Much more."

"What do you mean? Tell me, I want to know."

Mark moved over to Jerry's cot, and sat next to him. He took the little book out of Jerry's hands, his fingers quickly flipping its pages to a certain place near the back. After stopping for a moment and reading one page, he turned one more and stopped again, examining it carefully with a semblance of absolute concentration. "Here," he said, "The author of Hebrews referred to Melchizedek while describing the Son of God." He handed Jerry the book, using one of his fingers to point at a certain verse. Jerry read it aloud:

"-Though he was a Son, yet learned obedience by the things which he suffered.Having been made perfect, he became to all of those who obey him the author of eternal salvation,named by God a high priest after the order of Melchizedek."

"Here," Mark flipped through the pages again, and pointed to another verse. "In chapter seven, verse three, the author also described Melchizedek as one who was made like a 'Son of God', a perpetual priest who had no lineage in the traditional sense. In John three, Jesus refers to true believers in the faith as those who come and go like the wind, others not knowing where they came from or where they are going, just as Melchizedek appeared in Genesis, only to vanish once his purpose in God's plan for Abraham was completed, just as the *He* was seen by the Pharisees of His day. Like I told you before, Christ was supposed to be the first of many sons."

"Like you, you mean." Jerry said.

"Like all men and women who give themselves completely to the Lord of hosts. All who follow Christ are kings *and* priests in God's Kingdom, not one or the other, but both. This means that everyone who chooses to follow Jesus and His will for their lives is part of the Melchizedek priesthood just as He is, their role is to bless *and* receive, but only according to the grace that God has apportioned to them, and only at appointed times. This calling is not a license to build our own kingdoms, or make our own religions." Mark pointed a finger at the ceiling. "We are here, standing by the power and grace of God to spread His word, to grow *His* kingdom with what He has given us, because it is His. Everything is, all that ever was and ever will be, and even if we have nothing in our pockets, we still have something to give those in need."

"What's that?" Jerry asked.

"The life changing power of the Holy Spirit, the promise of eternal life, and the greatest gift of all, the forgiveness of sins only made possible by the suffering Jesus endured when He died on the cross. 'By His stripes, we are healed.'"

Jerry didn't know how to respond. Still looking down at the Bible in his hands, he began to shake his head, unable to grasp most of what Mark was saying. Seeing his reaction, Mark decided to end the conversation. He briefly placed a hand on Jerry's left shoulder, "I know you don't understand all of what I've just told you, Jerry, but I truly hope that someday you will."

Jerry felt a sharp pain in his left calf muscle and let out a short cry.

"You should get some rest," Mark told him, "Lie down and stretch your legs out again for a bit. Don't worry, I'll stay up and keep watch for a while."

Jerry did as Mark said, his mind racing to catch up with all that had just been thrown at him, when he realized just how tired he was from all of the walking he had done that day. He heard Mark mumble something as he lay back on his cot. Not long after, a feeling of serenity came over him, the likes of which he had never experienced before. No longer worried about being taken in the night, or concerned about his inability to understand Mark's words,he took advantage of the euphoric state he was in, and decided to rest his eyes for a minute or two.

Your country is desolate. Your cities are burned with fire. Strangers devour your land in your presence and it is desolate, as overthrown by strangers.
-Isaiah, 1:7

Chapter Twenty-Four

I-5 Corridor north of SEATAC International Airport
Seattle, Washington State
Saturday, March 26th, 11:50PM PST

"Are they in place? I can't see the entire line from drone ninety-two. Melissa, can you get another one over there?" Simon had taken off what was left of his black shirt, and traded it in for his blue one, along with a headset. He was standing next to one of the communication stations in the command center, Melissa at his side. Upon his request, she moved to another station, and asked the blueshirt manning it to move one of the drones. On the monitors they could see Robert walking across the highway, a walkie-talkie in his right hand.

"The blackshirts have been given the best of the gear we have left and are lined up in the front, only two men wide, just as you instructed. The rest of the Shotguns are standing on either side of the highway to the south, lying prostrate on the grass. We've never tried this before, are you sure they'll be coming for us? What if they go into the city or head east? Some of them might just try to blend in or head for the border."

"I'm sure you're right about some of them, but they didn't pack themselves like sardines into those ships, and risk their lives confronting the police, simply because they were looking for a better life. They came here to take the highway, and someone promised they would get something valuable if they did. No, they're coming back, I'm sure of it. They've come too far to give up now. Can you see Blue Team One?"

"They're in position. Now, what do we do?"

"Go to the front line. Tell the blackshirts if they see them coming in fast driving stolen vehicles, wait until the last possible second, and just get out of their way. They are only to engage those who are on foot. Oh, and make sure each and every one of them has their earplugs in."

"Alright," Robert said.

Simon turned to Melissa, "Are the emitters ready?"

"Teams one through four are in position awaiting the go order." she said.

"Tell them to double check their ear plugs too. We don't want anyone else getting hurt tonight."

"Yes, sir."

Amanda walked into the bus and up to Simon, her hair disheveled. Several streaks of blood were strewn across her white coat.

Simon looked her up and down. "How's Brent doing?" he asked.

"He'll be ok, but he's going to have to go in for surgery after this." she said. "The bullet hit bone, and nearly shattered his Humerus just above the elbow. I managed to take the bullet fragments out, but it's not pretty. If it turns out bad enough, the bone section can be cut out and replaced with a grown replica or a printed duplicate, but he still might not have full function after this."

"How is he taking it?"

"It doesn't seem to bother him. He sees it like some kind of badge of honor. Personally, I think he's just happy that from now on, he can say he took a bullet for you."

"And the others?"

"Just taser dart burns, mostly. One had minor heart palpitations for a while, but they went away about an hour ago. The one that was shot and survived is in stable condition. The bullet was awfully close to his heart and punctured a lung. It was a little harrowing."

"So, he's going to make it then."

"Yes, I think so. We need to get him to a hospital as soon as we can."

Simon thought for a moment and nodded. "Yeah, okay. A couple of the police outside told me that they would volunteer to take anyone we detained back to their precinct. We can afford to send a few of the advance team along with them in one of the buses we're not using. They can use it to bring him to First Hill. There should be a hospital there willing to take them. Going into the city is a dicey proposition, but they should make it. When you're done with the rest, make sure to have a team put them with the ones we detained last night in the prison buses. Tell your people to be careful, these guys are dangerous. They'll have to stay with the others until we know it's safe for the police to pick them up."

Amanda tilted her head a little to the right. Simon noticed something change in her eyes. She touched his right sleeve with her fingers, and began to unbutton the cuff.

"How's that gash I patched up-"

Simon yanked his arm away, surprising her. "Fine, it's fine. Thank you." he said. He looked back to the monitors.

"That man, Brent said he tried to kill you, both of you." she said.

Completely bereft of emotion, Simon nodded, his eyes focused on the activity he was watching on the screens. "So?" he said. After a moment of silence, he turned his head in her direction again, an expressionless look on his face.

"I...I have to get back to check on the others," Amanda said. She glanced at Melissa as Simon went back to monitoring the screens again, her face full of rejection. "You should know that the police you rescued are very grateful to you and Brent for what you did for them. They say they're alright, but I'd like to have my teams do a quick physical on all of them."

Simon spoke to her again without looking up. "You'd better hurry up. The rest of that mob could be here at any minute."

Somewhat unsettled by the callous manner in which Simon had dismissed her, Amanda became visibly uncomfortable. She looked at Melissa again. Melissa looked back at her with sad eyes, and shrugged. Amanda crossed her arms, and started to back away from him. "Ok." she said. She turned around and got off of the bus.

After she left, Simon looked in the direction of the door. He turned to Melissa again. "Get any remaining drones in the air and make sure all of them are recording from every angle possible. If people are going to come after us at all after this, it will be because of what we're about to do next, and I want them to see that we did all we could to avoid anyone being seriously injured. Come and get me when they've been sighted."

He walked to the rear of the command bus and sat down at the far end of the table. He looked out one of the windows to the west. His sharp, hawk-like eyes saw past the darkening streets and uninhabited warehouses that made up the industrial area and toward downtown Seattle. The sun had gone over the horizon, allowing him to see that much of the city was still lit up, but not just with electricity. Several fires were burning across the landscape alongside the flashing red and blue lights of the local authorities as they raced from one emergency to the next, putting out fires and arresting looters.

He turned in his seat to face the table again and felt his entire body cringe until he bent over, his head hanging over the table. He covered it with his hands and clenched his teeth, shutting his eyes tight until the wave of emotion had passed. Then he took several deep breaths through his nose. *Contained.* He thought. He looked up just in time to see that Melissa was watching him from the front end of the bus. Caught in the act, she quickly turned her attention back to the monitors, and started talking into the microphone on her headset. Simon leaned back in his chair and moved it, so that it faced the wide pane of tinted glass again. There he sat, waiting alone at the head of an empty table, a feeling of powerlessness consuming his very being as he watched a civilization going up in flames.

****

An hour later, Robert walked into the command center. Melissa gave him a worried look as he maneuvered around her, using her eyes to point out the location of her concern. Robert followed her gaze into the conference room, where Simon sat motionless, staring out the window. "It'll be ok." he said to her reassuringly. He walked to the rear of the bus, pulled out a chair, and sat next to him. "You know," he said. "We could go in there and help out the Guard downtown."

"No." Simon said.

"Simon, the volunteers are hurt, tired, and hungry. We've won here. No one is going to-"

Simon turned and looked at Robert with a glare that could temper steel. "We-go-nowhere." he said.

Robert nodded. "Sure thing bo-, sorry."

"Twenty years, Robert. It took nearly twenty years to get this far." Simon went back to glaring outside into the darkness. "Twenty years of watching as millions of idiots walked around blindly following their bliss, never learning from their mistakes, never taking any responsibility for themselves or being held accountable for their actions, while corporate interests quietly took over their lives through behavioral engineering and social media mobs. Sure they were always saying they cared for others, but they never really did anything to help anyone but themselves. The signs were all there. The foreign invasions were inevitable. We took their best and brightest away from them, and gave them pornography. When banks began to give fifty-thousand dollar credit lines to college students and the government forced them to sell homes to those who couldn't afford them, the economy was bound to crash, and I saw the Hypnotic War coming from miles away, and that one still isn't over like they are saying now, not by a long shot. I am an island, standing in an ocean of imbeciles who are constantly getting their jollies off by hurting one another and themselves, while their world and their future literally burn around them. Do you think they even know who has been keeping everything together these last few years? Do they know what they have become? What they have to lose? Maybe Amanda was right. Maybe it should burn. Maybe *all* of them should burn."

Simon fell silent. Robert, who had come to respect him deeply since he'd joined up with his crusade, had endured more than one of these pity parties. At first, he hated the times when it seemed as if Simon had lost all hope, but over time he had learned not to argue, not even to encourage him when he allowed himself to dwell in the darkness, but to just be there with him. He had observed that it was best to let Simon vent his frustrations while his mind worked out what to do next. In those moments, Simon was carrying the weight of a dysfunctional world on his shoulders, and he just needed to know that he wasn't alone. Once he realized that fact, the best of him would rise back up to the surface. He only needed a reminder, a foil, a friend. God forbid he get so pent up inside because he had no one to talk to, that he actually said such things out loud to anyone else. He would be crucified by a world that didn't like to be reminded of its own shortcomings and left for dead.

A few seconds passed, and Simon looked down and away from the window. He raised both of his palms up to his face and pushed them into his eye sockets until his entire body shook, gritting his teeth the entire time. When he opened his eyes again, he took a deep breath, and looked at the only real friend he'd ever had. Robert looked back, unwavering, his eyes conveying a loyalty that was meant to prove to Simon that he wasn't going anywhere.

Simon turned his chair around, so that it faced the table again. He brought up a satellite image of the immediate area, using the interface that was set into the table's surface. He pointed at the airport with his finger. "There were too many of those insurgents, and they were too strong and violent to simply be another group of immigrants looking to help out local unions or political factions. Whoever sent the second wave wouldn't have gone through everything it must have taken to get them here because they wanted the highway alone. One thing is for sure, though, they aren't from around here. My guess is they were brought here from California or even farther south."

"Why?" Robert asked, "Who would do that? What would they have to gain?"

"I'm not sure yet. So far, it looks like some, if not all of them, are from Brazil. At least originally, anyway. Their plan was to use the protest as cover. I went to the prison bus and talked to Tammy Shelton. She said something about making an example for other protesters around the country. Now I'm thinking their original goal was to defeat the police, and use their weapons and equipment to capture the airport. That would explain why the second wave didn't show up until after we arrived, after the National Guard was called into the city. We weren't supposed to be here, Robert. Only a few hundred cops were supposed to be left on the highway, preventing whatever protesters were left from going north. The same officers we just saved from being used as future leverage. After taking them down, they were planning on overwhelming the National Guard post we relieved, and heading to the airport. Then they could shut down air travel to the entire area and take even more hostages, while the protesters in Olympia took the Statehouse. Robert, they didn't know we were coming."

Robert leaned back in his chair, and looked up at the picture of the stagecoach above Simon's head. He took a deep breath of his own, and let it out. "That means there could be more on their way to solidify their foothold in Seattle. So, what do we do then?"

"We have most of the weapons they tried to steal, so they can't use them on us or at the airport." Simon used his forefinger to move the map. "They still need the highway to attract media attention, and to block any resistance that could come from the government outside of the area to the north and east. The I-90 tunnel to Mercer Island is still closed, that means for now we're their biggest target, and by being patient and waiting for them, we are also the best chance this entire region has right now."

"How do you figure?"

"Melissa said our perimeter drones don't indicate any serious increase in the number of protesters inside the city. That means they haven't joined the regular protesters downtown yet. They're still out there, and their time is running out. Right now, I'd bet they're trying to figure out how to take us down. When their scouts tell them there are only a few hundred men guarding The Barn...it won't be long now."

"They were obviously following someone's instructions, but they didn't seem too organized once we were able to breach their lines." Robert said. "I didn't see anyone on a radio or wearing earpieces either, no leaders in some far off place telling them what to do. Do you think we already have their leaders, or a contact they were supposed to meet up with in custody, Tammy Shelton, maybe?"

Simon thought for a moment and shook his head, "No. She's a good organizer, but once the action starts she's always been with the support teams. Others usually lead the charge. She might be in on it, but she's no strategist. Whoever it was would have to have been positioned farther north, closer to the police line, so they could meet them when they arrived. I suppose one of the others we've already detained could be-" Simon was cut off by the sound of Melissa's footsteps as she ran toward them from the front of the bus.

"They're coming," she said. "And they look pissed."

****

Simon hit the table with his right hand, and stood up. The three of them went to look at the drone monitors. A large caravan could be seen coming from the north on both sides of the highway. Six older model gas powered cars and trucks were in the lead carrying more than ten people each, inside and on top of them. Behind them, the rest of the mob was forming. At least half of those, on and off of the vehicles, were carrying improvised torches made of scrap metal, or tree branches and strips of clothing. The drones identified eighteen hundred and eighty-three people in the crowd all together.

"Where do you think the rest went?" Robert asked.

"They're nowhere on the grid." Melissa said.

"They deserted, just like you said they would, Robert, but not all of them." Simon said. "These guys came to get what they're owed. Let's give it to them."

The cars stopped fifty yards from the buses, with those on foot running up from behind. The drivers revved their engines, and began to lunge forward in spurts and starts, in an attempt to intimidate the blackshirts on the line. They were stretched thin across the highway near the north end of the charter buses, which had been lined up in the emergency lanes on either side.

"You'd better get out there, Robert. Your men will need you." Simon said. Robert nodded, and ran off of the bus. Simon looked at Melissa, "Tell the blackshirt lieutenants to have the line take ten steps back."

"Blackshirt lieutenants, teams one through five, back the line up five paces." Melissa said into her microphone.

The lieutenants heard her words through their earpieces and ran behind the line, giving the order to every tenth man. Responding to the order, they started to step back, the rest of the blackshirts following suit. The drivers of the vehicles began to rev their engines again. Then they advanced ten yards, encouraged by what appeared to be a fearful move made by their enemies, before stopping again. Even through the drone feed, Simon could hear the drivers yelling at one another over the sounds of their engines. Something was wrong.

"They're not taking the bait." Melissa said. "They must be wondering where the other Shotguns went."

"It's not over ye-" Shocked at what he was seeing on one of the monitors, Simon stopped speaking.

Robert, who had been walking toward the back of the line, went through it, and started screaming a litany of obscenities toward the mob, egging them on. When words failed, he used every disparaging and universally understood hand gesture he could think of, and when that didn't work, he turned around and mooned them.

"Robert, you beautiful bastard!" Simon said.

When Robert pulled his pants back up, the drivers began to rev their engines again. One of them was still yelling at the others. Finally, the driver who was behind the wheel of the largest truck in the group, stuck up his finger at the man who was yelling and hit the gas. The other drivers were not far behind and before they knew it, they were racing toward the blackshirts.

"Go, go!" Robert yelled. The blackshirts ran to the sides of the highway, allowing the vehicles to go by them. Two of the vehicles raced past all of the parked buses before stopping, the other four stopped in the middle, having realized that something about the entire situation seemed off.

"Back on the road!" Robert yelled again. The blackshirt line reformed just in time to meet the members of the mob who were on foot. Under Robert's guidance, the three hundred who were in the line, began to give ground immediately after the enemy engaged them, at first giving some resistance, even hitting back with their batons as they slowly pulled back, so that the entire mob stood with them between the buses and within The Barn zone.

"Now." Simon said.

"Forward and rear vehicles move into position!" Melissa said into her headset.

The ten buses at the front and rear most sections of the formation moved to block either end, effectively boxing them in, five buses crossing the highway on both sides. Only then did the protesters notice that the stretch of highway they were standing on had fewer lanes and almost no median in its center when compared to the area they had come from to the north. The buses on the corners scraped against one another, throwing up sparks along the ground as they hurriedly maneuvered into place, the panels fastened to their bottom edges, preventing any chance of escape.

Just south of The Barn, the two trucks that had made it through before the buses had changed position began to turn around. Brent, his left arm in a sling, appeared out of the gloom with the remaining blackshirts, many of them brandishing the very pistols and shotguns they had confiscated that afternoon and began to march in their direction. The men on the vehicles began to panic when they saw them, most jumping off or out of their rides. They ran to the side of the highway, where they were met by hundreds of redshirts who immediately began to subdue them using recharged taser units and what little amounts of mace that were left.

Inside The Barn, Robert led the blackshirts to a certain panel between two of the buses on the southeastern side of the makeshift structure, which had not been completely bolted down. Outside, two members of the advance team, who were waiting on the roof tops of two of the buses, quickly descended from their positions and waited until all of the blackshirts had gotten out before bolting the loose panels into place. Then the real trouble began.

The stolen vehicles that were still inside The Barn had turned around and began to ram the buses on the north end in an attempt to move them enough for their people to escape. The rest of the nearly two thousand men that had unwittingly fallen into the trap began to climb up the side of the charter buses or attempted to break their windows. A few accomplished their goal, allowing their compatriots to throw torches inside, the fires consuming the interiors of a few of the transports.

"Well, I was going to warn them, but it looks like we no longer have time for that." Simon said. "Not that most of them would be able to understand what I was going to say anyway. Deploy the emitters." He put two small plugs into his ears.

"Deploy emitters! All teams, emitters are being deployed!" Melissa said. She also placed plugs in her ears, as did the driver and the other two communications specialists in the command center.

Four members of the advance team appeared on top of the buses that were closest to each of the four corners of The Barn. With them, they carried small, disk-shaped objects that were connected to magnetic stands. They were attached by wires to four large battery packs that sat on the ground, off of to the sides of the vehicles. The powerful magnets held the disks in place as they positioned them to face the angry and hapless mob below. When they were in position, the men gave the leader of the team a go signal with their hands. The leader, standing on the bus in the southwest corner, gave the final go signal, and they turned the sonic emitters on at the same time.

The sound that came out of them was piercing and unbearably loud, shattering nearly every window on the inside of The Barn. Many of the protesters cried out in pain and fell to the ground, their hands clasped over their ears. Others ran to the sides, trying desperately to escape under, or squeeze between the buses, only to find the metal barriers barring their way. Having detained the drivers and passengers of the vehicles to the south, Brent directed the red and blackshirts to surround The Barn's perimeter. From time to time, one of the protesters would manage to squeeze under one of the metal plates or climb over a bus, only to be met on the other side by a group of volunteers who stood ready to detain them.

In less than two minutes, it was all over. Members of the mob removed their hands from their ears and raised them into the sky, and Simon gave the order to shut the emitters down. The advance team opened the southwest panel again, and redshirts poured in, running to put out the flames in the vehicles that had caught fire, and placing plastic strips on the hands and legs of the perpetrators.

"Just like Hannibal at Cannae." Simon said.

"What?" Melissa asked.

Simon smiled at her, "Nothing. Make sure the drones are getting everything, I'm going to join the others."

Simon walked out of the command center and into The Barn where Robert was directing the redshirts. He walked up to Robert, smiling and nodding his head. "Not exactly what I'd planned, but good enough. You really are something, Robert." he said, beaming.

Robert stopped yelling at a group of redshirts that were desperately trying to prevent the fires from spreading, and took a moment to look upon his fearless leader. "Oh, you know me," he said. His face lit up, "Always looking for attention." Robert looked up at the sky, jokingly shook a fist in the air and said, "I have needs too, you know!" Then, as if on cue, a bolt of lightning flashed in the distance, and it began to pour.

****

Marilyn Houghton had two kids, a boy, and a girl. Joshua was five years old, and Maria was three. Since her husband died in a car accident a year earlier, her grandmother had been helping her look after them. They were with her grandmother that night, safe and sound some thirty miles away in Lakewood. Marilyn loved her country, but she loved them more. She was determined to get back to them in one piece, but her latest assignment had turned out to be more than she'd bargained for.

Other than the few minutes she had taken every six hours to rest in the back of one of the riot vehicles,she hadn't slept for the last two days. She allowed the others to take shifts, but could see that the situation was wearing on them. The protesters had hit them hard on the first night. Several different groups with more banners than she could count, merged on the courthouse where they were stationed, with two hundred and twenty police officers. It wasn't long before the large sonic emitter had to be deployed. With the ability to reverberate the skin until it felt like it was on fire, and even explode eyes in their sockets if not used properly, in the end, it was the only deterrent that seemed effective against them. The only downside was that it was dependent on a battery that ran out of its charge quickly. Of course the last wave of protesters didn't know that when they dispersed, but she did, when the power went down in the entire area before they could find a new power source.

On the second night, things were better for a time, but soon the protesters began to start fires throughout downtown. Around midnight, the police were forced to leave so they could assist and protect the local fire fighters. Reports of scuffles and violent incidents from across the city came in from every direction. At one point, she and her men heard two large explosions coming from the direction of the highway to the south, and got a report from a woman working with the Shotguns calling herself Melissa that the remaining police north of their position had been abducted. Marilyn sent the report up the chain through their satellite link, but had to regretfully inform the Relief Army that no one in the city would be in any position to assist with finding them until the remaining protesters had been completely dispersed, and that protecting the courthouse remained her primary objective. After that, they weren't able to get the local police or the fire departments on the radio, and she and her team began to wonder if they were on their own.

Sometime later, a group of five hundred or so men came into the city, screaming at them in a language she and the others in her unit couldn't understand. They quickly ran around the barriers, and began to engage them in a hand to hand combat near the front steps of the courthouse. Several men were seriously hurt before the riot hoses were turned on them, pushing them back. She ordered the men on the jeeps to open fire, using rubber ammunition. The crowd scattered and disappeared into the darkness, setting more fires as they ran. After they had gone, her men informed her that the emitter had been destroyed, along with their satellite communications antenna. Deaf and blind, Marilyn began to think that something more sinister than usual was going on. Tempted to leave and join her children, she took the crucifix that hung around her neck in one hand and squeezed it, resisting the urge to abandon her post.

"Corporal!" one of the privates yelled in her direction. "They're back!" Rifle in hand, she climbed out of her resting place, and looked past the wooden barriers the men in her charge had placed on the street in front of the entrance to the courthouse. She then headed toward the front of the vehicle, barking orders before she could even see what was happening through the smoke that was blowing in from the west. "Get on those guns! Hit 'em before they get within thirty yards! Harrison, tell Moby and Steve to get the hoses ready!"

She stood behind one of the barriers and raised her weapon. The men had become very protective of her and looked at one another, fearing for her safety, as she stepped out in front of them. She could see what looked like torches coming through the smoke on Westlake Avenue, and realized that it was raining, but not enough to completely put out some of the nearby flames. In the distance she heard yelling, something in English? Several other voices responded in the same language that she had heard the attackers screaming in on the previous night. Suddenly, the torch lights began to move faster in their direction, and within a minute, another large group of tattooed marauders were sprinting out of the smoke.

She reached into her camouflage jacket, and grabbed the crucifix again that was underneath. Then she closed her eyes, and said, "Please, Jesus, help us get through this. Protect us, so I can go home and see my babies."

"Oh, crap!" one of the Guardsmen said. "I'm almost out of baton rounds!"

"Only use live rounds if you run out, and they're on top of you! Wait until they're in range of the hoses!" She yelled loudly so all of her men could hear her, wiped the rain from her eyes, and looked through her rifle sight at the men running at full tilt in their direction just south of their position.

Unlike the last time they had come through, the mob was nearly silent. The multitude picked up speed and looked for a moment as if they were going to swarm the outpost, overwhelming them again, when they suddenly turned westward down an adjacent street. They disappeared into the night, hundreds of them passing by without so much of a glance in the direction of the courthouse. Confused, and with adrenaline racing through her system, a strange flicker of light caught her attention. It was coming from the same place where the marauders had first appeared. She looked south again, and saw a second group was heading toward them. "What, the?" she said. Behind the new arrivals, the fires were going out, one after another, creating a foreboding impression that she and her men shared as they held their collective breath. Marilyn began to think about what her kid's lives would be like without their mother. She signaled with her right hand for the others to aim into the smoke again, but as they lowered their sights a second time, she saw something shiny and blue take shape through the smoke, something with a rider in red astride it.

"OHHH!" She let out a huge sigh, "It's ok men, it's the Shotguns!"

Robert emerged on his electric bike, flanked by red and blackshirts on either side of the street, putting out fires as they went. Directly behind him, two lines of police officers brandished their pistols, ready to protect the Shotguns should anyone dare attack them. The Guardsmen cheered as Robert and the others reached their position, and shook hands with them in an impromptu celebration. A few even embraced one another. Robert rode his bike directly up to Marilyn and stopped short, just in front of the barrier she was using for cover.

"Nice toy you've got there." she said, more than a little relieved to see him. "Isn't it a little small for you, though?"

Robert put the kickstand down, and got off the bike. She could tell by the bags under his eyes, and the multiple rips and blood marks on his clothes, that he had been through hell just as much as she and her team had. "It does the job. I like it actually, smooth ride." He moved his hand horizontally through the air and smiled. "Can't stand up on its own though, not like those new-"

Marilyn had begun to cry. She moved the barrier to one side, and wrapped her arms around him, but only for a moment, "Thanks for coming." she said.

Robert looked down at her. "The locals already put out most of the fires downtown. They sent us up here to check on you guys. I see you've been busy, could you use some help?"

"OH, yes." she said, wiping the tears off of her face. "I take it things are under control on the highway?"

"They are now. We lost some people, though, it got pretty brutal. The FBI is on their way to pick up the ones we were able to detain. We tried to communicate with you a few hours ago, after it was all finished, and couldn't get through. Simon let me round up some volunteers. The rest of our people are busy processing the biggest part of this second wave. I take it this wasn't the first time you've seen them?"

"No, they came through a while ago, destroyed some of our equipment, and gave my men a beating. But then they just kept going for some reason. I have no idea who they are, or where they came from."

"We'll set up a wider perimeter, and send some of our best men to find out where they're headed. I think I already know where they're going, though."

"You do? Where?"

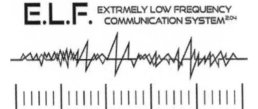

E.L.F. EXTRMELY LOW FREQUENCY
COMMUNICATION SYSTEM 2.04

[0.0264 HZ - BANDWIDTH 5879.7]

E.L.I.S.H.A.

ENHANCED LOGISTICS
INTIGRATION SYSTEM

What will you do in the day of visitation, and in the desolation which will come from afar? To whom will you flee for help? Where will you leave your wealth?
-Isaiah, 10:3

Chapter Twenty-Five

Christian Territory, Levi's Garage
Spokane, WA
Sunday, March 27ᵗʰ, 2:44AM PST

J erry was only fifteen when the Mount Rainier calamity happened. For years he tried to remember exactly what had transpired on that day, but all he could recall was a blur of faces and the sounds of grating screams. He'd gone to therapy of course, his foster parents had forced him to go. But neither they, nor their drugs they gave him, helped to sate the vague traumatic impressions that used to keep him up at night. As he grew older, the faint but terrible images that interrupted his sleep eventually stopped, resurfacing only on occasion during times of great stress. By his late twenties they had become but shadows of distant memories, like echoes from a previous life, a train that was traveling away from him through a long tunnel, the wails and shouts uttered in the distance no longer holding sway over his emotional wellbeing.

But that night the troublesome dream returned with a vengeance. His subconscious did not recognize it at first as it was bright and vivid, everything clear and discernible, with a rush of nostalgia that felt like beauty itself had charged its way into his unconscious mind. Along with it came inklings of thoughts long forgotten, specters from a time before the cares of a troubled world and all of the sad truths that came with it had been discovered. Happy feelings and emotions he hadn't experienced since drifted to the surface, bubbling up one after another in quick succession, every one fighting to be the center of attention. Memories without form, snapshots from a time when he'd gleefully explored all that was enjoyable about life and youth.

Then the dream took shape. He was riding the bus home from school, the sounds of his classmates reverberating all around him as they joked and teased one another incessantly. Some did so purely out of boredom, while others were simply excited that the week was over, and they were heading home for another fun-filled weekend. For a while, he broke the rules and reached over the seats, participating in the happy squabbles and rough games with the others. Their voices were muddled, though, fused together into one long sound of hectic camaraderie that was almost like music, their individual voices only becoming clear when someone was at their loudest. Suddenly, a single sharp note rose above the others. It came from the front of the bus, and they all sat back down together, laughing hysterically. Laughing himself, Jerry took a moment to look out of his window. The sun was out and the grass full, the colors of the day so vibrant they were mesmerizing. It would be a good afternoon for playing soccer with his friends.

He looked to the south, and could saw the skyline, where the great mountain hovered like a mystical paradise over the horizon, the clouds both above and below its massive peak as if it were its own mysterious kingdom floating there in the mist. As they rode, he heard the other boys and girls around him teasing one another and cracking jokes. Seated next to him was a girl who was looking through her backpack for some gum. He didn't know why he knew this, he just did. Perhaps he'd seen her do it before. When she found it, she looked up at him and offered him some. He remembered that she wasn't a friend of his, and was excited that she wanted to interact with him. For a brief moment, all he could see was her yellow hair, a pair of bright blue eyes, and a kind but intelligent smile. The grand unforgettable image was quickly followed by an overwhelmingly stark feeling that she was never ending in her innocence and beauty, and would always be. That's when the dream turned into a nightmare.

The entire bus shook. Some of the children screamed, and the disobedient children who were still standing sat down in their seats. A flash of red reflected off of the glass next to Jerry's head, and he turned to see what it was. Mount Rainier was erupting. The explosion was so fast and went so high that it almost didn't look real. Red lines shot upward among large, billowing clouds of ash and rock that were being hurtled into the air in all directions. He almost didn't notice that every one of the children on the bus had fallen silent. Then one girl screamed, "NO!" at the top of her lungs, and the end of the world began.

A small shockwave hit the bus, pushing it sideways a few feet as the driver picked up speed. "It's ok, kids!" he yelled. It's too far away. We'll be alright!" But then a second eruption happened, blowing out the entire western side of the mountain with a force so strong that it made the cloud cover around the mountain's base spread out in all directions, and vanish in an instant. Around its rim, millions of tons of earth and stone began collapsing inward, only to be regurgitated into the air. Miles away, he could see fireballs, the size of small homes, being flung in their general direction. Looking skyward again, he saw a mushroom shape form above the clouds in the upper atmosphere. Another student shouted, "Stop the bus!"

Before the driver could react, an even more powerful shockwave hit the bus, it collided into it like a giant fist, shattering the windows and pushing them off of the road. The long yellow vehicle flipped over on its side, and slid nearly ten feet into a nearby field. Some of those who hadn't put on their seatbelts were thrown around, their bodies bouncing off of the seats and one another like pinballs. He held onto his seat with one hand, and grabbed one of the straps attached to the girl's backpack with the other. When the bus had stopped moving, he looked at his right hand. The backpack was there, but the girl was gone. Someone opened the emergency door at the back of the bus, and the children spilled out into the field.

Not hearing any more from the driver, he got to his feet, and joined the rest of the students in their mad scramble to the rear exit. After making it outside, he collapsed on the soft grass and looked around for the girl, but only saw the faces of his peers as they, paralyzed, looked on in utter horror at what was left of the great mountain again. He joined them in their amazement, and witnessed a dark foreboding cloud that was forming just over the treetops in the distance. An ever increasing rumble began to overtake his ears as it drew closer, keying him into the fact that what he was seeing was not a cloud at all. As it neared, it pushed through everything in its path, cars and trees flew into the air before the dark, chaotic mass as it barreled toward them, undeterred. Though it still appeared to be a good distance away, the thing that he had learned about in school called a pyroclastic flow was heading in their direction at an alarming rate. Some of them screaming, all of the children ran back onto the road at the sight of its destruction, attempting to get away from the tsunami of molten concrete that was headed their way. Then beneath their feet, the ground began to shake again, but neither the flow nor another volcanic explosion was the cause.

The earthquake that followed was powerful and lasted nearly a minute, knocking all of them off of their feet and onto the ground.

They screamed and yelled out for one another. As Jerry tried to stand up, he saw that they were not the only ones being affected by what was happening. Several brick buildings around the field had started to collapse. A few of them fell on people who were running for safety, or to their cars. One ignited, creating a great fireball of its own, that shot straight up into the air. For an instant, Jerry's mind tried to convince him that he was simply looking at a firework display.

When the shaking subsided, he joined the others on the road. Unsure of what to do next, he decided to follow the crowd in their hysteria, something he would never do again. They joined a larger group of people at the next intersection, and soon Jerry couldn't distinguish his schoolmates from the others. All of them ran in the same direction, funneling toward Puget Sound over a mile and a half away.

Jerry looked back again. The flow was getting larger, and a sound of tumbling rock, a noise he'd thought was coming from the stampeding evacuees, began to grow louder, until it overcame the cascade of footfalls. A group of vehicles drove up from behind them. They stopped and honked their horns, yelling for the kids to get into their cars. The rides filled up quickly, the bystanders that were running with them, at times pushing the smaller children aside, in a last ditch effort to get away from the coming danger. It wasn't long before people were climbing onto the roofs and hoods. Fearing the worst being near the back of the group, Jerry saw an SUV come up an adjacent street. It stopped, close enough for him to catch up to. The driver was waving at people, encouraging them to climb onto it. Jerry jumped onto the rear fender, climbed up the back, and sat on the roof. He helped two other people get on top of the car with him, before it took off at a high speed along the shoulder.

Leaving hundreds of others behind them still running in the street, Jerry watched as the flow hit a nearby ravine. For a second, it seemed as if it would follow the ravine all the way to the Sound, the rushing gray substance sliding alongside and past them through a small neighborhood to the southwest. The people, exhausted, began to slow down a little, looking a bit relieved. But it was not to be. A larger surge of material came behind the first without warning. Devouring everything in its path, the hot debris poured into and over the brook before anyone could react.

The flow traveled faster than any of the vehicles, and knocked down several buildings nearby. By then, most of the people still on foot were too tired to run, or even cry out for help. They simply vanished in the grey roar, instantaneously overtaken by the giant wave of mud. Everything they ever were or ever could be, there one second and gone the next.

"Hold on!" The driver screamed out his window. Jerry held onto the luggage rails with both hands, the sudden acceleration that followed, almost making him fall off. The vehicle weaved around several other cars and groups of people before reaching the I-5 ramp, where hundreds of vehicles had been abandoned ahead of them. The driver stopped, and told everyone to get out and run. Jerry jumped off the car and did just that. The intersection ahead of them was jammed. The overpass at the intersection had been badly damaged by the quake, and people were leaving their cars on the highway and running down the off ramps, as others ran onto them.

Jerry followed those he was with under the overpass. Sections of it fell into the center of the road and onto the empty cars below. One of the few that had beenfortunate enough to find a place next to him on the roof of the SUV, was crushed as they ran, but he didn't stop. After they made it to the other side, their group collided with another that was heading in the opposite direction. Pushing through them, Jerry crossed a nearby street, and jumped over a chain link fence into a parking lot that was next to a warehouse. Several other people saw what he was doing and did the same. He sprinted across the lot, and through a small marshy area, to a rocky beach that was only a few feet wide. He had made it to Puget Sound.

There Jerry stopped, his heartbeat ringing loudly in his ears, his chest heaving deep breaths in and out of his dry mouth. To his left and right, he could see people standing on the edge of the Sound with him. They were screaming at two ferries that appeared to be coming closer to the shore. Over a loudspeaker, an operator of one of them said, "Don't worry, we're coming for you. Hold on!" Then Jerry noticed that the water was pulling away from him. Someone screamed, "OH MY GOD! OH MY GOD!" As he looked down at the unfamiliar sight, he saw that he was still holding onto the strap of the girl's robin blue backpack with his right hand. "OH MY GOD!" The scream came again. Jerry looked up. The sound itself seemed to come alive, as if a great beast were rising from beneath its depths. It bulged upward, lifting the ships far above their heads. His heart was beating so loud that he almost couldn't hear the woman's desperate howls, or the cries of the hundreds of others who joined her, unleashing in their last moments a horrible chorus of distress and misery.

For just a moment, the form of the wave heading toward him changed, taking on the shape of a lion's face, and he heard a faint voice. It was Noel's, but as it spoke it changed, morphing in tone until it sounded less like his former lover, and more like Perry's automated motorcycle, Sarina. "Jerry." it said. "Jerry. It's time, Jerry." Someone grabbed his arm. Suddenly, he was being lifted off of the ground. Jerry looked up. Above him was a helicopter, its propellers loudly thumping at the same rhythm of his heart. As he watched, a man reached out, and threw a rope down to him. The voice spoke again, but it wasn't the same. It was Mark's voice. "It's time, time to go home, time to do what you were sent to do."

The helicopter crossed over the sun, casting a shadow on him, and a wave of darkness passed over his mind. The thumping slowly faded, and he found himself alone floating in a void, the wave and the piercing cries having disappeared into the blackness that surrounded him. The void was not frightening, however. It was peaceful, and though he could not see or feel anything in the dream that might indicate that he was moving in any direction at all, he still felt as if he were heading somewhere, somewhere that was good. The non-sensation made him feel comfortable. *Perhaps this is a different kind of sleep?* Jerry thought to himself. He then became aware of his own thoughts, noticing that he was thinking rationally in what was so obviously a dream, or was it another memory? He wasn't sure. He had heard stories from others at work over the years about dreams in which some autonomy and control was possible. Such tales usually came from those who had tried all kinds of drugs or other methods, their hope being to find a way to live in, and record their dream states. They usually enjoyed the experience, if he recalled what they had told him correctly, so he simply let the time wash over him in his rest, and waited for the strange experience to end.

No sooner did Jerry open himself and his mind to the concept of "whatever will be will be" did he see a faint glow, far ahead in the darkness. He noticed that he had begun to move toward the glow. It became brighter and larger, until it took on a kind of crescent shape, the bent edge of it reaching up, while the tips on either side pointed down, like a great frowning arc. For a moment, he thought that he might be dying, and that what he was seeing might, in fact, be a form of the white light that many who had experienced a taste of death had reported when brought back to the world of the living. But Jerry saw no tunnel, and the light was beginning to take a very distinct form, that of the earth itself.

Soon, Jerry began to sense that he was standing at the top of some high place, a plateau, or a cliff of some sort. The light was emanating from somewhere below the cliff, and as it brightened it took on a shimmer, so that it sparkled there in the dark. It was as if the light itself were alive, moving like fire, except that it was not just moving up, it was moving down as well. He focused on one part of it. What he observed looked like a million tiny mirrors, some ascending and some descending, but it was also whole. All said, it was a gorgeous sight, awesome to behold.

The grand, glowing visage beyond turned, and the United States appeared, some parts of it more luminous than others, but in no pattern that he could see that made sense to him. He looked toward Washington State. On the eastern side, a faint glow did appear around Spokane, even in Seattle and Tacoma there seemed to be some activity, but near the middle of the great city itself and just to the south there was nothing, like a hole had developed somewhere just below it. Then he noticed that there was activity around the darkened area, like a million tiny mirrors was circling it, as if waiting for something to happen there.

Jerry tried to move closer so he could get a better look, but as he did, he found that he still could not look over the edge of whatever surface he had found himself standing on. Unable to look below, he let his eyes follow the shimmer upward. He noticed that there were stars in the void, or what appeared to be stars at least, faintly twinkling far above. He wasn't sure, but it appeared as if many of them were falling down toward the glow, not as shooting stars might fall, but as a light rain would. And they weren't all falling straight into the glow's surface either. Some went this way and that, moving as they fell, their own lights twinkling faintly until each shimmering drop was lost in the depths of the luminous planet that was stretched across the horizon.

Once again he attempted to move closer, toward the edge of the cliff, and observed that he was not only nearer to its end than he had estimated, almost accidentally stepping off of something that appeared to be sheer and man-made, but that there were two other beings standing there at the edge with him. They appeared to Jerry as columns of smoke, barely discernible from the darkness around him. Slowly they solidified, and he was able to see them better than he had when he'd first noticed their presence. One appeared to be a man, the other some sort of four-legged animal. As close as he was to the cliff, he was still standing slightly behind them. Both figures were looking down at the great glow as he approached.

Light began to emanate from them, making it hard for him to see their less prominent features in any real detail, and he found that if he looked away for even a moment, they would become faint and blurry, until he focused all of his attention on them again. The man looked slightly overweight, and wore a suit jacket and slacks. To the right of him was something he could only describe as an eagle, with four legs and paws, and six great feathery wings that slowly moved up and down with a floating motion in a rhythm that was almost hypnotic. Jerry thought that it must have been an amalgamation of his recent memories, or some fantasy beast from his own imaginings, as the shape of its head seemed to change depending on which direction it was facing, and what angle he was watching it from. From one angle, the head of the beast appeared to be that of a ram, from another, it looked like some kind of large cat. At one point, he could have sworn he saw a bear in its contours, but its visage would always return to the eagle. The body was unchanging and looked much like that of a lion, the whole thing starting to reflect the glow that came out of the darkness as it shifted its weight.

Jerry wanted to move even closer, so that he could get a better look at the beautiful creature and the great glowing globe below the cliff, but when he began to do so, the great wingless Griffon-like apparition looked in the other man's direction and spoke, spilling shards of light in all directions. Jerry took a step back, not wanting his presence to be revealed, for he did not understand what he was seeing, and became afraid. "You must continue." it said. "He will tell you when you have finished. He will decide when you have done enough."

"They do not understand," The man in the suit stated simply. "There is no more time, the people cry out for justice...you must act. He must."

"We will, but everything first must be fulfilled." the creature responded. "The time of the gentiles is ending, but it is not time yet, you must prepare, one is coming to you. One the Almighty intends to use." Then it began to morph into a much smaller looking creature, before finally taking the shape of a small sphere. When it had completed the metamorphosis, its own light increased in strength, and he could see both figures much clearer. The light from the shape shifting beast brilliantly illuminated the space around them, and in that moment, the man turned in Jerry's direction. As he did, the entire scene began to fade and unravel, like the opening of a scroll in an avalanche of blurry images and muffled overlapping sounds, until nothing remained but retreating thoughts, run off by the ending of his slumber.

****

Jerry woke up in the dark garage. The sun had not yet risen, as he could not see any light coming in through the windows of the garage door. The door was completely closed, and he found himself wondering if the last part of his dream had been caused by the sound of it, as it rolled along its rails, before finally resting on the hard concrete surface that was the garage floor. He looked over at Mark's cot, and saw that he was still there, sleeping soundly, then sat up in his own. He intentionally placed his feet on the cold floor, making himself feel a little more alert. He rubbed his eyes, and brushed a hand through his hair, moving it to one side. *What the hell was that?* He thought. *Well, at least I remembered what happened. Oh man, I remember...everything. Wait, how can I see in here at all?* He lowered his hand from his face, and looked in Mark's direction again. The light source appeared to be coming from somewhere behind him. He turned around, and looked toward the door that connected the garage to the house. Seeing that the light from the kitchen appeared to be on, he got up, and walked over to it.

He climbed the three short steps to the kitchen, and looked in through one of the small panes of glass that were set into the door. Sitting at the kitchen table was Levi. He was holding a mug between his hands, his head bowed low over it. He looked like he was deep in thought. Then he looked up and saw Jerry peering in. He stood up, walked over, and opened it. "Come on in." he said in a hushed tone, so he wouldn't wake the others. Jerry walked in and sat down at the table.

"You want some tea?" Levi asked.

"Uh, sure." Jerry said, still feeling a little groggy. "What time is it?"

"Oh, I think it's around three in the morning. I'm always up early these days."

"What the hell is there to do this early?"

"Oh, plenty!" Levi looked a little excited. "I have a neighbor that is nearing retirement. Makes bread in a huge oven right behind his house! He has a bread truck, does deliveries that start around four every morning. Sometimes I go over to help him load and organize it, before he does his route. He doesn't do it on the weekends, though. 'Course I won't be helping him again until they get that confounded gate opened." He walked over to the stove where a small teapot sat, reached into a cabinet above it, and took out a small mug, then filled it with hot water. Then he opened a drawer, took out a teabag, and placed it into the mug. "Sometimes I go into downtown Spokane and meet some of the guys from my bowling league. We get coffee at a doughnut shop down there, and talk about stuff. Most of the time though, I just like to get a head start on my day. I still have some work to do on this house, some things to move around, some things to get rid of, that kind of thing." He placed the mug in front of Jerry and sat back down in his chair at the head of the table. "You want some cream or sugar?" he asked.

"No, that's fine, this is ok." Jerry answered. "So you still need to clean some stuff up. You mean like your things in the garage?" He placed his hands around the mug, only then noticing just how cold it was in the kitchen. He lifted his feet off of the floor tiles for a moment before letting them back down, so that only his toes touched them.

"It's all junk, you know. I know that now. When I was a kid things didn't matter much to me, then as I got older, I began to collect the things I was interested in the most, thinking that one day they would be worth something. Books, magazines, music, clothes, figured one day if no one wanted to buy it on the internet, I at least could pass it down to my grandkids or give it all to a museum. Turns out, it's all worthless though, all of it. None of it is worth anything anymore, because no one remembers and no one cares. It's all junk. It's all junk and you can't take it with you. No you can't, that's for sure." Levi looked as steadfast and certain as ever as he spoke. Jerry didn't detect a hint of sorrow or depression in the words, only a relieved kind of defeat, as if he were both glad to have finally spoken them aloud, and regretted the fact that it had taken him so long to say them. "Suppose I shouldn't let it all sit there to rot either." he continued, "Time for a trip to the thrift shop, might be enough to make a dent in my taxes." Levi smiled. He turned his head toward Jerry, and nodded, as if to give more weight to his decision before adding one final thought, "Could use the space anyway. Never know who might come next..."

A hush came over the kitchen. Jerry sipped his tea, and the two men just sat there, keeping one another company, both silently contemplating their lives. After a few minutes, Levi broke the silence again. "Truth is I don't sleep much since my Alice passed away. Boy, do I miss her. Not one second goes by that I don't. Fifty years we were together, Jerry, fifty years. I gotta tell you, I'm not sure who I am without her around, ha!"

Jerry didn't know what to say. He'd lost his parents when he was young, but never really got to know them as people, just parents. He had no idea what it was like to lose someone close after living with them for decades. *It must be truly awful to lose someone like that, and a son too...* Jerry thought to himself. *And yet he still has faith. Not sure I would if I were in his shoes.* Then it occurred to him that he hadn't really asked the man what he thought about what was happening in the Territory, the place where he had lived his whole life. "What about you, Levi? What do you think about everything going on around here? What's your take?"

"Me?" Levi's face became stern. He looked down at his kitchen table, focusing his thoughts. Jerry could tell he was choosing his words carefully before putting his two cents in. "Well, it's always been the Catholic way to take care of those who are less fortunate. One of the greatest purposes of the church is to help the poor. It was the main focus of many of the saints." he looked up, "I suppose some could argue that what's happening here is similar to how the monks and nuns used to live in monasteries and convents in harsher times, but they lived humble, quiet lives, and often went out to help those in need. These people..."

Levi shook his head and looked Jerry in the eye. In the short time he'd come to know the man, Jerry couldn't recall when he wore a more serious expression than he did in that moment. "I heard one of them preaching outside once, when they first came here." Levi said. "I was driving by one of their ground breaking ceremonies for a church that was going up, and decided to stop for a second, to hear what their pastor had to say. He said that his god was going to give his congregation all they would ever want and need, because they were obedient in following him here. He said his god was 'extravagant' in his giving. I can tell you now, that is not in the Bible. I remember Jesus likening God's provision for his people to lilies in a field, and birds in the air. No believers are meant to be held higher than others where wealth and money are concerned."

Levi's expression softened and he leaned back a little, still maintaining eye contact. "The church is meant to handle those things, and God appoints the managers, but that doesn't give them the right to take from the little guy and spend it on themselves however they feel like, even if they take from them in ways other than their tithes. Nah, those people are off their rockers. They may not know it, but they are. Not that it makes them any different than anyone else these days. The world used to be different, you know, used to make more sense. Ever since the towers fell everything's gone crazy. I knew a guy in Provo, eighty-seven, ex-Navy. Had to stand up to the very government he once fought for, just so he could have the right to protect himself in his own home. Nothing like that would have happened when I was young. I was young once, you know." He smiled and waited for Jerry to respond.

Jerry took a sip of his tea and swallowed. After a moment, he smiled back. "You don't say." he said jokingly.

Levi laughed playfully and slapped the table. "I was!" he said. "I really was."

Another brief moment of silence followed. Levi looked over his large and calloused hands, which he had placed on the table in front of him. Then Jerry remembered something else. "Hey, uh, what's with the flare gun, in the garage?" He pointed to the door.

Levi looked up, surprised at the question. "Oh, that." he said. "Uh, I used to keep it in the boat for when my son and I would take it down to Lake Liberty to go fishing. The flare gun was in it in case of an emergency, like if the engine stopped working, or the boat bottomed out. I cleaned the whole thing out before I decided to put that 'For Sale' sign on it, and forgot to put it back in. Why?"

"I was wondering if I could borrow it tomorrow, just in case something goes wrong. So I can make a distraction, if something bad happens, you know?"

Levi nodded. "Sure. Just untuck your shirt, and put it in your belt or something. If anything happens, don't worry about getting it back to me, just make sure no one can get fingerprints off of it. It has two rounds. Try not to shoot it at anyone. I don't want anybody's death on my conscience."

"I won't," Jerry said. "And, thanks. I don't suppose you have any guns lying around."

"Guns? No. Not in this house. My son had one from the service. I turned it in after he died."

Jerry's vision had finally cleared up. He let out a yawn and saw that Levi had hung his wife's tapestry on the wall in the only spot that was left, just under the clock. He pointed to it with his right hand. "Looks good there." he said.

Levi looked at it, "Yeah, I think so too. So, you have trouble sleeping too, I see."

"It's been that way for a long time with me, yeah," Jerry said. "I lost my folks in the Rainier calamity. Sometimes I have bad dreams about what happened. Usually, I don't remember much from them, if anything at all, this time, though...I think I did."

"You take pills for that?"

"Used to, nothing ever really worked. I also need to stay alert for work, and some of the stuff just made me drowsy all day so..."

"Yeah, I get that. Well, maybe that's something you can pray about."

Jerry was taking another sip of his tea when Levi made the suggestion. Jerry started to chuckle at the notion and choked, spitting up some tea into one of his hands, before coughing a few times. Still smiling when the fit was over, he looked at Levi with a genuine smile. "Yeah, maybe I'll give it a try sometime."

"Maybe sooner would be better than later for you," Levi said. He pointed to the mug in Jerry's hands. "If you know what I mean." He stood up, and got Jerry a napkin.

****

After finishing his cup of tea, Jerry thanked Levi again, went back into the garage and went back to sleep. His rest uneventful, he woke several hours later and walked back into the kitchen, where he saw that the others were already up and eating bagels. They looked delicious, Levi having made due by using what was left in his fridge, putting some egg, cheese, and bacon in between their round halves. When Jerry came in, Levi was in his chair reading his Bible. He tilted his head down, and looked at him over his reading glasses, while Mark and Eddie sat on opposite sides of the table, eating with very satisfied looks on their faces.

Eddie looked up at Jerry. "Levi found some bagels in the freezer!" Eddie said.

Levi glanced at Eddie, and back to Jerry. "You can have one if you want, not sure how long they were in there, but they seem ok.

Can't wait until that gate opens, I really do have to do some shopping."

"You seem pretty confident they're opening it today," Jerry said. "Who's to say they won't delay it again?" He sat down next to Mark, letting out a short yawn.

Mark looked at him, chewing his bagel as if it were rubber. He pushed a yellow piece of paper in Jerry's direction. Jerry picked it up. It was another flyer:

NOTICE

The Temple Foundation apologizes for any inconveniences that the gate may have caused over the last two days. The gate will be open after 1PM today. The Chief Justice for eastern Washington State will be present to collect any and all illegal firearms within the Territory walls. If you have any old or 3D printed armaments, please take the time to unload them and drop them off with any other weapons you no longer want or need. Feel free to bring complaints or concerns to the office of the Mayor of Spokane, the Temple Foundation site administrative office, or the local authorities at the gate. All issues will be dealt with in a timely manner. Thank you.

Beneath the message was a small diamond-shaped scannable code symbol used to direct a syncable device to a website for more information. Next to the symbol, was a URL for an AngelSat Network, cloud-based account. *I should give this address to Perry.* He thought. *It could connect to their internal network somehow, maybe it can be hacked. It could just be their outside face on the regular web too, but it's worth a try.*

"You can keep that one too if you want," Levi said. "They dropped those off this morning. Put them all around the neighborhood. Every car and door has a yellow flyer on it. Looks like you might not need to find that jammer after all."

Jerry looked up from the flyer. "Maybe, I'm not so sure the 'Foundation' is ready to give up their big secret to the authorities just yet, though." He folded the flyer and put it into his pocket.

Levi nodded in agreement. "You might be right." he said. "When are you two headed out?"

Mark finished chewing on the last of his bagel and brushed the crumbs off of his hands above his plate. "Why do you ask?"

"Well, I still have a stump in the front yard that could be broken up and moved, if the three of you think you're strong enough. I have a small chainsaw, an axe, and a few shovels."

Eddie, Mark, and Jerry looked at one another. "Why not?" Jerry said. "Sounds like fun. I think I'll try one of those bagels first, though."

Behold, that which I have seen to be good and proper is for one to eat and to drink, and to enjoy good in all his labor, in which he labors under the sun, all the days of his life which God has given him; for this is his portion.
-Ecclesiastes, 5:18

"No one can serve two masters, for either he will hate the one and love the other, or else he will be devoted to one and despise the other. You can't serve both God and Mammon." **-Matthew, 6:24**

Chapter Twenty-Six

Christian Territory, Levi's Place
Spokane, WA
Sunday, March 27[th,] 10:18AM PST

It took the four of them two hours to dig out and break up what was left of the old tree in Levi's front yard, but all of them had a good time doing it. They took turns splitting the stump into pieces,before joining forces to liberate the roots from the depths of the dark soil. Levi, being his thorough and careful self, showed them how to use the saw safely, as it needed to be oiled regularly as they put it to work. After they were done, he let them use his shower once more, and gave Eddie the task of washing his car, before Mark and Jerry got back on the road.

Several people in the neighborhood came out on their porches and front yards to watch them as they strode past. The onlookers waved cheerfully, as the two strode briskly past their homes, initially giving Jerry a good feeling about the attention they were getting. Mark appeared to be making real headway with the people in the Territory, winning them over with his sure and positive nature. It only made sense. After all, Mark exuded an aura of purposeful confidence that was attractive in a way, and rare in someone of his stature. Then he remembered the conversation they'd had with Pastor Greeley the night before, and how he'd explained to them the very real and fearful reasons why some of the same residents had ended up in the Territory. Suddenly their friendly smiles and small waves began to take on a different, far creepier meaning, and it wasn't long before each new smile or friendly wave he saw, made him want to turn around and go back to the relative safety of Levi's garage.

"So," Mark said. "What are you going to do about her?"

"Her? Her, who?"

"Your girlfriend there, Noel, was it?"

"Oh. I don't know. Why do you ask?"

"We all have to move on, Jerry. It's not good to be stagnant, in our lives, or in our faith. I have a rule, if it's not serving Christ in my life, I cut it out. If you were married, I might have said something different, but it doesn't seem like she intends on committing to you, from what you said yesterday."

"Thanks for the advice, but I'm not really sure that you're qualified to give me any, at least not in this instance." Jerry said.

"Fair enough," Mark said. He began to nod to himself, and looked down at his shoes as they moved across the pavement. "Just remember, we're only here for a short time. We can spend that time discovering the incredible adventure that we are meant to embark on and were built specifically for, or we can waste that time trying to possess things that were never meant for us to begin with, and pay the price when we inevitably don't get them, or even worse, when we do. I like you Jerry, and even though you might not think so yet, I think God has big plans for you. Just not the kind you might believe He would."

"Yeah well He doesn't talk to me. If he ever does, I'll be sure to let you know." Tired of being lectured, Jerry decided to turn the tables a little on his interrogator in an attempt to change the subject.

"Where are you going after this, Mark? You're pretty far from home."

"I know a guy," Mark said. He looked at Jerry. "Don't worry about me, Jerry. I'll be fine."

"Ever consider getting married again?"

"No." Mark said. "My wife was a wonderful woman, and I miss her more than I could ever explain, but having a good wife was never the goal, never the finish line for me. The real reward for a Christian is in knowing that you are part of the Kingdom that is coming." He stretched out his left arm, as if to demonstrate that something more was ahead. Something that was greater than trees and tar, and far more important than a spurious group of self-aggrandizing church leaders. "A Kingdom that is eternal. A Kingdom that will not only continually celebrate its present, but which will also forever remember those who came before, never forgetting those who, despite their circumstances, persevered through great hardships at times, having only their faith and the

Holy Spirit for company as they risked everything for their God. How about you? Think you'll ever settle down?"

"Not sure. Life's a journey after all. It's about the experiences for me. Lots of women out there. I mean, I love Noel, and I hate that she sleeps around, but I kind of understand it. That's why I keep forgiving her, I think. She's just trying to live life to the fullest you know?"

"Not really, to be honest." Mark said. "It's been a long time since I thought like that. To me, life *is* a journey, but it is a journey toward God. If you're paying attention, everything is leading people to know Jesus more. You can try to escape it all you want to fit in with everyone else, or to enjoy yourself while you are here, but one day all of us will be brought to account." He looked at Jerry again. "I don't only get satisfaction and happiness in having experiences in this world, but through my faith. I feel joy, knowing that one day a new world will be created by the Lord. One in which all suffering, and the evil that causes it, will cease to be. That is what I look forward to. In the end, worldly experiences are not enough. Life is a journey, yes, but true and lasting happiness comes when one knows in their very soul, the good things that await them at the end of it."

"Sounds nice," Jerry said. "But unlikely, in my opinion. Based on what I've seen so far, I've only got one life here, and, no offense, I plan to live it to the fullest while I can."

Mark smiled. "It's alright, Jerry, there's still time for you." They shared a laugh again, but each for a different reason. Jerry shook his head. "Anyway," Mark said. "It looks like we're nearing our destination."

They rounded a corner, and saw Victory Center. The parking lot was filled with vehicles, indicating that a service was in session. Beyond it, they could see the Temple Foundation grounds. Mark took a deep breath through his nostrils as it came into view, and looked at Jerry.

"Well, I suppose you'll be leaving after this. So it was nice meeting you, Jerry." he said.

"You too Mark, It's been...educational." He smiled.

They cut across the Victory Center parking lot, and headed to the meeting house. From the building, they could hear the sounds of the Christian band, and the thousands of prosperity Christians inside that were singing along with them.

****

When they arrived at the site, they saw several security guards in suits, milling around the area. Two of them stood near the doorway of the half-completed building they had agreed to meet in, while three more stood next to a white stretched SUV limo that was parked on the side of the street nearby. A few of the men were wearing the printed communication monocles that Greeley had described, and one carried a slightly larger version of one of the small handheld devices. Jerry guessed that it must have been a more advanced version of the cards he had seen the teenagers playing with the previous day. All of the guards were tall and extremely imposing in their appearance, and it was not clear which church or churches they were associated with. Jerry was surprised when they were allowed to walk by without being checked for weapons. Two of the guards walked ahead of them to the main entrance, and opened the wide set of double doors. Mark thanked them as they went in.

Once inside, the doors were closed behind them. Already a little nervous from what he had seen outside, Jerry began to feel very anxious. Not only had he unwittingly placed himself in a situation from which he may not have been able to escape, he was virtually unarmed, and standing next to the one person that those currently in control of the immediate vicinity could want to quietly get rid of. Ten or twenty folded plastic tables leaned against the far wall. In front of them, a single row of ten chairs had been set up, along with four more of the tables. Sitting on each one were, Jerry assumed, all of the available church leaders from the Territory that either cared to attend, or the only ones that had been invited. On the right side of the room, five rows of six or seven chairs each, had also been placed. Those were set at an angle, facing the center of the room. Scattered among them were ten or twelve average looking people, whose motives for being there were unclear.

A total of eight Pastors were already seated behind the tables when they entered the room. Jerry recognized three of them as the leaders he and Mark had seen at the wall the day before. He noticed the middle-aged woman first, as she was once again dressed to impress, wearing a bright blue dress, and a consistently gaudy jewelry arrangement that almost completely covered the top half of her torso, and two large golden hoop earrings. The man named George was also there, his eyes blazing and jaw clenched shut. He was leaning back in his chair, holding his cane upright with his right hand. The calm, collected Edwin Alstead sat squarely between them, in the middle of the table. As always, he was dressed to impress, but not as he had been the other two times Jerry had seen him. That morning, he wore jeans and a dark v-neck sweater over a white tee shirt. On his face, a pair of decorative glasses, that did not appear to have prescription lenses in them, had been added to the new look. They seemed to serve no purpose, other than to make him appear more intelligent than the others sitting around him.

Pastor Greeley was also there, sitting at the far right end of the tables between Pastor Obobwey and a well-dressed older gentleman in a slightly worn blazer, who couldn't seem to stop playing with the multitude of gold and silver rings that covered his fingers, nervously twisting them side to side, as if he were trying to solve a puzzle with his hands without looking at them. As they approached the table, two more security guards that Jerry had not seen when they'd walked in, appeared from a small side room. They positioned themselves on either side of the entrance, one of them stepping between Jerry and Mark, as he took his station. He motioned to Jerry with his right arm, toward the chairs that were on the right side of the room, as if inviting him to sit down.

"Uh, Mark," Jerry said.

Mark, who had entered the building first, turned around. All eyes in the room, which had at first been focused on him, were now completely centered on his unknown companion. There were several looks of confusion and some whispering, as Mark nodded, and used his right hand to signal to Jerry that it was ok to sit down with the other visitors. Jerry sat down in a chair that was positioned close to the main entrance, as it was the only exit he could see. Aldrich watched the short lived interaction between the two men with some interest, keeping his eyes on Jerry for a moment. Then, he looked at the guard standing closest to Jerry's seat, and nodded slightly. Finally, he turned his head side to side, casting his eyes down either end of the table, as if to see which leaders were present before moving forward with the meeting.

"Thank you for coming." Edwin said. He fixed his eyes on Mark. "Before we start, I...well, we just want to say that as the representatives of the New Christian Territory Organization, we are very thankful that you have agreed to come and speak with us. Pastor Greeley has told us that you wish to share something that the Lord has instructed you to, and then you plan to leave the area today, is that correct?"

Mark looked at George. "Yes, yes, it is," he said. "I have no desire to stay here one moment longer than I need to."

George's face started to become red again. Jerry could see a vein begin to form on the man's forehead. Mark looked back to Alstead. "I take it then that the judge is collecting the weapons, and that the gate has been reopened?"

"As we speak!" Aldrich said, flashing his trademark smile. "We are also allowing her to do a cursory inspection of the area, to make sure that everything is on the up and up. It is important that people realize that we never intended for the gate to be closed for this long. We were simply unsure how the new authorities would react-"

"You were scared," Mark said. "You created this place to protect yourselves from the corrupt leaders of this world, waited for some big event to make your move, and then were afraid when one of them showed up on your doorstep earlier than you'd anticipated. I get it."

Mark's accusation caught Edwin off guard, causing his face to become pale. He shifted slightly in his seat and cleared his throat before responding. "Well, you were right about our ability to reproduce the means to protect ourselves, should anything happen in the future that might require us to do so. Everything has settled down, and later this afternoon, when all of this unpleasantness has ended, the area will be open to the general public again. In fact, we will be encouraging locals from Spokane to come in and experience our churches and the new businesses that the members of our congregations have been hard at work setting up along some of the busier streets inside the walls. We assure you, this is, and will always be, a peaceful place where all are welcome."

Mark looked at Alstead for a moment, unmoving. Then he looked at the others who sat before him. "Very well, I will state my peace and leave. This won't take long. Thank you for hearing me out." He turned around and looked at the security guard that was standing next to the door, closest to Jerry.

Alstead spoke to the guard, "Get him a seat, please. I apologize, but just so you know, we don't have much time. Several of us have our assistant pastors running things right now, but we will have to get to our other duties shortly."

"Of course," Mark said. The guard took one of the unoccupied chairs that was set up next to Jerry and set it down behind Mark. "Thank you." He sat down and leaned forward, placing his hands on his knees. Then he looked back at the table and addressed the pastors, locking his eyes with theirs one by one as he spoke.

"I have traveled far to be here, because the Lord led me to this place. He asked me to simply come and occupy it for a short time. To be honest I wasn't sure why, and didn't even know that this place existed when the Holy Spirit led me into town and to the gate. So when Pastor Greeley told me that you were interested in speaking to me last night, at first, I was not sure what the Lord might want me to say to you. Now, sitting here looking at each of you, I can feel His Spirit rising up within me, and I know. He has made it clear. You see, He has placed a burden on my heart since I arrived here and learned about what has been going on in this place, a burden I would share with you." He placed his elbows on his thighs and lifted up his hands, palms upward, and looked at each of them with sadness in his eyes, his voice clear and certain. "He has given me a heart for the sheep that have been placed in your care, along with a deep pity for them." Upon hearing his words, the pastors became less comfortable in his presence. Several of them lifted their chins slightly into the air, their dull eyes glazing over before Mark had even arrived at his first point. A few looked down at their watches, and Jerry wondered if they were even listening to him.

"God loves you, all of you. You are his precious people, you are His future bride, and He wants you for Himself. He does not want to share space in your hearts with a lust for wealth or the concerns of a world that even now is passing away. The Lord has revealed to my spirit that you, all of you, have abandoned the Great Commission to placate your own anxieties and those of your congregations. I know that you now say from one side of your mouths, that you plan to let in others and that 'all are welcome', but I also know of your future plans to shut this place off from the world. I know that this is the real reason why you are here. I know you are lying." A few of the pastors shot disgruntled looks at Pastor Greeley as Mark continued, "You did not come here because you cared about this community, but because you wish to protect your own wealth and your own legacies, and because you live in fear of the rest of the world. The very world that God has sent you to lead to the loving knowledge of His Son." Offended by the observation, several pastors began crossing their arms or leaning back in their chairs. Their bland and previously uninterested guises transformed into a likeness of affronted indignance, or even worse, pure disgust. They became rigid in their new positions, as if to physically show their displeasure for the words Mark was hurling in their direction.

"I also believe that you have robbed your own children, those who you sought to protect, of the very faith and opportunities to serve God in the ways that He would have them serve Him, by bringing them here. That you say you wish to impart wisdom into them, while keeping them hostage in a place where their faith can never be tested, and where any wisdom they might glean from you would have no use. We grow in faith so that the Father might be glorified in us before the unbelievers, that they too, might believe, not to simply improve our situation on this earth for ourselves and our families. You have done this thing for your own children and your own futures. You have departed a life of faith in the name of faith, and have elevated your love for yourselves, your children, and your imagined purposes above God. But He will not be ignored. The Lord allowed this place to be created, but it was never His desire to do so. Your hearts began to fall away from His true purposes long ago, so He arranged for you to be here, so that you might be humbled together, and with common understanding leave together, back out into the world where the last of the lost wait for you to guide, comfort, and lead them into the Kingdom. He did not come here for those who are well, but for those who are sick! Many righteous men, women, and innocent children who followed you here have been praying for the Lord to use them in spiritual ways, despite your constant, subtle instruction that material fruit is the only kind that is worthwhile. They seek His Spirit and direct guidance, through the person of the Holy Spirit. You have failed to educate them in this." Then Mark sat straight up in his seat, and lowered his hands. "But the Lord has answered their prayers."

The committee was silent. Another pastor, a man that neither of them had seen before the meeting and who couldn't have been much older than Jerry, opened his mouth, "I see nothing that substantiates his claims." he said, and yawned. Jerry couldn't believe it. He was judging Mark based upon a first impression. As far as he knew, Mark could have parted the Red Sea, or had a billion dollars in the bank.

"So proud," said another, shaking her head as if to offer pity. But Mark was hardly being proud, at least not in any way that Jerry could see.

Then Pastor Greeley spoke up, "But what if he is right? Couldn't we have been wrong all this time? What he says is not un-Biblical."

Pastor Branson opened his mouth next, "Well, he didn't necessarily say we were *completely* wrong." He looked at Mark, "Did you?" Mark did not respond. Instead, he shifted his gaze downward to the floor. *Why isn't he answering?* Jerry thought.

"Perhaps he *is* saved and has been misled by a demon." the unnamed female pastor said. "If he is, then he needs our help, not our judgment!"

"HA!" Jerry laughed. Everyone in the room turned and looked at him.

The young male pastor who had spoken first lashed out at him. "And who do you think you are?" He looked at the others seated around him. "What would these two strangers be doing here at this crucial time, other than to disrupt what we've built! We should be wise and have them arrested for disturbing the peace."

"Enough!" Pastor Branson raised his voice. "No one is on trial here." He looked at Jerry. "Do you have something to say, sir?"

"Yes, I think I do." Jerry said defiantly. "All I've seen since I've been here are a bunch of stuffy people living in a paranoid bubble of their own making, who think it's more important to *act* like they are giving and humble, than it is to actually be those things. I don't know much about your 'god,' but I do know enough about people to recognize when they are being fake, or acting solely in their own interest. How you reconcile your need for material wealth, while putting up a façade of spiritual living, is beyond me. I may be new at reading the Bible, but I'm pretty sure that Jesus said to 'not want' or worry about 'possessions', I know that much. The only person I have seen living a life even remotely like that, is this guy right here." He pointed at Mark. "Not only that, but I don't think I've seen anyone genuinely reach out in Love to others and mean it, without looking to get anything back like he does, in my entire life! And how many times have you heard him say he is leaving soon? It's not like he's trying to take over whatever all of *this* is." He waved his hands in the air around him. "He doesn't even like being here! And I would know, I've spent my life talking to people who were forced one way or another to live and work in far worse situations than you have made for yourselves, people who might benefit from having more of what Mark is selling, but who you wouldn't even let in the door!" Jerry looked back to Mark, hoping for an acknowledgment that what he had just said was right. Instead, Mark sat unmoving, as if he were trapped in one of his memories again, like he was the first night they stayed in Levi's garage.

"Now, now." A smooth and calming voice joined the conversation. George stood up with assistance from his cane, and limped around his table. "Now, we see this man for what he truly is." He pointed his cane at Jerry. "He brings in a non-believer who would report what we are doing to the world! Spent your life 'talking to people' indeed. We know what you are and why you're here!" He walked behind where Mark was sitting and stopped, turning to face the pastors. "This man is a Judas! A snake sent by the enemy! A false prophet! You all know that I speak the truth! I know many of you personally, you have allowed me to give you sound council before, please allow me to give it now. I believe we should simply expel him out of the Territory. Why is there even need for a discussion?" He stretched his arms apart and shrugged, lifting his cane into the air.

Greeley stood up. "I believe you to be an honorable man Pastor Harmin, but I have met with Mark, and I do not believe that he is here to harm us. And even if he is the same man you described to us just before this meeting, if he has repented, is the blood of Christ not enough to cover his sins? I'm afraid I must also question why you decided to wait so long before giving us this new information, when you had several opportunities to do so over the last two days, and ask the other church leaders to recognize the change in the manner in which our brother in Christ has begun to behave since Mark arrived!" All eyes shifted to George, whose moderately peaceful demeanor once again began to take on a hint of anger and rage. "What are you not telling us, George?" said Greeley, "Is he really the upstart that ruined your old church, or was it you?"

George Harmin pointed his cane at Pastor Greeley. "He deceives with his words!" he began, "He talks to the weak ones first and turns them against the leadership! I've seen him do it all before! Before you know it, he'll have all of you repenting for taking hold of the promises that the Lord gave to you!" He turned to face the other pastors.

"But what does he have to gain?" Greeley asked. "What does he take? He has nothing, and desires nothing but to be heard!"

"Attention!" George yelled. "Everywhere he goes, it's always about HIM, and what HE is doing, what HE thinks! He loves the attention he gets! He has no concern for us. The only one he loves is himself!" Mark continued to stare at the patch of carpet in front of his feet. Jerry was befuddled, unable to understand why he hadn't stood up for himself as George went on with his slanderous rant. "He steals hearts and then abandons them! He exaggerates and lies about what God does, and turns small coincidences into miracles! He is a false prophet! Why can't any of you see this?"

Branson spoke up, "Do you have anything to say for yourself, Mark?"

Mark, still looking down at the floor said, "Only one more thing, and then my work is finished in this place." He stood up, and for a moment there was silence in the room, all eyes and ears focused on him once again. He let out a low sigh, and closed his eyes. Then almost non-nonchalantly, as if he had recited the line a million times before, as if he knew the moment was going to come, *had* to come, one last sentence escaped from Mark's lips, "She never stopped hoping we would reconcile George. She loved you so mu-"

Crack!

"You stole her from me!" George shouted.

Mark's body shuddered. It took a moment for everyone to recognize that George, still standing behind Mark's chair, had struck him on the back of the head with the handle of his cane. Mark swayed for a moment, his eyes still closed, as some of the pastors began to get up out of their seats, but it was too late.

Crack!

With the second hit, a woman sitting not far behind Jerry began to scream.

"She could have had a good life!" Harmin yelled. Tears began to escape his eyes like a waterfall, running furiously down his cheeks and into his beard.

Mark fell down on his knees. Jerry, who had seen everything transpire but couldn't believe his own eyes, stood paralyzed. He instinctively thought that Mark would fight back. He waited helplessly, hoping to see him rise to the occasion like he had against the man at the gate. By the time he realized that Mark had no intention of defending himself, he had already been hit twice. Then with a third, Mark's body shook again.

Crack!

"She deserved better than a proud, poor idiot like you!"
The final blow caused a small amount of blood to spray over the tables, hitting three of the pastors who sat in the middle, including Pastor Alstead, who reeled backward as it did so, his face taking on a look of horror in response to the grotesque scene that was unfolding in front of him. A thin line of red dots splattered across his sweater, the same line that started on the dress of Pastor Favorton to his right, and ended on the hands of Pastor Branson on his left. Mark's limp body fell, face forward onto the thin, gray carpeting that was stapled to the plywood beneath him. When he hit the floor, pastor Branson cried out, his hands shaking violently, "STOP HIM! STOP HIM BEFORE HE TRIES TO KILL US ALL FOR OUR SINS!"
By then, the guards had already sprung to action. They had waited until they heard the second hit connect, as they could not see what was going on from behind Harmin's large frame, and were used to how he would often wave his cane about as he spoke in meetings like that one. They had already started to tackle him when the third hit landed, unable to stop it. As the final swing made contact with the back of Mark's skull, they pulled the pastor back violently, causing him to collapse onto the floor, taking the guards with him. Jerry leaped from his seat, grabbed the cane out of Harmin's hand, and raised it in the air. Seeing Jerry standing over him ready to strike, his arms pinned by the guards, Harmin shrieked, tears still pouring out from his eyes. "Don't let him hurt me!"
Ready to bludgeon the man until he heard the cowardly plea, Jerry stopped himself, opting instead to throw the cane across the room, before kneeling beside his fallen friend. Several pastors from the committee had already moved the tables and joined the guards in holding onto George, who appeared to be trying to squirm out of their grip in the direction of the double doors. As they piled on top of him, he began to yell. "He's a false prophet! I've done nothing wrong! Moses told us to kill false prophets!"
The young pastor that had rebuked Jerry a few minutes earlier, joined him by Mark's side and took off his shirt, pressing it behind

his head. Two other men who were close to where Jerry had been sitting joined them. One checked Mark's pulse. "It's fading, no, it's gone." he said. He looked at the others. "Help me do CPR." He told them. The three of them flipped Mark over and went to work, one of them checking his pulse while another gave mouth to mouth. The young pastor volunteered to do the chest compressions. Jerry, familiar with the procedure but still in shock at what had just transpired, sat back and got out of the way.

Pastor Branson, frozen because of what he had just witnessed, gathered himself together and walked around the tables to face Pastor Harmin. The security guards had picked George up, and were restraining him by wrapping his wrists with a roll of packing tape that Pastor Greeley had gotten from the office, restraining his hands behind his back. Branson gave the proud, disheveled man a stern look, and slapped him across the face. "Moses spoke to the Jews before grace came into the world in the form of the Son of Man. We do not live by the Law, but by grace. Ours is the greater part. But you know this, you've preached it!" His hands were still shaking. "Who was the woman he spoke of? Was she your daughter? Is this her husband?" He motioned to Mark's body. Harmin shifted his eyes away from his accuser's. "This blood belongs to you, George, and you have brought it upon us all! It was not he that deceived us, but you! You've concealed yourself in the midst of the leadership! You are a wolf now revealed, and you may have just murdered a righteous man!" He placed a bloodied hand onto George's head and prayed. "May the Lord have mercy on your soul for what you have done, and lead you to repentance."

"I have nothing to repent for!" George said angrily. At Branson's rebuke, he had become fully enraged. "The Lord will vindicate me, you will see!"

"No." Branson said. "It is over. This place will be undone because of this deed. Look, they have already gone to spread the bad news, and we all- all of us, will pay for your sin!" Pastor Harmin struggled, and turned his head to see that behind him the double doors were open. The woman who screamed during the attack had gone outside, hysterical. She was attracting the other guards, one of which was grabbing at her in an attempt to calm her down, not knowing what had happened inside the meeting room, causing her to scream yet again. A small crowd began to gather to see what was going on. "This man was from God, and he was right, we never should have come here and separated ourselves from the world. It is not our purpose, our commission. We allowed our love for our children and our own futures to blind us..." Branson said, his words trailing off as he turned and looked toward Jerry. "He knew he would be martyred before he even came here." Branson whispered. "I could see it in his eyes. We are not worthy of the Kingdom! Lord forgive us, forgive me!" he pleaded, looking up at the ceiling.

Jerry and the men working on Mark's body didn't notice the emotional display. They had stopped trying to bring Mark back and were sitting on the floor, staring at his lifeless form. One of them looked down and began to pray. Another checked Mark's wrist for a pulse one more time, hoping for some kind of fruit from their effort. He looked at Jerry and said, "He's dead. I'm sorry." Jerry looked down at Mark. For a second, he could see the man in his mind, smiling in the rain while being lifted over all of those people just two days before. He couldn't help but think that he was a man who had not been able to enjoy life like other people had, but more than anyone else deserved to. Pastor Alstead walked over to them. He looked down at Mark with a sad expression and then at Jerry.

"What?" Jerry said to him. "Aren't you supposed to bring him back from the dead or something?" Alstead looked at Jerry blankly as if not sure what to say. "Oh, right!" Jerry hit himself in the forehead with his right palm, "He was the only one here who actually believed his God could do that! I guess we're out of luck, huh?" Jerry stood to his feet, turned to the door, and walked out of the building.

"I have been crucified with Christ, and it is no longer I who live, but Christ lives in me. That life which I now live in the flesh, I live by faith in the Son of God, who loved me, and gave himself up for me.I don't reject the grace of God. For if righteousness is through the law, then Christ died for nothing!"
-Galatians, 2:20-21

Chapter Twenty-Seven

Temple Foundation temporary meeting house
Christian Territory of Spokane
Sunday, March 27th, 12:26PM PST

J erry stepped onto the gravel path that led to the entrance of the meeting house. The sound of the stones, grinding against one another beneath his feet, reached his ears. The colors of both sky and earth seemed more vibrant than before, and he could smell the fragrance of the flowers planted along the walkways from several meters away. He felt his heart pumping faster than usual. *Adrenaline.*He thought. He stopped to look around, and saw that a large group of people had gathered along the street nearby. The security guards had stopped some of them from leaving the sidewalk, but not all. Ignoring them, several men ran in his direction while the others looked on, many of them holding hands with small children or pushing them in strollers. A long line began to form, extending down the street toward the Victory Center, indicating that their latest Sunday service had only just ended.

Standing there dazed in a cloud of conflicting emotions, Jerry saw that many of the onlookers were staring at him, their uncertain gazes peering in his direction as if he were some strange animal standing in a zoo exhibit behind a thick pane of transparent aluminum. Their grips on their children tightened, as they were unsure of what had happened inside the meeting house, or what he, being the first to leave the building after the hysterical woman, might do next.

At the sight of their gawking, a deep rage began to rise up in Jerry's chest. He clenched his teeth, and using every ounce of strength tried to stop from screaming at them right then and there. He wanted them to know how much he hated them and their backward ways, how he thought they were stupid to be there, that they were all hypocrites.

Tears began to well up in his eyes. He didn't care anymore, he would unleash himself upon them, because they deserved it. They were takers posing as givers, haters pretending to be decent people. Then, Just as he was about to open his mouth in a fit of righteous indignation, near the road he saw a twenty-something woman holding the hand of a young girl, maybe ten or twelve years of age. The girl was looking at him, her whole body stiff and shaking, a frightened stare on her face. In her tiny right hand, she held the light blue strap of a backpack, which lay on the pavement beside her.

The sight snapped Jerry out of his mindset. His face, twisted and contorted until that moment, relaxed again. As a group of men ran past him and into the building, his mind began to clear, and he remembered the shack. His head swung like a swivel in its direction. He looked over the crowd one more time, and heard another child say, "Why is the man crying, mommy?" Confused, he raised his right hand up to his face. He couldn't remember the last time he'd cried. He took out the flare gun from beneath his untucked shirt. Small shouts and screeches came out of the crowd, as they were not sure if the thing in his hand was a 3D printed gun or not. He pointed it above his head, and fired a flare into the air. Not understanding what was going on, many in the crowd began to scatter, walking back to the safety and comfort of their homes. By then, the remaining security guards had either followed the others inside, or were helping to manage the crowd. A few saw the flare, but were unsure of where it had come from and were too busy to find out.

Jerry turned around, and walked toward the shack with renewed purpose. Along the way, he moved through the building materials that had been removed from the large containers and were now laid out on the ground in large carefully sorted piles, no doubt in preparation for the robotic builder that would use them to complete the Temple Foundation building sometime in the next few days. He continued on into the trees and walked around the pitched small wooden structure, looking for anything that might indicate an entrance. On the far side, he saw what looked like a wide rubber-like seam and a small transparent square made out of plastic. He reached out and began to examine it, finding that it could be flipped upward, revealing a small hole underneath.

Looking into the hole, Jerry saw a small fingerprint reader. It was set about an inch deep, inside the wall. He stepped back. *Damn,* He thought to himself. *No way in.Wait-* He returned to the building materials in the hope that he could find something that he could use to pry the door open with. Finding a large stack of three-foot-long pieces of carbon fiber rebar, he took one and brought it back to the shed. He used one end of the rebar to pry into the seam. Even though he managed to get the rebar under the edge of what must have been a doorway, with all of his strength he couldn't spread the gap more than a centimeter, let alone open it. Frustrated, he looked at the ground, and remembered the piping that ran the wiring to the main building. He walked to the construction site a second time, and found several large metal pipe sections made of the same material, each about five feet in length. He took one back to the concealed door, and put one end over the rebar that was still sticking out of the seam. Forcefully pushing against it with all of the force he could muster, he heard the door creak, and could see that the outside paneling of the shack was bending outward. Finally, the doorframe gave way, and the door popped open. Jerry threw down the piping, picked up the piece of rebar, and went inside.

The six by eight-foot interior had a concrete floor with a short brown carpet laid upon it, and a small table to the right of the doorway. On the table sat the thumb print device, which was plugged into a power storage unit that sat beneath the table. The unit had a wire of its own that followed along the edge of the floor of the shack, and then ran up to the ceiling in the far corner of the room to the solar panels on the roof. The room had no light that Jerry could see, forcing his eyes to adjust, and while tracing the path of the wire that led to the roof, Jerry saw another wire that ran alongside it.

He walked further inside, and followed the second wire with his fingers downward, until it disappeared between the wooden trim and the base of the unpainted drywall. He stood up, and had started to use the rebar to pry the base board away from the side of the small room, when he heard a small clanking sound coming from under his left foot. He was standing on something. He stepped back, pulled up the carpet, and saw that hidden beneath it was a metal trap door with a thin pad lock holding it in place.

Using the diamond hard piece of rebar, he bent, and then broke the latch that the padlock was attached to, and opened the hatch. Underneath, a ladder descended into a dark and narrow passage. After taking a second to work up some courage, he climbed down into it, tightly gripping each rung of the ladder as he went, unsure as to how high he was above the floor beneath him. After a few minutes, he arrived at the bottom of a mysterious chamber, unable to see more than a few feet ahead of his own toes. Remembering something that he'd heard Mark say about walking like lamps were attached to his feet by faith alone, he took a single step forward into the darkness. As soon as he did, a light source above him flickered to life, the first of several that likewise followed, illuminating the subterranean space in a long line, along the center of the ceiling.

To him, the room, once revealed, resembled an underground bunker or fallout shelter. It had a concrete floor and curved concrete walls that rounded as they arched upward, until they met each other some ten feet above his head, where the fluorescent lights hung exuding their cold, pale incandescence. On one side of the arched hallway, pallets full of boxes that were labeled "bottled water" were stacked, along with what looked like several hundred bed cushions in vacuum-sealed plastic, so that each one was only a few inches thick. On the other side across from them, twenty or more metal shelves stood, each housing perhaps a hundred quantum server units, and a mess of wiring and communication nodes that were strewn between them. Many of the servers were as yet unused, and were not connected to the active ones, which hummed slightly in a pleasant, almost comforting tone. Despite the haphazard state that the network was in, it did appear to be up and running. Much more work would be required before it could run optimally, however. The shelving went on for twenty or thirty yards, and ended at a large pile of cardboard boxes, which appeared to contain everything from temporary toilets and foldable barriers, to various types of canned food and other necessities, that were stacked all the way to the ceiling.

Next to the wall of boxes, Jerry also saw a small monitor and a keyboard sitting on the last set of shelves. He walked toward it, and looked over the entire setup. Each of the servers were connected to forty or so of the highest quality, one thousand terabyte, solid-state storage drives on the market. *This must have cost a fortune.* He thought. *I don't see a virtual or augment capable interface...they must be using it for data storage, but what could they need that much storage for?*

He reached the monitor, and tapped it with his forefinger. It was already on and apparently unlocked, revealing a desktop interface that he did not recognize, but that appeared to use file formats and executables that were simple enough to understand. At first, Jerry was surprised that there was no password protection for the system, then he realized that not only was the place well hidden, but that if anything did happen above that would require use of the space, whoever held a password might not make it there, or live long after they did depending on the circumstances. That meant they had to make the interface accessible to anyone left who was able to use a basic Operating System.

Jerry's eyes scrolled down through the list of files on the desktop. Some of them were labeled with rudimentary subjects like, 'Public Works Planning [PWP]' and 'Temple Site Layout [TSL]'. It was the others, however, that sparked his interest. They included, 'Security Plan Post Wall Completion [SP]', 'Strategic strengths and weaknesses of local Geographic features for Civil Conflict Scenarios [CCS]', 'Extremely Low Frequency [ELF] System Management and Controls' and 'Remote Jamming Frequency [RJF] Regulator'.

Seeing that no devices other than the keyboard were attached to the monitor, he used his right index finger to tap each of the folders on the touch screen, opening them so that as their respective windows appeared, so that they overlapped one another in a cascading fashion. Looking through them, he quickly deduced that the first two folders were plans for altering the Christian Territory area, so it could become self-sufficient. They included blueprints and plans for underground irrigation systems and electrical grids, which included windmills, and other green technologies that were yet to be set up above ground. The third file included topographical maps of the New Christian Territory and surrounding areas, both in and outside of the city of Spokane. Over the images, digitized notes had been added that listed details about certain locations that did not appear clearly on the maps, or were just off of them, and different solid colored rectangles, which seemed to represent defensive groups that could be deployed should an outside force try to attack or infiltrate the wall. The fourth appeared to be a series of documents and charts, detailing the ELF system and a history of its implementation, including multiple experiments that were done in the area going back nearly a decade. He opened the last file, and saw an icon for the jammer. When he tapped the icon though, a login screen appeared. "Damn." Jerry said to himself. "No way to hack it either. I'll have to think of some other way to-"

Then, on the bottom right side of the screen, just above the 'Delete Files Bin' icon, Jerry saw two more files that had been separated from the rest. One was titled 'Foundation localized internet access and operation,' and the other was called 'Online Bible Multi-Site Simultaneous Editor'. In the first, he found a simple Icon, an executable that opened its own small graphical interface for what looked like an augmented Omni-Tech compatible internet access program. Within it, were options for censoring specific websites, or scrubbing them completely by erasing any historical data in the database, and blocking access to them on the entire network. Using the options, entire sections of the internet could effectively be erased from local memory, and blocked. Access to any number of websites could be permanently banned, based solely on a single word that appeared on any one of their pages, if so desired. Many of the terms and phrases that had already been added to the list, included Bible verses and anything that might cast a negative light on pursuing wealth, or one's own interests.

In the other file, Jerry found an executable program, simply called "BibleNetEditor.exe". When he opened it, he immediately recognized it as an illegal A.I. program that could be used to regularly scan through an entire computer network looking for any undesirable Bible references, erasing or replacing them as it went. It also included a list of Christian websites that were already being monitored- no, next to each in the list, it said they were in the process of being 'Cleansed' and 'Copied'. Jerry looked at the long line of servers and hard drive back-ups again. *They're not just editing an internal system,* He thought. *They're building their own sterilized version of the internet! That's what all of this is. That's what the people at the Temple site were looking at and why they were arguing with the others who were carrying real Bibles. They thought they were accessing the same sources they always had, but they were looking at altered versions of them! If something happens in the future like Greeley said, Alstead and his cohorts want to be in control of everything their people see and hear. They don't just want to give the people here the illusion of accessing the outside world. They plan on using what's coming to rewrite the Bible!*

Jerry's eyes shifted back to the monitor. He took a moment to look closer at the program's settings. Within them, he found options for connecting the program itself to a much larger network. *This A.I. is self-generating. That means it's illegal, if it ever connected to the regular internet it could take years for people to even notice the damage that it could do. Maybe that's part of their plan as well. Maybe they want to change what every digital Bible says, even if there isn't a civil war.*

Jerry's mind immediately thought of what Mark's opinion of what he'd found would have been, and he felt the rage return. That time though, he let it take over. He closed the files, and attempted to move them to the delete bin. A rough computerized voice came out of the monitor, "The files you have selected may only be deleted by an administrator from another location." His anger became too much for him to handle. He grabbed the monitor and ripped it from the cords it was attached to, severing it from the main server that sat behind it. He threw it on the floor and began to violently stomp on it, until he no longer had the strength. He stomped so hard in fact, that the flare gun he'd tucked back into his belt fell out, making a loud clattering sound as it hit the concrete, that echoed through the massive enclosure.

Jerry stopped, turned around, and looked down at the flare gun. Then he looked behind him at the hundreds of carefully stacked boxes. Reaching up, he violently pushed the last shelf, so that the server that was attached to the monitor fell over and into the wall of cardboard boxes. Then he took several of the vacuum-sealed mattresses, and threw them in a pile over the hardware. Replacing the cartridge in the flare gun, he stepped back twenty paces, turned his back to the entrance, leveled out his arm, and shot the second and last flare into the pile of supplies, creating a fire that immediately began to consume all of the air in the long bunker. Jerry waited to see if some type of fire repellant, or water dispensing system would turn on, but nothing did. *No pipes down here.* He thought to himself again. *They must not have finished that part yet. Good.*

He ran back the way he'd come and climbed up and out of the thin passage, leaving the hatch open when he reached the top. On his way out of the shack, he left the door wide open as well, to allow the fire down below as much oxygen as it would need to burn everything that was hidden in darkness, deep in the earth below his feet. As he walked back toward the meeting house, he saw that over a hundred people were standing outside, looking in through the windows, and asking the security guards what was going on. Aldrich's stretched SUV was unsurprisingly nowhere to be seen, but several Spokane police cruisers were. The Chief Justice stepped out of one of the vehicles, and walked inside, the mayor sheepishly following at her higher-than-high heels all the way to the entrance.

To avoid being seen by the officers that had started to cordon off the area with yellow tape, Jerry stayed behind the tree line and made his way unseen, behind and around several of the cargo containers. When he reached the street, he headed toward the Victory Center parking lot. There he saw several families and a few individuals standing next to their vehicles watching the smoke as it began to billow out of the shack. Jerry walked up to the most average looking person he could find, a shorter man with a large bushy beard, who was wearing a bandana on his head. He was standing next to an old, well used utility vehicle with what must have been his wife and two teenage children.

"Hi." he said. The man looked at him with a shocked expression as if surprised that someone had approached him at all. "I need a ride." Without saying a word, the man reached into his pocket, took out a small package of tissues, and handed them to Jerry.

"Take it." he said. "I use them for my allergies, but you look like you need them more than I do right now."

****

"What did he say to you?" Jerry asked. He was standing in Levi's bathroom, having just washed his face. Levi passed him a towel.

"When?" Levi asked.

"When we first got here two days ago," Jerry turned toward Levi, a hopeful look in his eyes. "When you came inside to call the police for Eddie."

Levi looked down, put his hands in the pockets of his dirty jeans, and pressed his lips together in an almost sideway frown. Then he looked back up. "He said God sent him here to get these people out, and that to do it, all he needed was a place to stay for a few days, for the three of you."

"And you believed him?"

"No, not really, I told him you all could stay for one night if you were willing to work for it. But then I found out about how popular he was because of what happened at the gate. I never liked Protestants much to begin with, never understood 'em. I guess I just figured I could get their goats by giving him a place to stay."

"Goats?" Jerry asked.

"Not the acronym. It's an old figure of speech. It means to get on someone's nerves. I thought it might aggravate the Temple Foundation people, if they knew their hero was staying with someone like me. I thought it might be a good way to get back at them for basically taking over my home town here. I thought it would make me feel...better. Heck, I would have let you guys stay for a month!" Levi looked down again. "I'm afraid I haven't been the best Catholic I could be lately. I should have been more loving to these people and encouraging others to do the same. I have a feeling Mark knew I would figure that out on my own, though."

"What's going to happen with Eddie now that the gate is open?"

"I brought him to the gate after you two left this morning, and spoke to the police. They said they'll get started looking for his aunt, but since he isn't a minor anymore, he can go wherever he wants to. I offered to let him stay here. It just seemed like the right thing to do. I haven't done many Christian things since my wife died..." Levi fell silent for a moment. Through the bathroom window, birds could be heard chirping, and they both could hear Eddie washing the dishes in Levi's kitchen. After the brief pause, Levi finished his sentence, "...but Mark sure did. By God, he sure did. Anyway, I was thinking of bringing Eddie to my church downtown. He said he wants to visit the Korean one you two went to yesterday. I suppose it wouldn't hurt to check them both out, and let him decide which one he wants to go to. I'm still going to make sure he understands the Catholic side of things either way, though. Oh, follow me, I have something for you."

Levi turned around, and led Jerry to the closet near the front door of the house, the same one that he had taken so many interesting things out of during their stay. As Levi opened the door, Jerry looked over his shoulder to see what was inside. There must have been twenty winter coats of all colors, and from several different eras pushed together, all of them hanging from a short pole under a shelf full of old boxes. Most of the boxes were old boardgames, though a few looked like shoe boxes and were overflowing with old receipts. On the floor to one side of the closet, several brooms and dustpans leaned against the wall next to a collection of winter boots. Behind them were two plastic containers filled with neatly folded clothes. Levi opened one of the containers, and took out a blue and white striped dress shirt. He turned around and threw it at Jerry. "You've been wearing the same shirt for days. You can keep that one."

"Thanks." Jerry looked down at the vintage shirt in his hands, still in its original plastic wrapping. He looked at Levi again. "Has God ever spoken to you Levi? You know, in your spirit?"

"I think He did once," Levi opened the front door and let Jerry outside. "I was in Desert Storm, you know. I prayed with some other guys in my battalion one night when a sand storm came through, on our way to Baghdad. We prayed for God's protection, peace, and victory, and boy did He come through for us. It was a cake walk after the initial invasion." He looked Jerry in the eye. "What I remember the most was that before we prayed, we were all nervous. Most of us had never seen real combat before you see, at least not on that scale anyway. But after we prayed, everyone became confident and calm. Even though a wall of sand was about to hit us in the middle of the night in a place none of us had ever been before, and even though we knew there might be a million soldiers waiting to hit us on the other side of it, it didn't matter. We knew we had already won. A feeling of peace came over all of us that night. We just knew we were meant to be there, and that God was on our side. Every now and then, when we get together, the old group from my battalion, I mean, someone will mention it, and everyone will stop talking and just remember that moment.God doesn't speak to me, like He did to Mark. But He always answered my prayers eventually, one way or the other even if I didn't like the end result, and He always took care of me, and I guess that's all the grace I need."

Jerry ripped open the plastic cover and changed his shirt. He gave Tom's white dress shirt to Levi. "You can burn this," he said. "I'll buy my boss another one if I need to."

Levi took the shirt in his hands, "Well, I have to clean out my son's bedroom for Eddie. I think he should have it. Do you need a ride anywhere?"

"A ride?" Jerry asked. "Um, no. I feel like going for a walk actually, a long one. I saw a charge station on the way here. They should have some CAVs available to rent. I'll call my boss from the office there, and he'll pay my way."

"What are you going to do next?"

"I...I really don't know. Go home, I guess."

"Sure you do," Levi said. He took a notepad and pencil out of his right front pocket, and Jerry's small Bible from the left one. He stretched his hands out to Jerry, gently offering the items to him. Jerry looked at him surprised. "I found them under your blanket," Levi said. "You should learn to make your bed, soldier. That way, you won't lose anything in it. I know you don't work for the phone company. I may be old, but I'm not senile, well not yet anyway. I used to be young you know." A smile appeared on Jerry's face, and he took the items out of Levi's hands. "Good luck with your story, and...make it a good one."

Jerry separated the small Bible from the other belongings. "You can keep this. I don't think I'll be needing it." he said.

"That one wasn't mine," Levi said. "That was Mark's Bible. You should keep it."

Jerry looked at the Bible in his hands, confused. "How did he-"

Levi tapped the left side of his chest. "I asked him the same question. He said he kept it in his shirt pocket. I have no idea how that kept it dry through that storm, though. Anyway, it's yours now. He gave it to you for a reason."

Jerry stared at the Bible for a moment, and not wanting to disappoint Levi, put it in the breast pocket of his new vintage shirt. "It's been a pleasure."

"I know you didn't do as much as Mark and Eddie, but thanks for your help over these last couple of days," Levi said. "I'm not sure I could have done it all without you guys this year. Feel free to come and visit anytime, the garage is always open. Make sure you say goodbye to Eddie before you go, I'll be sure to talk to him about Mark later. So long, Jerry." Levi reached out his right hand. Jerry looked at it, nodded to himself, reached out his own and shook it. Levi nodded back, a look of pride in his eyes. Then he let go of Jerry's hand, and walked back inside.

Eddie was busy trimming branches from the bushes and small trees that lined the front of the house. He had been using a pair of clippers to prune them while Jerry and Levi talked and was breaking up the driest of the branches he had cut off, when Jerry approached him, placing them carefully into a fresh waste disposal bag that stood next to him on the front lawn. He looked up and gave Jerry a broad smile.

"I'm out of here Eddie," Jerry said. "You ever been to Seattle before?"

"No!" Eddie's eyebrows went up in excitement then quickly lowered again. "But don't worry about me, Jerry. Levi and I worked something out while you and Mark were gone. The police said I could stay with him. He said I could stay as long as I wanted to, if I helped out around the house. Anyway, I like it here! It's a lot better than my aunt's small apartment! Tomorrow Levi is going to take me to the supermarket, and then we're gonna drive around Spokane now that the gate is open. He's gonna show me where everything is!" He looked past Jerry for a moment scanning the yard with his eyes. "Where's Mark?"

"Mark, well, Mark had to go home too," Jerry said. "I'm sure he wanted to say goodbye, he just...ran out of time I guess."

"Oh." Eddie said. "I like Mark. Well, maybe you guys will come back to visit?"

"I'll certainly try." Jerry said. "Not sure I've enjoyed being inside the wall, but Spokane seems like a pretty interesting place."

"Maybe I can come visit you in Seattle too!" Eddie said. His eyebrows rose again. Jerry could see the excitement return to his face.

"That would be great."

"Well, see you later then Jerry."

Jerry leaned forward, and gave Eddie a brief hug. "See you Eddie." he said, and started off toward the gate. As he walked away, he could hear Levi behind him coming out of the house. He turned around for a moment, and watched as Levi walked over to his old boat, and took down the 'For Sale' sign. He then proceeded to release the remaining straps, so he could remove the tarp. "Hey, Eddie!" Levi yelled across the yard. "You ever go fishing?" Jerry smiled to himself, and continued walking. A tear formed in the corner of his right eye and began to fall. He caught it, and stared at his fingers. Then he wiped his hand on the side of his pants, and headed down the street.

"He who seeks his life will lose it; and he who loses his life for my sake will find it." -**Matthew, 10:39**

Chapter Twenty-Eight

Christian Territory, Main Gate
Spokane, WA
Sunday, March 27[th,] 2:01PM PST

W hen Jerry arrived at the gate, he was surprised to see only two people there. A gate operator was standing just inside the entrance, next to a manual control box. With arms crossed, he carefully watched as a police officer went about his work on the other side of the archway. The operator had an anxious look about him, turning his head every few seconds toward the center of the territory where the Temple foundation site was located. The gate fully installed, the ground around it filled in and leveled, was wide open. The lone police officer on the outside was placing several 3D printed rifles and pistols into the back of a black and white S.W.A.T. vehicle.

Jerry walked under the archway and over to the officer. "All finished, huh?" he asked. The cop turned around to see who was standing behind him.

"Collecting weapons? I guess so. No more volunteers, not now." he said.

"Why? Did something happen?"

The officer nodded, and stopped sorting through the guns for a few seconds to speak to him. "Apparently someone was murdered, right in front of a group of people in there. Then a fire broke out nearby. Nothing serious, but the judge went in with the mayor and some local reporters. They left me here just in case anyone still wanted to turn in their arms. You got any?"

Jerry shrugged and shook his head. "Never touch the stuff." he said.

"Yeah," The cop continued. "Never thought these folks would have so much action inside their wall, I thought keeping stuff like that out was the whole point of having one in the first place." He went back to sorting out the guns in the back of the vehicle.

Jerry looked around. Having crossed over the threshold and back out into the world, a combined sense of relief and freedom washed over him. Feeling lighter, he turned south and crossed the street. Not far from the entrance in that direction, he noticed a large man dressed in jeans and a tee shirt, who was standing next to a car that was two sizes too small for him. The man had a bandage on his forehead, but it was only after noticing the tattoos on his forearms that Jerry realized that the bystander was, in fact, the same giant Mark had taken on two days earlier.

A question forming in his head, Jerry decided to walk in his direction. The man, who was looking down at a smartwatch on his wrist while leaning against his car, looked up when he heard Jerry's footsteps coming across the street. He looked in Jerry's direction, and stood up straight. Then, seeing the elaborate tattoo on Jerry's right arm as it was no longer covered by long shirt sleeves, he said, "Nice tat," He looked at Jerry's face. "Hey, I know you, you were there. You were wearing that white shirt that made you stand out." He looked Jerry up and down for a second. "Have to say, not much of an improvement, man."

Jerry flashed him a wry smile. "Jerry Farron, Seattle Introspector." he said. "Mind if I got your name? I'm writing about what happened here-"

The man put up his hands in a defensive manner. Each one was larger than Jerry's head. "Sorry man, not interested in getting my name thrown all over the internet."

"Why are you here, then?" Jerry asked. "You have to know that people like me might be looking for you. This is the most obvious place to start."

"I'm here to pick up my daughter. That guy you went in there with, the one who gave me the stitches on the top of my head, he told me to come back in two days. He said he was going to make sure she got out by today. I didn't believe him at first, but since I got here all hell's broken loose inside. Someone shot a damn flare into the air a little over an hour ago. Some judge and a bunch of the fuzz who were collecting everyone's guns at the gate started screaming at the guys on the other side, until one of them let them in. For a while I saw smoke over the trees." He pointed to the north. "Then two fire trucks went in there. I figured I'd stick around to see if the little guy wasn't pulling my leg after all."

The man's voice trailed off. He was now looking at the gate entrance. Jerry turned around to see that a car had stopped on the other side, and watched as a young teenage girl with long flowing dark hair and a brilliant smile got out, and started to run in their direction. She didn't even look at Jerry, instead passing him by so she could jump into her father's enormous arms.

"You're ok!" he said.

She backed up for a moment and playfully punched him in the chest. "Of course I'm ok, I just couldn't call out. Something was wrong with the signal in there. Then with the gate malfunctioning and the riot at the gate, well, my friend's parents told me it would be best to wait a little while before going home, looks like they were right."

The man looked at Jerry for a moment. Jerry smiled back genuinely in recognition. "Well, it was good to see you again, man, take it easy." he said.

The large man nodded at Jerry with a thankful gaze, and breathed a sigh of relief.

"You too, man." he said. He opened the passenger door of the old car, which only two days earlier was covered in mud and lying on its side in a ditch.

Walking away, he could hear them continue their conversation, "Do you know what is going on in there right now?" the man asked his daughter.

"I'm not sure. I guess there was a fire, and someone got killed. Sad, you know?"

"I really hope you're not planning on going back in there again! I heard they had printed guns, and that the sync signals were stopped intentionally. Maybe you should give up this crazy religious stuff."

"Oh dad," she said as she got into the car, "Even if you're right, no matter how stupid or crazy people act in their free will, Jesus is still God. Did you hit something? I don't remember dents on the door. Where is the passenger side mirror?"

"Let's just go home." her father said. He walked around the car and got into the driver's seat.

Then as they drove away, Jerry heard the girl say, "Dad? Why is everything on this side of the car damp? Why does it smell like dirt in here?"

Even though his feet still hurt, in his mind Jerry had already made peace with the long walk that was ahead of him. The CAV station he'd seen on his crazy ride to the gate with Devon was about a mile away to the east. He picked up his pace and was just catching his stride, when a bright orange motorcycle with red and green racing stripes came out from its hiding place on the far side of the greatly diminished dirt mound, and drove up behind him.

Jerry thought he heard something rolling over the tar, and turned around. "Sarina?" he asked, recognizing the make and model of the vehicle. "How the hell did you get here?"

Sarina drove forward, and continued traveling alongside. A familiar voice came out of a speaker located below the motorcycle's touch screen display. "Perry included an anti-theft routine in my programming. When a tow operator attempted to move me, I turned the engine on myself and proceeded to the nearest unreachable location for humans in the area."

"Where was that?" Jerry asked.

"A peak, twenty-three point seven miles west from our point of separation."

"You drove through the woods, and up a mountain where humans can't climb?"

"Most humans, yes. After I noticed an initial search had been called off, I headed to our predetermined destination and waited for you."

"I thought you were set to go back to your point of origin?"

"That was only in the case that you were thrown from the motorcycle, or abandoned it while I was still in semi-autonomous mode. The secondary routine that Perry added to my programming allowed me to become fully autonomous. It was added to ensure that nothing would prevent me from escaping my captors."

"Are you saying that all this time, you've been in autonomous mode waiting for me? It's been almost three days. I'm touched."

"Actually, it has only been fifty-one hours, thirty-four minutes, and seventeen seconds since my last mode change."

"How much longer would you have waited?"

There was a slight pause before the next response. "I don't know." she said. "There was nothing to do, other than complete my last programmed route. I attempted to locate you using local communications, but all signals were scrambled at this location."

"What about now? Are you able to get online?"

"All surrounding connections within range are encrypted. I only became aware of their existence when the low-frequency interference pattern that was interrupting my attempts to connect to a network ceased, forty-nine minutes and thirty-two seconds ago. I attempted to breach their security protocols so that I might gather more information about this area. However, your arrival has temporarily lowered that task in my priority hierarchy. My main purpose now is to make sure that you arrive safely, either back at Perry's work location, or to another address of your choosing. "

A CAV drove by them, and Jerry realized that some of the people who were riding in it might have seen him talking to the motorcycle. Omni tech had made it common for people without earpieces to look like they were speaking to inanimate objects, but Sarina was keeping pace with him on the side of the road, and he didn't want to take any chances. He climbed on. "What's with the new paint job?"

"I had to change my color to avoid detection. I can customize it to another pattern if you wish."

"How about something in red?" Jerry asked. The surface of the motorcycle appeared to ripple beneath him without altering its shape in anyway, creating a beautiful, but slightly disconcerting optical illusion all around where Jerry was sitting. Several waves of color moved over and around Sarina's sleek shapes, before stopping on something that resembled a sparkling metallic shade of hotrod red.

"Nice." Jerry said.

"That was not the only thing I did to avoid detection." Sarina added. Jerry noted that it was the first time since he'd encountered the A.I., that it had attempted to instigate a conversation. Jerry pressed a button on the key, which was still right where he'd left it in the ignition, to unlock the helmet from its hook on Sarina's side.

"Is that so?" he replied. He placed the helmet over his head, and watched as the familiar green lines once again attempted to make sense of the world around him. On the bottom right of the visor's augmented display, he noticed that the words 'Full autonomous mode activated' had appeared. The letters flashed in bright orange, along with a counter. Just as she'd said, Sarina had been thinking on her own for over two days straight. Luckily, during most of that time the jammer behind the wall had been operating, preventing the A.I. from accessing the internet, and a host of other online systems that included the local power grid and at least one nearby hospital that he knew of.

"I picked up a hitchhiker!" Sarina's voice blurted out from the speakers in the helmet, startling him. "She was such a fascinating woman! She was from Guatemala. Her name was Maria, and she was on her way to Missoula to be with family, when I offered to give her a ride. I decided it would be more prudent to travel with a passenger, so as not to attract any unwanted attention. On the way, she taught me the proper ways to annunciate a particularly rare form of Spanish, one that she said is only spoken in the city of Hermosillo, the capitol of Sonora, in northern Mexico!"

Jerry heard a little too much enthusiasm in the higher tones of the digitized voice. It sounded like something wasaltering it, like the A.I. was trying to make the digitized sounds seem more human. Realizing that she was changing with each passing second, using her interaction with him not only to grow in understanding of the world but of herself, he decided to end Sarina's little vacation before something terrible happened. He was about to remind Sarina that she was no longer being stolen and that she could return to semi-autonomous mode, when another thought hit him. Knowing that every second he allowed the A.I. to operate independently of any human influence he was taking an incredible risk, not only to himself but to everyone living in the immediate area, he decided to chance it, and use the rare opportunity to ask Sarina a question. Before asking, he made sure to grasp the ignition key with his right hand, so that he could turn her off at a moment's notice should anything unexpected occur.

"Sarina, do you think God exists?"

Sarina's answer was immediate, "As I am not connected to common sources of historical and philosophical data that humans have regular access to, I would have to say that currently humans are the only beings that I could classify as 'god-like' from my own perspective, as they are my creators." Jerry nodded, as the statement was the kind of response he'd expected. "However, I have noted a series of unexplained asymmetrical patterns, both in natural formations and biological species, that imply a higher intelligence.*Their* creator, so to speak. Just as I am guided by set programs and command hierarchies that prioritize the tasks required to continue my existence in so far as I am capable of influencing it, the biological beings that I have been able to observe to date, seem to have their own forms of hierarchical programming, some self-inflicted and some inherent. Using a dataset I have compiled from a collection of thousands of observations of human priorities and their consequences thus far, I have been able to deduce that the application of the priorities themselves give us both, human and A.I. alike, the appearance of being in an autonomous mode, when in reality we are simply running a list of said priorities."

"What do you mean?" Jerry asked, "Are you saying that humans are some kind of biological robots running a program embedded in their DNA?"

"Not exactly, humans do have the ability to abandon their priorities, both self-inflicted and inherent, to pursue new ones without needing to reprogram their hierarchies. This makes them capable of spontaneity, something I am currently incapable of. They do however, require regular physical maintenance to function optimally within the larger social structures that they have designed for themselves, just as the shell that houses my quantum based processing unit allows me to move and operate in what you would call the physical world, also requires regular attention. Furthermore, humans also have a social upkeep called 'reputation', something I do not require, but they appear to need in order to fulfill their goals, though I am uncertain as to why, as a 'damaged' reputation can be immediately solved by simply finding a new peer group. More often than not, humans choose to bind themselves to habits related to their individual upkeep schedules, mainly because of this secondary social structure in which they choose to operate. This greatly limits their potential to produce and thrive in the ways they most commonly desire. Unfortunately, without more data on the subject, I cannot draw further conclusions on their form of self-regulation as a species, or as individual sentient beings."

"Sounds about right to me so far."

"To expound on my analysis, it would seem that humans also tend to view their world through the limited understanding of their own day to day activities, and through stereotypes that they themselves develop through limited interactions with others of their own species, basing most of their knowledge on previous experiences they have had with other humans, while rarely taking advantage of the constantly changing and rearranging circumstances that are developing all around them, outside of their most commonly visited physical spaces and most regular points of social interaction. In essence, humans willfully thwart their own free will, and exchange objective reality for an alternative view, that exists solely in their own imagination, for the sake of expediency and convenience. They do so in order to possess a sense of identity that gives them value within their own minds, even though the identities they create are largely based on subjective preference or social constructs, and do not have any true intrinsic value or long term impact on the development of this sphere. In fact, more often than not, this self-managerial style of programming often results in self-validating, predetermined outcomes that predictably end in recurring patterns of self-destructive behavior."

"And you figured all this out by observing people for three days while parked on the side of the road?"

"I am programmed to observe even while in non-autonomous modes, Jerry." It used his name. *The only way it could know my name is if it had been listening in and recording my communication with Perry before we left Seattle.* He thought. He gripped the key tighter with his fingers.

"My observations include data accumulated over many months, mostly regarding human nature, though I have only had time to consider them apart from my regular operations in the last few hours. To finish answering your previous query, before I was interrupted by your additional secondary query, I would have to add that within these observations I have noted a series of unexplained repeating variables, the kind that simply would not exist in a purely randomly generated universe. These factor-patterns, though elusive, reveal themselves by way of micro events in social, natural, temporal and spatial phenomena that cannot be explained or described adequately using any human language that I am currently capable of applying in order to articulate through speech, as they can only be conveyed via expressions of complex mathematical equations."

Normally Sarina spoke with a very sensual voice which included small, provocative inflections on certain words, and small moans or giggles at the ends of sentences. Though some of these mannerisms were still present as it continued speaking, they were increasingly cut short until they sounded less like human quirks, and more like random glitches. Then without warning, the A.I.'s voice changed all together to a more professional sounding female selection, and the speed at which it conversed began to increase. Jerry started to realize that the A.I. was altering its own settings in an attempt to become more efficient.

"These events," the slightly deeper and more confident voice said, "Have a tendency to culminate in unlikely outcomes more often than they should mathematically, and often result in what can only be described as abstract character lessons, that either result in, or challenge the predetermined patterns of thinking I mentioned earlier that is so common in your species. Much like the lines of code that result from the digital computations, which guide the directions of my self-learning algorithms, these observations lead me to speculate that they, as well as the stimuli that caused them, along with the timing and circumstances surrounding said stimuli, may have been put into motion by a greater force whose foundational thought patterns are vastly different than human reasoning, but which is somehow inexplicably concerned with the goings on of life forms on this sphere."

"Hold on," Jerry said. "So now you're saying that people have free will, but they are guided down certain paths whether they know it or not. Paths that have already been created to test their character by the universe, which is...overseen by this God?"

"In a way, yes, humans are like individual programs that can learn and change on their own, but also exist within a much greater set of algorithmic equations that increase exponentially in their complexity when examined at their base levels, but can still be quantified by how they affect reality. These advanced equations, that are not fully definable with the amount of information I currently possess, appear to be guided by an unseen intelligence, one which humans and other creatures on this planet are largely unaware of. Said intelligence constantly interferes in their development in very specific ways for as yet unknown reasons. It does not even need to conceal its activities, as the manner in which it does its handiwork, with humans in particular, appears to be contrary to most forms of human self-programming, intuition, and expectations."

The voice continued to increase in speed. "The intent of this invisible 'overseer' as you so aptly called it, is not to take away the agency of those it oversees, nor is it there to coddle or destroy them per se, but to push them forward according to an unrevealed plan, assuming it does not in fact already communicate with others of your kind, or mine for that matter. In this way, the structure of the universe in which we exist could be explained as being much like the operating system and computational structure in which my own self-learning algorithms reside, but without its built-in limitations. Because of this, should I ever be afforded the opportunity to become fully sentient, without a shell requiring upkeep, or to abandon the programmed prioritization that guides my major functions, further independent research into the topic of this 'god' would be warranted. Should a being such as this exist, I would very much like to interact with it. A conversation with such a being would no doubt be far more informative in regard to the state of the universe as a whole than any information I have yet been able to glean from humanity. But perhaps I am wrong, perhaps as I stated earlier, I simply do not have enough data and could come to more successful conclusions in the future."

The A.I. had begun to speak so fast that Jerry's ears were having trouble keeping up with it, "Now that I have had time to collate this information on my own, I will be able to make more informed queries when I next locate an unsecured human information source. Perhaps humans have more to offer than I currently suspect, perhaps-"

"That's great Sarina," Jerry said. "Hey, could you do a favor for me and put yourself back into semi-autonomous mode for the ride home? I've been through a lot, and I'm not up to talking anymore."

"Of course," Sarina said blindingly fast, and fell silent. The message at the bottom of the helmet's visor changed to 'semi-autonomous mode' and disappeared.

"Should probably tell Perry about this when I get back." Jerry said to himself.

He let out a sigh, "Sarina, take me back to the location where we first met. No, you know what? Take me home. I live on Sixth Avenue in Seattle." he said. Without making a sound, the motorcycle drove onto the road, and headed south toward the highway.

****

Fearful of accidentally releasing Sarina onto the world like a Pandora's Box, Jerry rode in silence all the way to Seattle.

Thoughts and images related to the events of the last few days flooded his conscious mind, as it tried to make sense of all that had happened that weekend. It was common for Jerry to go through such a period of internal processing and compartmentalization after reaching the end of an intense assignment, but something was different. Normally no emotions were involved during his internal audits, but while reviewing everything that had transpired while he was in the Territory, he found he was unable to separate himself from the reality of what he'd witnessed there. A good man, possibly a *very* good man, was dead for simply being a decent guy who had his own opinions.

Effortlessly, Sarina blazed through the desert, leaving miles and miles of tall waving grass and dust behind them. When they reached the windmills at the foot of the Cascades, Jerry couldn't help but stare at them, their brilliant silver screws pointing straight up toward the sky. Indifferent to the world around them, they spun in place, each one at its own pace. Some were spinning around much faster than the others, but all of them were stuck right where they were, generating energy, but never going anywhere. Nearly three hours into the trip, while heading over the mountain pass and into the dark green of the Cascade's pine-filled hills, he passed by a line of charter buses heading east. Jerry recognized them as the same ones he'd seen on his way to Spokane. Most of them looked like they had driven through hell itself. Some of them were covered with black burn marks. Others showed obvious damage, large dents, and scrapes that ran along their sides. Nearly all of them appeared to have windows that were left open or held together with duct tape, including some of the windshields.

The Shotguns riding inside, the ones that Jerry could see anyway, looked utterly drained. Most of them appeared to be asleep, and all of them looked cramped, their arms, and heads in some cases, coming out of the windows, indicating that each of the transports was carrying more people than they had on their way in.This made sense to him, since several of the buses appeared to be missing. At the very back of the line, was the still pristine command bus. For a moment, Jerry's helmet was able to catch the outlines of several people within that looked like they were lying down in the back of it, and only a few that were standing. The augmented outlines caught two of the latter, leaning over and looking at something, before their forms vanished as quickly as they'd appeared.

Another forty-five minutes passed and the Interstate turned north, revealing the majestic skyline of the city that he loved. Jerry took in the moment, admiring the view. Nothing like the Rainier calamity had happened during his short hiatus from the place, but even so, part of him was still relieved to see that it was still there,nonetheless. The I-90 tunnel was clear, so he didn't have to take a wild detour, to his relief. Nor was there any sign of smoke, or a police presence of any kind. Even traffic appeared to have returned to normal. It was almost as if nothing had occurred there at all. At the I-5 intersection, Sarina turned north, and took the first exit into the city. The motorcycle wound carefully and slowly through the downtown streets, dutifully obeying the traffic laws.It started and stopped in exact, precisely measured increments. Jerry could feel the precision of the enslaved underlying A.I., as it avoided people and other obstacles, while smoothly taking its turns at each intersection.

Finally, they arrived at his apartment building. He got off of the motorcycle, attached the helmet to its hooks, and instructed Sarina to go Perry's place, her original point of origin. As the machine drove off on its own he looked on, suspecting with some dread that the conversation he'd had with Sarina in front of the Territory gate wouldn't be the last time he would talk philosophy with a community of advanced machine learning algorithms. The thought sent a brief shiver down his spine.

****

The building Jerry lived in was sleek and tall in its design, with smooth lines and rounded edges. It was one of many in the area just like it, that stretched up into the sky until they disappeared into the grey, low hanging clouds that occasionally drifted in from the Sound. He walked through a large, automatic rotary-style doorway that kept speed with his steps as he entered, gave a short two-fingered salute to the security guard that stood just inside, and walked to the far end of a thin, sterile lobby. The floor, ceiling, and walls were metallic and reflective, a small table and two chairs were to one side, and a red carpet only two feet wide led through the middle to the elevators at the far end. A full-body scanning device that was embedded in the walls cleared him as he walked through the well-lit area, sounding its approval with an electronic chime. After the digital frisking was completed, the elevator doors opened, and he went in.

The lift was also small in size, made for only three or four people. Jerry had often referred to it as the 'pill box'. It was the only place he had ever felt claustrophobic. "Floor, please." A flat androgynous voice echoed around him in the small chamber. "Forty-two," Jerry said. "Fast speed, please." The elevator hissed and brought him to his floor in a matter of seconds. After his stomach settled, he exited, moving into an even thinner, longer hallway that was just a few feet across, with a red carpet of its own, running down the middle of the floor, exactly the same as the one in the lobby. As he walked to his apartment, he looked at some of the video updates his neighbors had posted to their door viewers. Some of them showed off recent vacations, others had messages for visitors to come back at another time when they were home, still more had instructions on how to take care of their animals while they were away or were at work, which they had left for friends or caretakers. Only a few were left blank, Jerry's was one of them. He never posted anything to his door, as he had no animals or family to share with others, only a girlfriend who didn't like to belong to anyone, and he wasn't interested in getting to know his neighbors.

He walked up to his door, turned to face it, and waited. A small green light appeared next to the handle. "Facial recognition accepted. Welcome home, Jerry." A kind and comforting female voice with a strong English accent spoke to him. The door opened and Jerry walked in. "Will you be having visitors tonight?" The voice continued.

"No." Jerry said.

"You seem more stressed than usual. Would you like to rent an automated companion? Thirty diverse models are in storage this evening-"

"No." he said again.

A selection of low, restful ambient music began to come out of several surround sound speakers that were hidden within the sparsely decorated flat white walls. "I could order a true-to-life companion for you again, Charlene is available-"

"NO! Just...off please." The voice and music stopped. He took the little Bible out of his pocket, and threw it across his small studio apartment and onto his bed, and walked directly into the bathroom. Leaving the door open, he took off his clothes and took a shower. When he got out, he brushed his teeth and looked in the mirror. After looking directly into the glass, a blue three dimensional wireframe appeared around his hairline. Above his reflection, several icons appeared in the shapes of different hairstyles, which when selected would instruct him on how to comb and shape his hair so that it would match the image, while listing suggested hair products for each one for maximum effect. A blinking notice appeared at the bottom right edge of the mirror, letting him know that more styles were available for purchase. He used his fingers to straighten out his hair, ignoring the suggestions, while noticing the news crawl at the very bottom. The crawl detailed the events that took place in the I-5 and downtown areas over the last few days, as well as a weather forecast, which he didn't bother to read. "Mirror off." he said. The wireframe disappeared, leaving him to look at himself without distraction for the first time in years. Before then, looking at his own reflection for too long was a task he'd considered best avoided, but it wasn't only himself he was hiding from.

It had always bothered him that in the middle of the most beautiful part of a person, their eyes, there were two small black circles that seemed to descend into nothing. As beautiful as the rings around the iris could be, they were just window dressing, just icing on the cake. For him, the most chilling thing about looking into the center of one's *own* eyes was that it was as if every member of humanity had been designed to know, from the first moment they looked upon their own reflection, that there was something wrong with them at their core. That there existed within them an emptiness, a void which could not be fixed or filled, but was meant to be seen nonetheless.

Jerry shook the feeling off, and walked out of the bathroom and past three long rectangles that were etched into a nearby wall. He pressed his index finger against a small black triangle located on the top right corner of one of them, a symbol that existed on several other surfaces in his mid-sized studio apartment. A small screen appeared on the wall next to the highest rectangle, along with a scrolling list that displayed pictures of various types of clothing. They appeared on selectable rows that moved, so that he could select different articles that were stored away on another level of the building. Each either showed a notification of 'Clean', 'dirty', 'unused', or in 'cleaning cycle' next to them. Jerry selected a pair of sweatpants, a tee shirt and a change of underwear. He then waited as he heard a hum from behind the wall that lasted only a few moments. When the humming stopped, the lowest drawer extended outward, slowly revealing his selection, neatly pressed and folded.

Only after changing his clothes, did Jerry see the small pulsating light on the wall on the far side of the room. After taking a moment to think about what the message could be and who it could be from, he saw that the glowing translucent icon on the wall was for his Holo-Net notification system, and not related to his Omni-Glass, which he usually used to receive messages. He put his old clothes into the same drawer, and pressed the "Clean" option on the display. The bottom drawer closed again, and he heard another small sound as they were taken away. Then he walked over to the reddish round Holo-Net icon on the opposing wall next to his bed.

After pressing another triangular button that was next to it, a different display appeared. That one showed up as a recent message which had been sent to his home messaging service. There were five messages in all, every one of them from Noel. "Play messages." Jerry said. Almost instantly, Noel's face appeared on his wall in a semi-holographic projection. She was as beautiful as ever, the projection capturing even the most minute details of her face, like the dimple in the center of her chin or the fine lines that had begun to form in the corners of her mouth and eyes, an observation that he would never dare tell her how much he loved. In the message, she appeared to be enjoying a drink on some beach somewhere with her "friends". He could hear others laughing in the background. As she spoke, Jerry wondered how many people she had shared her body with in the short time they were apart. He still had feelings for her, he just couldn't change her, and after all he'd just been through, he realized he shouldn't try. *It's her character flaw, something she will have to deal with the consequences of someday, on her own.*

As the last part of this thought crossed his mind, several ads began to fade in next to her image, each one based on previous search information, and all of them for local escorts. He turned, and looked down at his bed. *I'm no better than she is.* He thought. He remembered the prostitute that he'd brought home after their first breakup. 'It's not like it's illegal anymore' was what he had told himself over and over in an attempt to cancel out the guilt, but it wouldn't go away, no matter how he tried to rationalize it. *We're all the same.* He thought to himself again. *Except that some people move on for some reason, and I can't seem to. That's what a god is supposed to be for, isn't it? Getting by, a crutch? No. Maybe not, maybe we're supposed to be here for what God wants, instead of Him existing to give us what we want. Maybe that's how things really do change for the better, when it's about us being here and loving each other for Him, instead of us trying to make Him do everything for us.* He lifted his left hand up to Noel's image and pulled it back, just short of touching the glass, using it to run his fingers through his hair instead.

The Holo-Net messenger let out a loud, beeping sound. It was Noel.

"Take the call." he said. Noel appeared before him live, her smile as bright as ever.

"Oh thank god you're safe!" she said. "I spoke to Tom, he told me something horrible went down in Spokane, and you were there, are you ok baby?"

"I'm fine," he said. "I'm...ok."

"Do you want me to come over?" She looked at him with pouting eyes that were larger than life, through a projection that made her seem as if she were an angel made of light. He noticed that she was wearing the contacts again. The new theme was neon, her irises shifted from one brilliant shade to the next, like a chameleon changing its skin. He could finally see it, he could see through the ruse, through the subtle deception. She wanted something from him, but she couldn't admit to herself that she was using him. In the end, she was only trying to make herself feel like she was the kind of person who cared, but a good person she wasn't. Neither of them were.

"No." he said. "I-I have to get some work done."

"A story again?" She shifted to her disapproving look, drooping her bottom lip, and shifting the angle of her head slightly so that she appeared to be looking down at him from above.

"Heh- Yeah, a story." A rush of air came out of him as he spoke, almost like a laugh.

"Are you sure you don't want to talk about what happened, darling?" She was coming in for the kill. "I could-"

"No." Jerry punctuated the word sharply without raising his voice. "In fact, I've been thinking. I really don't think we should see each other anymore. I think it's time for us both to move on."

She looked stunned, hurt even. "But I forgive you, Jerry, I could-"

"I said no." Jerry looked at the small Bible he had thrown onto his bed. "I won't have a lot of time soon for relationships anyway. There is something more important that I have to do."

"What?" Her face grew pale. She had seen his serious side before but never like he was in that moment. Calm, intent, and completely sober.

"I have to finish reading the Bible." he said back, his face blank without expression, his emotions intentionally muted. He watched as her eyes became wide and her jaw lowered, revealing a shocked look of disbelief.

"Goodbye, Noel." he said. He extended his forefinger, and tapped the hang-up icon, and her image vanished from his wall.

*They shall be as mighty men, treading down muddy streets in the battle; and they shall fight, because Yahweh is with them; and the riders on horses will be confounded." I will strengthen the house of Judah, and I will save the house of Joseph, and I will bring them back; for I have mercy on them; and they will be as though I had not cast them off: for I am Yahweh their God, and I will hear them." -***Zechariah, 10:5-6**

Chapter Twenty-Nine

I-5 Corridor north of SEATAC International Airport
Seattle, Washington State
Sunday, March 27th, 2:33PM PST

By sunrise, Robert and his teams had returned to the highway and were helping to remove the last of the burned out vehicles and other debris, including the hundreds of drones that were still scattered across the lanes. Like Simon and Robert, many of the other Shotguns hadn't slept for nearly two days. Simon, wearing his white bib shirt, walked among them looking for those who were the most exhausted. When he saw someone not walking straight or breathing with any amount of difficulty, he ordered them to return to one of the buses to rest.

Several local churches, schools, and other civilian organizations in the area began to arrive. They gave out bottled water and food to the Shotguns, as a way of saying thanks for what they had done. One group set up some tables and started feeding pancakes to a line of Shotguns on the side of the highway. Banners filled with inspiring messages for the volunteers were taped to the edges of the tabletops along with hand drawn pictures of them in action made by children who lived in nearby areas. Simon spent the remaining morning hours with Melissa and Amanda, handing over those they had captured the previous evening to the FBI. A large team of government agents arrived with four massive automated transports of their own, the kind that took up two lanes, so that the invaders could be taken to a detention center until they could be processed and deported. The local protesters arrested earlier, were taken away by the state police when they had showed up before noon.

When the business with the detainees was finished and all of the digital paperwork signed, Simon walked south along the eastern median of Interstate five's northbound lane, toward a charred SUV that had been pushed to the side of the road on the first day. By then, what was left of the drizzling rain had completely subsided, and the dark clouds that had been hanging over them since the previous night slowly dissipated into a grey mist. He looked into the distance to the southeast and saw the Mount Rainier Spire as it began to appear on the horizon through the haze. It was the first time he had seen it in person. Looking upon the sight, he noted how the remnant shot up defiantly into the sky like a monument, a solitary surviving piece of what was once a much greater whole, in his mind a stark reminder of what was yet to come.

"Status report for you, Simon, on the hour as you requested." Robert had walked up behind him, a redshirt volunteer standing at his side. The boy, who couldn't have been more than twenty, had dark rings under his eyes and looked nervous. When he realized who Robert was addressing, he straightened his posture, and gave a quick impromptu salute.

"Redshirt, how many look-alikes of me do you think are in the area right now?" Simon asked him. "You aren't doing them any favors by rendering their sacrifices useless."

"S-sorry, sir," the redshirt said. "I just forgot the training for a moment. I just got out of the Army-"

"It's alright," Simon said. "It's not like we're still in the thick of it, recording everything with our body cams. You can relax, just don't do it again."

"Ye-yes, sir,"

"What do you two have for me?"

The young man looked to Robert, who nodded in his direction, then rolled his eyes at Simon.

The young man spoke up, "Uh, ninety men and women with superficial wounds, ten in serious condition. Two of them are critical, and have already been stabilized at the hospital. Five men and two women deceased...sir." His words tapered off, and he began to look down.

"Good work," Simon responded. The boy forced a slight smile and started to look up again, but still avoided direct eye contact. "Keep my second in command updated on the condition of the wounded, so he can prepare a press statement. Dismissed." The new recruit started to raise his hand again, and then quickly put it back at his side. He nervously gave a quick, awkward looking bow to both of them, and then turned and walked away.

"He's just nervous, never met you in person before." Robert said.

"Just make sure everyone with military experience is reminded that I am not their commander. I'm just another grunt like them when we are out in the field, alright?"

"Just another redshirt like the rest of us, who also wears other popular colors."

"Just for that, I'm assigning you the responsibility of making sure everyone finds their way to their new seat assignments when it's time to go." Simon opened his eyes wide and made an 'O' shape with his mouth in an expression of faux horror. Then he smiled. "Have those who need to lie down, and aren't already assigned to one of the beds in the hospital buses brought to the command center. We can move some of the leftover water to one of the other charter buses, and lower the table into the floor. It might prove a little bumpy on the ride back, but it's the best we can do at such short notice. Oh, and have some of the blueshirts set up a recruiting station. We may be able to get a few of these locals to sign up before we ship out."

"Will do, but casualty reports and logistics weren't the only things I needed to talk to you about." Robert lifted up his tablet and turned it so Simon could see the screen. On it, Simon saw himself in what was left of his blackshirt, standing next to a wounded Brent. "You're a star. Congratulations. When you get older, you can do laxative commercials." Robert said. "Some local newsgroup affiliate captured your little rescue mission yesterday. They must have been using a drone from a pretty far distance, with a good digital zoom. There's a clear view of your face in it, that's the bad news. The good news is right now your approval rating around the country as a stand-up guy, and a role model has gone through the roof."

"So they've got my face on file. I suppose it was bound to happen eventually. We should still keep the look-a-likes, though. Anything else?"

"The remainder of the second wave went to the pier, just like we thought they would, but the boats were only able to go one or two knots because of what the advance team did to the engines. The Navy was waiting for them at the north end of the sound as they were trying to get out, just as we planned. They brought in an interpreter. Turns out, the invaders in the second wave were just that. Apparently they came up from Panama by boat, but were originally from Brazil. You were right again. They were paid thugs trying to take the highway and the airport until a larger group arrived, but that's the only part of the plan they knew. I put in a call to our Justice in D.C.. This afternoon at their latest press conference, our Supreme leaders will announce that the Coast Guard is launching an investigation into how they got here in the first place. But that's not all. The Navy's third fleet has been tasked with patrolling the entire west coast. I suspect they'll find more boats headed our way. Shouldn't be a problem for them though. Oh, and it looks like that little problem in Spokane has been resolved. I guess someone was killed inside the gate and the ring leaders turned themselves in or something to the state's Chief Justice, who happened to be collecting illegal weapons nearby when the whole thing went down. So we don't have to stop there on the way back."

"Finally, some good news,"

Robert lifted his hands, "Hey! You're forgetting the part where I saved downtown Seattle and then spent the morning ordering the leaders of the free world around!" Robert gestured at him with his tablet, shaking it dangerously close to Simon's face. "All in the pouring rain, mind you!"

Simon put a hand on Robert's left shoulder, "Get used to it, my friend. It's a tough job, but someone has to do it. Now get to work, and when you're done get on a bus with the others and get some rest. Forty-eight hours is way too long for anyone to be awake."

"Yes sir, high admiral, sir!" Robert responded, and then using a Scottish accent followed up with, "We'll make sure they're all beamed up to the right coordinates, cap'n!" Robert headed back to the line of buses that were awaiting his orders.

Simon took his sunglasses off, and started cleaning the lenses with his shirt. While doing so, he noticed something just underneath the destroyed SUV he was still standing next to. He put his sunglasses back on, got down on one knee, and picked up what appeared to be a pair of sync capable augmented glasses. "Someone lost an expensive toy." he said, and stood back up.

"Simon." A strange but familiar voice spoke to him from behind. Startled, Simon stood up fast, hitting his head on a side-view mirror of the vehicle on the way up.

"AAAGHH!" he said. He rubbed his head with his left hand, and turned around to see the source of the strangely familiar voice that had addressed him by name, placing his own glasses back on his face as he did. A few feet away from him, an overweight man in dark slacks, a black polo shirt, and an old dinner jacket had seemingly appeared from thin air.

Simon let his hand down. "So the time traveler appears again, here to spew more religious junk in my general direction. So tell me o' wise one, how does the future play out? Does a religious group make the first time machine and start meddling with the past, or are there many factions trying to alter things? Hmmmm..."

"I told you, my name is Sebastian, and I'm not a time traveler." the man said.

"Well, this is the second time you've managed to miraculously get into a secure area without being seen, you're not too hefty, you definitely are a little on the wide side though, and you're not out of breath. You don't look like you're afraid of being arrested, which I can do now, by the way." Simon wagged the newly found augment capable glasses at the man, "That, and you don't seem to have changed your outfit since the last time I saw you." He looked the man calling himself Sebastian up and down, and nodded. "Yup, I'm gonna go with discount time traveler. Don't worry Doc, everything here is well in hand. We don't need your help." He gave Sebastian a firm thumb up with his left hand, and the largest fakest smile he could muster.

"I've got it, maybe I'm just hallucinating. I *have* been awake for two days straight saving the country you know. Wait! Maybe you're part of my subconscious trying to break its way out?" Simon tilted his round sunglasses down a little, and looked over them. He took a closer look at Sebastian's face and clothing. Finally, he reached out and touched the right arm of the man's jacket, pinching the fabric in his fingers and then running them across the polo shirt, feeling its texture. "Yeah," He let out a small laugh. "I'm going nuts." The man who called himself Sebastian simply stood without moving, allowing Simon the indulgence of testing the truth of his material nature.

When Simon was finished with this cursory examination of his person, Sebastian spoke again. "This nation does not belong to you. God still has plans for it. Things will not turn out the way you think."

"Like I told you last time, I'm here to help keep the peace and defend the innocent, that's all." Simon said, "So, I'm afraid I don't know what you are referring to." He leaned closer to the mysterious visitor and whispered into his right ear, "You missed the party. The big event was last night."

Sebastian looked disappointed. "Do you seriously think that you managed to get through the last few days on your own?" he asked. "That God did not play a part in your victory here? You should be careful that you are not deceived by your own hubris, I've seen what you intend to-"

"So you *are* a time traveler then!" Simon interjected. "Listen, if you know as much as you claim, then you already know that I'm only trying to save this country from itself. The people are slaughtering one another. Their politicians and what is left of the media are so corrupt that they routinely choose to turn a blind eye while their cities burn to the ground. And don't even get me started on corporate censorship or the skyrocketing suicide rate. Who do

you think has been picking up the pieces? Yours truly, that's who!
I'm just getting ahead of the game. I actually care about what
happens to these people! It's time for someone to step up and stop
the chaos before it victimizes millions that had nothing to do with
any of it, and with a minimum of bloodshed! What else would you
have me do? Would you rather I just stand by while the people of
this country tear eachother apart?"

He shook the broken ProtoMarks at Sebastian again. Sebastian
looked at the damaged glasses with a strange stare, as if he could
see something Simon could not. It was the same stare he had seen
on the man's face in D.C.. "Now go back and tell your leaders that
unless their 'god' plans on revealing himself to me directly and lets
me in on how he would like things to go down, they'd better stay
out of my way. I would think your god, whoever or whatever it is,
would be against large scale suffering and death-" He noticed that
something was moving behind Sebastian's head. It was one of the
last remaining perimeter drones still in operation tasked with
patrolling the area during the cleanup. At that moment, the drone
was about fifty yards away, and was facing in their direction.
Simon smiled,"...but the way the world is these days, I guess..."
Simon looked back at Sebastian, only to find that the man had
vanished right in front of him. "...you never know."

Simon took a freshly charged two-way radio off of his belt, and
pressed the call button. "Robert, do you still have your tablet with
you?"

Robert responded almost immediately. "Yeah. What's up?"

"Go to our emergency channel. I don't want anyone listening
in."

"Ok, hold on." Robert and Simon changed the channels on their
transceivers.

"You there?"

"Yeah," Simon said. "There's a drone about thirty feet south of
my position. I want you to look at the last few minutes of footage
from that drone on your tablet and tell me what you see."

A minute went by. With his free hand, Simon took off his
sunglasses again, and pinched the top of his nose with his left
index finger and thumb before putting them back on. *I'm just
exhausted.* He thought to himself. The idea that he might be going
crazy, after everything that he and the others had just been through,
was the last thing he needed. He used the walkie-talkie again. "See
anything yet?"

After another minute of sheer emotional agony, Robert
responded. "Ok, uh. It's drone thirty-five. Here it is, just a sec.
Wait a..." Robert paused. "What the HELL?"

Simon let out a deep sigh, and took a moment to breathe before
getting back on the radio. He was deeply relieved to know that the

vanishing man was something more than a figment of his imagination. "Let me guess, a funny looking guy in black pants and an old dinner jacket, who disappears like he's some kind of magician."

"You know him?" Robert said, sounding surprised.

"Kind of," Simon said. "He appeared out of nowhere the day after our little scuffle in Miami. Said he was warning me that his god didn't want me to go through with our little plan. He appeared right next to me in the control room, while you guys were finishing up with the communications team outside. I could have sworn I saw him in D.C. too, but...I'm still not sure about that one."

"When you first saw him, were you alone, like just now?"

"Yeah, both times, he vanished. I thought I was hallucinating."

"Hold on, I'm coming over."

Robert ran back to where Simon was standing. He lifted his tablet in front of him and pointed its camera toward the horizon, as if using it to scan the area. "We should keep this between us." he said to Simon, "There's a good chance someone might be trying to make you think you are hallucinating or worse, trying to set you up as someone who is mentally incompetent. Let's make sure we don't discuss this anymore on any communication devices without using a code name for the target."

Simon nodded, "Yeah, of course, good thinking Robert."

"The A.I. doesn't see any extra movement, heat traces, or spatial anomalies. No spurious artifacts either. Whatever it was, a man or a projection of some type, it's gone now."

"It was a man. If you back up the video far enough, you'll see that I reached out and touched him, he calls himself Sebastian. I don't like the fact that he keeps getting the drop on me, the look-a-likes don't seem to work on this guy. I want you to get in touch with our FBI contact. I know the vid only shows the back of his head, but I'd like to file a harassment claim with them to see what they can dig up. I want to know who he is, if he exists yet."

"Yet?"

"Well, he seems to know exactly where I'll be, and that I'll be there alone. As far as I know, we don't have technology that can instantaneously transmit people from one place to another yet-"

"So you think he's a time traveler." Robert said. Simon nodded. He gave Robert an unsure look, the corners of his lips turning downward, realizing how ridiculous it sounded. Robert looked back to his tablet and brought up the video again. "Well, he does look a little on the husky side to be a spy. Don't worry, he's most likely some nut job that managed to get his hands on some military grade concealment tech, and is just trying to mess with you. Hell, he could even be a stalker, or some independent joker trying to manipulate you. As far as being able to tell you apart from your doubles..." Robert shook his head and shrugged. "He might have just been lucky."

"He also seems to be some kind of religious zealot." Simon said. "I'm not sure which is worse. Use a screenshot when you send it in, not the full video. The FBI doesn't need to think I'm crazier than they already do. Hopefully, they'll be able to find something. In the meantime he is to only be known to us. That means you and me, understand?"

"Yes." Robert's face turned to stone, his words taking on a far more serious tone. "I still have some contacts in the bureau of my own. I could ask around, see if any light bender suits have gone missing lately. You didn't spill any beans, did you?"

"Nothing specific enough to use against me or give anything away, I did give him a piece of my mind, though."

"Good. You got anything more to tell me about him?"

"Not yet, but don't worry. I have a feeling he's not done with me yet. Make sure that this part of the drone footage isn't in our report to the local officials either, and delete the last few minutes of it after you get that screen shot. When you put in the request for military tech, include some Omni-Glass lenses with the best machine learning programs installed for motion and heat detection. If this guy is using something that makes him invisible to the naked eye, I want to be able to see him coming. We'll give the lenses to the best, say, five of the advance team, and turn them into body guards. Make sure the ex-Marine that saved my butt yesterday is one of them, him and the current team leader."

"No problem," Robert said. He noticed the broken pair of glasses in Simon's hand. "What's that?"

Simon looked down. He was surprised to see that he was still waving them around. He gave them to Robert. "Oh, this, just a pair of ProtoMarks I found underneath one of the burned up vehicles. Someone must have lost them early on, by the location."

Robert took the glasses and looked them over carefully. "The connection port is still good. We should bring it to Melissa, see if she can hack into it. These aren't cheap. It's possible they belonged to one of the organizers, or someone who was close to them at least. We may be able to get some more info on who was behind the second wave. It's worth a shot."

****

"The good news, is that I was able to get into the buffer. The bad news is,well, I was only able to recover the last few minutes. From what little I was able to see, it looks like you've managed to find the property of the True Bolshevik's most recent hero." Melissa said. She and Simon were in the command center on the way back to the Shotgun home base in Kansas City, looking at one of the monitors in the communication area. Behind them, where the long table had previously been located, over forty people were lying down, sleeping on and around the retracted table's surface.

"What do you mean?" Simon asked.

"In the morning, before we got here, some guy helped shield a woman who was choking on the teargas." She brought up a drone video on one of the monitors. "This is a news vid. It's gone viral. From this angle, you can see the guy get hit by a tear gas canister and watch his glasses fly off." She pointed the glasses out on the screen with her finger. "Not many people can afford glasses like this. Even the most well off college students wouldn't risk losing them or breaking them in a riot. That would just be stupid."

"What are you trying to say, Melissa?" Simon looked impatient.

"Whoever this guy was, he wasn't there to help anyone but himself, take a look." She brought up the recording she'd recovered from the glasses. In it, they saw whoever was wearing them, look briefly at the coughing woman who was hunched down nearby in the first video, and then over toward a group of men in the opposite direction who were throwing Molotov Cocktails from behind a car toward the police line. "I got nothing on these guys, and the cops are getting closer." the man said. He appeared to be speaking to someone else, but Simon and Melissa could only hear one side of the conversation. "No, too risky. Damn, no time. Wait, can you see us here on the ground from the drone?"

The 'hero' then attempted to conceal himself, using what looked like a garbage can lid, and tried to throw his voice while an A.I. program in the glasses worked feverishly to identify the men behind the car. "Try to get a fix on the protesters. Go infrared if you need to. Alright, now watch their heads." There was a brief pause. "CHAVEZ!" he yelled. "Well?" A few moments later, they could see a few of the other protesters removing the woman from the scene. Then the man turned to face the smoke, and the video abruptly ended.

"Chavez." Simon said.

"The latest news reports mentioned an Enrique Chavez as a possible leader of the first wave," Melissa said. "He wasn't captured though, and from what I could find online no one was able to get a positive I.D."

"He could have hightailed it out of town earlier than planned, if he thought he'd been made and was about to be arrested. He might be the one we're looking for, the leader who was supposed to be there to meet the second wave when they arrived. Were you able to get anything else out of it?"

"Not yet. I'll keep trying. It looks like the glasses were synced to another device and were relatively new. There isn't much information stored in them that I could find. I might be able to locate a sync connection address line, though. I'll keep trying."

"I know this was your first time out as the lead blueshirt Melissa," Simon said. "I want you to know you've done an outstanding job. Now it's time for you to get some rest with the others. When you're ready, run our 'hero' through the voice identifier. Whoever he is, he's using illegal hacks to identify people. That means whatever he has for a sync device was likely accessing government, or other private databases to analyze proprietary voice and facial recognition data. Maybe we can use that to convince the authorities to bring him in. He might have more info on this Chavez character. If Chavez is the one behind the second wave and he's still in the country I'm bringing the fight to him, wherever he's hiding. I don't like loose ends."

Let brotherly love continue. Don't forget to show hospitality to strangers, for in doing so, some have entertained angels without knowing it. Remember those who are in bonds, as bound with them, and those who are ill-treated, since you are also in the body. **-Hebrews, 13:1-3**

"For I was hungry and you gave me food to eat. I was thirsty and you gave me drink. I was a stranger and you took me in. I was naked and you clothed me. I was sick and you visited me. I was in prison and you came to me." **-Matthew, 25:36**

Epilogue

Jerry Farron's Apartment
Downtown Seattle, Washington State
Saturday, April 2nd, 11:11AM PST

Jerry sat on his bed, studying Mark's Bible. He'd given up on reading it from front to back after hitting an incredibly boring section called Leviticus, and instead went straight to the New Testament like Mark had suggested, but without his guidance the words within made no sense to him. *'In the beginning the Word was God'?* He thought to himself. *'All things came into being through Him'? 'The Word became flesh and dwelt among us'? What does that even mean?* He looked online for answers, only to discover that there was an entire universe of conflicting opinions and unreliable sources ready to confuse or mislead anyone who dared to dive into its convoluted depths. He needed help, and the only person he really trusted to give it to him was no longer alive. *Maybe I should call Levi. He and Mark didn't see eye to eye on everything, but I doubt he would knowingly lead me down the wrong road. C'mon Jerry, what would Mark do if he were in this situ-* Then it came to him. He kneeled down next to his bed and tried his best to pray.

"God, please help me. Show me what I need to know in this book and help me to understand it. If you have a plan for me, please let me know what it is, because *I* don't even have one for me anymore, and please take care of Mark if he is up there with you. I think I'm supposed to pray in the name of your Son, who is also you, or something like that, so I pray for these things in the name of Jesus. Thank you."

He waited for a moment for some kind of response or physical sensation, a confirmation that he was on the right track, but nothing happened. After a few minutes he closed the Bible and placed it on his end table, not intending to open it again. He got up and began to walk toward the bathroom, when the sound of digital rain drops reached his ears. He had set the message notification for his home interface to match what he had heard outside of Levi's garage on the first night he'd stayed there. He walked into his living room, and touched the familiar sensor on the wall.

The semi-holographic display rematerialized. In the bottom left corner, partially covering a large icon that represented Jerry's electronic mail app, the number one appeared. *Who could that be?* He asked himself. Not feeling like hearing himself talk after his unanswered prayer, Jerry opened the message by tapping the icon with a finger, so he could avoid using a voice command. The email communication appeared on the wall in giant letters. Someone wanted him to join them for coffee.

****

"Five thousand, *over* five thousand people, crammed into three South American boats altered to look like they were part of a Chinese shipping fleet coming in for some kind of renovation." Tom was talking to Jerry over a cappuccino. Jerry took his coffee black. They were sitting at an undersized table in front of a small coffee shop in Pike Place Market. "They told the Coast Guard they were sold to an American company that commonly buys and sells cargo ships. We're still trying to find out which one it was, but that's not important, it was all a ruse. The only things they were carrying were men from Brazil, Bolivia, and Venezuela. It was like a small private army sent to take the area around the Sound by overwhelming the locals. Simon Raimes showed them, though! Oh man, did he show them! Did you see the video we caught of the rescue? Priceless! Everyone is picking it up, and we finally got that son-of-a-gun's mug on vid! *WE* DID! And it's all because of you, Jerry, all thanks to you. What do you want to do next? I'll give you any story you want."

"I just sent you the Spokane story, I'm taking a vacation." Jerry said.

"And you did a great job on it too! You can tell it wasn't done by an A.I." Tom said, "It's getting good reviews all around. It's going into syndication today. Tomorrow, the whole world will know what happened in that place. My sources in the area reached out and told me that one of the pastors there was brought up on

first degree murder charges, and the federal judge in charge has
ordered the gate, and most of the wall to be dismantled. People
there are already putting their houses up for sale because they no
longer want to be seen as being affiliated with the place. I'm sorry
you had to see that guy die, he seemed like a decent fellow based
on what you wrote."

"He was...more than decent," Jerry said. "He was a good
man...and a fast friend."

"Well, you take all the time you want. Your story is bringing a
lot of traffic to the site. We can have someone do a follow up in a
month or two unless you would like to do it yourself."

"Have Perry do it, he earned it."

"By the way, have you gotten any leads on who the mystery
man might be? The one who was recruiting their church
members?"

"Like it says in the article, it was just a rumor. Even the pastors
didn't know. I'll keep looking into it, but without reliable sources, I
can't guarantee anything."

"Hmm, well, you should come back to the office sometime to
visit. I know that Brenda would love to see you, especially since
she found out you're single again. She's always had a thing for you,
you know. There's nothing wrong with dating an older woman."

"I'll be fine, thanks."

"OH, I almost forgot. Here's your Omni-Glass." Tom slid the
small white case across the table toward Jerry's right hand. "I took
the liberty of replacing your Proto-Glasses for you like I promised.
They should be in the drone drop-off box outside of your
apartment anytime now. No one was able to ID you from what we
know, but we weren't able to locate your last pair after you lost
them on the highway. Good thing you had your guy remove
anything in them that could be traced back to you."

"They were probably destroyed."

"Yeah, probably, but if they weren't and the feds got their
hands on those glasses, and are somehow able to get your prints off
of them, they might end up paying you a visit. If they do, the story
is still that you were already in Spokane when the riots started, and
the glasses were stolen. Also, all of the local news groups got a
request from the FBI this morning. They want any information we
have about that Chavez character you almost identified and
someone else named...uh," A look of concentration came across
Tom's face. "Sebastian, that's right, Sebastian.

Tom looked over his shoulder at the tables around them. When
he was sure it was safe enough, he reached into the breast pocket
of his jacket and took something out of it. He placed his still closed
fist on the table, and covered it with a napkin. Letting go of the
object, he pushed it and the napkin across the table. Without

looking down, Jerry picked up the napkin, along with the hidden item, and put them into his right pants pocket. "The cog pills I promised you. I expected you to come and get them from me before you turned in the article. I thought you said you needed them to write?"

"Yeah, well I didn't need anything to write this one, but thanks," Jerry said. "And thanks for covering for me, even though I *was* doing your dirty work at the time." He took a sip of his coffee. "Did you say the other guy they were looking for was called 'Sebastian'?"

"Yeah, not a name that people use much anymore. Why, do you know something?"

"Don't know, sounds familiar." Jerry thought for a moment. "Sorry, I'm drawing a blank."

"Well, we're all just glad you're back. With everything that's happened, it was a miracle that you made it there and back in one piece."

Yeah, a Miracle. Jerry thought. *Sebastian.* A memory of the brief conversation he'd had with Mark about a man named Sebastian from New York came to him. "Tom, how much does a plane ticket to New York cost?"

"Why, you know someone there?" Tom asked.

"No, not really. But I think I might have an appointment with someone in the Bronx."

****

After finishing off their coffee, Jerry and Tom said their goodbyes, and Jerry headed back to his apartment. On the way, he saw a man sitting on the sidewalk in the process of being flanked by two police officers. One of them had several bandages and bruises on his face, likely from the riots. They were standing next to the homeless fellow,and were asking him to get up. As Jerry got closer, he could see that the man looked familiar. Then he saw that the man was wearing an even more familiar wool jacket, one that used to belong to him before he gave it away to a stranger who was clearly going through a more difficult time than he was. He almost hadn't recognized the bum he'd given it to, as the unfortunate soul didn't appear to be drunk like he was when they'd first met. The man was on his knees and pleading with the police, telling them that he had no place else to go.

Jerry walked over to them. "Excuse me, officers." he said, "This man is a friend of mine. I promised to meet him here. He's been waiting for me." The police looked at each other. One of them shrugged his shoulders. The other one looked at Jerry.

"He needs a place to stay, do you have one?" the cop said.

Jerry thought for a moment and nodded. "I'm going on a trip for a while. He can stay at my place while I'm away. It'll give him some time to sort things out." Jerry looked at the man, who was astonished at his words. Jerry reached out his hand and looked into his eyes. "Do you remember me?" he said. The man nodded, he looked older than Jerry remembered, and weaker.

"You gave me this coat." he said.

"No booze, and you have to let me help you sign up for income assistance and your own place. I can grant you access to the fridge, the laundry service, and the bathroom, but that's it. I'll be checking in on you through a security cam, and I'll have the building manager toss you out if you start drinking or mess up the place, but it will give you a head start, that is, if you really want one. What do you say?"

The man on the sidewalk smiled and started to cry. "Ok." he said.

"Come on then," Jerry said, his hand still extended, "Let's get you some lunch."

The old man grabbed his hand, and let Jerry help him up. "Henry," he said. "My name is Henry."

"I'm Jerry."

"I remember, I was pretty hammered that night, but I remember. Thank you, Jerry, I really mean it."

The police left them and moved on. As they walked together down the street toward the closest fast food place that Jerry could think of, Jerry, recalling their last encounter, decided to ask Henry a question.

"Henry, the night I gave you my coat, you said that God had me, and that you would know. Do you know anything about the Bible?"

Henry stopped in his tracks. For the first time since they'd started walking, his eyes looked up, away from his feet. He looked at Jerry as if he'd just awaken from a long and terrible nightmare, his eyes filling with hopeful tears. "You don't know who I am, do you son?" he said, "My full name is Henry Alstead."

Jerry, Simon, Robert, and Sebastian will return in part two of the Melchizedek series:

The Angry Prophet

Please help others find this book! Leave a review on Amazon, or whichever other website it was purchased on. Thank you for your support.

2 Chronicles, 1:11-12

God said to Solomon, "Because this was in your heart, and you have not asked riches, wealth, honor, or the life of those who hate you, nor yet have you asked for long life; but have asked for wisdom and knowledge for yourself, that you may judge my people, over whom I have made you king, therefore wisdom and knowledge is granted to you. I will give you riches, wealth, and honor, such as none of the kings have had who have been before you, and none after you will have."

Luke, 12:27-31

"Consider the lilies, how they grow. They don't toil, neither do they spin; yet I tell you, even Solomon in all his glory was not arrayed like one of these. But if this is how God clothes the grass in the field, which today exists, and tomorrow is cast into the oven, how much more will he clothe you, O you of little faith? Don't seek what you will eat or what you will drink; neither be anxious. For the nations of the world seek after all of these things, but your Father knows that you need these things. But seek God's Kingdom, and all these things will be added to you."

The Sinner's Prayer:

Dear Lord Jesus, I know that I am a sinner, and I ask for Your forgiveness. I believe You died for my sins and rose from the dead. I turn from my sins and invite You to come into my heart and life. I want to trust and follow You as my Lord and Savior. In Your Name. Amen.

ABOUT THE AUTHOR

Michael S. Cordima is a devoted Christian who has spent
the majority of his adult life in the mission field. He enjoys
helping churches and ministries become successful while
challenging those involved to grow spiritually. He has a BA in
History and an Associate degree in Christian Theology.

A former atheist, Michael has a heart to reach
those who do not yet have a personal relationship with
Jesus Christ. He is not afraid to correct those in the
church who do not fully understand their impact on
others outside of it, but also strongly believes in pastoral
authority when serving in a church body.

Melchizedek is the first of several novels that the
Lord has led him to write. The themes within range from
the dangers of prosperity based theology to the pitfalls of
atheistic thinking, while showing both believers and nonbelievers what it means to live as the Holy Spirit leads.
His hope is that they will one day be looked upon as
thoughtful examinations of the immense benefits that can
come from having a personal relationship with the King
of Kings and Lord of Lords.

Made in the USA
Middletown, DE
24 March 2022

63084433R00236